Dark Arts

THE HORROR WRITERS ASSOCIATION PRESENTS:

EDITED BY

John Pelan

CEMETERY DANCE PUBLICATIONS

Baltimore

❖ 2006 ❖

Cemetery Dance Publications
132-B Industry Lane
Unit 7
Forest Hill, MD 21050
Email: info@cemeterydance.com

www.cemeterydance.com

Table of Contents

The Disease Artist

STEVE RASNIC TEM

"Because I couldn't find the food I liked."
—Franz Kafka, "A Hunger Artist"

The hardest thing is finding the right way to end. You are weak and in pain, the degree of weakness and pain dependent upon how many of the modern amelioratives you've decided to apply to whatever ancient or largely extinct illness you've selected for the core of your performance. Too many and your act fails to convince, too few and you are so distracted by discomfort and imminent mortality you lose the perspective necessary to make the performance an art.

He could feel Mickey, his lover of two decades, hovering in the wings off-camera. This was a broadcast performance, was it not? For the moment he could not remember, and there was too much sweat in his eyes for him to see clearly. He coughed up a glob of blood and felt it trickle down his chin. The hemorrhagic symptoms had always been the most difficult for Mickey to witness—somewhat strange in a medical professional, but maybe, with modern fluid control, lower level attendants encountered minimal blood outside its proper vessel. Mickey hovered, ready to end the performance prematurely, to apply more neural blockers, to end the mess. Mickey had always hated mess. It made them an odd couple.

Spread-eagled on the see-through bed, tilted steeply as if to launch into the crowd—the position was designed to display the plague tumors in the groin and

7

armpits, a balanced selection of egg—and apple-sized, a variety of buboes, boils, knobs, kernels, biles, blisters, blains, pimples, and wheals.

The lower portion of the bed would be thoroughly smeared with blood and diarrhea by now. The stench would be terrible, but some paid extra for an olfactory broadcast. People in the Dark Ages had believed they were being killed by a magical change in the very composition of the air. Back then everything had smelled, everything had been a mess. Here, all the stage techs would be wearing filters in their nasal passages, Mickey's the most powerful. Jerome wore the most porous filter possible, to experience his condition thoroughly, but not be overwhelmed by it.

"It's time to end this one." Mickey in his ear like the voice of the medieval god.

"Not yet," he subvocalized. "I haven't reached the moment yet."

"Death isn't a moment, Jerome. Death is forever."

Jerome knew his smile would look like either a grimace or delirium. "Not that moment. That peaceful moment when you understand what it means to be mortal."

"Save the bullshit for the interviews, okay? Let's get out of here—your vitals are looking a bit less artful."

Jerome blinked rapidly until his vision cleared. "I want to see some of the audience first."

God sighed dramatically in his ear. "It's your show."

The air in front of him was suddenly layered with images of crowds, small groups, individuals lounging in comfortable chairs, just a selection of those who permitted, or demanded, a two-way feed. Jerome recognized a number of the regulars: a wizened old man in antique lounging pajamas, the middle-aged French couple with their three teenagers, a small group of adolescents, several people with the image of The Disease Artist as the biblical Job emblazoned on the front of their robes along with the inscription *He destroys both the blameless and the wicked. JOB 9:22.*

Despite his convictions about the importance of his performances, he believed there were things children did not need to see, but he'd had little luck controlling their access. An increasing portion of his following consisted of children and teens, with particular interest from The Filthies. Having decided to forego contemporary personal hygiene technologies in favor of an unwashed look, The Filthies professed a belief in the "natural realities" of dirt and odor, and claimed that the bulk of contemporary society had removed itself from the "real" world.

"You put this stuff out there," Mickey would say, "and you have to live with the fact that people are going to make of it what they will."

Normally he would end a performance simply by closing his eyes for thirty seconds or so. Often at that point, the transformation of his body would appear to accelerate, skin turning color and erupting, sometimes showing actual decay faked within the transmission in order to show the eventual progress of the disease.

Sometimes a private client would request a demonstration of old-fashioned embalming techniques after the disease had completed its work. Such demonstrations were completely canned, differing from each other only in the diseased appearance of the apparently dead body. He'd never told anyone that these embalming shows were essentially re-runs, but then no one had ever asked.

The children's stares were attentive, questioning. This time he just started crying. Somewhere in his head God cried "Cut!"

꒷꒵꒷

From *The Disease Artist: A Performance Chronicle:*

His first performances were in prisons, for the population at large, or sometimes for an individual inmate whose crime was particularly heinous. In perfect safety, of course, his act broadcast from a studio to protect him from the inmates and the inmates from the disease he had chosen to nurse along and bring to some spectacular and dramatic conclusion.

These performances, not surprisingly, were somewhat controversial. It seemed now that there were as many prisons in the world as universities, with a commensurate number of advocates and activists. Everyone had at least one friend or relative in such an institution, and the common belief was that the performances of The Disease Artist constituted cruel and unusual punishment.

The warden who had ordered the performances claimed they cheered the inmates by demonstrating how much worse their conditions could be, and by putting them in touch with the "absolute value" of life itself.

The Disease Artist had his doubts—he could see the look on the faces of his captive audience when Ebola made him cry tears of blood. But at least he was performing, and that was what mattered. He appeared in a black-barred cage, pleased with how the backdrop showed off his poses.

The Disease Artist always made his talents accessible to members of the scientific community. But he insisted that they pay like any other customer.

꒷꒵꒷

As he passed through the restaurant Jerome could hear the intermittent whoosh of air jets: scent and disinfectant, so prevalent anymore that people rarely noticed them. Jerome noticed them. With each of his steps a push of air followed. He'd stop, and the jets in his immediate vicinity would stop. He had long believed that this daily orchestra of nozzle and pump paid him particular attention, tracking his progress through the world. When he'd start walking again, the hissing breath of dozens of hidden vents pursued him.

Intent on his lunch of steam, Mickey appeared not to notice his arrival. Mouth open over the wide nozzle, careful to avoid accidentally grazing his straining lips against the spout, he inhaled deeply. No mess, no worry, nothing to mar the teeth or stain the mouth.

"Have you ever thought," Jerome said, "about what it takes to turn a cow into steam? I mean the mechanics of it, what they have to do to that cow?"

Mickey glanced up, closed the spout. "Jerome, don't start." He wiped his lips carefully with a disposable disinfectant, although there was nothing to wipe. "This is beef now. Beef, Jerome. I can't remember the last time I saw a cow."

Jerome glanced at the menu, as usual couldn't find anything he liked, put it down again. "I'm doing cholera next week," he said. "Symptoms show up in 12-48 hours so you'll need to infect me at the last minute. I'll spend the next few days preparing mentally."

"Cholera's old news. You've done it half a dozen times already."

"It was important," Jerome said. "It was the world's first global disease. India to Russia to Europe. It was a full partner with the Industrial Revolution."

"People didn't know how to handle their excrement. It made its way into everything, including the drinking water." Mickey inserted his fingertips into his front pocket, which buzzed as sonics scrubbed the fingernails and tips. When he removed them they looked as transparent as glass. "I'll get everything ready. But don't let this one go on too long. You're doing too many performances. Your resistance is down."

"It's what I do." He wrapped his arms around Mickey, felt him shrinking away in aversion. Jerome could not remember the last time he had really held Mickey. As if Mickey's very flesh feared that some of him might rub off.

❦

Mickey modified the cholera strain so that the illness would last a week and a half rather than the usual two days, giving him more time to ease into the role, and time for more people to attend. This tampering was well-documented, of course, but no one seemed to mind. Ticket sales, especially for the live seating, were way up. Several entertainments concerning the early nineteenth century had been popular recently, and the kids, especially The Filthies, liked the clothes from that period. Whole troops of them climbed into the cramped seats. Jerome didn't believe anyone should be too comfortable at one of his performances, so he controlled the seating where he could. He also didn't like to see the same people in the audience for extended periods of time, but he gave discounts for repeat tickets.

Some people wanted to see The Disease Artist for a short visit each day, to note the subtle progress of the disease and form their own appreciation of its changes. Some liked to sit in the audience for an eight-hour stretch, content to listen to The Disease Artist's own chronicle of symptoms and perceptions. Many

10

appreciated most his careful attention to details and set design. For the cholera epidemic he had replicated a Paris of costume balls and mass graves.

And for a small additional charge they could touch the bare flesh of The Disease Artist himself. All innoculations included.

"It chose its victims erratically and suddenly," he announced, gesturing toward his legs and rib cage. "See how the skin becomes black and blue, how the hands and feet shrink within their gloves of skin." Suddenly he collapsed under the pain of extreme muscular cramps. The audience gasped and pressed closer.

Jerome felt his mind slip in and out of dementia much like a change of clothes. Long ago he'd recognized that first putting on a new disease was like putting on a new suit, being acutely aware of where it fit and where it didn't, in general feeling a little uncomfortable, and not quite yourself. But eventually the suit becomes you, and you gradually become something other: a lizard or a bird or a dragon. You become the body trying to find its kinship with the world. Through disease he had become the universe temporarily made conscious, so that the universe might know its own suffering.

He opened his eyes. People were rushing around. A small girl had crawled forward, trying to kiss him. "No!" he screamed. Trying to push himself away from the child, he had a sudden vision of filth leaving the body, of oils and hair and a variety of blood products pulled skyward in a silent exodus of fluids and skin flakes and white cells and sweat and this dew of urine and fecal fractions rising out of the mass of humanity and smearing the lens of God's eye.

He blinked. Blinked again. God's lips to his ears. "I'm getting you out of here," Mickey whispered.

"The problem, the problem is…" He felt himself choking.

"Jerome, calm down!"

"The problem is people have forgotten how to honor their mortality."

⌒∴∾

Jerome's sister had died five years ago, just before the height of his popularity. One of Mickey's colleagues at the hospital had called to say she was failing, but by the time Jerome reached the hospital his sister had already passed, to use the old word now back in common parlance. He almost didn't recognize her, wrapped in that thick, bluish, so-called "life blanket" the hospitals always used. The blanket appeared to have its own respiratory and circulatory systems, breathing in and out with groaning sighs and subtly changing shade like a living thing. It supplied oxygen and some medication, but more importantly absorbed the mess: the fluids, the odor.

Of course a death blanket was what it actually was—it was the clothing the contemporary dead person was expected to wear. But Jerome thought his sister looked better than she had in years. And that there was something terribly wrong with that.

He stepped up and kissed her on the lips. She seemed dry as a mummy, liable to flake away at any moment, that the blanket had taken something out of her.

He was struck by how thick the blanket was, how organic—it looked like some great flat fish or manta ray. Tentatively he reached down and touched the thing. It felt vaguely fish-like. He could feel something like scales. It seemed to push toward him slightly, gradually gripping his finger, then letting go, as if realizing he wasn't on the day's menu. *Sorry,* he thought, *some day you'll get your chance. But you already know that, don't you?*

He lifted the blanket away from her. He picked her up gently and carried her to the window, an astonishing thing to do. Her body in his arms was lighter than his memories of her.

ٮ؞ٮ

The Disease Artist watched as images of himself washed across the bedroom wall, having followed him there from every other wall in the apartment. Mickey had always insisted that they must keep informed. The coverage was of the panic at last night's *Cholera!* performance. Suddenly the images focused in on an old interview: he marveled at how young he looked. Since then he'd accumulated a number of scars he had chosen not to repair.

The caption along the bottom read *Interview excerpt, The Bulletin:*

Q: Do you feel pain when you take on the full symptomology of a disease?

A: We now have extremely effective pain-killers, of course, so theoretically I wouldn't have to feel any pain at all. But the look of a disease depends as much on the physical constraints that pain imposes as it does on the smell, color, and distortion of flesh. Pain also imposes certain attitudes which are necessary to a good performance. So part of the art comes from inviting pain into the performance, but regulating it so that the artist's perceptions remain clear.

Q: What about your audience? Are you causing them pain?

A: People have been genetically engineered to resist disease and limit infection. That pretty much limits their pain repertoire. Disease is an expression of how we view our internal mortalities, and eventually of course, our impending deaths. What I choose to do to the outside of my body is only an expression of the audience's internal fears concerning their own death and destruction. The closer the pageantry of my performance reflects some intangible unease the more powerful the performance is going to be.

Q: But to what purpose? Shouldn't society's goal be to eradicate disease?

A: I've never suggested that anyone but myself should be infecting themselves. But disease used to be as much a part of our lives as eating, drinking, sleeping. Of course it still is, but its effects have become so muted, so distanced from our consciousness that we usually aren't even aware that we are ill. I believe that our appreciation of our frailties in a world that will travel on without us has been stolen from us.

The philosophers and religious toastmasters speak of a paradise which was, or will be, free of disease. Disease has been our punishment for disobedience, they tell us, for following the unapproved ways. It is as if these diseases were administered by demons—in the old days they often had the names of mythological creatures—and can be alleviated through prayer and obedience. So we pray to modern medicine and we do what the professionals tell us to do. I'm not sure that's always a good thing.

"You shouldn't grant so many interviews, you know. If you keep yourself a bit of a mystery we'll make more money. And spouting off about the medical profession isn't to our benefit—they're still responsible for about a third of our income. Besides, in case you've forgotten, I'm a medical professional."

Mickey spoke to him from the shower. Mickey was always speaking to him from the shower. Most citizens who could afford it had a full communication system in the shower. A layered shower of sound, heat, water, and air was about the most relaxing thing a person could do in the modern world.

"Answering questions isn't what you do best," Mickey said, sliding into bed next to him. He put his hand on Jerome's chest, feeling the scar tissue there, pretending to be slightly repulsed, but his gentleness betrayed him. "Are you ever going to get your nipples back?"

Jerome glanced down at the two little patches of scar where his nipples should have been, a leftover symptom from his six months as a victim of Hutchinson-Gilford progeria, the rapid aging disease. In many ways it had been one of the most rewarding—as well as difficult and dangerous—of his transformations, involving surgeries, bone reduction, and genetic tampering. The result was not a perfect emulation of progeria by any means, but close enough for this world.

Most rewarding of all had been when the three remaining victims of progeria came to visit him and share the stage. "The bird people," Mickey had said of the four of them together, and thought it inexpressibly cute. Jerome had found them ineffably sad. During their limited time together they'd felt like the brothers he'd never had. Those with progeria resembled each other far more than they resembled the members of their own families. His recovery from progeria had been long, two years in the making, a process of countless surgeries and painful genetic experimentation, and costing far more than he'd made from the performances. But it had been an emotionally full time for him, and he'd retained the scars in lieu of nipples as a monument to the journey.

"No," he said finally. "I think this is the way they're going to be from here on out."

Mickey pursed his lips but said nothing. He slowly began touching Jerome's torso, checking out each scar, each monument to a past performance.

13

"Cut it out, Mickey. Please, not tonight."

"We haven't checked your skin thoroughly in awhile. That's my job, remember? Looking for hot spots, places where one of your little escapades is attempting a comeback?"

"I know, just leave it tonight, okay?"

"Hold on." Mickey reached over and grabbed a cleanser off the bedside table. "You got a little pustule coming back. That could mean serious stuff. Gross ...why can't you just have the measles sometime?"

"Dammit, Mickey." Jerome pulled himself out of bed and hobbled to the chair. Something in his leg was bothering him, but he wasn't about to tell Mickey that. "I'm just never *clean* enough for you, am I? That's what this is about."

"What this is *about* is that you're getting careless. You're supposed to run through one of the hospitals at least once a week, remember? Get checked out? That was the deal we made with the Health Services in order for you to practice this 'art' of yours. You haven't had a thorough check in three months."

"I've always passed. There's never been a problem." He'd stumbled over the word "passed," hoped Mickey didn't notice.

"So what are you afraid of? Why not get checked out?"

Jerome looked at him: his perfect nails, his perfect skin. His perfect hair: Jerome used to watch Mickey when he cleaned it, each hair pulled individually into a nozzle of the vacuumhead, stripped and scented, then a scalp scrub and scrape. When, to please Mickey, Jerome had tried the same thing, and the derma shaves, the full body wipes, he'd been injured or had had to stop because of the extreme discomfort.

"I've never been clean enough for you. I've never been tidy. I leave things scattered around, I carry things around with me, I can't let them go. I can't forget, I don't want to forget. I crave contact, Mickey. And contact is always messy."

Mickey responded by getting dressed again. As if in defiance he slipped on the shiny stiff clothes of his profession, clothing which would not crease and therefore trap dirt. His translucent nails glittered against the red material like jewels. Even from this distance Jerome could smell the particularly acidic aroma of the cleansing mouthwashes Mickey used to clean his teeth and gums and kill anything—even taste—that food might leave behind.

Jerome knew that Mickey sometimes swallowed the scouring wash even though there were strong warnings against it. "I'm a professional—I know just how much my body will tolerate." Once every two years Mickey, like half the population, submitted to a painful and dangerous blood cleansing.

Jerome's face suddenly blazed into existence on the mottled white bedroom wall. "Disease Artist may face charges in recent *Cholera!* mishap," the high-toned announcer said. There followed a collage of interview segments:

"Tuberculosis was the disease of the Industrial Revolution, syphilis of the Renaissance, and melancholy of the Baroque period. The message then was the same as now: disease is a sin, disease is not normal."

THE DISEASE ARTIST

"In ancient times epilepsy was considered a holy disease."

He sounded ridiculous, and trapped within the rough wall texture, he looked quite ill.

⌣∴〰

From *The Disease Artist: A Performance Chronicle:*
During the last year of his career, following the disruption at his *Cholera!* engagement, The Disease Artist enacted a number of manifestations in a relatively short period of time:

• His scrofula was remarkable in the brilliance of its "neck collar" rash, a bright red which awed the spectators. The accompanying suppurations were plentiful and, some said, spelled out intriguing messages if you understood the language.

• His short-lived sleeping sickness performance disturbed some of its audience when The Disease Artist manifested a morbid craving for meat, devouring a number of dead animal parts and then attempting to bite his partner of twenty years, Mickey Johnson.

• His portrayal of a memorable yellow fever victim, attempting to explain the breeding habits of mosquitoes while vomiting up large quantities of blood made greasy and black from gastric juices.

• His leprosy and his yaws were cancelled in mid-performance. There are no existing eye-witness accounts.

⌣∴〰

With Mickey gone and the government threatening to close down his career, The Disease Artist found that his recuperation times had lengthened and the side effects of his various recovery regimens were increasing. He had been experiencing severe shortness of breath for several days before he decided to return to his local hospital. But once the day's attendant recognized him, he ordered a battery of screening tests to check for any lingering issues.

Jerome waited over two hours for the attendant to return. He wondered how sick you had to be to actually see a full-fledged doctor anymore. Worm food. Mickey used to say that his art was coarsening him.

The hospital was as slow and quiet as most of the city's restaurants. And every bit as concerned with disinfection. The spray from the nozzles was a constant background music.

He did not know when hospitals had become places of such quiet. Now you could walk inside a hospital and be almost oblivious to pain and blood and the mess of illness. Of course this did not mean that the patients no longer felt the pain, no longer spilled the blood. There must be a higher survival rate in these new hospitals, but in their hush and tidiness they felt more like old-fashioned funeral homes.

A sudden rush in the corridor, figures passing, a whoosh of pressure, sharp perfume scent. Curious, he climbed off the gurney and walked into the hall.

In the next room activity was manic. Attendants rushed around a small figure in the narrow bed. Blood everywhere. The significance of this did not occur to him immediately. Blood everywhere. He stepped closer. A young woman lay beneath one of the blue life blankets, but something had malfunctioned, things had gone messy, and the girl was bleeding out through nose and mouth and from wounds invisible.

Suddenly Jerome realized he was alone in the room with the bleeding girl. There was so much blood, more blood than most had seen in decades, more blood than any small human had the right to contain.

⌣ ⁖ ᷄

Mickey thought he would retrieve the rest of his belongings while Jerome was out. He watched the apartment for days, and seeing no activity during that period he used his handprint to get in, both saddened and pleased that it had not been erased from the building's memory.

He found Jerome wandering from room to room, followed by jets of disinfectant and his own image from the day's newsreels. The stench was as bad as from any of Jerome's performances. He thought about checking the supplies of masking and cleansing compounds for the apartment, then remembered he didn't live there anymore.

"If I'm doing my job correctly, if I'm taking the particular malady far enough, some permanent physical damage always occurs: even after the course of the disease has been reversed, scars are invariably left behind. As far as mental scars, well, how can I even answer that?"

"They're saying I've retired," Jerome said, still walking, now swinging his arms in agitation, now scratching at visible sores. He did not look at Mickey directly. "This is some sort of documentary retrospective on my work. They say no one has seen me in months."

"...constant treatment for tissue repair and scar removal. It leaves a mottled, textured appearance to my skin (He shows the camera his arm.) Mickey says it's like touching an enlarged fingerprint: you find yourself trying to identify and interpret the ridges and whorls. Mickey? He's my assistant, no, more than that: my partner."

"I heard about the incident at the hospital," Mickey said. "That must have been awful. Those blankets ..." He paused. "Well those blankets *never* fail."

16

THE DISEASE ARTIST

Jerome stared at him as if unsure who he was.

"…molecular computers and various antibiotic vehicles handling most of the repairs. But their work is never one hundred percent complete."

"It really wasn't that bad," Jerome finally replied. "I mean, that's the way it used to be, right?"

"Relics and ruins get left behind: a discoloration in the skin, a twist in the joint, an internal pattern which persists. I am a relic and a ruin. I believe we all are."

"It used to be injury, pain, and dying, right? Used to be it was always messy."

"Mickey says that one of these relics is going to kill me eventually, and Mickey is probably right, but so what?"

"That's what my art's about, reminding people of all that."
"But so what?"
Mickey stopped and looked at him. "That's really what you think?"
"Well, of course. That's why the people come."
"It's just the human condition."
"Oh, Jerome. They already know about the likelihood of injury, of death. All that mess. But you still keep it tidy for them. Watching you is like looking at a painting or watching one of those old films. You keep the mess out of their living rooms."
"I should know. I've been doing this, *we've* been doing this, such a long time."
"No one cares, Jerome. No one even remembers. You ask those Filthies kids, or those Job characters, why those people used to die, why it happened, what it meant, especially what it means about them and being human, they're not going to know. They're just going to point to that picture of you on their cloaks, and sound out whatever slogan they have written there. That's all they know how to do."
Mickey thought Jerome might have stopped after that, but he was wrong.

᠁

From *The Disease Artist: A Performance Chronicle:*

The only film remaining of The Disease Artist's last performance is of rather poor quality, shaky and a bit out-of-focus, obviously taken with an antique film camera. Under normal circumstances this film would have been enhanced and brought up to contemporary standards, but a clause in the will of the original owner, The Disease Artist's long-time partner Mr. Mickey Johnson, forbids any form of alteration and/or augmentation. Few first-hand accounts of this performance have survived, most of those merely relating that The Disease Artist appeared to be in a state of advanced mental deterioration due to his disease, and babbled incoherently throughout the final days of the performance on any and all subjects which passed at random through his mind. This lack of specifics as to his final commentaries is particularly troubling in that the sound was turned off for most of Mr. Johnson's less-than-adequate filmed record.

Also puzzling is the choice of The Disease Artist's final ailment[128]: a rather undramatic assemblage of symptoms—weight loss, a barely visible swelling of the lymph glands, dry cough, fatigue and fever—symptoms indicative of a number of conditions. Only the white blemishes on the tongue, the red, brown, and purple marks on the nose and eyelids, and the various skin rashes are of any particular aesthetic appeal.

Only at the end of the Johnson film do we hear any clear statements from The Disease Artist. At one point he is heard to say, "It is our need to be remembered, to let other people know that we once walked this world." And at another, "To tell them how it was, how it used to be, how it felt to be there."

Clearly, we must take this as an artist's statement about what it must mean to be an artist in a world that does not always appreciate one's chosen art form. It is unfortunate that like the fictional Hunger Artist before him, who never found his defining food, our own Disease Artist passed from us without ever discovering his defining disease.

Footnote 128: The AIDS epidemic, of course, ran out of steam some fifty years ago. With the exception of The Disease Artist's final performance, there have been no reported cases since that time.

The Shape of the Empty Heart

GERARD HOUARNER

It occurred to Mark, staring at the rusted iron construction he had created in his Brooklyn studio, that the piece was as bankrupt as the formerly wealthy founder of a leading edge, venture technology company who had commissioned it. He sagged against the workbench, tossed the face shield aside, let the dead torch fall to the floor. The thing was hideous. "An articulation of the symmetry of interplay between art and commerce," he had written in his proposal, playing to his patron's conceits regarding creative expression in the business world. That man and his company were gone. Mark's inspiration had never arrived.

The down payment was gone. The piece was as ready as it was ever going to be. He could think of nothing else to do with it. He was stuck with the broken corpse of a monster that had never had the chance to live. The piece meant nothing, would have meant nothing except to the buyer. Possibly a critic or another sculptor or artist might study the piece and offer helpful advice, like: junk the pile of shit and find another career. But then the word would get out: he was no longer in creative control. He'd lost his edge. The talent was exhausted. Some might even gleefully pronounce the truth: talent had never been there. His reputation would be shot.

Mark wiped sweat from his face with the end of his T-shirt, closed his eyes to the glimpse of exposed, pale, bulging belly. Next door, speed metal raged as the resident artist concocted another drug-fueled splatter canvas for a Japanese buyer desperate for fresh Western hipness. That artist hadn't lost his inspiration. He hadn't lost his cash cow, either.

19

Mark coughed as residual smoke tickled the back of his throat. The bitter taste of his failed work coated his tongue, made him gag. He tore off the apron, ran down the back stairs until he was outside, in the filthy alley, sucking in chilled air tainted with the smell of piss, heart pounding as if to announce the arrival of a massive failure. The brisk cold snapped at his despair. The garbage piled around his feet prophesied the future, if he didn't find his focus.

He had been in this situation before. And worse.

He didn't want to visit the old man. The last time, years ago, his son David had gone with him. If he went again, who could he bring along?

There was no one left. There were no other choices.

᠊᠃᠊

Mark put the paper down and looked across the small glass breakfast table in the brushed aluminum kitchen and asked his wife, Lisette, "Did you know David's showing at the Girand Gallery was reviewed?"

Lisette stared at the espresso machine, ignoring their view of Central Park through the narrow window behind Mark. Her hands were stuck deep in the pockets of a thick, navy robe. Her grey-streaked auburn hair was pulled back into a knot, exposing the delicate bone structure of her emaciated face. She did not answer.

"Well-received, I might add," Mark continued, draining the black, sweet shot of coffee from his cup.

He tore the cup from his lips and threw it against the refrigerator. It shattered, fragments bouncing back to hit them both.

"That one cost $5," Lisette said. She stared at the ceramic fragments, as if trying to piece together what the shards might once have been.

"Henry says I should think about going deeper into mathematics-based conceptual art, or open a public studio and advertise myself as a performance artist," Mark said. Then he screamed, "Like I'm some kind of circus freak. Like I'm a whore putting out for art johns horny for what's hot and kinky on the market."

"It's a lot of work being a whore," Lisette said. "You have to be good at it."

Mark stared at Lisette, who went down on her knees to pick up pieces of his cup. There was no trace of a smile on her lips, not a single knowing, ironic glance in his direction. He waited for another barb, a signal that she was aware of, impatient with, and even disappointed in their life together. Eagerly, he searched for a sign of the hurt and the rage that should have answered his. But her attention remained centered on something beyond the floor and cleaning up, past his understanding, on the other side of the apartment they shared and the family they'd had and the world that contained both of them.

When she had built a tiny mound of broken cup pieces on the floor, she stared at it for a few seconds, then went back to her seat at the table. She prodded the half-eaten croissant on her plate with a fork.

THE SHAPE OF THE EMPTY HEART

"When an agent suggests you pursue things outside your interests, skills and range, your time is running out," he said, hoping to connect with his wife and spark a response from a secret measure of sympathy, or even a vein of resentment.

Their daughter Elizabeth wandered into the kitchen in a long, blue night shirt. Her gaze slid over Mark and her mother as she drifted from stove to refrigerator to sink while holding a CD player in both hands. Music Mark could not identify leaked out of the earphones nearly hidden under the teenager's short-cropped, dirty blond hair. She had her father's strong jaw and nose, Mark noted, reassuring himself of her beauty. And she had her mother's eyes.

Elizabeth kicked over the pile of ceramic shards, walked over the remains in her bare feet. A thin string of drool hung from the corner of her mouth. She bounced against the refrigerator door like a pinball machine's silver ball popping out from a bumper, then wandered out again, whatever need that had driven her to her parents or the kitchen forgotten. Bloody footprints marked her passage.

Lisette stood up suddenly, followed Elizabeth out, also in her bare feet. Like her daughter, she never flinched at the cuts made in her skin. Her blood mingled with Elizabeth's on the floor.

Joined by the bond of their wounds, the two women left a trail of blood for Mark to follow, as if in invitation.

He found another cup and poured more coffee.

꒯꒦꒰

If Mark had not needed to be an artist, his life would have been far less complicated. He could have been like his friends from school, getting through classes, graduating, finding wives and husbands and jobs and careers in a world where someone else was always demanding something, and the grind of daily existence shaped desires and warped needs. Those childhood friends didn't all seem unhappy. Yet some of them made more money than he did. Most of them could count on a paycheck.

It was the drive to make objects that possessed him. He filled drawers and closets in his old childhood room with school craft projects and, later, carvings, mobiles and constructions that spilled out into the yard and the garage. His parents bought him building sets and models, which he converted and used for far grander designs. He built the set for his high school play, and salvaged a National prize-winning statue from the wreckage of Buck Gershen's Mustang totaled in a drag racing accident. The award and a mild gift for mechanics let him into a college art program where he studied the rules of design, the engineering science of materials and how to put them together, the traditions of what had been done before and the emerging trends for the future in the art that seemed to fit his talents and need most comfortably: sculpture.

There had been a time when he thought he was reflecting an inner part of himself in his work, until one of his college professors pointed out there was

21

always a hole at the center of his constructs and speculated about what that empty quarter represented. No matter how hard he tried, Mark had never been able to overcome the stylistic stamp. It was inseparable from his need to create.

Then he became convinced, because of his predilection for combing trash dumps and junkyards for working material, that he was expressing the Western world's insatiable hunger for material things and its inescapable consequences. Another professor offered the possibility that Mark's insatiable hunger for junk might symbolize a more personal desire to feed off the artistic waste of his betters in order to fill the bottomless pit of his own lack of talent with what cultural leavings he was capable of understanding. Mark had dropped out of both professors' courses.

Caught up in his romantic vision of himself as the academic outsider with hipness granted by an exclusive muse few could understand, Lisette had married him while they were still graduate students. Her Parisian heritage and sophisticated manner put the imprimatur on his artistic ambition. For her, he was the bold American who was going to save her from her destiny as the wife of a government functionary, a diplomat at best.

It was a blow to them both when Mark was thrown out of art school. He was told he had nothing to say, and no talent to say it with. The work that had gotten him into the graduate program was re-evaluated, found lacking, another condemnation on the previous department head forced to resign under a cloud of controversy. His current work was not up to school standards. He was asked to leave. His parents looked on from a distance, smug in the certainty of the collapse of his youthful ego and his eventual return to a local job, possibly as a teacher, and settling down with a local girl. His wife's family pressured him to join their printing business. He stopped working in his art, inspiration gone as if he had never created a thing. But the hunger to make still gnawed inside the impotent shell of his self. He and Lisette took on a humiliating string of menial jobs as he wrestled with his muse and fought for attention.

He tried every desperate measure young artists attempt to kick-start their careers: distributed ridiculous manifestoes, attacked established artists, allied himself with up-and-coming rebels, joined a movement, donated pieces to charitable organizations, slept with agents, dealers, gallery owners, critics, other artists, even suppliers. He went into analysis. Tried Yoga. Hypnosis. Drugs. Magic. He discovered everyone ignored the ravings of unsuccessful artists and movements, and no one wanted donations of work from such entities. He lost confidence in his lovemaking skills when his affairs brought no results, and Lisette became disgruntled. He obsessed about his mother's lack of affection and his father's passivity, leading him to choose an inappropriate career as either a way to compensate for their absence, or a means of rebelling against their abandonment. He couldn't afford to stick around for the necessary years it would take to uncover the true root of his behavior. He also discovered he was physically graceless, a lousy drunk, and a dangerous drug abuser. Certain kinds of incense made him sneeze, ruining the atmosphere of spell-making.

THE SHAPE OF THE EMPTY HEART

He had been on the brink of giving in. A brief hospitalization had given him a taste of things to come on the path he'd chosen. With the need to create a steady ache in his mind and gut, like an appetite that could not be satisfied, he tried to choose between a retreat to home or a leap to Europe. Suicide lurked in the shadows of these bright options.

That was when he found the old man.

✌:∾

The building hadn't changed in thirty years, though its tenants had shifted from Italian to Chinese in the last generation as Little Italy shrank and Chinatown, bursting with legal and illegal immigrants ranging from wealthy Hong Kong expatriates to desperate slave labor, stretched through the Bowery and the Lower East Side.

Neither had the old man. He remained a short, wizened, dark-skinned figure made remarkable by the shock of shoulder-length white hair flowing from his balding pate. The length of his hair had never changed, and neither had his hairline. The wrinkles of his face had never deepened or multiplied, and the black eyes recessed in the folds of his flesh remained bright and glistening with intelligence. He said his parents were Indonesian pirates, and that the roots of his heritage drew blood from Africa, feudal Japan, and Imperial China. Mark had heard him speak Hebrew, Italian, French, and accepted the claims of Mandarin, Cantonese, Hakka, and a dozen Southeast Asian tribal dialects.

Mark had met him at a party held in an abandoned building close to the river. Introduced by a far more successful fellow student, Mark was told the old man was an inspiration. A spasm of nervous laughter had passed through onlookers before they hurriedly moved on.

"Why do you want to be an artist?" the old man had asked, between draws from an opium pipe.

"I don't know," he'd replied, still full of arrogance and outrage, nervous in the company of age, uncomfortable with the mix of sour and sweet smells. "Because that's what I am."

"Try to know."

"It's like I'm reaching for something," he'd found himself saying. "Inside, outside, I can't be sure."

"Have you found what you're reaching for?"

"No." The word was still bitter in his mouth, all these years later.

"Maybe you need a guide. I can show you the way. Where to reach, between the cracks, in the dark places. What to touch. What to bring back."

He'd brought his younger brother with him that first time. His parents never spoke to him again. His brother never left the institution.

23

The old man came downstairs to open the door. A young Chinese couple passed them on their way out, bowing to the old man, ignoring Mark.

"I didn't think you'd still be here, Sumarno," Mark said, shivering, his jacket too light for the wintry air that had blown in overnight.

"Why not?" asked the old man, stepping aside to let him in.

"After all these years…" Mark bumped against Sumarno as they maneuvered through the entry and the inner door. The old man did not yield, and Mark wound up recoiling softly into a wall.

"It's been seven years since your last visit."

"Business was good."

They went up creaking stairs, Sumarno leading. He took the stairs two at a time, leaving Mark behind. The paint on the walls had not changed in fifteen years.

"The world's changed a bit," the old man said, already on the next set of stairs.

"Yes. Times are tougher," Mark said, forced to raise his voice. "There's not so much money to spend on guys like me."

"I understand. How's your wife? Your daughter?" The questions drifted down through the stale air, through television babbling and grating Asian pop music.

"Fine. You can hardly tell the difference."

"I doubt that. And David?"

"He's doing very well."

"I saw a review for a show. I went to the gallery. Very fine work."

Mark let the conversation dangle until he had caught up to the old man on the sixth floor landing. Out of breath, holding on to the banister, he looked down on Sumarno and asked, "Why him? How come he didn't wind up like the others?"

Sumarno let them into his apartment. Water boiled in a kettle on the old stove in the first room, a dining room and kitchen. Mirrors, carved masks fleshed out with grass and feathers, and herb garlands hung from the walls. A closed door to the left led to the room Sumarno took the people Mark had brought with him in the past. One of the doors at the right end of the room, next to the tub sink, was the bathroom. The other went to a room he'd never seen Sumarno enter. The earthy smell and low-wattage overhead bulb gave the space the feel of a cave.

"Sometimes it works out that way," Sumarno said, taking down cups and a jar of tea. "Sacrifice gives birth to art, for those with the strength to cope with the loss. But you don't always need strength. Sometimes all it takes is innocence. Or ignorance."

"Yeah." Mark sat down, watching the old man preparing tea. David's condition had given him the courage to come alone. He hoped Sumarno could work the same miracle with him.

"You haven't spoken to your son?"

THE SHAPE OF THE EMPTY HEART

"David won't talk to me."

"Can't blame him, I suppose. You should have brought him at a much younger age."

"I didn't think I needed you, anymore. And you wouldn't take anyone else I offered."

Sumarno turned with a cup in each hand. He set them down on the table, joined Mark. They were crowded together like conspirators in a quiet café, plotting assassinations and the overthrowing of governments. "People can only give so much. There's talk in your family about what has already happened, I imagine."

Mark didn't answer. His parents thought he had brought Greg to a party and let him take drugs. Lisette's family blamed chemicals, smoke and poisons from his studio for their daughter's condition and tried unsuccessfully to have him convicted of attempted murder. Medical exams concluded she had suffered a stroke and absolved him of responsibility. Their daughter was diagnosed as mentally ill, and most blamed the same defect for their son David's sudden personality changes. He hadn't had to answer for the others he tried to use, the former classmates and ex-lovers, even strangers, before Sumarno told him the sacrifice had to come from those closest to him if he wasn't willing to submit himself to the process. But there were whispers of drug use, and his murky past with its string of broken associates served as a warning against getting too close for most people he dealt with.

"Speaking of giving," Sumarno continued, "who did you bring this time?"

"Nobody. Nobody left. Just me."

"You're making the sacrifice?" The old man avoided Mark's gaze, concentrating his attention on sweets, cans of tea, small scrolls and other paraphernalia cluttering the side of the table set against the wall. Gifts from students and clients, he always said. Small tokens of respect.

Mark was suddenly keenly aware he had never given Sumarno a gift. "Yes."

"At last," the old man exclaimed, clapping his hands once and breaking out into a smile. "Now we're talking."

⌁

After tea, they went into the room in which Sumarno had taken everyone Mark brought to him. Secure in Mark's company, seduced by the old pirate, they'd gladly followed Sumarno in for a treat, a look at a special artifact brought back from his travels, even a glance out the front window to check the weather.

He expected machinery, a rational construction, vaguely scientific, with straps, and electrodes, meters, cables. Instead, the room, twice as long as the first room, looked like a merchant's crowded alcove at a bazaar. Small Turkish and other rugs covered the floor in overlapping layers. A dense, irregular array of shelves packed with objects covered every wall, floor to ceiling. In the gloom,

25

Mark could only pick out an occasional book in antique binding, something of glass here, a shiny piece there, a soft thing squeezed between shell and bone and rock. The window at the end of the room, facing the street, was thickly curtained, and a few under-powered lamps, themselves antique, provided the illumination that deepened shadows and made an occasional piece glitter.

"Where do you sleep?" Mark asked, picking his way through a maze of wooden chests, urns, jars, crates. He moved slowly, afraid to send something crashing, or raising more dust.

"In the back room," Sumarno answered.

Mark looked behind him. The door was already closed. Without a squeak, just like every other time the old man walked in behind Mark's offerings. This time, the door had closed on him.

"Where does it happen?" Mark asked, looking for a couch, a seat, a hint of the procedure to follow. "Does it hurt?" He bit his lip. He'd never asked before.

He tried to remember the moment, waiting in the outer room, when he knew the old man had done what he promised. Particularly the first time, when Mark had brought his brother Greg as a joke, not expecting anything except to warn his teenaged sibling by personal example about crackpots and unrealistic dreams. He'd had hope, of course. Deep inside, where the emptiness he so desperately wanted to fill ached and burned and promised to drive him to madness. But what he really thought was that this final humiliation, the exposure of his last, ludicrous belief that he could find a way to create a thing that was both a part of and outside him while filling the empty places inside, would bring him to the decision point about his art, and his life. When the old man failed, he had told himself, he could go on.

He tried to remember when he discovered he was capable of art. He tried recapturing the feeling of fulfillment in connecting all the pieces of what he was into something larger than he could ever be. But instead, all he did remember were the people coming out of the room, Greg first, then the rest, a silent parade of ghosts helped along by the old man. Stumbling. Eyes glazed. Mouths moving without sound. Changed.

"It happens everywhere," Sumarno said.

A flash of light caught Mark's attention. He reached for the glitter, expecting to touch glass. His fingers slid across a cool smoothness. Before he knew what object he had found, he felt drawn to the feel of it against his skin and he started to ask Sumarno if he was selling what was in the room. He fell, tipping forward, first into bright light, then into darkness, his breath trapped behind a racing heart, his head spinning. His arms and legs spread wide as he tried to find solid purchase, but he continued falling, feeling lighter as he went faster with each passing moment. He cried out, but the downward rush snatched his voice, threw it away. Cold bit his fingertips, his feet, crept along his limbs, closed around his heart. He thought he was dying. He was already dead.

He woke with a start, braced for a hard landing. Sumarno held him in his lap, nestled between an iron-bound wooden chest of drawers and a half-finished marble bust of a wild-eyed, heavily-bearded man whose single, finished eye glared at Mark. The smell of fur and old wool choked him.

Sumarno helped him up, led him to the kitchen.

Mark slumped over the table while the old man prepared another cup of tea. The stove's heat, contained in the small, airless kitchen, warmed him. Reminded him he was alive. Ignited the hunger to make something.

To make himself. To reconstruct what he was, to complete the thing he might have been.

Mark sat up, feeling raw, scoured, inside. He struggled to understand the new perspective on his art, stumbled into blankness. No thought, no feeling. A void. He was sitting in a room with a stranger. He forgot his name. Was he dead? Was this hell?

A baby cried in the apartment next door, or in Sumarno's back room.

Mark. He was Mark.

He found himself, or what was left of him. A piece of the person he had been—more than a memory, an active aspect of identity, a living piece as vital as any organ—had been ripped out of him. There were things he could not name that he knew he could have done, couched in feelings he might have felt, but were no longer available. It was as if he had forgotten how to talk but retained the vague notion of verbal communication. Lost in the expanded territories of his emptiness, Mark burned under the glare of betrayal. He always gained something with Sumarno, never lost. He was not the one who was supposed to lose. He was supposed to gain what he needed to create. That was the bargain.

What had Sumarno done to him? Had everyone he'd ever brought to visit the old man formed an alliance and struck a deal with his secret helper to gain revenge? Not logical. Except for his son, they were incapable of such concerted action. Most could barely function in their daily routines. Was the old man plotting against him? Trying to steal his soul?

The baby wailed. The hunger in its voice resonated in Mark.

A new strength surged through him. Vibrant, desperate energy filled him. It flowed from hunger, from the fresh tracts of desert inside him, and it gathered mind and feelings into its current and dragged the many parts of him down a narrow channel through the skills and knowledge of his art. Worlds opened, others closed, as a rough alchemy transformed reality. Mark stood, suddenly restless, unable to contain the vision erupting in his head, through his body, from the fountain of inspiration that welled from fresh wounds. He was hungry. He knew how to feed.

"What's that?" he asked, holding on to chair and table to steady his balance.

"Nothing to concern yourself with," Sumarno answered, setting fresh cups of tea on the table. He took hold of Mark's elbow and sat him down. "You're here for inspiration, right?"

Mark giggled as he sat. Sumarno's trick had never worked as well. The power to create glowed inside him, leaked through pores, through his eyes, nose, mouth and ears. He felt like a god. He couldn't wait to get back to his studio.

⌣∴∾

His work soared. Metal curved through space, intersecting stone, absorbing plastic, embracing air. His agent did not believe he had made the piece Mark showed him, and watched as a second grew like an alien tree in the studio. The agent brought gallery owners, critics, buyers in for private showings. A magazine interviewed him about his breakthrough. An exhibition was booked. Museums queried about the availability of the new work.

Captured by his art, he slept on a cot in the middle of pieces yet to be assembled. Workmen delivered new raw material and carted out finished work, after it was photographed and catalogued by his agent, though he hardly noticed. He saw only what was under construction in his mind and in the studio. He felt only the hunger he rode, like a wild stallion galloping out of control under him, racing to stay ahead of his satiation. He could not stop. As far as he knew, his wife and daughter did not miss him.

He felt the physical drain of his passion after he finished his twelfth piece in three months. The torch fell from his hand. The loft's walls closed around him. He fled, shaking. The chill of late Winter air, seasoned with the faintest trace of Spring, hit him hard, brought him short. Had he missed the snow, the ice? The past few months lay like a collapsed house in his memory, with only the smoke of exultation rising from the ruin.

He checked the mail. Another magazine, with another review full of praise for his new work. Someone commented that his son's success had revitalized his own career.

David. His show was closing within the week.

Mark went back upstairs, put on his coat, took the train to Manhattan. Did he want to reach out, or gloat? He couldn't decide. He didn't know.

Speeding through tunnels while rocked in the metal cradle of a subway car, Mark felt the hunger in him deepen. As the distance stretched between himself and the nursery of his art, panic nipped and sliced. Was he feeling more vulnerable, more hollow, than usual? Had he been feeding on himself? Consuming the vital parts of his psyche in the service of his art? He stared at the reflection of his face in the car window. He forgot what he was supposed to look like.

He found the gallery. Walked back and forth in front of the windows, glancing in at first, then pausing to peer. A moving truck pulled up. A couple of figures emerged from a back room. David, slim and bearded, with eyes that were so much like Lisette's. Mark thought for a moment his wife was in male drag. David laughed, put his arm around the other man. A twinge of jealousy reminded him how cold he was. The other man, older, familiar, reciprocated the gesture.

THE SHAPE OF THE EMPTY HEART

The two met the moving crew as they entered. The cold seeped deeper into Mark, touched bone's marrow, slowed his heart.

The other man had the face he had just seen in the subway car window. He was the other man.

~:~

"Back so soon?" Sumarno asked, putting a hand on Mark's forearm, concern on his face.

He didn't wait to get up to Sumarno's apartment. "I saw myself. With my son. I wasn't hallucinating. It was me. I saw it, him. Who is he? What is he? What did you do?"

Sumarno's hand fell away, his expression shifted to neutral. He stepped out onto the sidewalk, pulling up the collar on his corduroy shirt. His hair whipped out with the wind gusts. "That was you."

Mark followed him, letting the door slam shut behind him. "I'm me. This is me," he said, holding out his arms.

"It was a part of what I took from you, the last time you came. The good father. Seemed a waste, in there with the rest of you. I let him out for a while. Kind of a payback for what I did to your son. Even I feel bad, sometimes."

"What about my wife?"

Sumarno looked up to, into, and finally through Mark. He shrugged his shoulders and unlocked the front door, stepped through. Mark caught the door before it closed.

Upstairs, the old man was already opening the door to the back room. Where he slept. He went in. Mark followed.

There was a bed, beneath a window with an air conditioner and blinds. A dark, narrow well was visible through the slats. The walls were again lined with shelves. But unlike the front room, their contents were distinct.

Sumarno passed his hand along a higher shelf. Stopped. Took down one of the jars.

"She's here. Along with your daughter," he said, pointing back to the shelf. "Do you want to see? They're all up there, everyone you brought. Your son, too."

Mark backed up to the doorway. "What do you do with them?"

Sumarno held the jar to his chest with both hands. A shape moved through murky liquid, like an eel. "Keep them. Care for them. Sometimes I let them out and we talk. Play games." He indicated the rest of the apartment with a hand flourish. "No TV," he said, with a touch of pride. "So we play cards, and we roll dice. We gamble for time, for pleasures, for sustenance." He pushed his shoulders back, straightened, and said with a slight scowl, "They feed me, as I find ways to feed them. We help each other to live on." With a shake of his head, he waved Mark away and put the jar back on the shelf. "I raise the young ones. Trade them. You're not the only artist in town looking for inspiration. What is offered in

29

sacrifice, I take. If the bond is close, what is needed is turned over to the one who makes the offering. What is left is for me. Most times, there is much left."

"You greedy little bastard," Mark said, taking a step in. "Why do you take so much?"

Sumarno's feet slid into a stance. His arms flew up, his hands lined up one behind the other, elbows aligned, like an arrow pointed at Mark's chest. Mark stopped, reared back, as if he had just stepped into a snake's den. His heart fluttered.

"I did not make the rules. I am just the guide and the guardian of this way. It was your choice to follow this path. Greedy bastard."

The echo of his words stunned Mark, especially coming from the man who had shown him nothing but politeness. He recovered, remembering what had brought him back. "What about me? What did you mean, 'you took the good father?' What else did you take?"

Sumarno waited a moment, then shook his head, relaxed, went to a shelf, reached for a jar. Before he could turn, Mark darted forward. Grabbed the jar, ramming the old man with his body and driving him onto the bed. He caught a glimpse of Sumarno's widened eyes before he ran out, down the stairs, into the street.

There was no magic, as far as he could tell. No procedure to follow for opening the jar, no ritual incantations or words of power to recite over its thick, oily contents. He simply opened the jar, put up with the sweet, incense scent, and waited.

The other man appeared at the edge of his peripheral vision. By the time Mark turned, he was looking at a reflection of himself sitting on his living room couch. Before either could speak, Elizabeth wandered in, listening to music through earphones. She smiled and ran to the seated man, ripping the earphones off, and said, "You're home early, Dad!" They hugged.

Mark stood. "Elizabeth, what do you think you're doing?"

His daughter flinched, bowed her head, gave the stranger on the sofa a weak smile, and left.

His reflection folded his hands in his lap. They wore the same clothes, had the same day's growth on their faces. Mark wanted to beat the invader senseless. Scar him. Make him different. An imperfect reflection.

There were a dozen questions battling the urge to violence. Mark stared at the jar, and the chain of circumstances explaining its appearance ran through his mind. The questions fell away until there was one left: "What's wrong with me?"

"You're not an artist," the other answered.

Mark rushed forward, loomed over himself. "Yes, I am. I have the reviews. The sales."

THE SHAPE OF THE EMPTY HEART

The other took one of Mark's hands and squeezed it between his. "Your success is based on what you took from others."

Mark pulled away, stepped back. "Not this last time."

"I grant you that," the other said, getting up. "But a little sacrifice doesn't make you an artist. Especially when you give up something you never used." He walked toward the bedroom, called out, "Lisette?" A noise, like a wounded animal crying in the brush, came through the door.

"What am I, then?"

The other's expression saddened as he put his hand on the bedroom doorknob. "A victim."

⋌⋎⋋

Sumarno found the studio. Mark didn't think the old man knew where he lived or worked, but then again, he did live a public life, and privacy was hard to protect in the art world. "I'm not giving the jar back," Mark told the old man, who remained in the service elevator, arms crossed over his chest, feet apart. He leaned back slightly, tilting his head further, to give the illusion he was staring down instead of up at Mark.

Sumarno looked younger. His hair was shorter, darker, and there were not so many wrinkles in his face. Even his voice, when he spoke, was charged with greater emotion. With rage. "The two of you can't go around free, like that. You're going to have to fight it out, sooner or later, to see who's in charge."

"I'm the one in charge, thank you, Sumarno. And I'll keep my other self safe in the jar for you." Mark kept the torch flame on, used the fire as a pointer. "You're not the old man from downtown, are you? You're the pirate. The one he was. The one he sacrificed to get this power of his. And his immortality?"

Sumarno pursed his lips in disgust. "One of you is going to have to come back with me, sooner or later."

"Aren't you going to try to take the jar from me? Use some street kung-fu, kick my ass?"

Sumarno pressed the elevator's down button. The door began sliding shut. "It is not up to us to settle who comes back."

⋌⋎⋋

His other self visited the studio later. Mark was finishing his thirteenth piece. It needed something. It felt empty. He was thinking of a glass centerpiece. A container buried in the heart of aluminum and steel and stone. A restless, viscous liquid trapped inside glass.

"I ran into your agent," his other said, getting off the elevator and casually strolling around the loft, pausing to study a table full of sketches. "Henry's quite taken with you, these days. Amazed by your rebirth, like everyone else."

31

Mark wondered what would happen if he trapped his doppelganger in a statue. Would he gain the power Sumarno wielded, to capture pieces of another's spirit, to feed on those shadow spirits and live forever? Would he see more deeply into the human condition? Would his art gain greater depth, a wider audience? Would his art, in turn, gain immortality?

How many pieces of people would he have to harvest, before the desert inside him bloomed?

Mark went to the flammable storage cabinet, removed the jar and lid. "You have to go back inside," he said, waving the open jar in front of him.

His other self glanced at the mouth, turned his nose up. "You have no idea how all this works, do you?"

"Sumarno said we'd have to fight. I'll beat you to death if I have to."

"Yes, of course, you would." He took a last look at the plans on the table, at the work near completion and the rest in progress, then approached Mark. "You're not going to give that back to him, are you?"

"No," Mark said, holding the jar out. He was disheartened that his sacrifice, or the reclaiming of his sacrifice, apparently had no connection to Sumarno's power. There were, he suspected, rituals and words involved. Perhaps greater sacrifices than he had already made. Maybe giving up his art was required. If so, Mark decided, he'd let his work carry him to others, to the future. He was not going to give up his art, not after everything he had gone through, and all he had achieved. "I'm going to put it, put you, in the piece I'm working on now. You're going to be a part of me, again. But in a useful way."

His other self stared at the construction dominating the studio. "I was hoping for a reconciliation, but you don't even want me back inside you. I guess I should have stayed out a while longer. But I was getting tired. It's not the same, walking around without the original body, or the whole of what we are at my disposal. People think they know you, but you can't be what they expect or want you to be, so you start to let them down. I don't need to do that to these people around us. Even though, with all the disappointment, some of them still might prefer the change of character." The other laughed. "The genie starts craving the bottle. It's safer in there. Peaceful."

Mark was not sure he had ever heard himself laugh in that way. While he sorted through his own shifting plans and dreams, the other stepped up to him with startling speed. Mark pulled the hand holding the jar back. Braced for an impact. Balled his free hand into a fist.

But there was nothing to hit. One moment, the other was charging him. The next, a shadow passed across his vision. His arm was pulled down with a sudden weight change in the jar. Some oily liquid splashed onto his hand. Then the jar's weight was only a little heavier than before, and a long, slick darkness glided through its cloudy depths.

Mark twisted the cap back on, still waiting for a greater power to possess him. When it did not, he resolved again to make do with his art.

THE SHAPE OF THE EMPTY HEART

⋞⋟

David had always known where the studio was, he just never dropped by to visit before. Henry had just left, ecstatic about the latest piece, the thirteenth in Mark's renaissance. They had probably met downstairs, talked of the change that had come over Mark. Maybe one or the other offered comforting platitudes of hope regarding Lisette and Elizabeth.

David came into the studio, but unlike most other visitors, let his gaze pass quickly over the new work and settled it on Mark. "Hi, Dad," he said, holding his arms out.

Mark took his son's hand instead of the embrace, shook it. They stepped away from each other, awkwardly. "I heard great things about your show," he offered.

David frowned. "Yeah, right, you were there, remember?"

The other. His son. Talking in the gallery. Mark nodded his head, looked away to hide his momentary disorientation. "Of course. It's just that I still keep hearing how great it was. You are."

"Are you okay, Dad?"

"Fine. Just busy. As you can see. This one's done," he said, sweeping a hand across the latest construction, with its secret heart of glass. "But I've got all these others to finish."

"That's why I came up. I decided to take you up on your offer."

Mark shuffled drawings on his work table as if searching for something he'd lost. "Really? I'm surprised."

"I know. My friends and my agent say I'm crazy. I should be concentrating on producing my next showing. But how many opportunities are we going to have to work together? I mean, it wouldn't be an actual collaboration or anything. I don't want credit. An assistant, like you said, is fine, so we can have a little time together to get to know each other. Catch up on all the changes we've been through."

"Ah, the assistant thing," Mark said, turning around, holding on to the table with both hands clenched so tightly they hurt. "Well, you know how I've always felt about assistants. They get in the way more than they help. Not that you would, of course, but right now I'm in the middle of some delicate work. Complicated. I have a hard time keeping it all straight in my head. I couldn't take the time to sit down and explain it. Have to move while the inspiration is still hot, right? I was actually thinking of later. When I've finished this series. Then we really could collaborate on something. You and me. Can you imagine what the dealers would ask for a piece like that? Mixed media, father and son, two rising stars? We'd make a fortune."

David's mouth opened for a moment. Then he cocked his head to the side, snorted, put his hands in his pockets. He headed back to the elevator without a word. Stopped. Turned again.

33

"They're all empty, you know," David said. "You're just putting frames around your emptiness. Even the new ones Henry showed me. Complex, layered frames. But still the same. I know. That's what I've been doing. That's all I could do, after you took me to that old man." He went to the elevator, held the door open. "Except this last piece," he said, pointing to the finished work in the middle of the studio. "That's a real breakthrough. You finally caught something real. Congratulations. You're a better artist than I'll ever be, after all. But I'll be the better father. You better fucking believe it."

The elevator went down. Silence settled over the studio. Dust particles danced in random rays of sunlight. Mark sat down on the floor. Stared at his latest creation.

It was an alien thing. Unrecognizable. Alive.

If Sumarno came back to reclaim his precious sacrifice, what would he choose to take back with him? Who was in charge?

Mark could not answer. His inspiration was gone, exhausted by the confrontation with his son. Or perhaps stolen. Not by David, or Sumarno. By the thing he had made.

It didn't matter. He had nothing left to offer.

No answers, no questions. No art. All that was left was the emptiness of his heart, which still hungered, more than ever, for the things it could not touch, for the shapes it could not fit, for the feelings that never came.

For Art's Sake

JOHN PELAN

Barton Harwood
Editor-in-Chief
Abaddon Magazine of the Arts

Forgive my sending this missive in lieu of my regular column. When you read of the monstrous prank perpetrated on several others and myself by Stonebraker you'll readily understand why I am no longer able to continue in the capacity of columnist for your magazine. It may be several months before I am again able (if in fact I am ever able), to regale the readers of *Abaddon* with shocking discoveries in the world of modern art. The avant-garde has seen many oddities over the years, artists that painted with their own blood, sculptors that made instruments of death into the most mundane of household furnishings, photographs of madmen at play, sights and sounds and shapes to jar the senses, to pointedly disturb. What Stonebraker has done is a transgression that goes far beyond anything that I've previously experienced…

Did I say it was a monstrous prank? What Stonebraker has done is an act so singularly repellant that several have died and others have gone into seclusion. What my eventual fate may be is anyone's guess… I awaken many times each night troubled by the most horrifying of nightmares, covered in a clammy sweat and nervously peering out the window for the first signs of a comforting dawn. After what I've seen it's unlikely that I shall ever know the comfortable feeling of a night of dreamless, restful slumber again…

JOHN PELAN

I've written columns on Stonebraker's work for you previously, you must remember the fuss from a couple of years ago regarding his photography exhibit? Crude and disturbing as a Buttgereit film, his images were deemed obscene and the gallery closed after only a week. I'm certain that you'll recall the full feature article on that particular show that succeeded in wringing cries of outrage from even our jaded readership. Who can forget the stark black and white imagery of his grotesquely deformed and maimed models performing the most repellant of actions?

There are however, always new levels of transgressive art to explore and Stonebraker has always excelled at finding new ways to shock and disturb his audience. His foray into short films (done pseudonymously, to prevent legal repercussions) will long be remembered as the final word in what the unenlightened would dismiss as "snuff" or "kiddie porn." The films were shot in Brazil and life is cheap there. If you've seen one of the rare tapes, you'll note that the most remarkable feature is the look of enthusiastic ecstasy on the faces of all the participants even while undergoing the most traumatic of mutilations. Who but Stonebraker would have hit on just the right combination of narcotics and hallucinogens to make such intrusive woundings not only possible, but actually pleasurable?

With his remarkable record of such amazing successes I dismissed my colleagues' assertions that Stonebraker had run out of ideas. That his silence of the last two years was not based in labors on a new work of genius but rather was the hallmark of the descent into a final phase of morbidity that would eventually have to conclude with his self-destruction.

"Nonsense!" I argued, whenever these statements were made. "Is it possible that such a great genius would burn out at such a comparatively young age?" (Stonebraker cannot be older than forty or so at the most.) The idea of such a talent becoming moribund and impotent at such an age is of course ludicrous. Whereas some of my acquaintances may have been surprised by the announcement of a new showing, I took it as a matter of course that the two years of reclusive silence was merely a cocooning for the larvae of some amazing new work that would burst forth on the scene like a poisonous butterfly.

The card was worded simply enough, but it fairly screamed by way of its implications:

The Foss Gallery Presents:

Stonebraker: The Final Face

Admission $5,000.00

*Monday ****/00*

8:00 PM

The "Final Face"? The face of *what?* And such a wonderful imagination as to charge $5,000.00 to attend the showing! I marveled at the man's audacity, it had to be Stonebraker that stipulated such a price; Foss was a shrewd businessman to be sure, but certainly not extravagant enough in his thinking to demand such

36

an outrageous fee! What sort of macabre blasphemies would the attendees see enacted before their very eyes? What could he possibly do to top the dreadful performance of some years ago where he presented a woman mutilating herself with a blowtorch?

If you'll recall, you declined to feature my follow-up interview with the woman, and in retrospect I must agree with your decision. Her words on paper seem to be nothing more or less than the chatter of a madwoman, but if you could have sat face to face in the hospital room with her as I did, looking into the once lovely face with its horribly ruined eye, you would have understood that her state was not that of a madwoman, but rather that of an *ecstatic that has seen her god.*

She'd performed her self-mutilation at Stonebraker's request for nothing more than the aesthetics of being what Stonebraker described as "a living work of art." I recall now watching the dim stage, illuminated only by the sharp blue flame of the torch as she directed its biting kiss to her thighs, nipples, and ultimately to her face. It was almost as though the torture was a religious ritual and she a devotee with Stonebraker as some perverse priest whispering encouragements as he led her through a brutal catechism.

With the idea that Stonebraker would have to top this performance or be exposed to ridicule I grudgingly acceded that I *could* come up with the money if I scrimped on other expenses for a period of time and sold off some of my own collection. Indeed, considering some of the pieces in my collection, the $5000.00 seemed easily attainable. I'd need to sell irreplaceable items, but they were as nothing to what might be a once-in-a-lifetime opportunity. With a scant two weeks before the event, I placed calls to two collectors of my acquaintance in hope of making arrangements to sell an unimportant piece or two from my collection.

Success on the second call (the first, to a wealthy ex-lover, was greeted with a recording); Sayama had long fancied my Dali bronze and was surprised to hear that I was willing to part with it.

"So tell me Siebert, what's the urgent need for money? I don't suppose you've gotten one of your *admirers* in trouble and have to pay for an operation?" I could picture him smirking on the other end of the line, Sayama was typical of many of the *noveau riche;* completely given to the notion that people would forgive his crudities simply because of his wealth.

"It's just that another piece has become available that I'd much rather have, the 'Lincoln' is of a small edition, it's quite unlikely that you'll find another for under $5000.00. For my part," I stumbled on, "the piece I'm after is unique and while it wouldn't be of interest to you, it's something I'd really like to have…"

He cleared his throat before continuing, I could picture him adding and subtracting values, considering that he was getting the piece at a bargain, conversely weighing in that he was doing me a favor by purchasing it at all. (After all, Sayama certainly had the means to simply buy another copy of the print in the more traditional marketplace.) Finally, perhaps coming to the conclusion that the transaction might be a marker that he could call upon at some point in the future, he cleared his throat and with the resigned air of a man who knows he's overspending, went on…

"Very well, I'll Fed-Ex you the money. However, I don't think you're telling me all of it… I don't suppose this has anything to do with an upcoming *event?"*

What a tremendous relief! I'd been reluctant to tell Sayama the truth of the matter for fear that he hadn't been invited and would perversely elect to blame me for his being snubbed. After all, the man's business was of the most crude commercial nature, the buying and selling of hideous old buildings in order to buy and sell more hideous old buildings. Such a prosaic occupation made him a bit of a pariah in our circles, to say nothing of his blunt and obnoxious personality.

"Well, there you have it Sayama, I didn't want you to think that I was strapped for cash to the point that I'd miss Stonebraker's show. Really, I do need to move some pieces that I've had for a while to make room for new acquisitions; I know that you've fancied the Dali, and I'm happy that it's going to an appreciative owner… I imagine you're flying in for the show?"

"Wouldn't miss it, Stonebraker's burnt-out, a fraud, $5000.00 to see him make a fool of himself is money well-spent. Do you really think he has anything of merit lined up? If you do, you're a fool, he's no doubt out of ideas, and this grand exhibition will consist of nothing more than air-brushed kiddie-porn or some demented crack-whore cutting on herself with a razor at his behest."

The man's arrogance was infuriating, the horrible thought crossed my mind *(what if Sayama was right)*, but I dismissed the concept as unworthy of consideration and replied as neutrally as possible… "We'll just have to see, whether it's a startling new work or the exposure of a fraud, it will be a memorable evening in any event. I'll have your piece shipped out to you tomorrow." With that I hung up and sat wondering who else in our circle of connoisseurs might have received an invitation…

༺༻

Imagine the anticipation of the next two weeks! Sayama's money came promptly and I thought that perhaps if I delivered it to Foss in person that I might stand a better chance of a preview of what Stonebraker had in store. As I've remarked previously, Foss was an avaricious, unimaginative man; one that could perhaps be startled by the sight of a large wad of currency into revealing secrets. The cab ride was short and uneventful, passing through the business district to that most disreputable section of town where Foss maintained his gallery. The slatternly women and haggard men shuffling through the grimy streets reminded me of several of Stonebraker's stark photographs of Balkan internment camps, people in which all hope had fled and death was something to be anticipated as a relief. There's something that gets into the eyes of people for whom there is no longer any hope, a horrible something that Stonebraker was so adept at capturing either on film or with his pen and inks.

The driver took no notice of our grim surroundings, dropping me off at the door of the storefront that now housed Foss' gallery. In mid-afternoon there was little to recommend a visit to the place, the light was such that works hung inside could hardly be shown to their best advantage and the profusion of the grasping and querulous derelicts did nothing to encourage one to linger in the neighborhood. I went through the front door clutching the precious sheaf of bills tightly under my jacket and was shocked at the sight that greeted me.

I'd expected an empty gallery, or possibly one undergoing considerable remodeling efforts (after all, to prepare for a show of the magnitude of a new Stonebraker exhibit is not a matter of simply hanging curtains and changing lightbulbs). What I saw instead was so grotesque as to force me to suppress an exclamation. The walls were covered with shiny beetles, beetles constructed of multi-colored foils in every hue, size, and species imaginable... Colossal ladybugs in violet and silver as large as my head climbed on the ceiling to inspect emerald-green stag beetles. Here in the corner of the room a gold and orange scarab nearly a yard across squatted like an alien idol. The display was colorful, to be sure, but also a testament to the banality of modern art... I could not believe that such a ludicrous spectacle was granted space in the same building that would soon serve as a theatre for the new work of a true genius. I looked at Foss, my expression no doubt conveying my feelings...

"Siebert! You look like you just had a bad plate of sushi," Foss chuckled and extended his hand in greeting. "I take it you don't much care for the beetles? Neither do I frankly, but they sell as fast as we can hang them up!"

I glanced at the card next to an ornate green, crimson, and blue stinkbug; $500.00! I shook my head and turned back to Foss, who was grinning like the Cheshire Cat.

"Takes a few of these bugs to finance the grand stuff, we couldn't possibly have brought off Stonebraker's fete here; we've had to rent another facility and pick up the tab for his laborers. Expensive as hell, but I suspect it will be well worth it in the end."

"You're saying that the show isn't actually here? I'm sure the card said..."

"Never mind what the card says, pay your fee, show up on time and you'll be provided for. I assume that's why you came by?"

Just like that he'd pounced. Well, I'd come to pay him and so pay him I did, though in truth I'd hoped that the sight of a cashier's check would have loosened his tongue a bit more about the event that was a scant few days away. Such information was not to be forthcoming, even though I lingered for a cup of the vile coffee that Foss serves to his patrons. He chatted on a good deal about Stonebraker and the upcoming display, but only in the vaguest and most tantalizing of terms. I left concluding that Foss had no more idea of what Stonebraker had planned than I did.

✌:〜

I returned home to find the answering machine winking its red eye in the dark of my apartment. Checking the number, I realized with some embarrassment that in my haste to raise money to attend the showing I'd placed a call to Daphne as well as Sayama. Daphne and I had a bit of a history, we'd been lovers for a time, and we parted on reasonably good terms, all things considered. She shared my interest in the decadent and the outré, but Daphne had more than just a deep and abiding interest in art; her desires were on a much more fundamental level; many were the evening we spent wracked by powerful hallucinogens or stuporous under the spell of the poppy.

Such minor risks were not at all disturbing to me, but rather it was her penchant for blood fetishism, which I found disturbing... While a bit of blood-play is innocuous enough, I was awakened one morning to find that she had opened a vein in my leg and was busily lapping up the flowing blood. As much as I enjoyed her company, I considered the risk of waking to a severed artery to be far too likely a possibility to make any further trysts prudent.

I returned her call, making offhand mention of selling some pieces from my collection, keeping such references vague so as not to let on that I'd already sold the one piece that I was actually in earnest about liquidating. It was no surprise that the conversation soon drifted to Stonebraker's upcoming display.

Of course she'd be there, with her new lover, perhaps we could chat more after the show... And so the conversation went, pleasant enough, but devoid of any real substance. I spent most of the night in restless anticipation as did most of our circle of connoisseurs, phone calls and e-mails flew back and forth like frantic insects buzzing about in search of hints or clues as to the nature of the show. No one seemed to have any real idea as to what could be planned.

Sayama theorized that we would see an actual execution performed on stage, that anything less than the ultimate transgression on human flesh would have to be considered a disappointment. There was the hint that Foss had dropped about laborers and construction in the old warehouse, Eaton thought that they must be constructing a theatre just for this occasion. Daphne cynically speculated that it would merely be a retrospective of his films, that this was all an elaborate ruse to raise seed money for another project.

This last had a ring of plausibility to it, but if the event was limited to the twenty or thirty of us that would consider $5000.00 a reasonable expenditure, then it certainly wasn't quite enough money to fund a major project. After all, a man of Stonebraker's connections could easily find patrons to advance him ten times that sum, should he wish to.

Finally, after an agitated and nearly sleepless night, the great day came. I spent most of the day poring over every scrap of paper that I could find relating to Stonebraker's previous works. Fortified with a pleasantly stimulating mixture of herbs I made my way again to the gallery...

FOR ART'S SAKE

~:~

A quick count indicated that there were at least two dozen of us stamping our feet in the cold as we awaited some word from our host. I surveyed my fellow enthusiasts, there was Daphne, with her new lover, a man I recognized from the papers as having a degree of notoriety for other pastimes that had little to do with the patronage of the arts. Sayama was there of course, his Armani suit looking strange and out of place on his pudgy frame. Others I recognized included many of our mutual acquaintances, people that have seen far too much over the years and would willingly part with the outlandish sum of $5000.00 as fitting price for relief of the ennui forced upon us by a repressive society.

The wind whipped old newspapers and sundry debris at us that clutched at our ankles like ragged hands while the cold was so bitter that one feared getting frostbite while smoking a cigarette. Finally, to our collective relief, a tour bus pulled around the corner and Foss clambered out smiling and nodding as he greeted each of us in turn.

"Hurry now, we've several miles to go! Only the most perfect of locations would suit him and we could find nothing in-city equal to the task!"

I squeezed on next to a sallow-faced man who introduced himself as "Blyth." I was shocked, after all, Edward Blyth (for it could be no other) had been expatriate for many years. There was the business about some sort of occult rite and two underage girls who had died horribly during whatever perverse ritual they were performing with Blyth and his associates. I was certainly surprised to see that he'd risked incarceration by returning to the country; but then, for a once-in-a-lifetime opportunity such as that promised by Stonebraker, I could see that he would consider the risk well worth it.

I looked over the rest of the passengers, reflecting that most of us had seen and done many things that the teeming masses would only imagine in nightmares. Once one has experienced the many rich varieties of the ecstasies of physical and sexual pleasures, an intellectual stimulus becomes all the more important. So it was with most of us, the wonders of hallucinogenic drugs and the narcotic visions brought on by the green fairy of absinthe were as passe as a burger and fries are to the average man on the street. When one has indulged in the wildest of sexual excesses, the prospect of routine coupling becomes almost distasteful in its banality. These were convictions shared, I'm certain by all of my companions on the slow and tiresome bus ride.

We needed a jolt of something new and provocative and inside a ramshackle warehouse on the city limits, we were sure that Foss and Stonebraker would not disappoint us. We pulled up in front of this unprepossessing structure and patiently filed off the bus to stand and stamp and fret in the bitter chill while Foss fumbled about with a large ring of keys before finally finding one to open the massive padlock that held the door's bar in place.

41

"He asked me to lock him and his assistants inside so they could finish their preparations undisturbed. There are tables with some refreshments already prepared. Please take your seats in an orderly fashion."

I was astounded at the work that had obviously gone into the place. The tables were neatly gathered in the middle of the room, one section had been blocked off with a huge stage-curtain with a roped walkway leading to a small cutaway section of the curtain. At the beginning of the walkway a speaker's podium stood, empty at present. Surrounding our tables were replicas (they couldn't possibly *all* be originals, *could they?)* of Stonebraker's sculptures. The revolting and twisted images based on victims of atrocities both real and imagined; the skeletal figure of a man wreathed in a pile of burnt truck tires, the huge bronze of Christ being fellated on the cross by a Roman Legionnaire, Joan of Arc being violated by a soldier's lance as she stood on her pyre. All of these, as well as images that blasphemed older, more archaic legends; Europa being violently raped by the bull, Persephone cuckolding Hades with Cerebus, Isis being sodomized by Set... To see this grotesque assembly in one room was almost staggering, the realization that this was a mere background, an appetizer as it were to the main attraction, was somewhat sobering.

As we glanced around we were served small flute glasses of dark-green, cloudy liquor by two slender girls dressed identically in black, vinyl bodysuits. I sniffed at the drink, recognizing it immediately for what it was. I was more than a bit dismayed, was Stonebraker hoping to mask a show of mediocre achievements by drugging his audience? An absurdity if that were to be the case, I peered around the room to see if the others were as nonplussed as I was at this offering.

I sipped at my drink feeling the bittersweet bite of wormwood and anise as the lights gradually dimmed, fading to a solitary luminescence surrounding the podium. Then, without warning, the light winked out, plunging the room into an absolute darkness. I heard a few of my companions gasp or curse as they were startled by the sudden change.

As suddenly as we'd been thrust into darkness, light was restored in the form of a solitary spotlight illuminating Stonebraker standing motionless at the podium. The man's presence was as impressive as ever, well over six feet in height and structured more along the lines of a football player than an aesthete, he radiated a ferocious energy and vitality.

"Friends," his voice boomed out, "I'm delighted that you could come here this evening! My work is as always of a unique nature; please consider that what I've created for you here tonight will eclipse the photographs, films, sculptures, and so on as surely as the sun burns more brightly than a feeble candle. My assistants have prepared the piece for your viewing. Due to the unique nature of what I have to show you, only one person will be allowed in the gallery at a time.

"Please finish your apéritifs. On the bottom of each glass is a number, the number is indicative of your turn to enter the gallery and see the 'The Final Face!' Please, examine your glasses, who has number one?"

FOR ART'S SAKE

There was a flurry of activity as the group downed their glasses as one and checked the bases for the prized symbol. There, two tables away, a thin man with a bald head and narrow goatee stood and brandished his glass. It was Eaton, a man I'd interviewed before about his fabulous collection of relics and occult artifacts. Stonebraker stood beaming as the two girls moved silently to Eaton's side and led him to the scarlet curtain that sequestered the "gallery" from the rest of the room. With a flourish, Eaton tossed the drapery aside and strode into the room.

We all waited, would his reaction be one of contempt? Was this exhibit to be revealed as nothing more than a colossal fraud? I watched the second hand of my watch laboriously complete its second revolution since Eaton had entered the room. Would he indulge himself in the full five minutes allowed?

The curtain parted and Eaton emerged, walking slowly. Looking neither to the right nor the left, he made his way back to his table and signaled for his glass to be refilled. Stonebraker smiled expansively from his place at the podium and inquired as to who held number two...

A woman that I did not recognize had the second viewing, she stayed in the gallery less than a minute before hurrying out and brushing past Foss on her way to the door without even pausing to retrieve her coat. Whatever it was that she saw, it was obviously profoundly unsettling to her. A dilettante perhaps, certainly not one of us that has had vast experience with the extravagant sights and sensations that have elevated our tastes far beyond that of the common people. It's a shame that someone like that was able to buy their way into this gathering and perhaps deny a spot to a more worthy connoisseur...

And so it went, some stayed for two minutes or more, some very briefly. None went so far as to give any hint of what they'd seen, a few left the room in a rush as had the woman who'd been called second. The few that stayed seemed to be lost in a reverie as they sat quietly at their tables. As number sixteen was called, I saw that it was Daphne's turn to enter the room. Now perhaps we'd get an inkling of what lay behind the curtain, certainly as jaded a sophisticate as I knew Daphne to be would not be easily impressed into silence.

She fled the room in less than a minute. I watched in amazement as she rushed out into the night. I could have almost sworn that she was crying, but that would be an absurdity... My number was called next. Just as I walked toward the curtain, I was startled by what sounded like a pistol shot from outside the warehouse. Recalling it was somewhat of a rough neighborhood, I thought no more of it at the time and flung aside the curtain to at last be alone with Stonebraker's masterpiece...

I came out of the room to find a scene of chaos, Daphne had shot herself just in front of the gallery. Her weapon was a little pearl-handled Derringer, a small gun, but when pressed against the temple, quite effective. Somehow in the confusion of screams and sirens with the vision of what I'd seen burning into my brain with an incandescent flame, I staggered a few blocks away and hailed a cab. I can't recall much in the way of detail of my ride home, only the twin images of Daphne's body on the sidewalk and the image that Stonebraker had displayed behind the curtain.

I apologize to you in advance for the fact that there shall be no more reviews or critiques from me for your magazine. No doubt you'll find another critic with the fortitude to view Stonebraker's next show. It simply is not in me to continue in this vein, the image I saw of hideous corruption and venality has made my very existence an unpleasant and laborious chore. The features of the thing I saw behind the curtain were old with a timeless evil, eyes that have seen so much and by their enthusiasms caused so much more. The face of the man that stared at me in that room was old beyond mere years, old in the experience of depravities that most people would not dare to contemplate. I don't know how anyone else could have looked at the image for more than a few seconds. I could not bear it for more time than it took to completely register what I was seeing.

I'm certain you know that there have been other deaths since that evening, other suicides; many of whom are no doubt acquaintances of yours. Sayama killed himself the next day, as did Eaton and Kolov. I take solace in my store of opiates and liquor, it's enough to blunt the awful reality of what I saw for a time. When the effect wears thin, there is the antique pistol on my mantel; it hasn't been fired in a good many years, but I believe it to be in sound working order.

I'm left to wrestle with the question of what it was that we really saw that night. Is it possible that Stonebraker is some sort of necromancer or hypnotist that showed us an image of his own device, his morbid fantasy of what our inner selves appeared to be? Or is it possible that he has indeed simply perpetrated a monstrous joke upon us all and that there was nothing more behind the curtain than an antique mirror in an ornate frame? I hope that I can formulate a satisfactory answer to this question before the compulsion to explore that greatest mystery of all becomes overwhelming...

Yrs.

Aaron

With Acknowledgements to Sun Tzu

BRIAN HODGE

When people find out what I do, and if we end up chatting long enough, I always know what's coming eventually. They can't help it. Sooner or later they won't be able to resist asking what's the worst thing I've ever seen.

"You don't want to know," I'll tell them. "Really. You don't."

It may have to be repeated a time or two, but this nearly always takes care of the situation. Like by this time they've started to notice the cues. How I'm not even close to smiling, the way I might if I was making them beg for it. My voice, too. It's accrued a lot of damage from cigarettes and drink over the years, so much so that somebody once told me that my voice reminded them of graveyards... which fits, because I've been through so many of them. The kind that have no gates.

Whatever it is that does the trick, these people seem to end up convinced: Maybe they really don't want to know the worst thing I've ever seen.

I'm not sure I could even give an honest answer. I've probably blocked it out so well that it would take a hypnotist to drag it back into the light of day.

"You're joking, right?" someone might ask, if I gave him a chance to get that far. "Why would it take a hypnotist when you've got the pictures? Whatever it was, you took pictures, didn't you?"

Fuck no. Who'd publish them? I'm not a pornographer. The kind of people who *would* want them, I'd never want to meet. Just as I would never take them to keep only for myself.

45

And when people find out the places I go, they often ask what it's really like there. Because they understand that, no matter how thoroughly photographs and film might document a war, no matter what juxtapositions of savagery, poetry, and loss they might convey, photographs and film never tell the whole story.

Sometimes they can't even contain what they do capture. I still remember the blue-black night skies over the deserts of Kuwait and Iraq during the Gulf War. Because the land was so flat and featureless, the skies pushed the horizons as low as they could go, and after dark filled with such a depth of stars that to stand and look into them for long left you feeling unmoored from the ground beneath your feet. No photo I shot then came close to capturing the immensity of an Iraqi night.

Can any one photo, then, come close to capturing the symphony of ruin that is the city of Baghrada?

Probably not, although I shuffle through them anyway, trying to imagine their destiny, how they will look in the pages of *National Geographic*.

I can see only their inadequacies. No matter how much suffering is conveyed by the ravaged eyes and architecture, no matter how much empathy is aroused, no matter how fast you run to your checkbook to write a donation for the refugees, still...to me, it's only surface now. Only ink and paper.

Because if Baghrada isn't necessarily the place of the worst thing I ever saw, it's the place of the worst thing I ever learned.

We arrived in late September, the days still warm but the evenings turning cold. From our various parts of the globe, we'd all flown in to Budapest, then cobbled together hasty travel arrangements and drove in across the border—got ourselves smuggled in, more like it, paying sympathetic locals to help get us in without attracting attention. It's been the way of mass murder ever since the rise of mass media: Whichever side is committing the worst atrocities is the one that doesn't want the story told to the rest of the world.

Five of us, ours was a union of mutual support and convenience, an alliance of acquaintances, friendships, and sporadically-entwined histories that went back as far as twenty-odd years. Doolan and I went back the longest, the two of us having met as younger daredevils in Peshawar, Pakistan, during the Soviet occupation of Afghanistan. It had been his first time out of Australia, and the two of us shared a room in the Khyber Hotel, a one-star pisshole that served as base camp for lots of foreign journalists before jumping over into the war zone. Both blond-haired and fair-skinned, we spent our last night there dyeing our hair and our new beards and even our skin, until we looked as native as we could, since the Russians had set a bounty on the heads of war correspondents. The next morning Doolan and I put our hangovers behind us and set off across the border to link up with the Mujahideen rebels and follow the progress of their campaign in the Panshjir Valley.

WITH ACKNOWLEDGEMENTS TO SUN TZU

Then there were the Barnetts, Lily and Geoff, freelance filmmakers based in London, who did a lot of assignments for the BBC. Doolan had gotten to know them first, a few years after he met me, running across the pair of them as newlyweds spending their honeymoon in the El Salvador of the mid-1980s.

Midori we'd known the least amount of time. She and I had met a few years earlier in the tribal slaughtergrounds of Rwanda. I was already familiar with her photographs, so to me it was like meeting a celebrity, although what eventually amazed me most was the quiet courage inside this tiny woman. Not just for the way she would run toward the places everyone else was running away from—we all did that—but for how much heart it must've taken her to pursue a life so alien to what had been expected of her by her family and culture in Osaka.

Our transportation to Baghrada was in two trucks, relics from earlier decades, and we captured images while on the roll. Now and again we would come across the remains of ambushed convoys littering the otherwise peaceful countryside, the kind of vintage trucks and other military leftovers that are the usual rule in Eastern Europe. Most had been reduced to burnt-out hulks, manned by scrappy tatters that had once been human beings, hardly fit for burial anymore, just continued gnawing by animals. Some were by now nothing more than grimy skeletons, joints wrenched apart by explosions or scavengers.

We'd all seen enough of these sights to take them in stride, although they still seemed to make our drivers nervous. Stocky, bearded men who'd brought meals wrapped in cloth, they would furtively scan hedgerows and treelines and hillsides for threats. Back in America, they would've been working in factories, in power plants, driving buses. Here, they were taking risks for enough pay to assure them of being able to feed their families for the coming winter.

Of course we took their pictures too.

We were safe enough, I figured, the road to Baghrada running two hundred kilometers through territory secured by the insurgent army that had risen up against Codrescu's regime. But the closer we drew to the city, the less it seemed to matter. It was as though we were driving into a vast corpse, and even if we weren't harmed by what had actually killed it, the decay would be sure to get us in the end.

"You ever stop and wonder," Doolan said, "why some places just seem to be magnets for this sort of business?"

He'd done his homework, obviously. He knew.

Situated between a river and mountains mined for ores, Baghrada has been of strategic or economic value to over a millennium's worth of marauders. At one time or another, it has been set upon by Mongols, Ostrogoths, Saxons, Ottoman Turks, French, Serbs, Germans, Russians, and probably by armies that history has forgotten. Thirty years ago, they even found evidence of a Viking settlement there, although by all indications it had thrived in peace. Someone has always wanted Baghrada. It is a city with thousand-year-old scars, and as we came upon it, we saw that the wounds had been laid open once again.

Its peacetime population had climbed toward a quarter-million, but it would be some time yet before anyone might calculate what it had been reduced to. From a distance, only the smoke seemed alive. Lazy plumes rose into the sky or smudged against the tops of surviving spires and towers, wafting in the wake of the artillery barrages that had driven Codrescu's soldiers into retreat. The fires beneath the rubble might burn for months, a mixed blessing over the coming winter, with the poorest of the poor willing to blacken their lungs for the privilege of huddling against a still-warm heap of bricks.

Twice we went through checkpoints—once for free, the other time needing to bribe our way past, paying tribute to scruffy men in woolen vests, the impromptu peasant uniform of the rebel militia. Most of them carried Russian-made AK-47s slung from their shoulders with an insolent ease.

Deeper into Baghrada, its bones came into view. Buildings raised centuries apart had been blasted together, sides or ends collapsing and the husks jutting with oak beams, steel girders. People still lived inside the raw shells, at least in the more stable ones, second and third and fourth floors like platforms now, stages on which families waited and watched, hoped and prayed, their daily subsistence turned into the dioramas of museum exhibits.

It sometimes shames me to admit that I've always found a grotesque beauty in devastation. Seared landscapes and charnel fields and cities that lie writhing for block after pulverized block, they're all works of art in…whatever is the opposite of progress.

And yet, in the midst of it, life continues. Beauty—*true* beauty—endures. Grass as green as Ireland sprouting against the sooty gray of broken masonry. A fresh-cut rose laid by an unknown hand atop bricks, as if to remind them what red really is. An old man, one eye turned milky blue by a cataract, taking the gift of a sandwich in his tobacco-yellowed fingers and ripping it in half to share it with his droop-tailed dog.

The lens sees all, passing no judgment but approval.

⌁

On the First Day of Creation, according to a very old story, God divided the darkness from the light, and called the light good.

No recorded value judgment on the darkness this early in the experiment, although it appears to have acquired a bad rap soon after.

But photographers, at least, have been grateful for the act ever since.

⌁

After we got our gear stowed in our hotel rooms—which brought back fond memories of the Khyber, Doolan joked—all five of us headed for the roof. Something we always did naturally. Everybody seeks high ground in wartime.

WITH ACKNOWLEDGEMENTS TO SUN TZU

From this lookout, beneath an evening sky gray as slate, we scanned what remained after the latest onslaught upon Baghrada. We looked down upon nearby streets and distant roads, and the scattered signs of life within. Death too. Always death. Death doesn't just walk in these places—it swaggers. We saw workers using makeshift gurneys to carry three bodies exhumed from rubble; from elsewhere came the inconsolable wail of an unseen woman in mourning, until she was drowned out by the faraway chop of helicopter blades, the staccato chatter of small-arms fire.

And God help us all, tired as we were, for the way we perked up at that. We wanted to be there.

The Barnetts were filming already, camera balanced on Geoff's shoulder and Lily doing an impromptu voiceover. She's always had this way of looking camera-ready even after two hundred kilometers of rough road. And as I watched them work, I suppose it was not without envy.

Eventually the two of them, and Doolan as well, went back down to leave me alone with Midori.

"Why don't you marry her?" Doolan had asked me in Budapest, before her plane had arrived. "By now, you're probably the last two people left on earth that could actually live with each other."

"It's not for failure to ask," I'd told him.

"What's that prove?" he'd said. "Asking's always come easy to you."

True enough. Over the past twenty years, three other women had already said yes. Then they'd all eventually said forget it. Nothing against them. The fault was clear. It wasn't so much the danger—during my entire career, I'd been wounded only once, although close calls hardly come any closer. A piece of Russian shrapnel had sliced a chunk from the back of my neck. A different angle and it could've chopped out vertebrae and spinal cord.

Instead, my marital failures came from having doomed myself to a life of restlessness no matter where I woke up. Whenever I was home, I was itching to be out in the field. But after I got there, I missed whoever and whatever I'd left behind so much that it was like a toothache. Whatever happiness I was chasing around and around, it felt like I was always 180 degrees on the other side of the circle from it.

So they left us alone, Midori and me. Because, in close quarters, you really can't keep much of anything a secret from anybody.

We'd held each other in some strange places. A rooftop in Baghrada and the smoke from a dozen distant fires were as normal to us as a park would be to others. Then we always ended up going our separate ways. Even though I still dreamed that one day the same window and its unchanging view would finally be enough for us.

"I never told you," she said. "The day the World Trade Center was attacked, I was in San Francisco."

"You should've called me." Because Midori had never seen where I lived in Seattle. Just as I'd never seen her apartment in Tokyo.

"I had planned to. But then that happened, and I realized we both would be going to Afghanistan soon. And that that would seem more real."

I knew what she was really saying: that neither of us could have enjoyed the other when we both knew the kind of war that was imminent.

She pointed at one of the nearest smoke plumes, followed its climb with her finger.

"After the attack, those cheap newspapers you have in the queues at markets, on their covers they showed photos of the burning towers. But they'd retouched the clouds of smoke so it appeared that devil faces were in them. I thought it was such a shameful lie at the time. But maybe in that there was a kind of truth after all."

"I thought Shinto didn't believe in the devil."

"The world is bigger than Shinto. I don't know what to believe."

I nodded, because there were times I had sensed it too, walking upon bloody streets or battlefields and recognizing with painful acuity that here was a place bereft of anything remotely resembling God. Instead, a void had been left.

Rarer, but worse, were the times when even the void seemed absent, because something else had filled it with a lingering residue of terrible purpose. There had been times when I'd focused upon slaughter with one eye toward truth and the other toward aesthetics, and it was as though something had been peering over my shoulder, looking at the same scene, the way a bricklayer might stand back to inspect his pattern.

I heard the snap of a shutter, fell back into the here and now to see that Midori had just taken my picture. I always found it hard to tell her not to do that, because it felt like bad luck. Not that she would've listened. To her, war has all kinds of faces. And to me, she'd always been a small force of nature with a mop of glossy black hair, as immovable as a rock in her determination, and her age a secret, in that way of Asian women.

She would give her heart more easily to refugees, I think, and maybe they sensed that, even if they couldn't speak a single word of the same language. In country after ravaged country they would look at Midori with such openness and yearning it was as if the most wounded regions of their souls were naked to her, and her gift in return was to show their plight to the rest of the world. She could look at eyes and reveal entire histories.

"What were you thinking then?" she asked, camera lowered. "You were so far away."

"I forget."

"And now you're here with me again, but you're lying."

"When I was growing up, I had all these books about World War Two," I told her, because I had to give her something. "I didn't actually read them much, except for the captions under the pictures. Everybody always remembers the famous shots that stand on their own, like raising the flag on Iwo Jima. But I was always most drawn to those shots that felt like freeze-frames, one slice out of an ongoing story. I'd look at a picture of a guy jumping out of his foxhole, or ducking for cover, and I'd wonder, 'How much longer did this guy live? Did he ever make it home?'

"I've never forgotten this one picture of a pair of German soldiers. Not an action shot, they were only looking at the camera. It must've been near the end of the war, because one of them was just a kid. At the time I didn't know enough to realize they were drafting boys by then. His face looked so incredibly smooth and his helmet was too big for him. It looked like the cap of a mushroom on the stem. But the other guy... you took one look at him and just knew he'd been at it ever since 1939. He needed a shave and had this thousand-yard stare. I used to wonder what he'd seen to look that way. So... I guess what I was thinking a minute ago... is that I know. That's all."

It still had a hold on me, that war, in ways that no others have. Particularly the German side. I've never felt that I've fully understood it, or that it even can be, but I'm not talking about factors like resentment over the terms of the Treaty of Versailles. What mystifies me still is what could so totally consume a nation and its rulers as to gear them toward war with such ruthless efficiency. From top to bottom, an entire society mobilized for destruction, disposal, and conquest, and yes, there were those who were immune to it, but they were few. It's always frightened me that one country, so small when seen in context on a map or globe, could overrun its neighbors and fix its sights on the rest of the world, then continue to pour forth resources both human and material, erupting like a volcano, until it exhausts itself from within.

And I marvel at the way beaten men, who could not all have been evil, could turn over their rifles, turn around, and walk home to live out the rest of their lives in peace, as if they've only come through an especially bad dream.

Never again, the victors say, pledging vigilance, and they mean it with every fiber of their being. But they all die off eventually, and good intentions don't make for much of an inheritance.

So it frightens me sometimes, that if something like Nazi Germany could happen once, it could happen again, somewhere.

I let a thing like that slip, though, and people usually just scoff.

What are you worried about? You live in the only superpower left.

I don't find that nearly as comforting as they intend it to be.

Midori and I were still on the roof past nightfall, when the darkness became one with the mountains and the streets, and little pockets of the gutted city below us began to glow with unquenched fires.

"If I were to die, while working, and you were there," she said to me, "would you take my picture?"

"I don't know." Could I really be that cold-blooded? Strangers were one thing, but Midori? Just contemplating it hurt my heart. "Would you want me to?"

"That's what I'm asking," she said, because once again I'd misunderstood her. "Would you please take my picture?"

⌐:⌐

Sometimes I dwell on battles and aftermaths I'll never see, never can see, because time and technology have superseded them.

I consider the proximity required to fight with swords and battle-axes, with maces and war-hammers, when you really would have to wait until you saw the whites of their eyes. And the red of their wounds. I think of the savagery and the damage, easier to grasp than that of two-ton bombs, yet more nightmarish too, because it all came down to muscles: limbs hacked to cordwood and kindling, faces and chests pounded to jelly, heads cleaved from their shoulders.

How colorful the ancient killing fields must've been, those sprawling banquets for ravens and wolves. Not just the blood, but the shining metal and the dyes used for the bright proud banners under which they fought and fell.

And the noise, the pageantry. The cacophony of thundering drums and bagpipes and huge blaring horns. War as theatrical production. They must've found it terribly exhilarating as they stampeded toward one another unleashing their fiercest cries.

At least until all they could do was crawl.

⌐:⌐

Over the coming days we networked, cultivating relationships among the locals to work as guides, drivers, translators. We made some vital inroads with the officers of the militia and planned excursions along with them as their campaign continued. Geoff and Lily filmed an interview with the commander who now had Baghrada under martial law, and who seemed cool enough on the surface, although experience told me he was sweating out the possibility of a counterattack by Codrescu's army.

We'd been there almost a week when I received an invitation to the police station, a forbidding gray building now used as a military headquarters and, as I learned, a holding area for prisoners regarded as more important than garden-variety soldiers. They had one now, a wounded colonel in Codrescu's army, left behind during the retreat and captured two days earlier trying to escape over the border where we ourselves had entered the country.

"We thought you might enjoy a chance to hear his side of things," said Danis, a lieutenant I'd warmed up to, whose English was good enough that he'd acted as go-between when language proved a barrier. "Of course he lies. They all do when they are caught."

They took me to his cell, and Danis remained behind to translate. At our approach, the colonel scrambled upright onto the wooden cot bolted to the wall and a shadow scurried away. He'd been playing with a rat. Or perhaps preparing to kill it, for food.

He didn't look like much now, wearing ill-fitting civilian clothes instead of a uniform. His left arm hung in a sling, useless after his elbow had been shattered by a bullet. He sported bruises, some fresh, and would've been a stouter man before, but after two or three weeks of reduced rations his skin seemed slack. The only reason I was seeing him now was because the others were finished interrogating him, had spent two days wringing him out like a sponge until what remained was fit only for the monotony of captivity.

I fingered my camera, then thought no, the time wasn't right yet. I wanted him relaxed enough to let defiant arrogance creep back in. I wanted a portrait of a man convinced he was held by people whose blood was inferior to his own. Instead, he looked downright quizzical, as though he thought he should know me.

Danis had a duty guard open the cell door. We had little to fear from the colonel, but they still took the precaution of cuffing his good hand to the wrist of his wounded arm. We were given stools to sit close enough for normal conversation. I started up a small recorder with a built-in condenser mic and tried a few questions, which Danis relayed. The answers I got back were hardly worth the breath expended, a few words delivered without conviction.

Finally the colonel muttered something to Danis, who looked embarrassed at having to be so rude as to pass it along.

"He, ah… says you are boring him. He asks if you have nothing better to do than discuss politics and policies and maneuvers."

"Ask him what *would* hold his interest," I said.

Danis posed the question, and at this the colonel straightened his back against the stone wall. He smiled at me, briefly, then his gaze roamed the cell while his tongue, like the tongue of a frog, pushed out from his jowly face to wet his lips, and his gaze fixed on a small barred window near the ceiling. He had no view here. But he had air.

"Baghrada has always been a beautiful city, yes?" the colonel said, through Danis. "But it is even more beautiful now, I think. You wonder why I think this? I will save you from asking, if you wish."

He waited, patient and confident, knowing that I would nod yes.

"Can you tell me," the colonel went on, "that as a boy you did not once take a frog, or a lizard, and pin it living to a board and cut it open to see what it looked like inside? Can you deny this?"

All the answer he needed must have flashed across my face, my grown-up's judgment of what had been childhood curiosity. I could still remember the window I'd sliced into the bluegill's side; how a throbbing air bladder popped like a tiny balloon when I stuck it with a sharp probe, and speckled my face with pondwater.

"Was it not beautiful inside to see?" he asked, growing rhapsodic while Danis gave me his words in a deadened monotone. "Was it not made yet more beautiful by knowing it could never be made whole again?" He smiled up at the window through which he could see only sky, as though imagining all that lay crumbling beneath it. "Everything else is but a matter of scale."

Over the years I've noticed a quality to certain people, not all of whom were behind bars, but most probably should've been. There is something fundamentally wrong with them, down to the core, and the longer they live, the more it seems to manifest itself in a baseness of appearance that I can only call degenerative. Old serial killers look this way, especially while reminiscing.

As I watched sweat collect in the iron-gray bristles of his hair, then ooze down the creases and folds of his face, I knew that the colonel was one of them. He may have been a military man, but he was first and foremost something else. He blinked little pig eyes and stroked the chapped red skin of his bad hand.

"Imagine a young woman, or a girl even," he said through Danis. "A fresh pretty thing, she has spent her whole life in one village and knows almost nothing of the world. Her priest may have told her it is a place of miracles and she believes him, because every day she wakes up to mountains. Then imagine the look on her face the first time she is forced to confront all the things that can happen to her and to her body, from soldiers who can do anything they wish, for as long as they wish. She was beautiful before... but now she is made... perfect..."

The further the colonel went on, the more difficulty Danis had remaining detached while translating. His breath whistled in his nose. He had three sisters; I knew that much about him. Finally Danis surged to his feet and punched the colonel in the face with one fist, then the other, to knock him back against the wall. The man leaned against the stones and dribbled blood as he laughed.

Obviously the interview was over.

"As you can see," Danis said, trembling, "the colonel is a sick man."

But he still had more to tell, several moments' worth, and Danis looked at him as if comprehending only half of it, if that much.

"What did he just say?" I asked.

"It makes not much sense to me," Danis said. "He says... perhaps he has done a poor job explaining the work he does... but he says you of all people should understand—I'm trying for the correct word—should understand the... aesthetics. Then it becomes stranger still. He says he does not know if what we all seek to appease, whether or not we realize it, is an it, or a them... but that it is everywhere, watching everything, and that the rats are its eyes."

Danis paused to spit on the floor near the bunk.

"But as I told you already, he is a crazy man, I think. You should see the book we found in his belongings."

The colonel interrupted again, speaking to Danis but staring directly at me. The unfamiliar words seemed to hang in the air as Danis looked from one of us to the other.

"He asks," Danis said, hesitant now, "if that scar on the back of your neck is still as prominent as it used to be."

I ran the past minutes through my head, concluding that I hadn't turned my back on this man even once. I knew better, a habit ingrained from conversations with fitter, more dangerous men. Even if I had, could he have seen through collars and hair? And so, all I could think of in that moment, again, were the times I'd turned my lens upon slaughter... sensing a presence peering over my shoulder... so close sometimes I could feel on the back of my neck its cold sigh of satisfaction.

"I don't see any reason to continue with this," I said.

Danis flexed a sore hand and called for the duty guard to unlock the cage.

Maybe because none of us were expecting much from a man in the colonel's condition, this was what allowed him to get as far as he did. When the iron door opened, he was suddenly off the cot and across the cell, bulling into us, knocking Danis and me off-balance and into the guard. His wrists were still cuffed together, but he could run. He ran past us, over us, up a flight of stairs; ran as though he'd dreamed of this moment for days.

Astonishingly enough, he even made it out of the building and as far as the street. But by then other guards were following. They didn't chase him once he was in the open. Danis and I made it outside in time to see them aim their weapons at his back in an almost leisurely manner.

I've seen men die before, many times. In my experience it's either frightfully quick or agonizingly slow. They drop like stones or linger for eternities. I even filmed it once, my first time in Afghanistan—a Russian soldier crawling from a burning troop carrier in a convoy ambushed by Mujahideen rockets. I can't know what he really saw, but will never forget the sight of him floundering across the ground like a half-squashed roach, his blackened and bloodied face beseeching me through the lens. Ever since, whenever I've heard anyone speak of the glories of war, I've wanted to show them that footage.

The colonel, though... he died like no man I'd ever seen.

The bullets only seemed to propel him farther. He stumbled along with gouts of blood splashing the chewed-up street beneath him, yet still struggled on. He ran off-balance, as a man might with both hands bound before him, then another volley finished the job on his wounded elbow, clipping his arm in two. The severed half slipped from the sling and he dragged it behind him, still cuffed to his intact arm, for another ten or twelve incredible paces, until the best marksman dropped him to the street in a heap that seemed loath to ever stop tumbling.

For a few moments, not a one of us could do anything but stare.

Just three thoughts:

Not for a second could the colonel have believed he could escape.

So it seemed to me like a performance.

He died like a man in a movie.

⌣⁚⌣

On the Seventh Day of Creation, according to a very old story, God rested.

Presumably He thought this rest was every bit as fine as everything else He'd already called good, the just rewards after some very hard work, whose crowning achievement walked on two legs, sharpened spears, and harnessed the power of the atom.

Even today, people wonder when, where, and how it went wrong, a system so exquisitely balanced as this watery blue third planet from the sun, where even the harshest upheavals of nature cannot undermine the inherent tranquility.

The answer seems obvious.

Like a watchman snoring through footsteps, the old Bastard was asleep on the job.

⌣∶∾

That night, in bed with Midori, I could hardly bring myself to touch her.

Even under the most normal circumstances I was never unaware of how small she was, although usually this just meant a subtle amazement that no matter how strenuously we made love, I wasn't going to break her.

But that night, even though we both were too exhausted and drained to do anything except lie there, I still could only think of her fragility, how exaggerated it now seemed. How breakable she really was.

By now we all knew about the rape camps, the barbed-wire enclaves deep in the mountains where Codrescu's campaign of ethnic cleansing extended to the next generation. Although they got carried away sometimes, his stallions did.

I'd seen proof.

I'd forgotten, by the time the colonel had been gunned down, that Danis had mentioned a book he'd had on him when he'd been captured. Did I want to see it, Danis asked as they were scraping up the colonel's remains; did I want to know what kind of man he really was?

I did. I didn't. I did.

Danis first had to secure permission; then, in a room in the police station, where they catalogued evidence of crimes in both war and peace, he took the book from a cabinet and set it on a table before me. A hardback book, once slim, now bloated, as if things had been stuffed between its pages. I couldn't read the title, but realized what it was from the author's name. In China, nearly five hundred years before the birth of Jesus, a warrior named Sun Tzu had written a strategy manual so perfect that it was still used in the modern era, by everyone from Mao Tse Tung to Wall Street corporate raiders. At first, *The Art of War* seemed a reasonable thing to find on a military man.

"Just open it," Danis told me.

The text was gone, I saw, made irrelevant, the pages used for backing as in a photo album. Now they were stiff with tape and glue, paste and pictures. It didn't matter where I opened.

The first snapshot I saw showed a blurry uniformed soldier striding out of frame on the right, away from a woman kneeling before a stone wall and above a tiny heap on the ground. A wet telltale blotch stained the stone. I had heard, of course, of babies being swung by their ankles; had never, until this moment, seen evidence of it.

WITH ACKNOWLEDGEMENTS TO SUN TZU

Flip at random to another page, more evidence—this time that the colonel, if indeed he was the photographer, had known firsthand about the systematized defilements he spoke of. He'd known firsthand of many things, even worse, about which he hadn't had the chance to gloat.

There is no need to describe any of the dozens of others.

But they lingered. Like a contamination.

I carried them with me through the streets of Baghrada. Sat with them as I ate cold salmon from a can. Took them to bed with me, where I could only bring myself to touch Midori's hip with my cheek and not my hand, pressing my stubbled face against the creamy warmth, above the bone, and I thought, *This could be broken. For sport. They do that here.*

No, there's no need to describe any of the others.

Just ask myself why the colonel had indicated that I, of all people, should understand the aesthetics of the work he did.

Mind games, I told myself, played by an insane man who said his work was done for something that employed rats for its eyes. An evil man who collected and possibly even took the sort of pictures I'd always drawn the line at, said I would never shoot. Because I was so much better than he was, right?

Which hadn't stopped me from looking at them.

Every. Single. One.

An insane and evil man who had somehow seen through me to my scar.

༺༄༻

On the First Day of Destruction, it's anyone's guess how it really happened.

But it's easy enough to imagine groups of short, squatty men cloaked in ragged furs they themselves had skinned, carrying crudely effective weapons they themselves had fashioned by firelight, with total absorption. The skirmish may have been over the fresh carcass of a giant antelope or bison, or a particularly inviting shelter.

The one's hands and thick broken fingernails were stained with the ochers used to create lovingly detailed likenesses of their prey animals on cave walls. But as the cudgel, fired to a hardness near stone, smashed the other's skull into splinters and sent him pitching to the ground, this was nothing like hunting, where lives were taken with an attitude that approached reverence.

It's easy enough to imagine him looking down at the bloodied brains oozing into the dirt, breath gusting like the wind through his broad nostrils, and muttering whatever was his word for good.

༺༄༻

Beneath Seattle's rains, in the loft where I sometimes live, sometimes work, and sometimes just stare at the walls, they hang from a line stretched between a shelf and a nail. They hang not like laundry but like snakeskins, clipped at the top and weighted at the bottom to thwart their stubborn tendency to curl.

For those who shoot pictures where the people are shooting each other, there are two categories of work. There are the photos snapped quick and dirty, often digital, sent in for immediate consumption. Then there are the ones we save for later, time capsules preserved in rolls of film; their colors are richer, their shadows starker; we tell ourselves they mean more, that they'll be around longer. That some of them may even be remembered.

As I lift the magnifier to one eye, like a monocle, and lean in close to scan negatives along the wet dangling strips, each one is a surprise, a treat.

I may have developed them, but not one of them is my own. Instead, as I see for the first time what she saw there, I'm peering through *her* eye.

I see the faces of Baghrada, their rare smiles and their frequent tears. I see the very definition of squalor, throughout a city and a countryside and a populace laid to waste. I see myself on a rooftop far from home, and how she really saw me, and I wonder how she ever could've loved someone so marked by his years and how they were spent, then wonder why she couldn't have loved me just a little more.

I wonder, too, if it's my imagination, or if I really can see better than I used to; if it's true what I've always heard about sensory compensation. Total deafness in one ear, eighty percent in the other—that should be enough to earn a little kickback.

It seems important that I should preserve those last things I did hear clearly. That I should be able to press a button and replay them, if only in my mind...and I suppose I can, it's just that I'd gladly give up that last monaural twenty percent to be rid of them.

Laughter. I can still remember the laughter, and how it drew us.

She'd made arrangements to head out the next morning on a trip to one of the rape camps, liberated but with many of the women still there, because now it was an impromptu field hospital. With the colonel's picturebook still so fresh in mind, I wanted to ask her not to go, but knew what an insult this would be.

The Red Cross is there, I told myself. *She'll be fine.*

Laughter.

As we walked near the hotel, it came from a block away, or two. We stopped, because hearing that sound was like seeing the sun again in a world of night. We'd heard so little laughter since coming to Baghrada. Better still, it was the laughter of children, lots of them. Anything that was causing this much joy, in this place, was cause for us to run, to immortalize it before it could disappear.

And at first, as we came upon them, it seemed so normal. Just a group of boys at play in the middle of the street, laughing and cheering during a spirited game of soccer. The same scene was probably going on at that same moment in Berlin and Madrid and Dublin and Chicago, places that knew peace...but if it could still be found here, then to me that meant there was hope. There was light.

WITH ACKNOWLEDGEMENTS TO SUN TZU

We shot and advanced, shot and advanced, together, but Midori was the first to see, through all the flashing legs and kicking feet, that their ball had a face and a beard and broken teeth.

I find it easy to blame them now, for everything. That if we hadn't sought them out, then we wouldn't have been in the wrong place at the wrong time. That if we hadn't been so transfixed by their laughter, then the reason for its sudden cruel turn, we might've noticed moments or minutes earlier some sound warning us that Codrescu's army had launched its counteroffensive against the city they'd lost.

Laughter, and the shrill whistling approach of an artillery shell—these are the sounds I remember last.

From then on, it's mostly imagery, a few sensations. Boys, and pieces of boys, flying through the air. A sick whirling weightlessness as I flew too. The taste of the street and the wet warmth of blood down one side of my neck as it ran from my right ear. A thickened isolation caused by an almost total absence of sound, the world closing in like a muffling blanket.

Take it, she told me when I found her. Just lips to be read, movements that vaguely matched a hazy muddle of sound at my left. *You're bleeding.* Wasting neither time nor words, because how could either of us have forgotten her request on the hotel roof? *Take it now.*

But to do that, I would've first had to let go.

⌁

In the legacy of which I've inadvertently become curator, it is the last picture on the last roll:

Midori lying in the rubble, with an arm reaching into frame from the left to cup her cheek. It's my arm, but could be anyone's, and that's all that matters. It was unthinkable to me that anyone should get the idea she died alone. Technically the photo is an abysmal failure, marred by a cracked and dirty lens. The world, I think, will excuse these flaws…even if it's now a poorer place for her absence.

And so, back to the original conundrum:

Can any one photo come close to capturing the symphony of ruin that is the city of Baghrada?

There is one, but it exists only in my mind, because neither Doolan nor the Barnetts nor anyone else was there to take it:

A man kneeling in a street, calm and poised even though he's surrounded by carnage and chaos. He can manage that because, like a priest administering Last Rites, he has a purpose. You see him only from the back, and even less of the body he kneels beside—an older child or a small woman. They, too, could be anybody, and the ambiguities are important. They are far from the first.

But it's the background that really makes the shot: the rising black plumes of smoke in which some might see cruel faces, the shadowy corners where rats scurry for a better view, and all around, a jagged still-life of walls and roofs

59

whose utter devastation might even be called beautiful. So tragic, made as though by a master artist turned vandal, who in despair has turned against his own epic painting.

We are not only the brush strokes upon his canvas, the scene seems to say. We are also the bristles of his brush, and the edge along his blade.

Hurdy Gurdy

PEADAR Ó GUILÍN

"You ready, boy?" asked Grandfather.

Snowflakes and pedestrians drifted by. I helped Grandfather set up his hurdy-gurdy, stopping every few seconds to blow into my hands.

He smiled through rimey whiskers. "I'll be gettin' you gloves today, boy. Don't you worry, your mammy did the right thing. You won't starve in *my* care!"

He inserted a roll of music around the drum. His arms moved stiffly, enough to make me wince sometimes. But he knew what he was at. He made a few final adjustments with a screwdriver. "Hold this for me, and don't you cut yourself."

The end of the screwdriver had been sharpened almost to a knife point.

Grandfather pushed me back against the wall. "Watch, now, little one. It won't affect you much if you stay behind it."

Nobody else paid us any heed. They rushed to work or charity shelters through a growing blizzard. Grandfather turned the handle of the ancient hurdy-gurdy. For some reason I had expected cheerful music to issue forth, bouncy stuff to make passers-by forget the depression long enough to drop us a few coins.

But this music had me thinking instead about mammy, crying her eyes out when Angie died. "I can't feed you, Podge," she said, "I can't feed neither meself nor you."

"What about Grandfather?" I had asked, "Will he help us?"

61

She looked at me, mouth agape, tears dripping over her top lip. "Who told you about him? Who told you? Don't you mention him again, you hear me? Don't you go near him!"

I knew she couldn't really hate her own father. She had been stinting herself on food over me and Angie and she just couldn't think straight. She'd have more food and time to earn it without a ten-year-old to look after.

The music wafted between snowflakes and into ears. Sad stuff. I had tears in my eyes worse than a girl. I staggered forward but Grandfather pushed me back against the wall. I saw other people crying too. Men and women falling to their knees in ankle-high snow, rich and poor. Grandfather worked harder at the handle. His breath steamed out in little spurts like he was an engine running short of coal, but he didn't stop until the people were crying so hard they lay down raking at the frozen earth.

"Now!" said Grandfather.

He hobbled across to the nearest sobber. She wore a maid's uniform with laddered nylons underneath. We got right up close where I could see the moustache she had tried to cake over with make-up.

"Here, Podge, I'll show you how it's done."

He took the screw driver from me and demonstrated how to hold the sobber's head back.

"This here's the jugular," said Grandfather with a wink, "you best stand back if you're going to be using that one! But the eye is best. You never get messed with the eye." He shoved the screwdriver through a veil of tears into her eyeball. She jerked and spasmed and poor Grandfather was too old to keep her down. I could almost feel his shame. "You do the next one," he said, red-faced, "I'll get her money."

A business man lay not two steps away. I bet he had a car, a driver maybe. He must have decided to walk today, through the snow. Pick up presents for his son.

"What're you waitin' for?" Grandad asked.

What if the man had come here looking for me? Maybe I was his little boy and he was sorry for leaving us, me and mammy and Angie. The presents could have been for me. And hugs and trips to the hockey, with the other lads to see us pass hand in hand and mammy in a new dress proud as punch.

Grandad took the screwdriver from me.

"Wait!" I said. The man was still sobbing. They all were.

Grandad knelt down beside the man. "Wait!" I said again. "Why are they crying?"

"They're mourning," said Grandfather. "They're mourning the end of the world."

"The world is ending?"

"Sure," said Grandad, "but we still have to eat."

In went the screwdriver. The man called out a name and lay still. It hadn't been my name after all.

62

HURDY GURDY

Later, Grandfather took me to the toyshop. The security guards didn't want to let us in with our poor clothes.

"I preferred it when we still had police," said Grandad, but a few fifty Euro notes had us inside in a flash. It was good we had cash—rich folks shops wouldn't barter like normal people.

Grandad bought me a remote control car with batteries and everything. I felt ashamed I hadn't been of more help, especially when he beamed at the shop assistant and put his arm around my shoulder: "My grandson," he said, "anything he wants!" Then, he whispered, "We'll pick out a present for your mammy too and we'll send it to her in time for Christmas." My heart swelled.

Grandfather also bought me an ice hockey stick and other extravagances that emptied the rich daddy's wallet.

"Don't you worry, Podge," said Grandfather, "we can always go play some music." He winked and it made me feel awful, for he was too old to do the work himself and I knew I wasn't grown up enough. The sight of blood had made me feel sick as a mink, though I could not admit it to him. I kept thinking about the rich folk who were waiting at home for the ones we had harvested that morning.

Two days later and the blizzard cleared. Grandad and me wrestled the hurdy-gurdy through snow to the lakeside. Grandad sent me off to the supermarket to borrow a shopping trolley. When I got back, he had already slid a sheet of music over the drum. His joints popped audibly and he grimaced.

"It never hardly snowed when I was your age, Podge. We always thought global warming would make things hotter. Did most places, but half drowned us and froze us. Not your fault, boy! You look sick! I wasn't giving out to you."

I tried to smile and stood back as Grandad asked, hockey stick in one hand, trolley gripped in the other. The sun shone down on the lake. Rich folk skated in continuous loopy circles. Their shrieks and laughter filled the air while their bodyguards looked on nervously.

"Look at their coats, Podge! Good mink! Ermine gloves!"

Grandad looked like he could do with some himself. Arthritis had curved his fingers into claws. I offered to turn the handle of the hurdy-gurdy for him, hoping to help without having to wield the screwdriver.

"I don't know if you could… Your mammy had the knack, but…" Grandad shrugged. He showed me how to hold the faded ivory handle. It passed into the drum and where the two met some artist had painted a map of the world which spun as the handle turned. Grandad warned me to keep turning steadily and not to be distracted by "strangenesses" I might feel. A few people by the lake glanced at us. A little rich girl dragged her mammy over. She waved, hands like paws in her mittens. Grandad winked at her. To me he whispered, "Those gloves are too big for her anyway. Let's start, Podge, these 'uns will be wanting music to go with their skating."

I turned with all my might and the music blared forth all jolly and bouncy. "Too fast!" hissed Grandad. "Slowly does it!"

I went easier so that the map of the world spun less frantically. I wondered at the strange lands, at the children who lived in them, the animals I had seen in books I couldn't read. The soles of my feet felt warm and the heat passed up from the ground, through me into the ivory handle. I sped up my turning, but the lovely heat left. So I slowed until summer embraced me again.

"Good boy!" shouted Grandad. "You can play! You can play!"

Sure enough the endless circling of the skaters began to falter. A portly man crashed into the backs of a couple. All three hit the ice, but no one complained and nobody helped them up. Sonorous notes covered the rich folks in a blanket of sorrow 'till none could take the weight. All went first to knees and then to back or belly, sobbing for the end of the world.

"You don't have to use the screwdriver if you don't want to, Podge," said Grandad when my arm could turn no more. Instead he handed me the hockey stick he had bought me and warned me to strike firmly.

He had a stick of his own and together we tottered out onto the ice amongst the sobs and the wailing. It wasn't so hard after the first few. I didn't look at their faces, I didn't think about the ones who would miss them. Instead, I hit one and thought: "This is a dress for mammy." I hit another and thought: "These are gloves for Grandad." "This one will get us Christmas dinner."

The blood spattered across the ice. Exertion warmed us and built sweat inside our thin clothes. We clubbed the rich and took their fur coats. I filled the shopping trolley with their pelts, my pockets bulged with notes. We worked our way from the far end of the small lake back towards the hurdy-gurdy. Poor Grandad spent as much time heaving in breath as he did working. Once I think he tried to shout encouragement to me but was panting too hard.

I kept working until I was sure we wouldn't have to come out again for the rest of the winter. "This one will feed us for January and this one for February..." My arms ached as never before. Blood and red bits ran down the shaft of my hockey stick every time I lifted it into the air. We worked now in almost complete silence. A pack of wild dogs were fighting over a few of the carcasses but most of the sobbing had stopped.

Two pairs of eyes sought my own. The mammy and the girl with oversized gloves held each other, blue eyes wide, all limbs a-tremble. Neither had tears in their eyes. I heard Grandad's shuffling footsteps come up behind me.

"They're not crying, Grandad," I said. "I'll—I'll give the handle a few more turns." I felt myself shaking every bit as violently as the two on the ice before me.

"Won't work," said Grandad. "The girl is protected by her mammy. Mammy has to stay strong for the girl. You'll have to just get on with it, Podge, then we can go for a nice hot cup of tea."

I raised the stick.

Lines spread out from the corners of the woman's eyes, just like mammy's. "It's not too late for you," she said. Her voice was kind. My arms wobbled under the weight of the stick. I saw faint dimples that must have deepened beautifully when she smiled. Without fur and make-up she might have been my aunty.

Perhaps somebody started turning the handle of the hurdy-gurdy at that point, because I fell to the ice weeping uncontrollably. Distantly, I heard poor Grandad finishing the job. The job he had trusted to me.

"Worse than his mammy," Grandad muttered. I wanted mammy so badly then.

Grandad spent the next few days wrapped in blankets coughing into a handkerchief. Sometimes I saw blood come up though he tried to hide it from me. During the day I scavenged firewood from nearby ruins or bought food from the market. I made tea for us maybe twice an hour. Grandad thanked me every time, but avoided my eyes. Once he glared at me for trying to sneak into the cellar where I wasn't allowed. I didn't even want to go down there into the dark with the rats and whatever secrets Grandad had. I think I was just trying to provoke him into shouting at me and getting it over with. I deserved to be shouted at after all he had done for me.

On the third day, however, the cough began to ease. He caught me as I walked to the stove and swept me into an embrace so fierce I thought his old joints would pop.

"I'm sorry I let you down, Grandad," I said.

"No, Podge, I'm sorry." His arms tightened and there was a catch in his voice, "You put in as good a day's work as I ever seen. I drove you without five minutes for yourself and you only ten. I'm so proud. Forgive this old man."

Then his voice changed again. Became so sad. "Who will take care of your mammy when I'm gone, Podge? Who?"

"I will, Grandad," I said. The thought of her starving as the winters grew ever colder was too much to bear. I dreamed sometimes of finding her, thin as Angie, curled up on a step.

"Poor Podge," said Grandad, "you're too young for the necessary." He coughed, a hacking splurge of a cough that brought black stuff and a foul odour up from the depths.

"Don't leave me, Grandad!"

"One more trip," said Grandad, "I don't think I could last any more than that."

"You can stay here, Grandad. I'll buy firewood and blankets and... and soup! Hot soup! We got so much we don't need to go out again before summer!"

"I'll be gone in summer, Podge."

I knew it was true. He looked worse than Angie had looked and her dead and frozen a week.

"One more time, Podge, to make you the type of man that can look after my lovely Margaret." He coughed himself into exhaustion and sleep. I lay down next to him, hugging his spindly body, willing it to keep breathing. It did, like a saw over mahogany, all night long.

A week of sea lion stews brought colour back to the old man's cheeks. I went to market every day to get fresh meat and firewood for our cauldron. I bought presents for Mammy which I placed on her doorstep before running away. Once she must have seen me and her lonely voice pursued me in echoes down the road.

I never told Grandad about these trips, but he always smiled at me on my return and never questioned my absences. He showed me how to care for the hurdy-gurdy, had me buy polish.

"It's a barrel organ, Podge, that's the proper words, not hurdy-gurdy like most people say. Belonged to my grand-mammy. This sheet's the music, see them holes? They tell the pipes to blow and make the music, if you had different holes you'd be getting different music."

"But what's it for, Grandad? Why do we have to... why do we..."

"If somebody hurt your mammy, Podge, you'd get them wouldn't you? Rich folks killed the world, Podge. The likes of us take her revenge. But we have to be strong to do it, boy, we can't be chicken." As he spoke he put an arm on my shoulder to take the sting out of his words. "I'll make you strong. I won't go to my grave until I know you'll do the family proud."

I kept polishing and didn't look up. My knuckles clutching the rag grew white.

Clouds of gulls flew in from the coast, showering us with feathers as we crossed the frozen canal that had once been O'Connell Street. The heads of statues poked up through the ice; in one case, a dramatic pair of hands poked above the surface as if a man lay drowning beneath.

A fair had sprung up here for Christmas-time, patched tents, clowns and jugglers. Sweet sellers and rival Father Christmases fought for the attention of a hundred children and their daddies. Everywhere screeches of delight, laughter.

It felt good to be out. Money in my pockets and an adult holding my hand made me the equal of any other boy in the crowd. My stomach still knotted at the thought of what Grandad hoped to achieve here today. But we had left the hurdy-gurdy and hockey sticks at home and I was sure we'd spend the time looking around and shopping for treats.

Nearby, a daddy in tattered coat, hands wrapped in bandages, led his son through the crowd. I imagined them living in a squat like ours. I pictured the daddy gathering sticks and scraps of green paint to make a Christmas tree. I saw presents, stolen at great risk or borrowed against the cost of a month's labour. Grandad saw me looking at them.

"Good boy," he said, "good. These should do the trick."

"They're too poor!" I sputtered.

"Nonsense," said Grandad, "look at the shoes on the kid!"

Sure enough the son had shoes no more than a few years old. His clothes shone next to the rags the father wore.

"There are plenty richer here."

HURDY GURDY

Grandad shook his head. We weren't here for the money, not this time. We had come to make me a man. He shuffled up behind them and engaged them in conversation.

"Your kid looks cold," said Grandad after a while. "We found a stash of old furs, me and my boy here. Sell you some for a week's labour."

While they bargained, the boy, half my age, maybe, hid behind one of his father's legs and peeked around shyly from time to time. I stared back as menacingly as I knew how. I mustn't have been very good at it, because he just smiled back at me, a big gap where his baby teeth had fallen out.

"You don't believe me? Come back and see for yourself," Grandad winked when the man looked away. "Maybe you could do an hour's work right now!"

Grandad took my hand for the walk home with the other two. He squeezed as strong as he still could and once whispered, "Me and your mammy's gonna be so proud!"

The daddy's eyes practically popped out when he saw our collection of furs: mink and otter and fox. Creatures from as far away as Siberia, said Grandad.

"Paddy! Don't touch that!" The boy, Paddy, like my real name, sprang back from the mahogany finish of the hurdy-gurdy.

"It's all right," Grandad smiled. He took the daddy by the arm. "I won't trade though 'till I see what you can do. We have a window needs boarding in the next room."

The man grinned until he dimpled and took off his jacket. "Wait here, Paddy, good boy," and to Grandad, "Take me to it!"

Grandad pulled out some tools I never knew he had from under a pile of fur coats. He handed all of them over to the daddy except for the screwdriver which he gripped as tightly as his arthritis would allow.

My stomach flip-flopped. "Grandad! Can't he fix it some other day? Can't they come back?"

"Be a man, Podge," he said, "look after the little one. Show him your hockey stick." The two adults disappeared into the next room where presently the sound of hammering emerged. Grandad had obviously decided to get the window fixed for real while he was at it.

I felt a tugging at my sleeve. "So, where's your hockey stick?"

I rested a hand on the hurdy-gurdy. At least when they were lying there sobbing I could pretend I was putting them out of their misery.

"Show me it!"

At that moment the hammering stopped to be replaced by a gasp and the sound of somebody falling.

"Get out!" I hissed at the boy, "Your daddy's not comin' back! Get out!"

I opened the door to swirling flakes and a drift that pushed its way into the kitchen. I tried to bundle the boy out, but he pulled away from me and ran instead for the cellar.

"Not there!" But he couldn't have been much more than five or six. He must have thought he could hide there until his daddy came out of the other room.

Instead Grandad shuffled through, screwdriver in shaky hand, bloody to the wrist as though he had tried to clean the kill in order to cook it.

"Where's the boy, Podge?"

I pointed to the door, but I could see he didn't believe me by the disappointment on his face. I felt terrible for lying to him. Grandad sat down on a pile of furs with his back to me.

"Take your hockey stick and bring him, Podge."

"Grandad?"

He didn't answer.

"It would be great to have a brother, Grandad, somebody to play with. Maybe— maybe he could help us with the music? And we have loads of furs and money. The three of us could live snug here Grandad…"

"Shut the back door, Podge. Then do what I told you." As I moved to obey he kept talking. "We can't be letting people go, Podge. They talk, they always talk, even the little ones. We are revenge, Podge, why else did Earth give us the hurdy-gurdy? What else could it be for? We can't be letting her down. You an' me an' others like us in all the countries for all the final generations. If you will not do what's in your blood you're no grandson of mine. You're no better than one of them."

His final words chilled me. I took my stick and walked to the door. One quick blow and it would be over. "It's the best thing," I thought. Life without a daddy was no life at all.

I took a torch from where it hung by the door and used its light to guide me down rickety wooden steps into a world of jumping shadows.

"Paddy?" I called softly. Piles of old suitcases blocked my way, smells of damp and rot. Did Grandad keep bodies down here? I swung the torch around and called out again. I wished Paddy'd just come out of hiding and get it over with. I would turn off the torch just before so I wouldn't have to look at him when I did it.

I brushed against a box perched on other boxes perched on suitcases. It crashed to the floor spilling dozens of pieces of paper. I picked one up. Rats had gnawed it, but I still recognised it as a 50 Euro note. I flashed the torch into another box: rotting furs and more money in a bulging suitcase. I could have lived a hundred years and never spent half of what Grandad had left to rot around the cellar.

I brushed against something else. It gasped.

I looked down and saw Paddy crouched in misery at my feet. A worm of snot rested on his upper lip and wet patches under his eyes reflected the beam of the torch back at me.

I raised the stick expecting him to cover his head, but instead a smile lit up his face.

"It's a real one!" he said. He stood and took the stick from my unresisting hands. He made a few swipes with it, knocked over a few more boxes.

"Podge!" Grandad's voice floated down the steps towards us. "Oh, Podge!"

The door slammed shut. I didn't think it had a lock, but fear filled my belly. I clambered over a pile of suitcases, intent on getting up the steps, but Grandad had already reached the hurdy-gurdy and begun to play.

All at once it was like I opened my eyes to find I had killed Mammy. Like I had blocked my ears to her screams, sat on her dying body for warmth as I drank my tea. No son had ever been so ungrateful as I. The pain of it! I saw myself hurt her in a thousand ways, killing her with my greed. Tears dripped down my face, damp earth soaked through my coat to the skin, but the music kept playing and I kept hurting Mammy. In one scene she screamed outside in a blizzard, banging again and again on the door while I tried to sleep, too lazy to let her in. Another scene saw me flavour a watery soup with her freshly snipped fingers; still another saw me send her again and again to the well for water with a leaky bucket. Rather than repair it, I cursed her for a lazy hag even as she fell exhausted at my feet.

I heard more weeping nearby and felt sure that the other person must have become aware of my wickedness too. But I couldn't concentrate on anyone else.

I cried and cried for my own evil until even when the music had stopped I couldn't bear to be with my own thoughts and hoped desperately Grandad would come soon with his screwdriver.

The other person's sobs reached fever pitch. Paddy? Little Paddy? Were those footsteps creaking on the stairs? Thank God for divine punishment! Thank God! Let it stop!

As I writhed in my sorrow, my hand touched another and it gripped me. Paddy! Poor little Paddy! I was the wicked one, not him! Let Grandad punish me!

I snapped awake and sat up, vision blurred. Grandad stood over Paddy with the screwdriver in his shaky right hand.

"No, Grandad! No!"

He turned to look at me, his eyes like caverns after a flood.

I put myself between him and Paddy. "No," I said again, "we were wrong." A strange delight began to fill me as I spoke. In my love for him I thought he would be as happy with the discovery as I was. "I know what the hurdy-gurdy is for now, Grandad. I know!"

His voice seemed to come from far away, sweat sheening his face. "You think I didn't know, little Podge?"

He tried to push past me. His breath came in huge gulps, his body like a feather against mine. One final heave and he collapsed backwards over a pile of suitcases, dust billowing and rats scurrying. I believe he had stopped breathing before he hit the rotted bank notes that cushioned his fall.

Paddy and I have brought our music all over now. The melody won't come for him when he turns that ivory handle, but he sets the sheet on the drum and brings tea to the audience after we wake them from their experience.

Many who hear us will spend the Summer planting trees. Some will freeze to death when the snows come, for they refuse to burn coal. Few who've seen the hurt they've done their mammy can ever bear to hurt her again.

My Mammy was glad to hear we didn't hurt the people. She's mammy to both of us boys and sometimes she comes with us and makes the music.

I miss Grandad. I remember how happy he was when he bought presents for Mammy and me. But he's happier where he is now, with the earth.

The Art of Madness

EDO VAN BELKOM

I'd been aware of Daren Musenda's work for a few years, had heard all of the outrageous and over-the-top praise from the critics, but I'd never imagined any of it was deserved.

But it was.

Musenda's paintings were remarkable.

No, more than that… they were utterly brilliant.

I'd arrived at the Driftwood Community Centre early on the opening night of Musenda's new show, hoping to get a few minutes to look at the man's work alone, without the push of bodies and the fawning of people *who don't know art, but know what they like.* When I entered the room where sixteen of his paintings were hung, my eye was immediately caught by the largest painting which was hung on the wall directly across from the entrance to the room.

Once I looked upon it, even from a distance, I couldn't look away. I was drawn to it, my eyes dancing across the canvas in a rush to take in all its detail even though I knew I'd be able to look at it for as long as I liked.

And so I stood there, taking it all in.

In awe.

Years ago as an undergraduate art major I learned that there were basically two schools of thought concerning art. One said art was inspired by the collective unconsciousness and expressed that which is beyond appearances, namely inner feelings, eternal truths and the like. The other said that art is concerned with the representation of appearances and gives us pleasure through the accuracy and skill with which it depicts the real world.

Amazingly, Musenda had done both.

He'd reproduced the world around him in such a way as to make his paintings more real than the life they were meant to portray. But these were no one-note Norman Rockwell renditions that brought a smile to your face before you quickly turned the page, these were brutally realistic portrayals of the darker side of the life he knew so well. Every inch of canvas shouted out with gut-wrenching emotion that demanded to be noticed, to be contemplated, to be considered.

In front of me was a painting measuring four feet by six called "Drive-By Mother and Child." In it a young black mother was sitting on a tattered couch in the living room of her home with her young son in her arms. The boy—no more than ten years-old—had a wound in his chest that was bleeding badly. The woman's eyes were open wide in terror, her mouth was in the midst of a scream, and her right hand hovered over the boy's head as if she didn't know what to do. The boy was looking up at his mother with ghostly white eyes that had been all but drained of their life. The boy's mouth was barely open, but it seemed as if he were trying to say something. Perhaps he was trying to ask for help, or trying to tell his mother that it hurt, or that he loved her, or maybe he was just asking her "Why?" The entire painting was seen from the outside of the woman's home through her living room window. There was a spider-web sort of crack in the glass around a small bullet-sized hole in the window's lower-right corner. Further outside the window frame was the front of the house, its peeling paint and rotten wooden siding covered with graffiti and spotted by the heads of rusting nails.

I swallowed to wet my curiously parched throat.

Musenda was as good as they said he was. Of that, I no longer had any doubt.

Here was a realistic rendition of a scene that was sadly a weekly occurrence in the artist's world, but in addition to displaying masterful technique it also carried with it an emotional impact that I had thought was unattainable by a static work of art. The curtains in the window seemed to move with an unseen wind, the light from the television in one corner of the room seemed to flicker, and the tears streaming down the woman's face appeared to be fresh, as if the shooting had taken place just moments before the image was painted.

Standing there in front of the canvas, I could almost hear the woman's softly muted cry through the bullet-hole in the window.

So I moved closer and the sound got louder.

That stopped me cold, and for a moment I looked up at the painting knowing such a thing was impossible.

I had heard *something,* though.

But what?

I stepped up to the painting and positioned my ear scant inches from the hole in the window.

THE ART OF MADNESS

The woman was crying, calling out the name of her boy between sobs that heaved up from her broken heart.

My body shuddered and I was overcome by a cold sweat.

I turned away from the painting and glanced around the room, looking for another one to, to... experience.

It was in the corner of the room. Another large canvas measuring three feet by five. I hurried over to it and learned it was called "Prisoner of War." I didn't quite understand the significance of the title, but the painting still chilled me to the bone.

A young black man lay face down on the sidewalk, one leg hanging over the curb onto the street. There was a hole in his back where a large calibre bullet had ripped apart the flesh and touched a section of his spinal cord. The man's legs were splayed in awkward directions as if they'd collapsed under him and remained bent and bowed as he lay there unable to be moved. There were shiny brass shell casings lying on the concrete between his legs and on the street. Blood was beginning to pool under the man's body, running down off the curb and into the gutter. His left hand was empty and resting on the pavement. A fifty-dollar bill was just beyond his reach, fluttering slightly in the air as if moments before it had been part of a larger wad of cash that had been torn from the man's hand. His head was turned to the left, the cheek resting on the cold concrete of the sidewalk. The man's eyes were open, suggesting he was in pain, but more important were the whites of his eyes which were bright with fear, as if he knew the shot had paralyzed him from the waist down and he'd be sitting in a chair for the rest of his life—if he survived at all. Past the man's body on the right, were several figures running away from the scene and toward the shadows in the dark upper corner of the painting. One of them had a gun in his hand, another carried a fistful of cash. Judging by the color of their clothes, the ones who were fleeing were members of the man's gang. That was important because they were running away, abandoning one of their own at the very moment he needed them most. On the other side of the painting, a strange reddish glow seemed to be encroaching on the scene, as if a police car was pulling up, but not yet arrived.

I stood there staring for several minutes, and slowly the significance of the painting's title occurred to me. The man lying on the sidewalk was indeed a prisoner of war, paralyzed and made a prisoner in his own body for the rest of his life in a gang war that was being fought over a corner of some hood. I could almost hear the shouting from the people living on the street who were just now coming out of their homes to see what was going on. I could also hear the faint screech of the police car's tires as it came to a stop in front of the downed man, and the footsteps of the policeman's boots as he strolled, not ran, over to where the man lay lifeless from the waist down.

It was all so...alive, like I could see movement even though I knew there was none.

Like right there!

I could have sworn that I saw a drop of blood streak down the white curb to the gutter, creating a new blood line where none had been before.

Wanting to see it again, I stepped closer and concentrated on the man's wound. It was red and fresh, and glistening with moisture, as if the red on the canvas wasn't paint at all, but the man's very own blood, still bubbling up from his body.

There was another movement of light, as if more blood had pulsed up out of the wound.

It was impossible, of course, but that's just what it had looked like.

What technique was this? I wondered.

Was it even a result of the artist's work, or a trick of lighting to make the highlights move across the canvas and create the appearance of movement.

I had to know.

So I moved even closer to the painting...

And was struck by the smell of blood and urine wafting out from the canvas. It was a sharply pungent smell, but not overpowering. I leaned in toward the painting and sniffed at it, and the smell became stronger.

I stepped back, revolted and amazed. Musenda had not only captured the moment's image, but its smell as well.

Incredible!

I looked to the man's wound again, still bleeding, then looked around the room to see if anyone had arrived while I'd been enraptured by this second painting.

The room was still empty.

So I leaned in closer to the canvas, and lifted my right hand to touch it. My right index finger floated less than an inch from the man's wound. I could almost feel the heat escaping his body through the hole in his flesh.

But that wasn't good enough.

I pushed my finger forward, expecting to touch the cold, dry canvas, but instead my finger went through it, into the man's hot, wet body, all the way up to the second knuckle.

I gasped and pulled my hand away from the painting.

Then I glanced down at my fingers and found that the tip of my index finger was covered in blood.

⤞⁘⤝

I spent the next few weeks doing a little research on Musenda. Some of it I knew already, but a lot of it I didn't.

He was born and raised in the Corridor, a five mile stretch of high-rise, low-income housing projects that stretched along Jane Street from Shepherd Avenue to Steeles. It was one of the most densely populated areas in the city and, not surprisingly, the one with the highest crime rate. Knowing the neighborhood he grew up in, it seemed natural that he'd wind up painting the sorts of images he did.

Paint what you know, right?

What seemed unnatural was his name. While Daren was common enough, in his case it was actually a Hausa name from Nigeria pronounced "Dah-ren" which literally meant born at night. His last name, Musenda, was an African Baduma name meaning nightmare, which is given to a child when its mother has had an especially vivid dream right before the child's birth.

Maybe he'd been destined to paint these things.

Or maybe not.

There had been things that were too familiar about the images in the paintings for me to believe that they were simply creations of Musenda's mind. A little bit of digging in the back issues of the North section of the *Star* and I'd found what I was looking for.

Within the last year, there seemed to be stories in the paper that roughly matched up with the paintings in Musenda's show. For example, "Drive-By Mother and Child" seemed a snapshot of the July 16th article,

> *Killers drive by wrong house,*
> *Boy 9, shot dead in family room.*

I found another match to the painting, "Prisoner of War" in an article dated September 27th,

> *Man paralyzed by gunfire*
> *when drug deal goes wrong.*

These discoveries led me to believe that Musenda wasn't so much a brilliant artist, but merely a man who used his brush to hold a mirror up to the world around him. There was no real interpretation or expression to his paintings, he simply painted scenes he'd observed looking out his front window.

Almost like a landscape artist.

Sure, his technique was brilliant, almost perfect in fact, but he wasn't putting anything extra into the artwork. He was little more than a photographer, only he used a brush instead of a camera. He was Norman Rockwell, if Rockwell had grown up in the Corridor instead of on American Pie Avenue.

I smiled and thought about that for a while, until something I'd seen in the catalogue that I'd picked up at the Community Centre finally clicked in my subconscious and I compared the information in the catalogue with what I'd discovered in the newspaper.

According to the catalogue, "Drive-By Mother and Child" had been offered up for sale in July, meaning it was finished shortly after the article appeared in the paper. But more important than that was the preparation time a painting like that would require. There would be weeks of sketches and treatments before things were right for oil and canvas. That meant that Musenda had to have begun the painting well before the incident occurred.

At first I thought it was merely a coincidence. After all, crimes of this nature happened all the time in the Corridor and it seemed plausible that the painting could have been completed just a few days after the shooting.

Then I checked the date on "Prisoner of War" and found that it had been put on sale in September. That was curious because there had only been four days between the shooting and the end of the month. Musenda must have been working on the painting weeks before the shooting actually occurred.

The discovery left me cold.

I checked a few other paintings in the show and was able to find events in the Corridor that directly corresponded to the completion of paintings by Musenda. The headline, *Homeless man beaten for an empty bottle of wine,* corresponded directly to the release of "Poor Soul." And, *AIDS cases on the rise in Corridor,* appeared within a week of Musenda's painting of two youths sharing a needle called, "Connect the Dots."

Coincidence each and every time? That seemed more and more unlikely. But if it hadn't happened by chance, then how had it happened?

I was suddenly struck by a terribly dark thought that turned my stomach.

Maybe Musenda was somehow involved in the crimes that wound up in his paintings. Maybe he did some rough sketches of the image he wanted, but realized simple black lines on white paper didn't carry the emotional impact he needed to finish the artwork.

And so…

And so he staged the crimes to get the sight and smell and taste and feel of the images he wanted. Maybe he even enacted the crimes, just as a still-life artist might set up a bowl of fruit to get the right mix of light and shadow.

The thought was too disturbing, too utterly bizarre to even merit further consideration, but there were facts that couldn't be ignored: the dates of the paintings and the crimes, the terrifyingly realistic renditions of the crime scenes, and of course, the blood.

What if the blood from the paintings matched the blood of the victims? What if instead of paint, it was the victim's blood up there on the canvas?

My body shuddered at the thought of it, and I knew right then that I'd have to tell someone about what I'd discovered.

But who?

I paid a visit to the police that afternoon.

⊱⋅⊰

"You wanted to see a detective?"

I had, but now that I was looking at one—an older man with a bad haircut, loose tie and checkered shirt one size too small—it didn't seem like such a good idea anymore. "Yes," I answered.

76

"About a murder or something?"

I nodded. "More like a *something.*"

"All right, let's go in here."

The detective led me into an interview room and offered me a cup of coffee. I declined.

"So what is it?" he asked.

And so I told him, carefully explaining all about the crimes occurring in the Corridor, how they all showed up in Musenda's paintings, and how the dates in the catalogue matched those of the crimes. All of the events were clearly connected and a little digging on a detective's part was sure to reveal that Musenda was somehow involved in the crimes and using human suffering to infuse his paintings with life and energy. It was obvious to me, but the more I talked, the less obvious it seemed to the detective.

"The paintings appeared after the crimes were committed, even after they were reported in the papers," he said, making a statement, but making it sound a little like a question at the same time.

"Yes, but these kinds of paintings aren't created overnight," I argued. "A twenty-four square foot painting requires weeks of sketching, preliminary paint work and color tests. There's no way the man could have produced any of these paintings to coincide with the crimes unless he knew the crimes would be happening weeks in advance."

"So, what you're saying is this Musenda character is murdering people so he can make better paintings."

There was a bit of a smirk on the detective's face then and that's when I knew there was no hope of ever convincing the man without some sort of smoking gun—but I'd come this far and had to keep trying.

"No, he doesn't commit the crimes so much as stage them, so he can know what they really look like, get the details right, you know sight, smell, sound…"

"In a painting?"

I was about to mention the blood, but at this point I didn't think it would do any good. Instead, I just said, "Yes, in a painting."

The man glanced at his watch, then looked at me for a long time. I couldn't begin to imagine what he was thinking, but my guess was that he was either going to call in the other detectives so they could have a laugh too, or call in a doctor to check on my state-of-mind. Turned out my second thought was closest to the mark.

"Are you on any medication, Mr., uh…?"

"Landen."

"Are you?"

"No."

"Any history of mental illness?"

I let out a sigh. "No."

He looked at me again, staring really, probably trying to figure out what I was up to instead of what he should be doing, which was worrying about Musenda.

"What do you do for a living, Mr. Landen?"

I hesitated, then said, "I'm an artist."

"An artist?" He said it like he'd just unscrewed the top off a big can of worms.

"Yes."

"Like Musenda?"

"Not exactly, I do more expressionist artwork."

"Oh, you mean like abstract art, that sort of thing."

"Sort of, yes."

He was quiet again, obviously thinking. "So Musenda must be getting a lot of attention for his work. A black artist, painting scenes from the Corridor... I bet the critics are just going apeshit for his stuff."

"He's been in the media a lot lately, yes," I conceded.

"And you don't think he should be." It was a statement more than a question.

"Not at all, he's an excellent artist and deserves whatever recognition he's getting."

"But you think he's killing people to make his art better."

"Maybe not killing people himself, but he's probably been involved in several deaths, yes." We'd covered this point before, but now the detective seemed to be more interested, like he'd made his own connection between the art and the crimes.

"So if Musenda got into trouble with the law, maybe even put in jail, that would be better for you."

I was stunned. I'd never even thought of it in those terms. "That's not my motivation in reporting this," I stammered.

"It would even be a victory for the kind of art you do over the kind he does, right?"

Well, apparently I had read the detective wrong and he was far more perceptive than I'd given him credit for. He was right, of course, but all I could do now was deny that it had been my intention. "I don't get ahead by pulling someone else down. That's not why I'm here."

"No? Then why are you here?"

"People are getting hurt, and Musenda's profiting from it. I'm just trying to do the right thing."

The detective got up from his chair then, walked around the battered wooden desk that had been between us and put a hand on my shoulder. "Look, Mr. Landen, I don't know much about art, but I'm sure there are some people who think that what you produce and call art is a crime." He seemed pleased with his put down.

"But there's blood on Musenda's paintings," I said, knowing he wasn't listening any more, but not knowing what else to say.

"Thanks for coming in, Mr. Landen," he said, ignoring my words and opening the door.

"No, I mean it, there is blood on his paintings. Real blood."

"I've got work to do," he said, his voice polite but firm as he gestured again toward the open doorway.

That was it. The interview was over. Nothing more I could say would make any difference. "Thanks for your time."

"Don't mention it."

⌣∴⌣

I tried to put what I knew about Musenda's paintings out of my mind. After all, if the police didn't care about them, why should I? Anyway, I had a show of my own coming in the spring and a commission for a huge canvas for the lobby of the new bank tower going up downtown.

I was going to be busy for the next six months and wanted nothing more than to forget all about Daren Musenda and his portraits of life in the Corridor.

Trouble was, Musenda wouldn't let me forget.

The invitation came on a Monday. It was from Musenda himself, saying he'd heard I'd shown interest in his artwork and asking me if I'd like to visit with him in his studio Thursday afternoon. My initial reaction was, no way. Musenda was trouble and it was best to stay away from someone like that. But, of course, I was too curious about the man, his art and technique, his motivations, his muse, his demons… to say no.

And so I called him up and told him I'd be there.

"Excellent," he said in that deep East African accent I'd heard so often on Sunday morning television arts shows these past few months.

"See you Thursday."

He hung up without another word.

I couldn't do any work for two days.

⌣∴⌣

On Thursday I headed out around ten in the morning and arrived at Musenda's Jane-Finch studio just after eleven. It was located on a side street off the Corridor in an old warehouse building. I climbed the three flights of stairs to Musenda's studio and the man greeted me at the door before I even had a chance to knock.

"Come in," he said, his voice sounding thick and dark. I knew that Musenda was a big man, but I hadn't known how big until that moment. He was huge, on every plane, standing well over six-and-a-half feet tall and weighing at least two-hundred and fifty pounds. His hands were big too, the fingers thick and beefy, causing me to wonder how it was he was able to move a paintbrush so deftly. He stepped back from the doorway and said, "And welcome."

"Thanks for having me," I said.

"No problem."

"So, this is your studio?" I knew it was a stupid thing to say, but I honestly couldn't think of anything better. I wanted to ask him if he'd killed anyone lately, or how he knew I was interested in his work, but there would be time for that stuff later. Right now, there was a need for civility, since this was nothing more than a meeting of two artists, colleagues.

"Would you like some tea?" he asked, gesturing to two chairs and a table sitting off in one corner of the studio.

"Do you have any coffee?" I didn't want to be difficult, but I'm not much of a tea drinker.

"No, only tea."

"Tea will be fine then."

He smiled at me, and his face suddenly became unsettling as his lips peeled back, revealing a ragged set of teeth that seemed to be more suited to a ripsaw than someone's mouth. "You'll like my tea," he said. "It's very soothin'."

I nodded, then glanced around the room while he brewed the tea. Aside from a faint foul odor, and the fact that the entire place was painted black, Musenda's studio wasn't all that much different from the studios of a dozen other artists I knew. Sure it could use some better lighting, and could be kept a bit more tidy, but the studio had a feel to it that suited his subject matter. This place was dirty, gritty and that probably helped him get the darkness of his world onto the canvas.

That... and the fact that he staged crimes in order to flesh out his paintings.

He was done brewing his tea and approached the table with a tray that held a dirty yellow ceramic pot and two mugs from a local bank. We'd be chatting soon, so now seemed like as good a time as any to break the ice. "So," I said. "How did you hear about my interest in your work?"

He said nothing in response to this, only poured the tea into the two mugs. Then, he said, "Drink."

I sipped at the tea. It was bitter and there seemed to be some sort of spice in it that burned the back of my throat. I took another sip just to be polite, then put the mug down onto the table. "Do we have a mutual friend or something?"

Again Musenda did not answer.

Instead, he lifted the teapot, raised it over his head, and brought it crashing down onto the back of my skull.

⌒:⌒

When I came to, I was still sitting in the chair, but now my arms were tied behind my back and bound to the backrest. My ankles were wrapped in cord and lashed to the chair's two front legs.

My head felt as if it had been cracked open like a walnut. My clothes were wet from the steaming tea that had drained from the shattered pot and the skin around my neck and shoulders was pink and tender. It was painful for me to move even an inch, because my shirt rubbed against the flesh and burned like fire.

80

There was blood on some of my clothes, my blood most likely, but it didn't look as if I'd been cut all that bad.

After assessing my injuries and my predicament, all I could say was, "Why?"

"You are conscious," said Musenda.

"Why..." I repeated. "Why'd you do this?"

"You have talent, Mr. Landen."

"What?"

"You have great talent. You saw the true nature of my art, and I can't allow that."

Either the blow to my head was worse than I thought, or Musenda wasn't making any sense. "What are you talking about?"

He came around in front of me, grabbed the back of the chair and spun me around until I was facing one of his large canvases. The chair stopped moving, but my head seemed to turn another couple of times. I felt like I was going to throw up, but somehow I managed to keep it down.

"You should be proud, really. Only a handful of artists have been able to really *experience* my work."

When he said the word "experience" he held his right hand out in front of him like he was holding grapefruit. It was obvious to me that what he'd meant was that I'd been able to smell his paintings, hear them, feel them. I wasn't proud of the accomplishment at all. In fact, this was one talent I wish I'd never been blessed with.

"But while others have *experienced* my art, you're the first who has tried to do anythin' about it." He went over to his work table, picked up a pencil and began making lines on the canvas. "I admire you for that."

"You did kill people, then," I said, the words giving me some strength. "So you'd know just what the scenes looked like, so you could paint them. Make them more real."

"I've never killed anyone," he said with a smile, exposing that sawtooth mouth of his. "Not yet anyway."

I found that I was repeating myself, but asking a different question. "Why?"

He laughed, which surprised me. Then, he said, "Why not?"

"You've hurt people, for what?"

"For my art," he said, coming over toward me. "So many artists in the world, livin' in squalor, starvin' in garrets, sufferin' for their art." He shook his head. "Not me. Why should I suffer for my art, when I can just as easily find someone else to suffer for me. There's sufferin' goin' on in every inch of the Corridor, most of it for no reason. So what if I take some of that pain and use it for my art. This way, none of these people suffer in vain."

"It's not right," I stammered, knowing the ache in my head was dulling my ability to put together a cogent argument.

"So what?" Musenda said, getting back to his sketches. "There are a lot of things not right with the world."

For the first time I noticed what it was he was sketching. It was a picture of a man, tied to a chair, just like I was. His head was drooped lifelessly over onto his right shoulder as a gout of blood poured out from the huge rent in the left side of his neck. There was one other man in the room, he held a blood-stained knife in the fist of his right hand. The expression on the man's face was one of accomplishment, as if he was happy to see the other butchered. As if the one in the chair was getting exactly what he deserved.

Musenda drew a few tentative lines on the canvas, looked over at me in the chair, then made the lines darker.

"What are you doing?" I asked.

"Workin'."

"Are you going to hurt me?"

"Yes... a little."

I didn't understand at first, but slowly his meaning became clear.

"This one's called, 'Rat's Reward.'"

"No," I cried. "I won't tell anyone..." But of course, I already had. "I was wrong to go to the police... Whatever you do to create your art is your own business..." But like a fool I'd already made it mine.

Musenda took a brand new brush out of its package and fanned the bristles out with his fingers.

Then he moved closer to me.

"Are you going to kill me?" I asked, ashamed of the fear in my voice but powerless to do anything about it.

"No," he said, showing me that smile again. "I'm goin' to make you live forever."

And then he drew the dry brush across the left side of my throat. I could feel the flesh split apart, and the warm rush of blood flow down my neck and over my shoulder.

Before everything went black, I took a last look at the canvas in front of me.

There was color on it now.

A rich, bright red.

The canvas slowly came to life.

The Power of Preserving Pictures

LEAH R. CUTTER

"These are worthless," Ikuno said, slamming the box of paint tubes down on the table. "Give me my money back!"

All the chatter in Osamu's tea house died. The sound of the continual clash between waves and shore seeped in from outside, filling the room. The quiet fueled Ikuno's anger. Not only had Ama no Haruzumi, his best friend, cheated him by buying paints that cost three times what Ikuno usually paid, he'd goaded Ikuno into making a scene. They'd be the topic of gossip all over Okushiri, the tiny mountainous island where they lived.

"But they're mahouteki paints—magic—much better than the ones you usually buy!" Ama said in protest. "They'll make you famous!"

Ikuno dropped his voice to a hissing whisper, though he knew that the sharp-eared old men drinking *saké* at the low table next to theirs would hear him anyway. "Ama, there's no such thing as magic paints. That witch cheated you. And me. There are only good paints, and skill. I have skill."

Ama snorted.

Ikuno ignored him, and continued. "I needed good paints. Paints that let light through. What am I going to use for this next commission? You know I don't have the money to replace them! I need my money back."

Ama didn't reply. Ikuno glared at his friend. The day hadn't gone well for Ikuno. First he'd dropped his favorite *icchou*, shattering it and scattering sharp rocks of black ink across his workroom floor. Then he'd fallen on the steep track going from his mountain home to the village, and had torn his jacket. At the post

83

office a letter from Ikuno's son awaited him, saying he and his family wouldn't be visiting that spring. His son had given an excuse of too much work, but Ikuno knew it was because his son was ashamed of his poor father, ashamed that Ikuno couldn't take the family out to dinner when they came, couldn't afford treats for his grandchildren.

And now this. Ama cheating him. He didn't even have a receipt for the paints. 6000 yen! It was too much to bear. Ikuno regretted giving Ama so much money, but Ikuno had also needed more paper, and only the mainland store had the heavy, hot press paper that Ikuno used.

"Give me my money back," Ikuno said, stiffly rising from the floor pillow where he'd been seated.

Ama stayed seated, arms folded across his chest, his full lip pressed together in a stubborn line. He glanced at the paints, then at Ikuno, as if saying, "There's your money."

Ikuno grabbed the paints and marched out the door. It wasn't until he'd gone through the village and started up the mountain that he remembered he hadn't paid for his tea. Well, Osamu could just take it out of Ama's hide.

⌒∴⌒

Ikuno didn't believe the two foreigners when they told him how much they admired his work. However, he did believe their money. They must have had money to fly with a translator to where he lived. And they offered that money to him. Not a lot. But some. Enough to pay his tea and *saké* bills for a year. And why?

The broad-headed Chinese pond turtle. The fat one said it was endangered and that the Wild Animal Stocking Source, a spin-off of the World Conservation Union, wanted to use Ikuno's painting to gain recognition of the animal for their breeding project. The one who spoke through his long nose added that if they could get a famous artist like Ikuno to paint a picture of the turtle for them, their organization could get more money. Which they would give to him. Ikuno believed they would pay him, that they wouldn't swindle him, unlike that bastard Ama, his supposed best friend.

So Ikuno agreed. They spent the rest of the afternoon signing documents, poring over photos of the turtle and agreeing that the picture would be *suisaiga,* water color, and *sumi,* ink, then drinking toasts to each other's good health. The crickets had begun their evening concert before the foreigners left, bowing out of his room incorrectly. Ikuno thought of making a joke about it with their translator, but decided not to. He needed their money, and they might not find the humor in it.

After the noise of the foreigners stumbling through the woods had faded, Ikuno went out onto his front porch, stretched a little and thought about making his own way down the treacherous mountain path to Osamu's. He wanted to drink some *saké* and celebrate this new commission. But who would he celebrate with? His best friend Ama had cheated him yesterday, giving him those cheap paints, charging him so much for them, claiming they were magic. A cold wind rattled the bamboo next to his house. *Torihada*—chicken-skin—raised across his shoulders and neck. He shivered, sighed, and went to bed.

In the morning, Ikuno ate some noodles and soy while watching the sunrise. He loved his view from high in the hills, even if the path was a little steep for his old bones, and sometimes impractical in the winter. If he sat just right, he could only see harbor and the ocean: the trees hid the power lines and bare TV antennas of the village below.

When he felt at peace and ready to paint, he went inside to his studio, the little room he'd added to the south side of his two-room shack. Sunbeams slanted through the paper walls, casting a milky light on his table. He reached for his brushes, his water jar and his good ink. He prepared the space like he had prepared his mind, placing each item in readiness, with an ease that made it seem automatic, and a carefulness that made it seem like ritual. However, when he reached for his watercolors, his rhythm broke.

That bastard Ama no Haruzumi had cheated him, bringing him this box filled with cheap tubes of water color paints. He sneered at the name of the paint manufacturer—*kuroneko*. A company called "Black Cat" should make Chinese fire crackers, not paints. He opened a tube and sniffed it. An oddly compelling, sweet yet medicinal smell came to him. He squeezed a bit of paint out onto his forefinger. At least it was solid color, and hadn't separated. He rubbed it between his forefinger and thumb. The paint had a silky texture he hadn't expected: cheap paints generally felt more oily.

Ikuno sighed and looked around his workspace. He was all set to paint. He didn't want to tramp down the mountain, take the ferry back to the mainland and spend all day buying paints. He didn't have either the time, or the money. He'd have to use these paints, even though he didn't want to.

Ikuno attached the turtle photographs around the edges of his canvas using flour water paste. He studied all the angles of the turtle, paying as much attention to it as if it was the actual incarnation of the God of Fire and Thunder. Certain of the inferiority of his paints, Ikuno concentrated hard.

Ikuno filled a recently cleaned pallet with the *mahouteki* paints, shaking his head at the gullibility of Ama. He didn't allow himself to get angry now: he needed to keep his concentration on the painting. He tried different ratios of water and paint, working hard to get the consistency and translucency he wanted.

Then he started to paint. He paid as much attention to detail as Ito Jakuchu had in his Domestic Fowl painting—the one where it seemed Ito had painted every feather on every bird.

After three days Ikuno finished. The turtle swam away from its viewers, the back of its broad head barely visible over the top of its shell. It had just reached the shore, its foreleg extended, nails scraping the mud, almost as if it were begging. The turtle existed between things, between water and land, between extinction and life.

Ikuno took the long trek down the mountain to the post office to send the painting to the foreigners. He was grateful they'd left him money so he didn't have to pay the air freight. Then he decided to stop at Osamu's, drink some warm *saké,* and relax.

As he walked through the public room, many old men sitting at the low tables greeted him, including Ama. Ikuno acknowledged all of them, except Ama. He sat on the floor at a window table overlooking the sea. Two of his other friends joined him. Ikuno let them buy him *saké* to celebrate his good fortune.

Suddenly Ama stood in front of their table. Ikuno's words dried up in his throat and he took a sip of *saké* to hide his embarrassment.

Ama broke the silence saying, "Everything I told you was true."

Ikuno didn't reply.

Ama continued. "The art store was closed. I didn't know where to go for your paints. Then this old woman approached me. She said she was a *mahoutsukai* and had magical paints. How did she know I wanted paints when she saw me looking in the art store? It sells more than paints. But she knew. She was no *inchiki,* she sold me good paints. You will become famous using them!"

Ikuno laughed, but not nicely. "You should be a *rakugo,* a story teller, eh? But your tale hasn't enlightened me, or given me chicken-skin. I want my money back!" Even though he hissed the words quietly, he expressed himself with enough vehemence that the chatter in the room died.

"I thought our friendship was worth more than a few Yen," Ama said, drawing more attention to their quarrel.

Ikuno squirmed, chagrined. Everyone was watching them. They'd already caused enough gossip. He looked away, out the window, and heard Ama leave the table. He thought he heard the word *nigiriya,* miser, as Ama left the room.

"Drink my friends, drink," Ikuno said when he turned back around. His friends toasted his health and talked about how the rains would come soon.

When Ikuno called for the bill, he choked when he saw it was double what he'd expected to pay. Because Ama had left without paying, Osamu had included Ama's bill with Ikuno's. Ikuno and Ama were best friends, right? They'd paid each other's bills often.

Ikuno paid, furious, certain that Ama had left without paying on purpose, possibly trying to get Ikuno since the last time they'd been at Osamu's together, he'd been the one to leave without paying. He felt like a fool. He stomped up the hill to his house and sat on his front porch, but even the beautiful view couldn't calm his heart.

꒰꒱

The money from the foreigners arrived nine days later, with a note and contracts for another commission. His painting had become very famous because all the broad-headed Chinese pond turtles had died of an airborne plague that had claimed many amphibians in recent years.

THE POWER OF PRESERVING PICTURES

Ikuno paid what he thought were appropriate taxes on the foreign commission, then put the rest of the money aside. Now his son didn't have to feel ashamed of his father. His grandchildren could have all the treats they wanted when they came.

The next commission was for a Japanese mountain goat. The note said the painting must be finished for a conference in less than a week's time. Ikuno hadn't bought any new paints, and though he wanted the commission, for a while, he was afraid to use the paints Ama had bought him, afraid they were *majutsu,* black magic. Hadn't all the turtles died?

However, there wasn't time to buy new paints, and he didn't want to waste the money he'd spent on the *mahouteki* paints, so he used them. A mountain filled the right side of his painting. One *yagi* stood on a narrow pass. The reddish-brown hair around its neck reached its knees, like an old monk who'd never shaved. Its small eyes looked as ancient as the mountains it roamed. Another goat in the background leapt toward the empty space on the left side of the paper, as if across a chasm, away from the viewers, full of life and energy.

A month later a note from the foreigners came saying that the goats had died too. No one connected their extinction with Ikuno, but he did. He put the *mahouteki* paints aside, swearing never to use them again, though the pictures he'd painted with them had given him great fame. Everyone on the whole island knew who he was now.

Ikuno wanted to share his good fortune with his old friends too, with Ama. Ikuno missed his old friend, missed Ama's house by the sea, missed the long nights sitting and drinking *saké* and talking. However, Ama still refused to pay him back the money for the paints. He claimed it was the paints that had made Ikuno famous, and that Ikuno should be paying him.

Ikuno considered not accepting the next wildlife commission—a rare bird with brilliant blue tail feathers that trailed behind it, like the Phoenix. However, the money was too good. Because the foreigners paid cash, there was no official notification of how much he received, so he didn't pay taxes on all his money. For this painting though, he didn't use the cursed paints, and the species didn't become extinct.

Ikuno accepted more commissions. Sometimes the animals he painted went extinct, not always. He told himself the first two had been coincidence.

One evening the next spring while he sipped *saké* at Osamu's, listening to the sea go out, Ama came in and sat at the table next to him. Only a few men lounged there that evening, so the whole room heard Ama's story about an artist who became famous because he paid his reviewers. All the work he did was *jouhitsu,* worthless and unworthy. He became a *nigiriya* who sold all his friends for money, caring more about his fame than his companions or family.

Ikuno knew Ama told the story to goad him, but he pretended not to hear. Ama left when he finished the story. Ikuno found that, though he breathed a little easier after Ama left, the night also seemed colder and darker.

Then Ikuno found that Ama had stuck him with his *saké* bill again.

Ikuno wasn't drunk enough to make the mountain path up to his house dangerous. He was drunk enough to mutter and swear under his breath. He wanted to teach Ama a lesson. Ikuno's fame wasn't because he paid his reviewers. He had skill. He painted with great talent and veracity. He'd show Ama. He'd paint Ama's portrait, though he usually only did landscapes and animals. It'd be so good, Ama would never have to look in a mirror again.

The moon through the paper walls of his studio washed everything in ghostly light. In his mind's eye Ikuno saw Ama, seated like a fat toad on a rock. He'd paint those flabby lips, those hard pebble eyes, that nose so swollen from drinking it was as big as a foreigner's.

Ikuno hadn't meant to use the *mahouteki* paints for the whole portrait. Just for the important parts, like for Ama's nose and mouth, to make those disappear. However, he found that he couldn't put the black cat paints down. When he added the water to the now dried paints in the pallet, a dusty smell rose from them, like a spider's web. It caught him tightly, not hindering his movements, but forcing him to paint. He did Ama's whole face with the *majutsu* paints. Dawn light brightened his room, and still he worked. When the woman who brought his groceries came, he yelled at her like a *kyoujin,* roaring for more *saké.* He didn't listen to her talk of the plague in the village.

Ikuno finished that night. Fevered dreams of dead goats chasing dead turtles, leaping across the ocean, going from one great bed of algae to the next, filled his sleep with wonder and dread. When cool morning arrived he felt ashamed. Ama was his best friend. How could he treat him so? He went to burn the piece.

The painting sat in the middle of his studio, dominating the space. Ikuno couldn't take his eyes off it. It was much better, more realistic, than he would have imagined, given his impulsive start. A shadowy mountain stood in the background with a hint of a trail stretching from it. Ama stood on the path turned away from the viewer, as if he was leaving, but he still looked back over his shoulder, one hand outstretched, entreating the viewer to follow.

Ikuno decided to give the piece to Ama as a peace offering. They were both old men. He didn't want either of them to die angry and be reincarnated as a vengeful ghost, haunting the other. He rolled the painting up and tramped down the mountain path.

Ikuno walked quickly through the maze of streets in the village to Ama's house. He slowed himself down more than once, only to realize a few steps later that he was almost running again, like a school girl on her way to her favorite aunt's house. He'd missed Ama. Why had he let himself stay angry for so long?

Ama's house overlooked the sea. Ama loved the sound of the waves like Ikuno loved the sound of the mountains, though each criticized the other's taste. Ikuno said he couldn't hear the sea over the motor boats and village noises. Ama said he never heard the mountains, just the wind and the crickets.

Many people stood outside Ama's house, along with an ambulance. Ikuno made his way to the front, asking what had happened. Suddenly everyone pushed back, away from the stretcher the ambulance workers carried, saying, *ekirei,* plague. The yard emptied. Ikuno stood alone, twisting his rolled up painting in his hands, the sole mourner as Ama's body passed by. Then he went to Osamu's to find out more.

Only a few men sat at Osamu's tables, drinking seriously and silently. Ikuno ordered his *saké* and sat alone at a table covered with handbills. First he drank a silent toast to Ama, praying his spirit would forgive him. Then he read the first handbill.

In poorly translated Japanese it said Armageddon had arrived and that he should convert now, start believing in the Jesus-kami and save himself before the plague took them all. Ikuno remembered the woman with his groceries had said something about a plague. Before he could ask anyone, a formally dressed stranger came in the door and asked, "Is Ikuno Sugawara here?"

Ikuno wondered if it was Ama's lawyer. Maybe Ama had forgiven him, and had left him something in his will. He called the stranger to his table.

Without introducing himself, the man began. "You owe the government 80,000 yen in taxes for all the foreign commissions you've received over the past year."

Ikuno blinked and took a sip of *saké,* shocked. How dare this man confront him in public? Ikuno had paid what he'd thought was appropriate for taxes. Maybe not as much as he officially should have, but what man did?

Pig-like eyes stared at him across the table. This man didn't care that Ikuno's best friend had died that morning, or that a plague killing everyone ran loose in the world. All he wanted was his money, and the power he achieved by bullying people weaker than himself.

Ikuno wasn't intimidated. He stood up, pointed a finger at the government man, and spoke like Nai no Kami, the God of Thunder. "I will not hear your false accusations! I've paid my fair share of taxes! First Ama accused me of being a miser. Now he's dead and you're here representing his spirit. Why won't you leave me in peace?"

Embarrassed, the government man left. However, Ikuno hadn't had enough. He sprinted up the mountain path to his home.

He ran out of paper after he'd completely covered three and a quarter walls of his studio with it, from ceiling to floor. He couldn't paint the evils of society like Masami Teraoka. He couldn't paint avarice with his magic paints and make it disappear. But he could paint all the people in the world. He didn't have to paint every single individual, just the suggestion of them all, with their backs to the viewer, walking into the sea, leaving the earth behind.

Ikuno refused to die of a plague like everyone else. He wanted an honorable death, like *karoushi,* death from overworking. He painted in a fever for three weeks. The woman who brought his groceries only came up twice, the second time telling him that the plague had spread to every continent and the world had gone mad, no place was safe anymore. He'd have to get his own food—if he could find any—she couldn't come again.

During the last week Ikuno was so fevered he could barely stand, but he still dragged himself off his *tatami* and painted. Millions of heads, suggestions of every race and kind of human, old ones, young ones, rich and poor. When he knew he wouldn't be able to paint any more he painted another figure a little apart from the others, with a paintbrush held over his head like a baton, marching into the sea. Then he had to go lay down.

And soon a fresh canvas, without people, was laid down over the earth.

The Death Technique

JOHN B. ROSENMAN

I discovered the Death Technique the day after my twelfth birthday. Perhaps it was puberty that made it possible, or the fact that I simply did the right thing at the right time.

It's more likely, though, that I was genetically predisposed to discover the DT, that it was in my nature to lie down one day and concentrate on a realm somewhere beyond this one and start to dissolve as a result. Well, "dissolve" isn't the word. "Decompose" is more like it, as in ashes to ashes, dust to dust. "Decompose," as in there goes my right eyeball, there goes my left. And darned if I can't feel my bones emerging from where my flesh used to be.

Actually, the first time it happened, I was anything but blasé and philosophical about it. You can't be, you know, when you first feel your gums start to recede from your teeth and smell the stench of your own advancing decay. Feeling your pancreas commence to liquefy isn't soothing either.

Later in life, though, the experience did become soothing—in fact, deliciously peaceful. There was nothing finer than lying back and letting your body act out this cellular rehearsal for the final drama. Once you're reduced to a skeleton and a small pool of shrinking protoplasm, you find you've acquired an admirable sense of proportion and of what really matters. And the knowledge that you yourself, not God or Chance, can personally monitor the process precisely and pass the barrier into the next world at any time, is, well, comforting. How many people do you know who would find their worst fears laid to rest if they knew they held the keys to the kingdom?

91

But you've got to be careful. Folks don't appreciate finding you in a state of advanced decay. Most of them, in fact, believe that your entrails and viscera ought to remain on the inside.

I learned this lesson when I was seventeen and forgot to lock my bedroom door. It had been a terrible day at school, for my art teacher had finally told me what I had long feared: that I was clumsy and had no talent. All my love for art was meaningless, a cruel mockery.

To forget his words and my own immense pain, I lay naked on my bed and contemplated a spot just beyond the boundaries of this universe. Then I let the DT unfold.

As usual, decomposition and liquefication of my body served only to enhance my senses. Indeed, I was able to leave my body and look down in triumph upon my corporeal collapse. Despite the odor, I thought, "Oh death, where is thy sting?" Even when I started to drip on the floor, I felt no concern. After all, from previous experiences, I knew that with a minimal exertion of will, I could reconstitute myself in minutes, leaving not even a stain on the bed or carpet.

Then my mother opened the door and entered the room.

I must confess I can't do justice to her expression. She stopped halfway to my bed, and her face turned a color I had never seen before. Most amazing was her mouth, which opened incredibly wide. From a space three or four feet above my own remains, I watched her start to tremble as if she were conducting an electric charge. Then she screamed and bolted from the room.

I heard her fall once or twice as she stumbled down the stairs.

Panic. Fear. What should I do? My secret was out!

Drawing on resources I little understood, I willed myself to reconstitute. Molecules coalesced; cells healed. My flesh knit and became whole again, drawing blood and entrails up from the bed and floor.

But would it be quick enough? As my face reformed, I could hear my mother's hysterical screaming downstairs and my father desperately trying to make sense of it. "What's wrong, Edith? Please calm down and tell me. What—"

Mom's voice rose to a shrill peal. "He's lying there, and... and d-d-dissolving! I could see his bones! The bed was covered with blood. And Frank, his *e-e-eyes* were gone!"

Hearing my father's footsteps cross the living room and start up the stairs, I accelerated my healing. I knew I must be faster than ever before, that I must push my powers as if my life depended on it.

As Dad's footsteps reached the landing, my last wound healed. I rose, grabbed my robe, threw it about my naked body, and lay down with a smile.

He entered my room, his face stricken, expecting the worst. When he saw me, he stopped.

"Eric," he gasped in relief. "You're all right?"

I frowned. "Yeah, why not?"

"Y-your mother. She..."

THE DEATH TECHNIQUE

Mom crept in slowly, her hands clasped in agony. When she saw me whole and smiling, her mouth fell open.

"Eric—you're alive!"

"What is this?" I asked. "Of course I'm alive!"

Dad turned and held my mother. Now his concern was for her.

Mom was still looking at me. "Oh, thank God. Son, I could have sworn you were dead a minute ago! You were…"

I shrugged. "Well, I have felt a bit out of sorts lately."

"Out of sorts? You were rotting on the bed! And…"

Hating myself for what I'd done to her, I rose and went to give her comfort. "But Mom, I'm all right. Look!"

"But how—"

"It must have been the light. It can play tricks at times." Avoiding my father's eyes, I kissed her cheek, determined never to put either of them through this again.

⌣∶∾

Time passed. I graduated from college, got married, then divorced.

After the failure of my first marriage, I contemplated suicide. Maybe, I thought, a freak and failed artist like myself wasn't meant to be happy. Maybe, the next time I sought Peace, I'd be better off if I pursued it all the way and let it truly be the Death Technique. From the beginning I'd sensed that if I permitted the process to pass a certain point, I'd be unable to reverse it. I'd simply pass out of this world altogether.

Later, I found Sarah, the woman I should have married the first time, had two kids and a dog, and taught art for free at a community recreation center. I told myself that as long as I could guide and develop some young kids' talent, my dream wasn't dead after all.

Ironically, it turned out that my real talent in life wasn't art but something I originally had little interest in: politics, or more accurately, running other people's campaigns. In college I had met a student whose policies I liked, but whose bookish image made him a huge underdog for Senior class president. Almost before I knew it, I had taken him under my wing, repackaged him from top to bottom, and managed him to a near-landslide. After graduation I continued such work and eventually became the campaign manager for Starret Granton, an up-and-coming politician I deeply admired. Life was good, or so I told myself. When it came to politics, I was a Picasso.

But the truth is, the experience with my mother had changed me. Before that day, I had viewed myself simply as a person with an interesting knack. True, I knew it was a knack I had to keep to myself, for if it got out, my whole life would be changed forever. I would be seen as a freak who made anything in *Ripley's Believe it or Not!* pale in comparison. But as long as my DT remained a secret, I was just an ordinary guy.

No more. After the near calamity in my bedroom, which made my mother see a shrink, I was Clark Kent with a hidden "S" emblazoned on my chest. Only the "S" stood for Strange and Supremely Scary. For the first time I realized my "talent" could make a difference, only unlike Superman's, it would be destructive.

Did my talent have no purpose? Would it serve only to shock and horrify? If so, then I was the equivalent of a two-headed baby and must carefully avoid ever putting myself on display.

Remembering my mother's horrified face, I resolved at once never to use DT again. Instead, I tried 97 types of TM, communing with everything from my Inner Self to the Mystic Soul of the Universe. But nothing I tried gave me the sense of peace and tranquillity that DT did. Let me emphasize: when I relaxed and let my spirit leave my body, I felt freed and fulfilled in a way I could find nowhere else. I was even able to forget my failed dream of becoming an artist.

But then I met Sarah, who became my second wife, and somewhat later, my behind-the-scenes skills at politics caught Starret Granton's attention. From then on, I was basically happy and able to put my "quirk" on the back burner of my mind, though now and then the same questions returned.

WHY AM I ABLE TO DO THIS? DOES IT HAVE ANY PURPOSE?

⋰∴

"Eric," my wife said softly, "you can't let him suffer anymore."

"Him" was Socrates, my 17-year-old Irish setter, who was dying of cancer and old age. The problem was, I hadn't done what I knew I should have, which was to take Socrates to the vet, hug him one last time, and let the vet put him down. I had told myself a hundred times I should do it, but I just couldn't.

I was a coward. And even worse, I was a coward about an animal I had loved for a long time.

Sarah sat beside me on the living room floor, watching me gently stroke Socrates. She started to say something, then thought better of it.

Socrates, I thought, *tell me what to do.* I sniffed, and a tear fell on his fur. I knew he was in terrible pain as he struggled forward to lick my hand.

His fur. Once it had been so soft and long, with a rich, reddish sheen. How often he had run up and rubbed his silken sides against me! Now his coat looked dull and faded, as if someone had turned out a light inside him.

"Eric..."

"I know." I started to slip my arms gently around my pet so I could carry him to the car, but instead placed my hand on his weakly panting chest. *Decompose,* I thought, *melt like I have inside so often.* I imagined his heart, seeing it soften and lose its shape, like a badly molded lump of artist's clay. But I did it only a little, just enough to matter.

I waited. Felt his chest rise and fall, rise and fall ...

Then he stopped breathing and the small light that had lingered in his eyes simply vanished.

"Honey…"

"It's all right," I whispered, choking back tears. "He's gone."

⌣∴∾

The next day an event occurred that changed my life. I was walking past Starret's office when I heard his baritone voice. Something about its tone made me stop and listen.

"I want your endorsement, Governor. I hope I make myself clear."

Was the governor in Starret's office? Starret, who was running for his first term as senator, hardly seemed to merit such an honor.

"Very clear," the governor's familiar voice replied. "But I would have preferred to handle this over the phone."

"I'm sure you would. But let's be frank. I've got you over a barrel. If you don't play ball with me, I'll leak your love affair with the drug companies to the press. I wonder what voters will say when they hear you've pocketed a half mil for vetoing drug reform."

"The two have nothing to do with each other."

"Please, Governor. Bullshit the voters, not me."

Silence. Heart pounding, I listened, thinking of whispers I'd heard and ignored about Starret's ruthlessness, about backs he'd stepped on. Suddenly I was ashamed I was this man's campaign manager!

I left numbly and returned later, when Starret was alone. "Hey, Star," I said, peering around his door with a tight smile. "Got a minute?"

He leaned back in his plush chair, a smile spreading across his handsome face. "Sure, bud. You know I always have time for you."

I closed the door and went to a chair before his gleaming mahogany desk. Sitting down, I considered working into it gradually, then just plunged in and asked if what I'd overheard was true.

He tapped his desk, hesitating. "The truth?"

"Yeah," I said. "No bullshit."

"Okay." He leaned forward, resting his elbows on the desk. "Sure, I'm squeezing the governor a little."

"Blackmailing him, you mean."

He shrugged.

"And on top of that, you called him in here to rub his nose in it, assert your clout."

"Didn't hurt."

Far away, a car honked faintly. My hands were sweating.

"I didn't know about this."

"As my campaign manager, it's time you did."

I cleared my throat. "I don't think I can continue, Star."

"Why not, Eric? It's just politics, no different from business." Still smiling, he tapped the desk. "To tell the truth, I'm glad you overheard. I'm tired of hiding things from you. Besides, you were bound to find out anyway."

"Hiding things," I said. "What do you mean?"

He laughed. "Really want to know?"

"I... have to."

"Okay." He leaned back with a soft roll of casters. Keeping his eyes fixed on mine, he started talking.

Ten minutes later, I was sopping wet, watching the man I had once admired hint proudly at ruining several people's lives. He was vague, cagey with the details, but he left no doubt about the kind of person he really was. How could I have been so blind? Or deaf? When you tallied up his total, you found that Starret Granton was a goodlooking, sincere-sounding fraud. A John Kennedy without soul.

Finally he stopped talking, and it was my turn. I hesitated briefly as a strange thought stirred inside me. If I only had the skill to paint such corruption, to capture this man's evil on canvas for all to see! But I remembered grimly that while I had been born with an intense desire to be an artist, I totally lacked the talent required.

Bitterly, I suppressed the old pain. "You made a mistake telling me all this," I said. "I'm... going to stop you."

"You are?"

"Yes. I'm your manager. I'll quit and tell the press why."

He acted shocked. "Eric, that would really disappoint me. I have considered you my friend."

"After listening to you, I don't think you have any friends, Starret."

"Oh, but I do," he said smoothly. He leaned forward again, his eyes drilling me. "And one of them did a little digging for me. Call it excavation of the past that revealed some interesting buried secrets." He winked, enjoying this. "Which is why I doubt very much you'll be telling anyone."

"What makes you so sure?"

"Eric," he said softly, "would you like to know a few things about your wife?"

❧

"How do you like your meatloaf?"

I looked across the table at her sweet oval face. Sarah was wearing one of those cashmere sweaters she loves so much. Tan-colored, it matched her light brown eyes perfectly.

"It's great," I said. "As usual."

I took a bite, smiling at her. For a while, I had wondered if Starret's revelations would change the way I felt about her. We had been married for twenty years, and never once had she told me what her drug habit before college

96

had forced her to do. At first, I had scoffed at Starret's claims, but I couldn't deny the evidence he had shown me.

I gripped my fork, tempted to confront her, perhaps show her one of Starret's choice pictures. But then, I thought, I would be just like him, wouldn't I? Using the past to hurt and gain some kind of advantage.

"Eric, is everything all right?"

I studied her face, which I had kissed a million times. No, I thought. Knowing makes no difference at all. But the fact that Starret could so callously use Sarah to get at me *did* matter. More than anything else, more than all the sins and double-dealing he had hinted at, it served to make his inhumanity real.

I rose and went to the window, passing a painting of Sarah I had done several years before. Competent but undistinguished, it was the best I had ever done, the best I could ever do. Though Sarah had told me often how much she liked it, I knew in my heart that it was a mockery of the love I felt for her. Why couldn't I paint the pictures and portraits I wanted? Why had I been given this great desire to create but denied the talent to do so? It seemed like a cruel, heartless joke, and I imagined God laughing.

I forced such old, familiar thoughts away, and focused on the problem at hand. Starret. He had meant to regain my loyalty by blackmail and by destroying my love and respect for my wife. But the only person I disdained now was Starret himself. I gazed at an icicle on the gutter which was beginning to melt. Funny. In a way Starret had decomposed before my very eyes.

I sighed, caught in a moral quandary. Starret was far ahead in the polls, and I knew that becoming senator would only enhance his ability to hurt others and cause harm. Even worse, I was absolutely certain that he would do so as soon as it was in his self-interest. Still, did my knowledge give me the right to play God and attempt what I was thinking? Suddenly I was frightened more than ever before by this power I had and wondered if I was mad for even thinking about using it. Mad or not, if I did use it, how would I be any better than Starret? And if I failed, what would I do then?

On the other hand, how could I live with myself if I simply sat back and did nothing?

"Eric," Sarah said, "is anything wrong?"

I studied the icicle, which went drip...drip...drip. "No, honey," I said. "Everything's fine."

⌣∴⌣

It was a big event, a $100-a-plate dinner at which the governor was officially going to endorse Starret Granton for the U.S. Senate. Starret sat to the governor's immediate right, sipping from a glass of ice water. I sat several seats to their left down the long table, having managed to take just two bites of my overcooked chicken.

At last the governor was introduced. He rose and reached the podium in five steps, and the packed hall listened to him recap Starret Granton's illustrious, public-spirited career and make him sound as if he were the Party's Last Great Hope. As he returned to his seat amid thunderous applause, I rose and headed quickly for Starret.

But before I could reach him, Starret's new bodyguard intervened. He placed a meaty hand against my chest as Starret stopped behind him.

Stunned, I feared the man could feel my racing heartbeat. Starret must have had doubts his blackmail would keep me quiet, and asked him to watch me closely tonight for any suspicious moves. Still, with five hundred people watching, I knew that Starret didn't want any embarrassment.

I forced myself to smile and looked past the bodyguard at Starret. "I just want to shake my boss's hand!" I half-shouted over the applause.

A second passed. Then another.

"It's all right, Mike," Starret said.

The bodyguard gave me a long, skeptical look, then moved aside. I stepped toward Starret with a bright grin, seized his hand and pumped it.

"Congratulations, Star," I said. "I'm with you all the way!"

He frowned. My excessive enthusiasm at this moment was irregular. But then, I was his campaign manager, congratulating him and wishing him the best. I watched his frown melt into a smile as the applause died.

"You're staying with me, Eric?"

I grinned. "Till the end!"

His smile widened. "I'm glad. I hoped you would. Stay on board, and we'll both go a long way."

Not if I can help it, I thought. Cranking up my smile a few watts, I squeezed Starret's hand harder, thinking of my dog's heart. "Congratulations again, Star!" I said.

Finally I released his hand, patted his shoulder, and left the table. As Starret went to the podium and began speaking over the mic, I moved as discreetly as I could toward the front of the hall. A few diners gave me curious glances, but they had paid big money to hear Starret, not watch me. Besides, I was obviously attending to some business for my man.

I posted myself near the entrance doors and waited, watching Starret closely.

But Starret's rich voice filled the hall, and nothing whatsoever happened.

Gradually I realized how foolish I had been. Yes, Judas had betrayed Jesus with a kiss, but ending this bastard's career with a handshake was something else entirely. Even if I was right about my helping Socrates to die, that did not mean I could accomplish something of *this* magnitude.

"I SEE GREAT THINGS FOR THIS STATE, OPPORTUNITIES I WANT TO SHARE WITH YOU TONIGHT!"

THE DEATH TECHNIQUE

At the podium, Starret was in fine form, his stirring voice and chiseled, movie-star features mesmerizing the crowd. I watched him raise his finger for emphasis.

"THE ECONOMY HAS NEVER BEEN HEALTHIER, AND IF BUSINESS AND GOVERNMENT CAN WORK TOGETHER..."

He faltered, staring at his finger. Peering close, I could see why.

His finger seemed to be melting, dripping on the podium.

Starret's composure crumbled, but he was a political animal of the first rank, and his instincts quickly kicked in. He thrust the offending member behind him and raised his other hand.

"WE... WE CAN WORK TOGETHER IF WE REMEMBER TO CHERISH THE PEOPLE'S TRUST. IF WE..."

No good. His whole right hand was starting to melt now. Starret lowered it quickly and struggled to continue.

But even if the diners hadn't begun to murmur, a dissolving palate can wreak havoc with oratory. Though I was over twenty yards away, I partly shared his deterioration. I could feel his flesh melt on my bones and his tongue wither in my mouth. And I could feel something else too, something that brought joy to my heart and tears to my eyes: the realization of a dream that I had thought forever lost.

Moment by moment, as I watched, Starret became my masterpiece. That it was grisly and gruesome, a macabre, morbid masterpiece did not matter in the slightest. For now at last, the vile ugliness beneath Starret's handsome, charming facade was displayed for all to see.

And I, the man without talent, had done it! Which meant that I possessed an artistic gift after all, a genuine calling and purpose in life. All my hope and longing hadn't been foolish or wasted. If I wanted, I could be the Dali of Death, the Degas of Decomposition!

Starret's voice died. Across the great hall, he looked at me.

I smiled.

He lurched then and tried to leave the podium. But by now he lacked the strength and succeeded only in collapsing over it. Swaying against the podium, he mouthed silent cries for help.

As people started screaming, the governor and a few other luminaries at the main table rose to aid Starret. But they stopped in horror a few feet away. The DT had accelerated, and Starret's handsome form was rapidly becoming formless. Flesh melted and ran like wax down his entire frame. His right hand abruptly fell off, spewing blood and liquefied flesh. What remained of his face was crumbling, and one of his eyes tumbled from its socket.

Mayhem. Before the main table, a cameraman stood with bulging eyes, his mission forgotten. But perhaps he could be forgiven, for by this point, Starret Granton was clearly dead. You could even see his white bones, streaked with gore, beginning to emerge from his shrinking flesh.

Ignoring the screams, I turned and left without looking back.

⌣⁚∾

Later there was a press sensation, and a hundred theories to explain Starret's demise. A new virus perhaps, or a rare hereditary condition. Fearing contagion, most of the people had themselves tested. What remained of Starret Granton was examined as closely as possible.

Nothing was found. Starret's gruesome decomposition remained a mystery. Consoled and consulted by friends and reporters, I could only shake my head and dry my eyes.

Eventually the excitement died down. One day I told Sarah I'd been offered a new job, teaching art full-time at a community college. One of the best things about it is that it has absolutely nothing to do with politics.

We moved out of state, and I began a new life—in more ways than one.

I can't say that I have found *the* purpose of the Death Technique, but I definitely believe I've found one of them, which is to purge the world of some of the evil people who hurt others for their own gain. And if, in the process, I experience a bizarre artistic fulfillment, an aesthetic exaltation, then so be it.

Was I right to take Starret's life? Balancing all he had done and all he would have done if he had lived, against the continuance of his selfish life, I find that I have little trouble sleeping nights. And when I do, it's only because I think of my mission and the responsibility implied by my gift.

There's an American far more prominent than Starret Granton. You all know and admire him, and indeed, would be shocked if you learned even a fraction of what I have. Compared to him, Starret was a saint.

This man is a billionaire, a captain—no, make that a general—of industry.

And the path he's trod is stained with blood and broken lives. According to a reliable report, his tentacles reach even into the Oval Office itself.

I can hardly wait to shake that man's hand.

Body

TIM LEBBON

Love is …

Lyle had a tattoo of an eye between his shoulder blades. The tattooist had used the tines of a tarantula to prick it through his skin, deep down into the flesh, deep and painful so that it would never, ever fade or be damaged by scarring or sunburn. It was wide-open, all-seeing and all-knowing, and it had the same emerald green iris of my own eyes, green with golden flakes. Lyle said the gold was like sheddings from the sun, but I had often thought it more likely to be a vitamin deficiency. In the camp we ate the best food in the land, prepared by the most experienced cooks and served with the finest wines. But luxury was our hosts' main objective, not healthy eating. After all, we were as good as gods.

The eye was green, and it was as big as my hand, and it only ever blinked when Lyle flexed his muscled shoulders hard enough. He never covered it up, even in the cold evenings when the desert heat dissipated to the clear skies and stars hung like frozen snowflakes over the landscape. It was only ever concealed when we made love. I would reach around his back and scratch at it with my nails, smother it with my palms, in a secret attempt to see whether I would feel it as well.

I could not, but I always tried.

Because Lyle said the eye tattoo was of me, and for me. He said that when we were separated at last, it would help him find me in the dark, help me see where he was when I searched. Through the long tunnels of pitch black, the arteries clogged with desperate bodies, the organs where slaughter and birth took

101

place side by side, it would see. So Lyle said. Through the pain of death and the agony of rebirth, it would see.

I knew how much he loved me because they would never let him keep it. When his time came and the pampering and worship was over, the eye would be taken from his back with a hot knife or a boiling splash of iron. The wound would be cleaned, of course, because infection and death would only put rot into the system. But the pain would be exquisite.

Lyle knew this.

Love is blind.

⌄ː◡

"They're taking Brandon tomorrow." Lyle came into my tent and sat cross-legged on the rug, taking a pipe from his robe and lighting up. The tang of dope hazed the atmosphere and I breathed in deeply. "Did you hear me?"

I nodded. For a second I'd been shocked, but then I always was when it was someone I knew well. "Yes. Brandon. Is he pleased?"

"Wouldn't you be?"

I smiled and waved a hand at him. "Don't play with me, Lyle. You know what I mean."

He puffed again on the pipe, letting out a spiralling cloud of smoke. I crawled across to him and pretended to bite it from the air, breathing in, feeling it tingle my nostrils and only wanting more.

Lyle was looking into my loose robe. "He's been offered the final day's prayers, the cleansing and purification by Jacobus, but he's chosen to leave the camp instead."

"Really? That's... strange."

"Brandon always was, a little."

I took the pipe from Lyle and drew deeply, enjoying his look of fake anger. Brandon would disappear from this world tomorrow. I'd grown up with him in the camp, enjoyed his company, been his friend. The only thing I wanted to do now was to get high.

"You're only jealous," I said. "You know what he thought of me."

"He wanted to screw you, same as everyone in this place. They all want to screw you. But none of them ever will."

"Why should I let them when I have you?" I could feel the dope working already, stretching my senses and sending smoky fingers down my backbone, relaxing bunched muscles and calming my mind. My heartbeat had doubled. I was sweating, and wet.

"Shall we go and watch?" he asked. We *always* watched, he knew that, but perhaps he was just playing along in the game. He could see the look in my eyes and he knew what it meant. Even as I reached out and wormed my hand beneath his robe, grabbing him, squeezing, still he played. "I'd like to say goodbye. Brandon will like it too."

102

BODY

I squeezed once, hard, angry that his attention seemed to have drifted. Then he pushed me over and was on me, in me within seconds, and we lost ourselves and left the camp as free souls the only way we knew how.

It was the same every night, every day. Our love was deep, our lovemaking desperate. And for those few minutes we forgot.

Love blinds.

༄

We went to watch Brandon leave this world, just as Lyle said we would.

There were hundreds of Chosen weaving between the tents and heading for the camp gates. Many of them carried offerings which they knew would never be allowed. Some of them looked grim, but most smiled, happy in the knowledge that they would be allowed to leave the camp today, at least for a while. Happy too that the future was being brought one soul closer. It's ironic that inside the fence was the nearest place to perfect any of us had ever experienced, yet we all craved time away. Perhaps it was simply a desire to see the truth of things in an attempt to make ourselves feel better.

Lyle and I walked hand in hand. In his other hand he carried a pot of honey. I'd told him that he'd never be able to hand it to Brandon, but he smiled and shook his head. "I never really believed I could. It's a gesture, it shows we care, and he'll see us all carrying these things."

"But it's such a waste!"

"You really believe any of us will go without because of this?" he asked, and I bit my tongue. I could see his point. These false offerings were just another part of our preparation, another luxury spared us at the expense of everyone else. And besides, Lyle intended it as a reference to us. I never needed reminding of our love, but I'm sure Lyle thought I did. When he licked me, he said I tasted of honey.

The routes between the tents had been baked hard so that the dust was kept to a minimum. The tents were all but permanent, with running water and air extractors worked by hand pumps, the slave pumpers hidden away in holes in the ground, and changed at night when they tired or died. Foodstuffs brought in were exported from across the world, and anything we wanted was given to us. Brandon had once asked for a fillet of fresh sea bass. The sea was a thousand miles in any direction. It took a week, but he got what he wanted, and then threw it away because it hadn't been properly cooked.

In the desert there was never perfection, because nature did not allow it. But we were given the best there was.

When we reached the gates we had to wait while the guards divided us into groups. One guard was assigned to every fifty Chosen. They kept their weapons meekly hidden away, holding their robes around their belts as if trying to hide hard-ons. I enjoyed staring at them, trying to see the weapons, making them uncomfortable. I knew that I was beautiful, and these men—rugged desert types,

103

fighters, mercenaries, instilled with an almost supernatural awe of us Chosen—would find my gaze almost unbearable.

"We're really on the way now," Lyle said, the excitement evident in his voice. I was looking forward to our outing as well. We left the camp once or twice every moon to trail across the desert to the monolith, but each trip felt fresh and new, an adventure in itself. We saw things out there that we weren't allowed inside the camp. Not good things—those were never denied us—but bad things, the truth of things. Perhaps that's why we liked these journeys so much… because they told the truth.

And especially at the end, when Brandon was stripped of luxuries and comforts, honour and dignity, truth would be punching us in the face.

☙

It was a walk of several miles to the monolith, but we could see it every day, lived in its shadow for a couple of hours each and every dusk. It didn't block out the horizon, it *was* the horizon. Black, stretching for miles to the north and south, higher at either end than in the middle, swallowing the light, crushing the desert, a constant reminder of why we were here and where we would eventually end up. Many Chosen called it simply The Answer. A reminder to the slaves as well, those tens of thousands of workers who were shipped in from around the globe to starve and die, or perhaps to be killed if their blood was required. It was a tomb or a folly, a city or a graveyard, one or the other or all of them depending upon what mood one was in whilst considering it. I had always seen it as an end of things, like a black hole against reality through which we would all eventually pass.

For every question… *The Answer.*

Lyle squeezed my hand tighter as we approached the slave village. Ahead of our huge entourage, slaves paved our route across the desert with white lily petals. Their cool moistness stuck them to our bare feet. It was respite from the hot sand, at least.

When the slaves drew level with the ramshackle village outskirts, they doubled their efforts. As they hit the ground the petals turned red from spilled blood, so more were piled on, and more. But the blood was tenacious. Lyle and I were halfway along the column, and by the time we reached the huts and hovels and wretched humanity, our route was paved red.

"Someone's had a bad day here," Lyle said, glancing around and trying to spot the bodies. "Look at all this wasted blood! Heads will roll for this."

"Already have." I nudged him and nodded further along the road. There were stakes in the ground along the path, each one topped with a head. Eyes and tongues had been eaten away by the desert wildlife, or perhaps stolen by still-living slaves. Tongues were meat, pickled eyes were charms. I thought of Lyle's tattoo and shivered, squeezing his hand for comfort.

"Don't be soft," he said, and I could hear similar whispers around us as other Chosen saw what we had seen. It was a sight we never really got used to. The slaves were worse than animals; rarely looked at, certainly not spoken to. Yet this mutilation was always distasteful.

"I'm not," I said, trying to translate the hard squeeze into something else. "I'm just thinking about us." And then I was. Us, lying there in my tent with fine silk curtains shifting in the desert heat, sweat linking us, Lyle buried deep and joining us further, his tongue, his hands…his love, binding and blinding and safe.

"There's more ahead," he said. He lifted the pot of honey to his nose, breathed in deeply and looked at me from the corner of his eye, smiling. As always, he'd known exactly what was on my mind.

"Is it the blooding?" I asked. Seconds later cries came from the front of the procession, and I knew what we were about to see. "Come on!"

I pulled Lyle through the crowd, smiling and apologising as we nudged people out of the way. None of them became angry or aggressive. Some even groped a feel beneath my robe as we went by, and I knew that Lyle was probably receiving the same treatment. Sex was something that kept the Chosen the way we were, a luxury indulged in unfettered and unforbidden by any religion or law that might govern anyone else. Today, with Brandon going, everyone else knew that they were spared, for however short a time. As always after the building in, the camp would sing to the sounds of love and lust.

We forced our way nearer the front so that I could see the blooding. It was a basic, animal part of the ritual, but one that I relished and enjoyed. Sensual and gorgeous, it allowed the Chosen to have a say in his or her fate. If Brandon selected a good, healthy slave with whose blood to bathe himself, then it may well save his life.

The monolith watched us all, black and blank.

And then I saw Brandon for the first time that day. He was naked, but adorned with lily petals where they had stuck to his sweating skin. He looked like a half-plucked bird, and I had to stifle a laugh.

"What's wrong?" Lyle hissed.

I shook my head, smiling, and he knew not to ask again. Some things, even here, were private.

Brandon was surrounded by several ceremonial guards. We only ever saw them during the processions to the monolith, although I guess they were always close by in case one or many of us had a sudden change of faith. None of us had ever been the subject of a guard's wrath. We'd only ever seen them strike out against slaves. But then the deaths were remote and meaningless, flashes of red in the summer sun, and we took little notice.

Standing before Brandon and the guards were seven slaves. They all wore a look of resignation, but that switched to fear as he walked the line, inspecting them before he selected his sacrifice for the day. He reached the last slave and turned, looking back at us Chosen and smiling broadly, raising a cheer when we realized he was playing, and a frown and shiver of fear from the slaves.

He caught my eye and his smile grew wider. His mouth moved and he spoke my name, but above the cheering and laughing I could not hear. I looked down at his body, some of it obscured by lily petals, the important parts clear and visible, and for the first time I wished I *had* screwed him. It was a retrospective wish, but even its thought sent a chill down my spine and made me grab Lyle's hand tighter, warding off the mental indiscretion as hard as I could.

Brandon turned back to the slaves, walked their line again and touched a young female on the shoulder. She was immediately shoved forward by her companions, eager to escape their own deaths for a short while longer. Brandon took the knife proffered by one of the ceremonial guards, pushed the woman to her knees, held back her head and slashed her throat. She gagged, coughed, put her hands up to catch her draining blood. He had to stab her three times in the chest before she was silent.

The crowed cheered.

Brandon collected some of the blood in a bowl handed to him by a second guard. It took a few seconds, he had to hold the body at various angles as the blood flowed, and then the slave's heart ceased its pumping and the gush faded to a dribble.

The crowd cheered again, and I joined in as Brandon drank some of the blood and poured the rest over his head. He shouted out, words I couldn't hear, and then rubbed the blood across his face, chest and genitals, standing then with his arms held wide so that it would dry quickly in the desert heat.

We proceeded on towards the monolith. Lyle still held my hand and I couldn't help but think of a time when he would not be there, or I would not, one of us chosen to be the one, cast to the front of the column and respected, loved and adored, and I was glad that it was Brandon today because that meant it wasn't either of us. Being Chosen was an honour above all honours, it was our raison d'etre. But for all that, I didn't want to die.

It was said that none of us would *ever* die, but I could not accept that as total truth. Through all the years I had been Chosen, I had kept a part of my own mind, secretly shoved away at the back where it could hide from indoctrination and "teachings." On those rare nights when I chose to be alone I'd stare up at the clear desert sky, trying to count stars and understand just what was happening to us here. And sometimes, when the dark was doing its best to suck all the heat and I wished for Lyle's body to keep me warm, I would know. Madness. This, all of this, was madness.

I could never question what we were told. Not even to Lyle.

The remaining six slaves were herded along by the ceremonial guards. They would be killed and their blood used to bathe the stones that would build Brandon in. Every stone that made up the monolith—each block seven by seven by seven, because that was how many years old the Emperor's daughter had been when she died—was blooded. They said it was to give life to the rock, and help the body live when the time came.

BODY

It stood before us, miles away but big enough and close enough to touch. We walked into its shadow, and its chill was like the purest paranoia. Somewhere deep in the heart of that thing, in chambers built before Lyle and I were even born, lay the remains of the Emperor's dead little girl.

It took another two hours to reach the monolith, and a further two hours for the Chosen to climb the narrow paths leading up its steep sides. On top, the sun blazed down once more. Hundreds of slaves lined the route to Brandon's cell, heads bowed, hands holding out cups of cool pure water.

"I wonder if he's relishing the sun," I said.

"Of course he is," Lyle said. He was holding my hand again after the long climb. Our sweat fused us together. "Maybe that's why he wanted to leave the camp for his final day."

"Where did he go?"

"It's said he visited the slave village." Lyle whispered this, glancing at me once to warn me not to react. "It's said he was in love with a slave girl."

I was stunned. So stunned that my eyes went wide and the sun dazzled me, casting ghost spots onto my vision. Even the phrase *slave girl* was something of a contradiction; we barely distinguished them as human, let alone attributing sex to them. And to fall in love with one...

I wondered if it had been the slave he'd slashed and killed for the blooding. It made sense, even if it was the sense of a madman. Blooded by his love. And the blood dried on his skin was all he would be allowed to carry in there with him.

"You're quiet," Lyle said, louder now. Everyone was chatting, no one would pay us any attention.

"I'm thinking of romance."

"I'll show you romance as soon as we're back at the camp," he said, and I didn't bother trying to explain. Lyle and I told each other everything, even our dreams, but this time I did not. Perhaps my own small rebellion had begun.

We reached Brandon's cell. It was a hollow in the monolith's top surface, its proportions seven by seven by seven, big enough for someone to stand and walk four paces either way, and that was that.

This was why we were chosen.

It had a hole in one corner through which Brandon's waste would pass, winding and dribbling down through the huge structure to the massive drains built generations ago. There was no water barrier in there, and even out in the open we could smell the rot of it.

This was why we were sought out as children and brought up in luxury.

In one wall of the cell, three holes as big as fists would disgorge fresh air, food and water. The air was pushed through by dozens of manual pumps located around the base of the edifice, each run by a gang of fifty slaves. Similarly the food and water chutes, the food mostly soup and other fluids, the water generally warm and dusty. The slaves running these were lucky because they were allowed to develop muscles. And they were well guarded.

107

This was why we *were*. This was our reason, our purpose of existence and the fate for every one of us.

Brandon stood at the edge of his cell and the ceremonial guards stood either side, glancing over his body for any signs of adornment or hidden belongings. They looked between his toes, under his tongue, in his anus, and declaring him clean they stepped back.

"I wish we could leave him with something," I said.

"Don't be stupid!" Lyle hissed, amazed, even though he himself had brought along the jar of honey.

Brandon was allowed nothing. A few people went to show him the gifts they had brought, and he eyed the gifts and thanked the people and looked back up at the sky as they took them away again. He was shaking, I could see the streaks of dried blood on his skin shifting tone as his muscles spasmed. He was trying desperately to control the fear.

In two opposing lower corners of his cell, dull grey slabs marked where one day Brandon's escape would be found. They would fall away and he would find another life, *make* another life, be part of a new beginning. One day.

There was chanting from the ceremonial guards, and the head priest Jacobus appeared from nowhere to give his blessing. It was supposed to be a celebration, but we had seen so many people built in that by now it was nothing new. Like waking up and making love and falling back to sleep, this was something we were all too familiar with.

Brandon was lowered into his cell by the guards. For a few moments his eyes went wide and I thought he was going to shout, panic, scream, shame himself and embarrass everyone else. Lyle held me close and we both stared, shifting slightly so that we could see through the crowd. Neither of us wanted to lose sight of him.

Jacobus chanted, his voice low and roasted by the sun.

The guards let go and we heard the sound of Brandon landing on his cell floor.

"See you all!" he shouted. He was supposed to remain silent, paying his respect to the old Emperor's dead daughter, but if he had something to say nobody could stop him now. "See you all sometime soon! Don't be too long, now! Stay in the sun too long and you go mad, you want to be in here with me, in here in the dark where everything is possible. Come on, don't be long! Go and ask the Emperor when we can finish!" The crowd was utterly silent. Only those right at the front would be able to see him now, and they had probably averted their eyes.

And then came the grinding of stone on stone, vibrating through our feet, as the first of the four blocks was pushed into place to seal him in. A guard slaughtered one of the slaves and cut off his head, wiping his gushing neck across the grey stone. Fifty slaves pushed, fifty more pulled on ropes, and the rock covered a quarter of the cell.

"There are people in here I can't wait to meet again," Brandon shouted, and while the second rock was blooded and heaved into place he told us who they were, why they were important to him and what he'd say when he met them once more. Some must be his enemy, he knew that, but it was simply the nature of things. "And if they are, I'll kill them," he said, and the second stone slid into place.

We were denying him the sun, light and fresh air. We were giving him only darkness. "It's wrong," I whispered, but Lyle elbowed me hard in the ribs. I looked at him, unable to decide whether it was fear or anger I saw in his eyes. He believed totally, he was utterly loyal, but I guessed that he must be aware of my deeper scepticism.

As the third block slid in Brandon began to weep. His voice was quieter now, dulled by the huge blocks above him, swallowed by the millions of similar rocks and cells below where we stood.

The fourth rock began its noisy journey. A slave screamed as she was stabbed, pressed against the stone and stabbed again, her violent death giving the stone more blood to soak up.

"Goodbye sky!" Brandon shouted. "Goodbye all!" And then the stone slid into the fourth corner of the square, and Brandon was built in.

There was silence for a while, broken only by the indifferent cries of birds floating in the warm air currents rising above the monolith. Lyle clasped the jar of honey to his mouth and inhaled, perhaps thinking of later. I thought only of Brandon. It may be totally silent in there, or perhaps he was shouting. Either way, he would not know when we left.

I guessed he was already mad. In my darkest, most secret moments, I thought we all were.

At some point the ailing Emperor would give the order to halt the building and open the valves. All the cells were linked by tunnels and chambers, and the thousands of Chosen built in over the decades, those who had survived, would at last have their new freedom. Inside. In the dark. Flowing like blood, fighting and mating like individual cells, congregating into central organs, breathing, drawing air from the outside. And in the Emperor's madness the monolith would be given life, become a life itself, rescuing his long-dead daughter from the ravages of the afterlife. Allowing her, at last, to take his place.

Yes. Perhaps we were all mad.

∽∴∾

The walk back was quiet, subdued, and dark. The sun was sinking behind the monolith and the whole journey took place within its shadow. Lyle still held my hand, the honey jar clasped in his other hand, but he was quiet. He smiled, looked around, acting as if he didn't have a care in the world…but I knew that he was thinking.

We were *all* thinking. Musing upon Brandon's fate and that of the thousands before him. Our own, as well. Eventually we would all be in there waiting on the Emperor's word. And if he died before giving it, or changed his mind, or decided he loved his daughter more in memory than he ever could in some strange returned life…then maybe we'd be there forever.

I'd never thought like this, not really, but Brandon's eyes had shocked me. And Lyle's whisper that he'd been in love with a slave girl, perhaps even the one he'd blooded himself with…all these things drove slivers of shock into the solid wall of belief I'd built and nurtured over the years. And perhaps these splinters bore the sharpened edges of truth. I feared that, just as I feared my own inevitable fate. I feared the truth.

I was terrified that everything was wrong.

When we arrived back at the camp it was twilight, the heat dissipating to the clear, dark skies, the mercenary guards standing back and letting us in. They knew what was about to happen, they'd seen it so many times before. Some of them even still stayed behind to watch.

Lyle let go of my hand and drew me to him, kissing me and stroking the small of my back. He breathed into my ear, kissed my neck, but still I could not close my eyes and see past those strange thoughts. I watched as one couple dropped their robes and started making love there on the sand, just inside the camp entrance, the woman squatting over the man and offering us all a frank view of where they were joined. Others hurried off to their tents or dropped to the ground to do the same, in pairs or groups or, on occasion, simply on their own.

I closed my eyes and saw Brandon staring back.

"Come on," I said, pulling away from Lyle, grabbing his hand and heading for my tent.

"Why not here?" he asked.

I smiled at him and loved him, loved the way the dregs of sunlight lit his eyes, fell on his skin, darkened the tattoo on his back until it looked as though it were asleep. He was my rock, not that monstrosity back there taking up half the sky and filling our world. *Him.* "The things I want to do are for us alone," I said. "Open that honey. Put your tongue inside. Taste good?"

He dropped the jar and walked with me.

The cooling night was alive with the sounds of love and sex. The love was calm and caring, the sex loud and cathartic, an expression of life on this day when we'd all seen one of our own pass from this world and into another.

We reached my tent and Lyle was guiding me inside, hand inside my robe and hooked under my belt. His fingers were cool against my warm skin, as if—

I thought of corpses and the living dead, those who had been shut away inside the monolith for as long as I'd been alive, or longer still. Sitting in the dark, talking to themselves, freezing or boiling or going silently mad. The slaves were still made to pump the food and air and water, because there was no way of knowing how many were alive and how many dead. All alive, Jacobus would have us believe, all alive and awaiting the Emperor's word to bring the monolith to life, become its vital components. *All alive.* I thought not.

Lyle lowered me gently to the cushioned floor and parted the robes about my legs, kissing my thighs, licking and kissing higher. I gasped and arched my back, staring up at the ceiling of the tent. The material billowed for a moment as if the final breaths of the dead had set it moving. I heard a sigh outside, but it must have been someone else making love.

Lyle knelt up and entered. We smiled and kissed and closed our eyes, and for a while we escaped the camp and our lives along with everyone else. I forgot about everything, narrowed my vision, concentrating only on what we were doing. Our familiarity made it passionate, each movement holding us together for a moment longer.

It was a necessary escape, as if to stay here was to admit complicity in Brandon's fate and face one's own. The guards stood around the edges of the camp, smirked, watching those who were rutting in the open. They grinned through the fence. Little did they know that, for the few dark hours of this night, none of us were really there.

※

There were eagles in the sky the day Lyle was chosen.

Years ago, they'd come down from the mountains far to the north, exploring and foraging and finding the monolith, huge enough to be called a mountain in its own right. And here they had stayed, riding the warm currents and picking off the desert creatures dwelling in the shadow of the monolith or the quarries further south. Sometimes when they flew low the guards would try to shoot them down, but they always missed. Everyone in the camp watched the eagles on occasion, but I wondered if any of them felt what I did: jealousy. I coveted the freedom these birds had, the *choice,* and once I even said it to Lyle.

"But we're as free as anyone," he said. "The only thing we can't do is move." In a way I knew that he was right, because we had *everything.* The Emperor's original order that we should have the best the land could give still stood. But Lyle was right. We couldn't move. And we were all destined, eventually, to be shut away in another world.

So I watched the eagles and considered their freedom, trying to give myself their wings.

I knew that something was wrong as soon as Lyle came into my tent. He hugged and kissed me, and I reached down to his groin. He was limp and disinterested. There was sweat running between his shoulder blades as if the tattoo were crying.

"What is it?" I asked, but I knew. He would not meet my eyes, so I knew. Maybe by not looking at me he was already trying to let go.

He twirled the loose end of my belt around his finger, brushed my hip with his other hand and sighed. "I'm going tomorrow," he said. Then he looked me in the eye, and I was startled by what I saw. No sadness, no fear, only joy. "They've chosen me to go tomorrow!"

"But…" So much in one word. I could not think of anything else to say. *Don't you love me? We'll lose each other. You'll die.* It all should have been said but Lyle would not have understood. This was all wonderful to him.

I started crying instead, and he hugged me and kissed me on the forehead. Brushing my tears away with his thumbs, he looked again into my eyes. "What's wrong?"

"You're going."

"We'll be together again, you know that. When the time comes—"

"It's never going to come!" I hissed, tearing away from him. "That thing the size of a world will be there forever, full of dead people. And if the Emperor ever does deign to give the signal—if he can manage it before he dies—do you think all the doors and traps will work?"

Lyle stared at me open-mouthed. He was welling up, and the realisation that my disbelief had upset him so much made me feel like a murderer. I was dragging out his faith—his own faith that belonged to him and no one else, however much I loved him—and trying to slaughter it.

I had no right.

"Oh Lyle…" I said, shaking my head. "I love you so much. I just want to be with you." *I don't want to lose you,* I meant to say, but the two were so different.

"You'll never lose me," he said. He hugged me again, and I reached down and cupped him, squeezing, wondering why he was still unresponsive.

"No," he said. "No more. I have to pray. I have to cleanse myself. Please… I *will* see you again, tomorrow. I'd like very much if you walked behind me. But the last time we made love is the time we must both remember forever."

"Lyle—"

"I'd hate for us to make love when you're so sad and bitter," he said, and I knew that he was right. He turned and walked from the tent, and I stared into the tattoo, watching myself go.

⚓

Lyle spent his final day praying and preparing for his building in. I went to see him only once, but I was turned away from his tent by a ceremonial guard. Only Lyle could have given this command.

So I wandered the camp. There were a thousand Chosen living there, and I knew almost all of them by sight. I recognised faces and smiles and distant stares, acknowledged them when they spoke to me, ignored them when they did not. I looked into faces and wondered what thoughts really went on behind them.

Could I be so different? If I could recognise the futility in what we were doing, as well as revel in the honour that being Chosen bestowed upon us, surely others could as well?

BODY

I thought of Lyle and our time together. It was the past already, even though he had yet to go. He'd been my true love ever since we were children, growing up together in a nomadic commune in the western desert until a caravan of ceremonial guards had stumbled upon us one morning. A quick word to our parents and we were whisked away, without even a goodbye kiss. I could still remember the sight of my mother's smile bidding me farewell, the contented look in her eyes as she watched her nine year old daughter crying her way out of her life. I'd forgiven her, eventually—we were told to forgive, cleanse and forget our previous lives, and at first I had all but lived by that—but I'd never forgotten that particular sight. Me sad, my mother happy. It hadn't seemed right. It still did not.

Lyle had been with me ever since, and I'd been with him. Transported into a camp of children and adults, a place without the usual social and familiar hierarchies, our love had blossomed quickly and been encouraged by everyone. Our love, our physicality, my ability to become pregnant stolen from me by a toxin in my food the first week we were there. At the time I hadn't known what had been done to me, but as the years went by and Lyle and I continued making love each and every day, I knew that I had been made barren.

Even back then I had wondered whether this was really the way for the Emperor's dream to be realised.

Neither of us had ever strayed. Casual sex was a way of life in the camp, group sex and homosexuality encouraged and enjoyed by a vast proportion of the population. We watched with interest but never joined in, because we were so perfect for each other. Neither of us could imagine anything better. *You should try everything,* one of the Chosen had once said to us, but we merely smiled and looked at each other and said, *we do.*

And now I was losing him.

Throughout that long afternoon of wandering, avoiding conversation, trying to steer around the edges of the camp where there were fewer people, I resolved to do whatever I could. I was resigned to losing Lyle, for the simple reason that he so wanted to go.

But I would ensure that I could still be with him.

I owed that to myself.

⌐:∾

"I'm going to be happy," he said, standing before me as naked as I had ever seen him. He'd removed the necklace I'd given him when we were eighteen—I wanted to ask where it was, but I was certain he'd now consider it unimportant— and even his thumbrings had been cut off. There were small wounds weeping blood where the cutters had caught his skin. I wanted to tend them and kiss them safe, but I didn't think he cared.

"I hope so," I whispered. I was so close to tears that I could barely talk. I didn't want him to see me crying, not this early.

"Of course I will." He reached out and clasped my upper arms, pulling me to him like a friend to a friend. I tried to turn my head and kiss him—smelt his skin, that faint spice that he exuded however much he washed—but he pulled away and smiled. "Now—"

"I don't want you to go!" I said, glancing around in case any of the guards had heard. They'd given us a minute alone inside Lyle's tent, but he'd be called soon. Naked, he'd walk across the desert and leave me. Forever. I never for an instant believed that we'd ever see each other again. "The Emperor is crazy, and we're mad for following him!"

Lyle's face dropped slightly—perhaps only I could have seen that, the change was so slight—and he turned away from me. "I love you," he said, and looking back he whispered his single, solitary statement of doubt. "But even now isn't the time for disbelief."

He left the tent, and we were never alone again.

Not exactly.

⌁

The procession followed the usual route. Lily petals rained down and stuck to our feet. I walked several paces behind Lyle and his escort of ceremonial guards. Every now and then I looked up from my feet and saw the eye tattoo staring back at me, and I felt as if I was in two places at once.

Lyle never looked back.

There were hundreds of Chosen behind us being escorted by the bored mercenaries. Many of them carried gifts they would never be able to give Lyle, an offering as foolish as the tradition it honoured. I almost laughed out loud when I saw one man struggling under the weight of a healthy, fat goat. He'd be walking back with it, he knew that, but still he hauled it for miles across the baking desert. Being Chosen didn't necessitate a sudden drop in intelligence, did it? Did these people—and I realised that I was starting to distinguish myself from them now, a dangerous, foolish thing to do—ever think about what they were doing?

"Blooding," one of the guards said softly, but I was near enough to hear.

We'd come to the slave village and there were seven slaves lined along the road, wretched looking creatures without a complete outfit of clothes between them, cursed by sores and sunburn and half-dead already. None of them drew away as Lyle walked the line, and none of them looked at him. That was forbidden. Right now he was as close to a deity as these untouchables would ever experience.

Lyle touched a female on the shoulder and she stepped forward, letting slip a high-pitched squeal of fear.

I edged forward until I was standing directly behind the guards. I was two steps away from Lyle, although he didn't seem to notice me at all. That hurt.

A guard handed Lyle the knife and he brought it up from waist height, slashing the woman from stomach to chin, stepping back as her insides tumbled

114

out and she thrust her hands into the steaming mess, trying to hold it up from the sand, crying, screaming until he reversed his stroke and slit her throat. He dropped the knife and grabbed the woman by the hair, bringing her to his chest so that her leaking blood pumped down over his stomach and crotch.

For an insane few seconds I was jealous—we had never tried this, that was for sure, and I was certain I could see movement in Lyle's penis—but then I darted forward, snatched a handful of the woman's guts and slapped them across his back.

A guard hauled me away but I managed to hit Lyle one more time. The sickly-warm mass made its mark. Lyle looked at me, and I think he knew what I was doing, he knew, I could see it in his eyes and—

—and he smiled.

I was sure then, even though I knew the truth, that everything was going to be all right. I let myself live the lie as the guards dragged me back and dropped me in the sand. I retained it as I stood and walked on with the Chosen, heading toward the giant monolith that was a tomb for thousands and hope for one. Even as we climbed the sides and headed across the top to the cell that had been prepared for Lyle, I wallowed in the illusion.

It was the only way I was able to stand there and watch him buried alive.

He didn't moan or cry or rage. He was built in just as all the best of the Chosen were, and will be. He sat quietly, content in his fate, perhaps even believing that one day he'd be free inside this monstrous structure, free to live a new life and search me out.

Me. He didn't look at me at all after I'd blooded him. The mess from the slave's innards had dried on his back, masking the tattoo and hiding it from the ceremonial guard's cursory search. I'd done it for me, but it saved Lyle a lot of pain as well. I hadn't even thought of that until then.

He stared down at his crossed legs as the four great blooded blocks were heaved in above him. Perhaps he had taken what he told himself was his last look at the sun, and one more would be just too unbearable.

He remained sitting like that as the light was taken from his world.

⌒:∿

I like to think it was me. I like to lie in my tent and imagine that Lyle had known what I was doing with the slave's blood, and after that he couldn't face seeing me again. Because his love was too strong, and he didn't want to shame himself, and really, truly, he knew it was all a lie.

The eagles are still there, but they are the offspring's offspring of those which had circled on the day of Lyle's entombment. I've gained thirty years and as many pounds, and a reputation as trouble amongst the other Chosen. They don't mistrust me, exactly, but they know I'm not like them. And they don't really avoid me. But sometimes days go by without me speaking with anyone. I don't mind. They let their beliefs buffer them against the truth. They go to the monolith and watch one of theirs built in, and they come back and screw through the night to escape the insanity of this. In reality they are only escaping the truth.

The Emperor died years ago without uttering the order to give life to the giant stone corpse. They're still building it higher and wider, and imprisoning more and more Chosen, simply because they don't know what else to do.

I don't mind. I know that after thirty years Lyle is still alive. Because every night, when I close my eyes, I truly see the darkness.

And that is my escape.

The Final Staging of Ascent

TOM PICCIRILLI

Clay still wasn't sure if *Ascent* was supposed to be performance art or interpretive dance or what. As the electron cloud hovering around his skull kept skipping into higher-ring energy states, he could feel the fillings in his back teeth beginning to heat up.

This sort of surreal shit went out with *Albee's Box* and *Quotations from Chairman Mao Tse-Tung,* back in '69 when the love generation was figuring out they'd fucked it up as badly as the rest of them. Clay wandered around the stage dressed like Charles Manson, the wig and beard all teased out, the swastika drawn on his forehead with a fine point Sharpie marker. Hunched over, wide-eyed and insane, trundling along like you saw in news clips. Every three minutes or so he yelled out, "Sharon Tate lives inside my womb!" That was it, his entire role.

Darton, the director, stood backstage, giddy as a new bride. *Ascent* was his first "piece" and his mother was in the audience. He sneaked around the proscenium curtain on occasion and waved to her. She'd wriggle her fingers back at him while taking bites from a rope of licorice, lips with about a quarter inch of waxy maroon lipstick on. Clay could feel himself coming apart.

It sometimes got like that. He could do all of Hickey's hardcore monologues in O'Neill's *The Iceman Cometh,* as well as the entire body of Shaw's *Man and Superman,* including the often edited "Don Juan in Hell" third act that went on forfuckinever. But instead of taxing his talents he'd somehow been reduced to this. It gave him some pause, he had to admit, wondering when he'd made the first wrong step and what had happened after that.

117

Paige, the playwright—he had to call her something—wore a complex grimace that worked every muscle of her face and neck. She was twenty-five and handsome in an old world way, discerning and capable if a little too harshly angled. But now she looked only frustrated and prune-ish, ready to chew through her cheeks. Clay guessed this wasn't how she'd envisioned the performance to turn out. She should've come to rehearsals more often.

"Sharon Tate grows inside my womb!"

He was starting to draw chuckles from the audience and he thought he'd play to that. Sort of a, *Hey, this isn't my fault, they're forcing me to do this shit, I'm in the same burning boat as you people. We're all suffering.* Darton had put the tap on him three days ago claiming to have the last minute role of a lifetime for Clay. And here he was, folding into his own seams.

There were only two other actors on stage: Mags, who actually had something of an intricate portrayal going, forced a show of depth as a woman lost without her murdered lover; and Barter, who tried to seduce her with his flaccid good looks and oiled pecs. He was either a new paramour or the ghost of the old one, Clay hadn't quite worked it out yet. Jesus, the guy was greased but he hadn't waxed his hairy shoulders. It almost made you gag looking at those tufts slicked down like flattened squirrels. The Parblazer lights threw gleaming streaks in front of the house, and every time Mags touched Barter you could hear the ugly squeak of their slippery contact.

The set design even had some audience members sitting on the stage, which took up almost the entire arena—no wing space and very little backstage area. All the lights were visible instead of being hidden by the curtain. When the actors weren't onstage, they were sitting off to the side, watching, just like the rest of the audience. Instead of pulling them into a different world for a couple hours, the idea was to widen the performance to encompass the rest of the theater. It was sort of working, he thought, but not in the way that Paige had meant.

Barter went after Mags onstage the same way he hunted women all around the bars—seething, buttery, with a smug grin that made you want to take a swipe at him with a brick. Mags had a real expression of pain and fear on her face as Barter grabbed at her again, hanging on to her skirt as she tried to whirl away. Curls looped off his forehead and swung into his darkly pitted eyes. He let out a soft snicker only Mags and Clay could hear. The beam spread of lights were cooking Barter's blood, and wafting trails of steam rose from his coppery chest. Clay wondered if he should knee Barter in the nuts, just get it over with. Nobody in front would know it wasn't part of the show.

Here was the part where Mags started doing a few ballet steps, pirouetting while Barter sort of skipped and pranced alongside her. But you could tell it embarrassed the hell out of him so he barely lifted his feet, doing a funky shuffle to keep up with her. Then he put his hands on her hips and raised her while she arched her back and aimed her hands like she was going off a diving board. There it was. He carried her a few steps as she rolled in his arms, and as he set her back down on the floor they continued their dialogue like nothing had happened.

THE FINAL STAGING OF ASCENT

Large black veins bulged between Paige's eyebrows. She leaned heavily to one side and had to put a hand out against some of the set design lumber to keep from going over. Okay, so it wasn't supposed to be interpretive dance so far as she was concerned. Clay kept cocking his head, the buzzing of voices in his convoluted gray matter and ganglia growing louder.

"Sharon Tate...!...well, you probably already know what she's doing by now. Hey, anybody know a good Italian place around here?"

Darton kept making kitchy-coo faces at his own mother. Christ, Clay was starting to get a little uncomfortable watching the Oedipus complex in action, so he decided to get out there, to exit.

He didn't know how his performance might look from the limited view seating stage left of the orchestra, so he drew up inside the nervous electron cloudburst while neurochemicals slithered free from the corners of his brain.

His pineal gland kicked in, third eye staring through time and searching himself out. There, finding himself in some other role from the past, and urging that guy forward.

Come on, man, come over here and take a look at this.

He split himself off. There was a soft pop of static electricity in the shadows near the main doors, a sudden whiff of ozone.

Then he was up there too, walking down the aisle, until he took an empty seat next to Darton's mom. She had the same Neanderthal characteristics as her son—heavy brow ridge, jutting square nose, anthropoid arms, as she bit off chunks of the licorice and wagged her hands. She had about six pounds of candy in her lap.

Mom turned and nodded when he was suddenly in the seat. He was dressed like J. Perripoint Finch from *How to Succeed in Business Without Really Trying,* the Jersey Mead Center production he'd done two years ago. Clean shaven, in a suit, had a nice red power tie on, staring down at himself in Manson gear, screaming about his womb. *The fuck?*

"Hey there," he whispered to Mom Darton, "how you doing tonight?"

He looked like an idiot on stage, he saw, leaning back in the seat, crossing his legs. How had he ever gotten talked into this? He lumbered around Mags and Barter with no idea of what he should be doing, projecting, feeling, with his fists clenching and unclenching. The fake Manson beard was scraggly and coming loose, and the swastika—*ah, shit*—the swastika was pointing the wrong way because he'd drawn it on himself in the mirror. *Goddamn it.*

J. Perripoint Finch really wanted a taste of licorice though. Mom was going at it pretty good and his mouth was beginning to water. "Could I have a piece of that?" he asked. She stared at him with a stunned, simpering smile but forked a twist over. He smiled and thanked her, looking back at himself down there playing a fool.

"Sharon Tate is eating Malomars inside my womb, I swear!"

119

Sometimes it sure felt that way. A dagger crept low in his guts and prodded at his softest tissues. The glue on the fake beard made him itchy as hell, and he was getting a rash.

He glanced over at Paige, who was doing strange and exquisite things with her hands. Her long tapered fingers caused a twinge of arousal. They'd made love once in the parking lot of Shea Stadium when the Mets were down twelve runs. Afterwards, with the air conditioner purring, they went to great extremes not to talk about theater or art at all. They whispered casual lovers' talk and discussed a little of their lives, their childhoods, pets, morning cereals, favorite deodorizers. Other meaningless clutter of tongues until they'd both been so bored they'd broken down in each other's arms. Not weeping really, just stopped cold, both sitting in the back seat with their clothes disheveled and their thighs drying, waiting for the world to set them back into motion again.

Paige was murmuring to herself as the audience laughed in the wrong places. Three reviewers sat out in the darkness taking notes, sharpening their deadly witticisms that would eviscerate the piece in ink tomorrow.

Paige went, "Oh, Mama, I should've listened." Her mother was a producer on Broadway who'd told Paige to write a musical. A period piece set in another century, something grandiose that you could put a rose or an orchid on the cover of the playbill. That's all anybody wanted. Symbolism, elements of opera in their own tragically flawed, blunted lives. Even if the play bombed you couldn't really be singled out, everybody took some of the heat.

But in this—in this—

Clay thought it might be fun to suddenly launch into *Uncle Vanya* or *Waiting for Godot,* do something to shake everybody up. Mags was really trying to bring dimension to the piece, playing it as straight as she could while Barter kept groping her and getting cheap feels.

Her voice sounded like she was pulling it up from the cave of her childhood. "And no matter what I'm doing I can feel his hands on me, still, the way he brushed past my breast when he got home at night, battling through the door as if he were still struggling through all the rest of the world." Whatever else was going on, at least Mags had found the depth and honesty in Paige's words. The tears in her eyes, though, were because Barter kept pinching her.

Clay decided to pass up his one line and go talk to the audience for a little while. It couldn't offend Paige anymore than she already was. There were only twenty, twenty-five people in the house and a few of them were backing out of the aisles already. Experimental theater wasn't for everybody, but they usually didn't know it until the play began. Clay sure despised it and still couldn't figure out how he'd gotten here.

He saw one reviewer named Hardwick sitting pretty much alone in the third row, center, scratching notes in the dark and quietly chuckling to himself. He'd once dated Paige but it had ended badly, and now he'd get a modicum of revenge. She'd told Clay that Hardwick liked hash, and when he got too high he'd try on women's underwear and walk around like that for a couple days. Clay thought about climbing over the seats and giving him a wedgie just to see if he had lace panties on.

Paige was about to scream, he could see it. He walked over to her and said, "We'll fix it, we'll make it all right."

"What the hell are you talking about? Why are you back here? They're leaving!"

"That's probably a good thing at this point, but they're not all going. A couple of the critics are still out there."

"Hardwick?"

"Yeah, him and Johnny Saramango from Channel 22."

"Oh Christ. They're not only masochists, they're sadists too. They're gonna flay me alive."

"Wait, Johnny's already gone. Let's pull the plug and hop a freight to Tuscon."

"That's not far enough after this," Paige said. "*Ascent* is going to be right up there alongside *Carrie, the Musical* and *Starlight Express.* I'm ruined."

Clay thought about it, figuring the show was too small to do much damage to her except now it'd be famous and everybody would talk about it without ever having seen it. "I can do something."

"What?"

"Get a few fillers out there, laugh in the right spots, cheer and clap."

"How the hell you going to do that? You can't pay a stranger enough to ruin his afternoon watching this. I'm gonna kill that fucking Darton."

"You should've come to rehearsals."

"No need to tell me. If I ever do another play I'll sit on the director's lap holding an ice pick to his throat right up through dress rehearsals."

Clay twitched as he hit a higher energy ring, trembling with the hairs standing out on his arms. "Let me see what I can do."

"You're gonna leave? You're the only one getting them to laugh when they should."

He wanted to say, *Oh shit, you mean I'm supposed to be funny?* but he let it slide.

He went back out there and tried to shove Barter aside, but his fingers slipped on the oil and Clay nearly took a header into the first row. "Time to go," he said. "Charles Manson is God and he requests you meet him at the pearly gate, right outside. Let's mush along."

Barter stared at him like he was a lunatic, still trying to get a cheap feel on Mags, his hand open and sort of palming the bottom of her left breast.

Barter hissed through his teeth, "Are you crazy, man? We're still in the middle of a show."

Clay ran with it, feeling better. "I'm Charles Manson, you fucker, and you're part of the Family! What I say goes. Let's move it before I call Squeaky in to cap your ass. She might've missed Gerald Ford but she's gotten a lot of practice in since then, can plug a nickel at forty yards!"

Barter swung on him and nailed Clay just under the heart. Clay felt sparks skittering along his teeth and over his fingernails, the stink of frying ozone so heavy around him that he couldn't get any air. He wheezed and his brain felt too juicy, the ions screaming into their nuclear pools. He tried to push Barter off him but slid aside again. Barter drew back his arm to launch another fist into Clay's face, but it never got there.

Somebody suddenly stood in front of Clay, defending him, enraged.

It was Tony from *West Side Story*, a role he'd forgotten he played, way back in junior year in high school, but they'd done it without any of the music or dance numbers. Tony standing there with the knife out before him, right after Riff has been stabbed by the leader of the Sharks, Bernardo, and Tony leaps forward almost accidentally, jamming the blade into Bernardo's stomach. Stabbing Barter in the gut and watching him stumble backwards, gushing blood.

"Oh fuck," Clay said, trying to calm himself down.

But it was no good. They'd broken the fourth wall down, audience and performers part of one large pseudo-reality farce. You didn't know where your existence ended and the fantasy of the stage began. Hardwick was still writing, unsure of what was happening but leaning forward, getting into the play a little more. Clay motioned him to step up and Hardwick actually shook his head, unsettled.

Mags squealed as the blood splashed her, but you could see some relief in her eyes now that Barter's hands were finally off her. Paige grunted as if in pain back there, looking at Tony and Tony staring back about to shriek his big line.

"Maria!"

It was a poor high school and the cheap props had looked so lame that the Jets and the Sharks brought in real knives, fucking around with them in the halls, scaring the jocks and playing with the switchblade buttons until they broke off.

Darton and his mother both had the exact same expression on their faces, as if they'd just sat in Jell-O. Darton came out from behind the curtain and walked over to Barter, who'd finally quit thrashing and just lay there with his hands around the knife handle. The director had let it all slip away from him, and he kept hoping that somehow he'd set this scene but had just forgotten about it. Barter cried out, "Get me a doctor, somebody...Jesus...somebody...look at this, look here, oh Christ..." And was dead.

Darton turned to the audience and let it go, right on cue. "Is there a doctor in the house?"

Hardwick and a couple of the others burst out laughing. Clay nearly let out an insane giggle too, but there was too much pain deep inside the root of his head. The air kept spitting sparks around him, his clothes smoking in spots, the Manson beard curling up at the edges. He split and kept splitting, one after the other.

There he was coming down the aisle as Schaffer's Salieri, Beckett's Krapp, and playing the soldier Simon in Bertolt Brecht's *The Caucasian Chalk Circle*. Filling seats one after the other. He was both Rosencrantzs, the one from *Hamlet* and the other from Stoppard's *Rosencrantz & Guildenstern Are Dead*.

THE FINAL STAGING OF ASCENT

Prospero, Banquo, Stanley Kowalski, the guy who carries the torch, the guy who touts the trumpet, the guy who is in attendance, Biff Loman, Third Man, a peasant, a servant, guy who goes in for a shave and gets his throat cut in *Sweeney Todd, the Demon Barber of Fleet Street,* Second Man, First Man, gravedigger, courtier, a Norwegian Captain who says, "Anon."

Paige stared wide-eyed but sort of grinning too, having worked with him so often before and knowing it was him, all of him, out there.

"It's a little gift I have," he told her.

"Christ, but...but—"

"Yeah, it was kinda cool before I killed somebody."

And yet that didn't seem to bother her much. Maybe because Barter was such an asshole, or maybe because they were heading into someplace new, way out and beyond the fourth wall.

The critic was still enjoying himself, and Paige liked the look in Hardwick's eyes. It got good to her, seeing that reaction, knowing they were finally involved with something that had her hand in it. Hardwick turned in his seat and saw all the other characters parading through the house, unsure if it was still part of the show or not. He dropped his pen and it clanked and rolled. Banquo picked it up and handed it back to him, Hardwick unable to close his mouth. He'd shredded the Bayonne Players presentation of *MacBeth* and just kept blinking, clicking the ball-point pen. He looked back and forth from Banquo to Clay, finally realizing that there was something else going on. Clay grinned at him, and so did Paige.

It was fun watching them all packing inside. Clay tried to put them in order and see just how all of them led through the history of his life to this role, but he couldn't do it. There was no way to make sense of his fall from grace, it hadn't happened slowly or quickly so far as he could figure, it had just happened. He looked over and Mags was still trying to rub the blood off her, just kept getting her hands more and more red, like she was playing Lady MacBeth. He said, "Mags, it'll be all right."

"What?" Her voice was the same, as if it had been drawn up from a well she'd been trapped in as a child. She was never going to be the same after this. "What?"

"Mags, calm down."

"What?"

"Go sit and take it easy, honey."

Tony handed the knife to Clay and led Mags off the stage towards one of the back rows. He hugged her and kept rubbing her back, looking around and wondering where all the west side tenement buildings were. He asked, "Maria?" and she answered, "What?"

Darton ran out to his mother and pretty much sat in her lap. J. Perripoint Finch was still wrestling with his rope of licorice. He reached down into Mother Darton's lap and grabbed all the other candy, started handing it out to everybody else. They all chewed away, ravenous, and Clay didn't know why. He hated licorice.

Hardwick glanced down at his notes and then back up. Paige whispered to Clay and said, "Can you have them bring him down?"

"Where? To the stage?"

"Set him up next to Darton over there."

"You want to show him how it was supposed to be done. How you intended it to be before Darton screwed the show."

"Yeah."

"Sure." He waved the knife in the air and gestured for them to bring Hardwick over. "You want me to…?"

"Can you learn the other parts this quickly?"

"Sure, I'm a professional."

He got over there and took Barter's role, oiling up, continuing to populate the audience. He'd played one of the transvestite chorus girls in *Torch Song Trilogy*, just a single scene he and some friends had put on during an early acting class, and here she came with her plastic knockers and platinum wig, down the aisle to take over Mags' role. The stench of burnt ozone was really bad, and a few of his characters got up and opened the windows. Members of the audience getting into it now—some of them with liquor on their breath. He used to drink a lot in those days, to loosen up before a performance and still all the extra voices and memories in his head. Rosencrantz was really fucked up, making a lot of noise and trying to give the bedroom eyes to Mags. Jesus, he'd been a real schmuck.

And the demented Oswald Alving from Ibsen's *Ghosts,* dying of syphilis and losing his mind a piece at a time in the script, with Clay doing everything he could to make it happen in his life too. Taking everybody to bed no matter how they looked or behaved. Up there right this minute, sitting in the theater with his arms crossed, chewing his bottom lip and thinking thoughts so big he couldn't keep them under wraps inside his skull. Clay considered sending him away, but figured they all deserved to be here, for one reason or another. They were no more ghosts than he was himself.

"Hey, Rosencrantz, give it a rest, man, pipe the fuck down."

Rosencrantz turned a puzzled frown on him as if he'd never seen Clay before, but he shut up.

They brought Hardwick over and sat him next to Darton and his Mommy. Clay grabbed Barter's corpse by the leg and dragged him across the stage, leaving a thinning river behind, and laid him out at their feet. The guy was still sneering and the blood and oil pooled around their shoes. He put on a more worthy performance at the moment than ever before. Darton kept staring down at the body like he wanted to start giving orders again, yell something like, "No no, I said with feeling! Again, do it again!" Barter's body flopped the other way, playing the dead man to perfection.

Mom went, "Oh my!" Really pulling it up from her diaphragm, she must've done a little stage work herself when she was younger. He noticed she had a light and well-trimmed downy mustache, dyed blonde a while back but the color starting to fade back in. A few stray billy goat hairs corkscrewing across her chin. They were kind of cute, really. She kept chewing.

Grabbing at Hardwick's notes, Clay scanned them quickly and whistled. "Damn man, you're one harsh son of a bitch." The critic's mouth was still hanging open and Banquo shoved in a piece of licorice.

Clay asked, "Hey, tell me, are you wearing a pair of satin bikini briefs under your slacks?" He really wanted to know, but Hardwick's tongue was unfurled too far over his lower lip, with the candy just hanging out the corner of his mouth. "You let me know later, okay? Sit back and enjoy the show. You're going to see something special in a few minutes."

Hell, yeah, he was.

Paige plucked the blade out of Clay's hand and tossed it on the floor. They found seats a few rows back and settled in. She helped him out of the burned beard and wig and tried to spit-polish the swastika off but he'd used a permanent marker. He laid his head on her breast and she pulled him closer, both of them warm and comfortable now that they weren't forced to make stupid small talk. Everything that mattered had opened up before them.

All the men and women are merely players, Clay thought, closing his eyes and hitting the top energy ring. He was the cast. He was the audience. Thinking, this is the last stage, the final staging of *Ascent,* and of course, as we gnaw and glare and step over the puddles, the play goes on.

ᛁ Hear You Quietly Singing

LUCY TAYLOR

Jennifer Kruger had always believed that when your number was up, it was up, and there wasn't a damn thing you could do about it. Maybe such a fatalistic attitude came from living and working in Vegas for the past six years—she'd seen lives made and destroyed at the whirl of the roulette wheel or the toss of the die at the craps table, a randomness that was more obvious on the casino floors but never-the-less, she thought, reflected the malicious caprice of the world at large.

On the last night of August, with the sun baking down so hot you could barbecue ribs on the sidewalk, Jennifer's luck seemed to have finally taken a turn for the better. After years of working the seedy clubs in North Vegas, she'd landed a singing gig at the Odalisque Lounge at the Mirage. Publicity was coming her way—she'd been written up in *Vegas Weekly,* a guide to local entertainment, and had her picture displayed wearing a slinky red gown just past the *Welcome to Las Vegas* sign at McCarren Airport. Around nine p.m. Jennifer crossed through the casino and made her way to the dressing room area behind the stage of the Odalisque Lounge. There she teased and sprayed her abundant black locks into a sleek, curving cone, made up her eyes so that they resembled a pair of exotic, tropical fish, and poured her twenty-eight-year-old surgically enhanced body into a backless, black lamé gown that clung to her curves as closely as the crimson polish she'd painted on earlier adhered to her nails. At close range, under normal lighting, she looked like a slightly desperate callgirl, but on stage, under dim, gold-tinted lights, her look matched her voice: sinful, smokey, and lush.

Just before going onstage, Jennifer made her way back onto the casino floor and played a few hands of video poker on a dollar machine. She drew three aces, discarded her other two cards, and then drew a fourth ace—an easy win of five hundred dollars.

My lucky night, thought Jennifer, as she returned to the lounge. The pudgy, already slightly tipsy emcee was just introducing her and Jennifer launched into her opening number—a torchy blues song that permeated the room like smoke in an opium den.

Jennifer didn't know it yet, but tonight her number was up.

☙

Singing had once been magic for Jennifer, back when she was just Jenny DeSoto, growing up alone under the lackadaisical eyes of a philandering mother and an alcoholic father in DeKalb, Illinois. Back then, singing had freed her emotions and unleashed forbidden feelings. It connected her to something greater than herself when she felt lost and alone.

Even now Jennifer's singing could bring tears to some people's eyes and kindle longing and warmth in hearts long gone cold, but somewhere along the way her own heart had shrunk and closed down.

A disastrous marriage right out of high school hadn't helped nor had the long seasons of neediness, financial and otherwise, that drove her into trysts with men whose fiscal wealth was exceeded only by their emotional impoverishment. She came to rely on drugs and alcohol to burn off her depression and sex to quell the anxiety that rode the knobs of her spine like a knife edge when she woke late at night, sometimes by herself and longing for a lover, other times with some stranger astride her, wishing she could drag him down into her loneliness and drown both of them.

No one who heard Jennifer sing, though, could have imagined the degree of discontent that reigned in her soul. Her voice was by turns mellow and mirthful, plaintive and penetrating. Such was the intimacy in her voice that some of the men who heard her imagined that they knew her, became enraptured with the illusion of some counterfeit connection and came to think of her as theirs, even if they'd never shared so much as a drink or a bed with her.

☙

The man who sat in the audience listening to Jennifer that night was just such a man, although his delusions of possession were grounded in a reality that he'd rewritten over the years. He'd thought he loved Jennifer once and that she had loved him. That she could have divorced him still seemed inconceivable. Such things didn't happen in a just Universe and, if they did, only proved what he already believed, that the Universe was arbitrary, unfair and ultimately insane, and that the deck was stacked irrevocably against him. Any act, therefore, was justified.

I HEAR YOU QUIETLY SINGING

∽:∾

Jennifer came back to the dressing room around midnight. She took off her make-up, changed into street clothes, and was on her way to her car in the employee section of the casino parking lot when she noticed a green Chevy pick-up with Michigan plates and a vanity license plate that read ROOFMAN parked next to her black BMW.

"Nice picture of you at McCarren," a voice said.

Her heart caught, and she turned around automatically.

A face she knew, a face she'd actually once gazed at with love, leered at her drunkenly and said, "Gotcha!" Before she could even beg for her life, the bullet from the barrel of the .38 Smith and Wesson was already on its way. It careened into her skull just behind her right ear and came out above her left temple, dropping her in a heap on the concrete and spraying an arc of blood on the truck's bumper and the vanity license plate.

∽:∾

When Jennifer was a little girl, her favorite times were those spent with her grandmother. The old lady sang her lullabies and she encouraged Jennifer to sing, too. "God gave you a gift," her grandmother said. "You must put it to the best possible use." As she got older, Jennifer looked at her grandmother's life and saw it as bleak and depressing, a widowed nurse caring for people who needed to be in a hospital but were too poor or too stubborn to go. Once in a while, at family gatherings, her grandmother would play the piano and sing something upbeat and bawdy, but most of the time her songs were melancholy and sometimes not even songs at all—Jennifer had heard her sing to some of her patients when they were very ill and the songs sounded odd and unearthly, like the sound of an oddly-pitched flute.

After high school, Jennifer remembered her grandmother's advice and resolved to make the best possible use of her gift—she would use it to get out of DeKalb and then to bring her all the things of this world that she craved and that her upbringing had denied her.

Unfortunately, she delayed her escape by marrying the first man who fell in love with her—a roofer named Kevin Grimaldi, who promised to love her forever and never let her go, and while the first part of that promise he quickly forgot, the second part he made good on.

∽:∾

For Jennifer, there was no tunnel with a white light at the end of it, no benevolent figures welcoming her to some celestial realm. She heard music, notes that were low and atonal, and that seemed to emanate from inside her. A song unlike any she'd ever heard, which she somehow realized was the sound of her life ebbing away, of her soul slipping out of her body.

No, please, I'm not ready to die yet, she thought.

And gradually, like an exhaled breath being gradually drawn in again, the weird song was absorbed back inside her.

꒰˙ᵕ˙꒱

The doctors working on Jennifer figured her for gone. Her skull was penetrated in two places and the trajectory of the bullet had torn away pieces of grey matter. Still she kept surprising them by continuing to live. At the end of a week, she'd come out of her coma and could sit up in bed. A miracle, they said. Jennifer's luck had been one in ten million.

꒰˙ᵕ˙꒱

Jennifer didn't feel lucky. In fact, she wished she were dead. She woke up to absolute silence, a silence so vast and bottomless that it felt like being buried alive. As soon as it became obvious she couldn't hear, more tests were run. Then one of her doctors got a pad and pen and started writing out a treatise on the extent of the neurological damage, but Jennifer had only one question: *When will my hearing come back?* The doctor said maybe someday, but the look on his face said otherwise.

And the thought pierced her heart like the point of a knife, *I have Kevin to thank for this.*

꒰˙ᵕ˙꒱

A pair of detectives came and interviewed her by writing questions in a notebook. She told them she hadn't gotten a look at the person who'd shot her. No, she didn't have any enemies, no old boyfriends or ex-husbands she'd angered or drug dealers she hadn't paid, nobody who'd have any reason to want her dead. She even pretended the five hundred dollars she'd had in her purse had actually been two thousand, painting her attempted murder as a robbery hastily executed. Her shooting didn't get much attention in the Vegas papers, either. A billionaire casino owner o.d.'d on heroin the same night, which relegated her attempted murder to a paragraph underneath the obits.

꒰˙ᵕ˙꒱

I HEAR YOU QUIETLY SINGING

Alone in her hospital room, she sang a few lines from a song, but the sensation of feeling the notes vibrate in her throat without hearing the sound was so strange and scary she abandoned the effort. One of her doctors, a portly, balding neurosurgeon named Wyeth came into the room and said, "You have a beautiful voice. I understand you're a singer."

She couldn't hear the words, of course, but she was becoming adept at lip reading. She shrugged. "Was a singer. Not anymore."

He looked at her sadly, as though he wanted to comfort her but didn't know how. Jennifer shut her eyes and pretended to be falling asleep.

Suddenly her head jerked up. "I hear something!"

Dr. Wyeth stared at her. "What?"

"Music, singing. I'm not sure."

Wyeth's lips moved, but she heard no words. He tapped on the table with a pencil—nothing. The sounds she heard seemed to emerge from a silence deep within Dr. Wyeth. Then they faded back again, teasing her, playing hide and seek.

"It's you! You're singing!"

"No, I'm not."

"I hear you, dammit!" She was furious that he would mock her.

Wyeth called in colleagues and conferred with them. New tests were run and for a while, there was excitement. The doctors thought Jennifer's hearing might be coming back. The only sounds she could hear, however, were the odd, flute-like notes that seemed to hover around Dr. Wyeth and that no one else could hear. Soon it became clear to her that this was some kind of aberration or illusion and that her hearing was not coming back.

Kevin did this, she thought.

And in the silence, she started plotting ways to thank him.

During one of the times when Jennifer's parents were separated and she was living with her mother, they'd been terrorized by an ex-boyfriend of her mother's who threatened to kill them both, who followed them in his car and called in the middle of the night with nasty messages. The police came by, took the complaint, and did nothing. They said her mother should get a restraining order, when even Jennifer knew that what she needed was body armor and a .357.

Before the former boyfriend was sent to prison for an unrelated crime, Jennifer and her mother had moved out of four different apartments, had their phone number changed more times than she could remember, and lived in fear for over a year. During that time, Jennifer had made herself a promise—if anyone ever stalked her, if they ever tried to kill her and failed, she wouldn't bother going to the police. She'd buy a gun and dedicate the rest of her life to getting even.

The day after Jennifer heard music surrounding Dr. Wyeth, a nurse told her that a different neurosurgeon would be treating her from now on.

"Why? Where's Dr. Wyeth?"

The nurse began to speak, then caught herself and instead wrote something on a piece of paper and handed it to Jennifer: *Dr. Wyeth had a cerebral hemmorhage last night. He's dead.*

⤳∴⤶

Jennifer walked through the children's wing until she found the room she was looking for. A six-year-old boy had been admitted the week before, suffering from head injuries after having been hit by a car. She had stopped by his room before and his mother, a pale, heavy woman, was always there, sitting in a chair by the bed, sleeping on a cot in the corner.

"How's your little boy doing?"

The mother looked up, startled. She didn't realize Jennifer was deaf and spoke rapidly, but Jennifer could read her lips enough to get the general idea, that the child was doing better and would recover, that the mother was so grateful. "God's answered my prayers," the woman said. "The doctors say he's going to be fine."

Jennifer tried to smile, but it was hard to do because she was listening, listening, with her whole being, her whole heart. The child was sleeping in blissful silence. The music that Jennifer heard, that had drawn her to this room, emanated from the mother.

"He's going to be fine. He's got a long life ahead of him," the mother said.

Jennifer couldn't look at her, but turned and walked rapidly back up the hall.

⤳∴⤶

At the end of November, Jennifer checked out of the hospital, reclaimed her car from the lot where it had been towed, and drove north on Interstate 15. She crossed Utah and Colorado and headed for Kansas City. Her destination was Michigan, but along the way she planned a stop to see her mother, whom she hadn't spoken to in years. The old woman's kidneys were failing, and she lived in a nursing home. Since this would be her last trip east, Jennifer wanted to say good-bye.

⤳∴⤶

At the Westminster Home, Jennifer found her mother sitting at a cardtable, playing gin with a trio of elderly women. Jennifer had tried to prepare her for the changes in a letter she'd written earlier—the dramatic weight loss, the change in hairstyle, and oh yes, the fact that she was now deaf and had to pass notes back and forth when her lipreading abilities failed her.

So changed was Jennifer, though, from the glamorous entertainer she'd once been, that it took a few seconds before Mildred DeSoto could be convinced that this was, indeed, her daughter. Her pinched and wrinkled face remained composed, but tears welled in her eyes as she suggested they go somewhere to be alone.

Mother and daughter talked for awhile, Jennifer encouraging Mildred to write notes and reading her lips when she could.

"In your letter, you said somebody shot you."

Jennifer shrugged.

"Kevin always said he'd come after you if you left. Was it him?"

"I don't know who it was."

Mildred turned away and stared out the window, lapsing into a temporary silence while Jennifer remained in her own silence, which was permanent and infinitely deeper.

"Do you hear that?"

"Hear what?" her mother said.

"That music."

"The old coot down the hall keeps his t.v. set running night and day. It's probably why he's senile."

"No, not the t.v."

The sound she heard could not be ignored. Like a streak of red paint on white canvas, it threaded its way through Jennifer's silent world. Leaving her mother, she walked up the hall until she found the sound's source—an old woman with skin the color of urine and a tube running out of her arm, who stared blankly at the ceiling.

Jennifer sat down by the bed. The music wasn't continuous. There would be a short strain of melody followed by silence, then long, haunting notes that sounded to Jennifer like someone chanting far, far away.

Closing her eyes, she concentrated on the notes and tried to replicate them. She felt foolish—what if the sound existed only in her own head? What if, as one doctor had suggested, it was nothing but a trick played by her damaged brain, the auditory equivalent of a phantom limb to an amputee?

But she sang a few notes, mimicking as best she could the sounds she heard.

Another strain of sound, more plaintive and drawn out, echoed in Jennifer's mind. Again, she took a deep breath and repeated it back.

The old woman's eyes, open and amazed, focused on Jennifer. A look of wonder and deep peace came over her face. Whatever the sound was, it meant something to her. She reached out to put a withered hand on Jennifer's arm, her lips forming the words, "Yes...*sing.*"

Jennifer stared into the old woman's face and knew what she was hearing was life unraveling, the leave-taking of a soul. Such intimacy was unbearable, and she felt herself recoil.

She knew the woman wanted her to keep singing, that somehow this eased the way, but she couldn't continue. She hated the sound of a life winding down, hated most of all the fact that she was the only one who could hear it. That made her a freak, didn't it, a creature living between two worlds?

She ran out of the room, found a bathroom, and stared at herself in the mirror. Saw a haggard woman—no longer young—with a hairstyle straight out of Dachau, a dented skull, and hands that quivered like tripwires. And an interior world as silent as snow except when she heard people dying.

I have Kevin to thank for this.

She thought of the Glock in the car's glove compartment and the only thing she longed for more than the moment when she put a bullet in his brain was the moment after that, when she put one in her own.

Her mother came into the bathroom and handed her a hastily scrawled note: *You're going to find Kevin, aren't you? Let it go. Let him think you're dead.*

"I don't even know where he is."

She was lying, of course. She knew damned well where he was—or thought she did. Whatever attributes Kevin might possess, imagination was certainly not among them. He was a creature of habit who would no more willingly part with his past than he had let go of her.

Kevin's mother owned some cabins in the U.P., Michigan's Upper Peninsula, that she rented out to tourists—fishermen, hunters, and campers in summer, snowmobilers and ice fishermen in the winter. Even if he believed she was dead, Jennifer knew Kevin would go there. He was, at heart, a mama's boy and murder or attempted murder would have sent him scurrying home.

She left Kansas City early the next morning, driving through thick snow that swept down from Canada and blanketed the Midwest, closing down highways in Oklahoma and Kansas. The snow didn't bother her. Its icy cold and utter white silence matched what was inside her heart.

～:～

Fat flakes of snow spattered against Jennifer's windshield as she drove northeast through Wisconsin toward northern Michigan. Living in Vegas, she hadn't driven in winter conditions in years, and her Toyota Camry was lacking both snow tires and four-wheel drive. Twice she spun out and barely missed ending up on the side of the road.

Around mid-afternoon, she followed a snowplow into Indian Lake, watching the right side of the road for her destination, hoping she'd recognize it. She and Kevin had honeymooned at the Hiawatha Lodge in the dead of January. This was the place he'd hung out in his youth, the place, he had confided, where he'd go if he were hiding from the law. Never mind the fact that his mother owned the place—this was Kevin's idea of a hide-out.

Just getting there almost killed her. She'd forgotten how, from the west, the lodge appeared just at the point of greatest hazard, where the road steepened sharply and curved right. She glimpsed the sign for the Lodge a second too late and twisted the wheel hard to make the turn. The car skidded, tires fighting for traction on the icy road. A stand of fir trees loomed ahead and for a second that was where she was headed, over the drop and into the trees, and all of it took place in silence, even her cry of terror before the car regained the road.

As she'd expected, Kevin's mother had retired long ago from the front desk. A hefty middle-aged blonde, who acted as though Jennifer's deafness were a personal affront, took her money and gave her the key for #14.

"Does Kevin Grimaldi still live here? We went to high school together."

"He hangs around sometimes, but he don't live here," said the woman. She was speaking too rapidly. Jennifer took paper and pen from her purse and pushed it across the counter to her. A sour smirk appeared on the woman's face, but she printed, *B.J.'s Tap* followed by a question mark. "There, or some other ginmill."

Jennifer checked out her cabin—a tiny, two-room affair jammed with enough homespun knickknacks and wall hangings to fill up a handicraft store—then she went cruising.

Kevin's green pick-up was white now and it wasn't parked outside *B.J.'s Tap* but behind the dubiously named *U.P.Inn,* but the license plate still proclaimed the driver as ROOFMAN. Jennifer got out a piece of paper and printed on it in big letters, "Gotcha!" She applied a thick coat of lipstick and pressed her mouth to the paper. She then wrote *Hiawatha Lodge, cabin #14* and slid it under the windshield.

⌒⋮∾

All evening, she sat in the dark with the Glock on her lap. Around eleven, she saw lights in the parking lot. Her heart jumped and she crept to a window. It was a trio of snowmobilers passing through on their way to the trail that led to the rental place next door. They were coming back very late—she wondered if they'd lost their way up on the mountain, if there'd been a bad moment when they thought they'd be spending the night in the cold and the snow.

She remembered the time Kevin had gotten her on a snowmobile—during the first year of their marriage, before the drinking got out of control and turned him into a frightful parody of himself. She remembered the terrible noise as they caromed through the snow, and the herd of elk that stampeded up the slopes to escape the roaring, exhaust-belching machines whose characteristics would in time come to remind her so much of her husband's.

They'd gone too far and gotten themselves lost as night was falling. Jennifer remembered the panic she'd felt, not just of the cold and the darkness but the woods themselves, their very vastness seemed ominous, as though they were capable of swallowing her alive. Kevin had reassured her. He'd pulled out a flashlight and after consulting a trail map for what seemed like hours, had planned out a route and gotten them home.

They'd made love the rest of the night, the adrenaline rush of being lost fueling their ardor.

She'd loved him then, his coolheadedness under pressure, his competence in finding the right trail. How strange and sad, she thought, that love can be here, as powerful as a thunderclap one moment and then disappear, like a sound dying back into nothingness.

The snowmobiles passed by the window like ghosts, their lights muted by the snow, their riders bundled against the frigid night, hunched low and helmeted on their mechanical steeds.

She watched them go while her heart slowly returned to normal.

⌣⠆⠰

One o'clock and still no sign of Kevin. Had he found somewhere else to go drinking? Had the wind blown away her note or had he been too drunk to notice it? Or had he found it, but been so panicked at the idea that she was still alive that he'd taken off without even bothering to look for her?

Unlikely, she thought. On his home ground, Kevin didn't rattle easily. If he thought she might be here, he'd most likely want to be sure.

She looked at the gun and thought about the irony—when she fired, it would make a tremendous explosion in the small room, it might even damage her eardrums, yet she would hear nothing. And if Kevin didn't die right away, if he screamed, neither would she hear that, and she almost regretted it—she had dreamed of the moment when he begged and pleaded and whimpered in agony with a bullet in his knee or groin before the second bullet carved a trough between his eyes.

Turning back toward the window, she suddenly saw lights—not in the parking lot, but on the road up above—highbeams splashing across the blackness. A vibration shuddered through the soles of her feet. The crossbeams on the ceiling swayed above her head as light flooded the room. Seed catalogs and corncob dolls and handpainted wooden daisies dropped from the walls as the far wall of the cabin suddenly imploded and a section of roof crashed down. She threw herself on the floor, covering her head with one arm and cradling the Glock with the other.

When the floor stopped shaking and nothing else fell, she dropped the gun and crawled through the wreckage to get outside. The highbeams of the pick-up illuminated the area like day. Kevin's truck had plowed through the trees from the road above and crashed through the back wall of the cabin.

She stared at the wreckage, disbelieving.

Had Kevin, a driver who must have made this turn a hundred times, lost control of the truck on the icy road, or had he given way to a drunken impulse to try to murder her by hurling his vehicle through the rear wall of her cabin?

"Kevin?"

She peered into the cab and saw him folded bloodily between the driver's seat and steering wheel.

Blood was dribbling from his nose and pumping from his chest, where the steering column had punched through his sternum. His eyes were open, wild with fear. "Help me."

She willed herself to either exhult that he'd spared her the trouble of killing him or to hate him for cheating her out of the satisfaction, but found herself incapable of either.

His lips moved. She couldn't hear his voice, but she could hear him dying. When she took his hand, the distant music became more clear and she could sing it back to him.

And while the life was draining out of him, she felt the hatred leaving her, not only for her former husband, but for herself and the world she'd always thought had cheated her.

Jennifer Kruger, Jenny DeSoto, for the first time in her life, they didn't seem to matter anymore. They seemed, in fact, to be fading away, but she was still there.

And I have you to thank for that, she thought, looking at Kevin.

A few minutes into her song, he seemed to relax and grow peaceful. Soon after that, blood gushed from his mouth, and his heart stopped. She let his hand fall and walked back toward the main lodge to call an ambulance. Her world was silent once again, but she took comfort knowing that the one thing she could hear was the one thing that really counted, knowing that now and for the rest of her life, she would be listening, listening.

Learning to Leave the Flesh

JEFF VANDERMEER

I.

Browsing through the Borges Bookstore, on a mission for my girlfriend Emily, I am suddenly confronted by a dwarf woman. The light from the front window strikes me sideways with the heat of late afternoon and, when she upturns her palm, the light illuminates all the infinite worlds enclosed in the wrinkles: pale roadlines, rivers that pass through valleys, hillocks of skin and flesh. A matrix of destinies and destinations.

Before I can react, the dwarf woman takes my hand in hers and stabs me with a thorn, sending it deep into my palm. I grunt in pain, as if a physician had just taken my blood sample. I look down into her large, dark eyes and I see such calm there that the pain winks out, only returning when she shuffles off, hunchback and all, out of the bookstore.

⚜

The walls rush away from me, the shelves so distant that I cannot even brace myself against them. I bring my hand up into the light. The thorn has worked itself beneath the surface and might even burrow deeper, if I let it. I examine the blood-blistery entrance hole. It throbs, and already a pinkish-red color spreads across my palm like a dry fire. The hole itself could be a city on a map, a citadel

139

torn apart by the angry pulse of warfare that will soon spread into the countryside. A war within my flesh.

❦

I leave the bookstore and walk back to my apartment. The boulevard, Albumuth, has a degree of security, but only two blocks down, on graffiti-choked overpasses, young teenage futureperfects carouse and cruise through the night-to-come, courting pleasures of the flesh, courting corruption of the soul. Albumuth is my lifeline, the artery to the downtown section where I work, buy groceries, and acquire books. Without it, the city would be dangerous. Without it, I might be unanchored, cast adrift.

As it is, I drag my shoes on the sidewalk, taking every opportunity to run my fingers along white picket fences, hunch down to pet cocker spaniels, converse with smiling apple grannies, and stare into the deep eyes of children.

Even now, so soon after, the wound has begun to change. I manage to pry out the thorn. The hole looks less and less like a city in flames and more like part of my own hand. Rarely has a portion of my anatomy so intrigued me. No doubt Emily has traced the lines between my freckles, explored the gaps between my toes, run her hands through the sprawl of hair on my chest, but I have never examined my own body in such detail. My body has never seemed relevant to who I am, except that I must keep it fit so it will not betray my mind.

But I examine my palm quite critically now. The wrinkles do not share consistency of length or width and calluses gather like barnacles or melted-down toothpaste caps. Abrasions, pinknesses, and a few stray hairs mar my palm. I conclude that my palm is ugly beyond hope of cosmetic surgery.

I reach my apartment as the sun fades into the blocky shadows of the city's rooftops and scattered chimneys. My apartment occupies the first floor of a two-story brownstone. The bricks are wrinkled with age and soft as wet clay in places. The anemic front lawn has been seeded with sand to keep the grass from growing.

Inside my apartment, the kitchen and living room open up onto the bedroom and bath to left and right. In my bedroom there is a window seat with triangular, plated glass through which I can see nothing but gray asphalt and a deserted shopping mall.

In the kitchen and living room, my carefully cultivated plants behave like irrational but brilliant sentences; they crawl up walls, shoot away from trellises despite my best efforts. I have wisteria, blossoms clustered like pelican limpets, sea grapes with soft round leaves, passionfruit flowers, trumpet vines, and nightblooming jasmine, whose petals open up and smell like cotton candy melted into the brine-rich scent of the sea. Together, they perform despotic Victorian couplings beyond the imagination of the most creative *menage a trois*.

Emily hates my plants. When we make love, we go to her apartment. We make such perfect love there, in her perfectly immaculate bedroom—a mechanized grind of limbs pumping like pistons—that we come together, shower together afterwards, and rarely leave a ring of hair in the bathtub.

II.

I suppose I did not think much about the thorn at the time because now, as I lie in bed listening to the dullard yowls and taunts of the futureperfects riding their cars halfway across the city, the wound's pulsating, pounding rhythm leads me back to my first real memory of the world.

Orphaned very young, my parents lost at sea in a shipwreck, yet not quite a baby to be left on a doorstep, I remember only this fragment: the sea at low tide with night sliding down on the world like a black door. Water licked my feet and I felt the coolness of sand beneath my legs, the bite of the wind against my face. And: the *plop-plop* of tiny silver fish caught in tidal pools; the spackle of starfish trapped in seaweed and glistening troughs of sand; ghost crabs scuttling sideways on creaking joints, pieces of flesh clutched daintily in their pincers.

I do not know how old I was or how I came to be on that beach. I know only that I sat on the sand, the stars faded lights against the cerulean sweep of sky. As dusk became nightfall, hands grasped me by the shoulders and dragged me up the dunes into the stickery grass and the sea grape, the passionflower and the cactus, until I could see the ferris wheel of a seaside circus and hear the hum-and-thrum hollow acoustic sob of people laughing and shouting.

Whether this is a real place or an image from my imagination, I do not know. But it returns to center me in this world when I have no center; it gives me something beyond this city, my job, my apartment. Somewhere, magical, once upon a time, I lay under the stars at nightfall and I dreamed the fantastic.

I have few friends. Foster children who move from family to family, town to town, rarely maintain friendships. Foster parents seem now like dust shadows spread out against a window pane. I can remember faces and names, but I feel so remote from them compared to the memory of the wheeling, open arch of horizon before and above me.

Now I have a wound in my palm. A wound that leads me back to the beach at dusk, of my grief at my parents' death, that I had not drowned with them. Living but not moving. Observing but not doing. At the center of myself I am suggestibility, not action. Never action.

My parents took actions. They *did* things. And they died.

III.

Despite my wound—not a good excuse—I drive to work down Albumuth Boulevard, turning into the parking lot where tufts of grass thrust up between cracks in the red brick. The shop where I work occupies a slice of the town square. It has antique glass windows, dark green curtains to deflect the gaze of the idly or suspiciously curious, and stairs leading both up and down, to the loft and the basement.

My job is to create perfect sentences for a varied clientele. No mere journalism this, for journalism requires the clarity of glass, not a mirror, nor even a reflection. I spend hours at my cubicle in the loft, looking out over the hundreds of rooftops, surrounded by the fresh sawdust smell of *words* and the loam *must* of reference text piled atop reference text.

True, I am only one among many working here. Some are not artists but technicians who gargle with pebbles to improve the imperfect diction of their perfect sentences, or casually fish for them, tugging on their lines once every long while in the hope that the sentences will surface whole, finished, and fat with meaning. Still others smoke or drink or use illicit drugs to coax the words onto the page. Many of them are quite funny in their circuitous routines. I even know their names: Wendy, Carl, Daniel, Christine, Pamela, Andrea. But we are so fixated on creating our sentences that we might well pass each other, strangers, on the street.

We must remain fixated, for the Director—a vast and stealthy intelligence, a leviathan moving ponderous many miles beneath the surface—demands it. We receive several paid solicitations each day that ask for a description of a beloved husband, a dying dog, a sailor on shore leave soon to rejoin his ship, or a housewife who wishes to tell her husband how he neglects her all unknowing:

> *He hugs her and mumbles like a sailor in love with the sea,*
> *drowning without protest as the water takes him deeper; until*
> *her lungs are awash and he has caught her in his endless dream*
> *of drowning.*

Ten years ago, we would have been writing perfect stories, but people's attention spans have become more limited in these, the last days of literacy.

Of course, we do not create *objectively* perfect sentences—sometimes our sentences are not even very good. If we could create truly perfect sentences, we would destroy the world: it would fold in on itself like a pricked hot air balloon and cease to be: poof! undone, unmade, unlived, in the harsh glacial light of a reality more real than itself.

But I am such a perfectionist that, in the back-water stagnation of other workers' coffee breaks, in the *tap-tap-tap* of rain trying to keep me from my work, I continue to string verbs onto pronouns, railroading those same verbs onto indirect objects, attaching modifiers like strategically-placed tinsel on a Christmas tree.

By my side I keep a three-ringed, digest-sized notebook of memories to help me live the lives of our clients, to get under their skins and know them as I know myself. Only twelve pages have been filled, most of them recounting events after I reached my fifteenth birthday. Many notes are only names, like Bobby Zender, a friend and fellow orphan at the reform school. He had a gimp foot and for a year

LEARNING TO LEAVE THE FLESH

I matched my strides to his, never once broke ahead of him or ran out onto the playground to play kickball. He died of tuberculosis. Or Sarah Galindrace, with the darkest eyes and the shortest dresses and skin like silk, like porcelain, like heaven. She moved away and became an echo in my heart.

These memories often help me with the sentences, but today the wound on my hand bothers me, distracts me from the pristine longleaf sheets of paper on the drafting boards. The pen, a black quill that crisply scratches against the paper, menaces me. My fellow workers stare; their bushy black eyebrows and manes of blond hair and mad stallion eyes make me nervous. I sweat. I teeter uneasily on my high stool and try not to stare out the window at the geometrically-pleasing telephone lines that slice the sky into a matrix of points of interest: church spires, flagpoles, neon billboards.

A woman who has finally found true romance needs a sentence to tell her boyfriend how much she loves him. My palm flares when I take up the pen; the pen could as well be a knife or a chisel or some object with which I am equally unfamiliar. My skin feels itchy, as if I have picked at the edges of a scab. But I write the sentence anyway:

When I see you, my heart rises like bread in an oven.

The sentence is awful. The Director leans over and concurs with a nod, a hand on my shoulder, and the gravelly murmur, "You are trying too hard. Relax. Relax."

Yes. Relax. I think of Emily and the book I was going to get for her at the Borges Bookstore: *The Refraction of Light in a Prison.* Perhaps if I can project from my relationship with Emily I can force the sentence to work. I think of her sharp cadences, the way she bites the ends off words as if snapping celery stalks in two. Or the time she tickled me senseless in the middle of her sister's wedding and I had to pretend I was drunk just to weather the embarrassment. Or this: *the smooth, spoon-tight feel of her stomach against my lips, the miraculous tangle of her blond hair.*

So. I try again.

When I see you, my heart rises like a flitting hummingbird to a rose.

Now I am truly hopeless. The repetition of "rises" and "rose" knifes through all alternatives and I am convinced I should have been a plumber, a dentist, a shoeshine boy. Words that should layer themselves into patterns—strike passion in the heart—become ugly and cold. The dead weight of cliche has given me a headache.

At dusk, I ask the Director for a day off. He gives it to me, orders me to do nothing but walk around the city, perhaps take in a ball game in the old historical section, perhaps a Voss Bender exhibit at the Teel Memorial Art Museum.

IV.

I spend my day off contemplating my palm with my girlfriend Emily Brosewiser, she of the aforementioned blond hair, the succulent lips, the tactile smile, the moist charm. (My comparisons become so fecund I think I would rather love a fruit or vegetable.)

We sit on a lichen-encrusted bench at the San Matador Park, my arm around her shoulders, and watch the mallards siphoning through the pond scum for food. The gasoline-green grass scent and the heat of the summer sun make me sleepy. The park seems cluttered with dwarfs: litter picker-uppers armed with their steely harpoons; lobotomy patients from the nearby hospital, their stares as direct as a lover's; burly hunchbacked fellows going over the lawn with gleaming red lawnmowers. They distract me—errant punctuation scattered across a pristine page.

Emily sees them only as clowns and myself as sick. "Sick, sick, sick." How can I disagree? She smells so clean and her hair shines like spun gold.

"They were always there before, Nicholas, and you never noticed them. Why should they matter now? Don't pick at that." She slaps my hand and my palm thrums with pain. "Why must you obsess over it so? Here we are with a day off and you cannot leave it alone."

Emily works for an ad agency. She designs sentences that sell perfection to the consumer public. Before I ever met Emily, I saw her work on billboards at the outskirts of town: "Buy Skuttles: We Expect No Rebuttals" and "Someday You Are Gonna Die: In the Meantime, Buy and Buy—at the Coriander Mall." At the bottom, in small print, the billboards read: "Ads by Emily." At the time, I was girlfriendless and so I called up the billboard makers, tracked down the ad agency, and asked her out. She liked my collection of erotic sentences and my manual dexterity. I liked the gossamer line of hair that runs down her forearms, the curves of her breasts with their tiny pink nipples, the fullness of her lips.

But her sentences have become passé to me, too crude and manipulative. How can I expect more from her, given the nature of the business?

So I say, "Yes, dear," and sigh and examine my palm. She is always reasonable. Always right. But I am not sure she understands me. I wonder what she would think about my memory of the arc of sky above with night coming down and the sea rustling on the shore. She did not argue when I insisted on separate apartments.

The circle on my palm has gone from pink to white and the way the wrinkle lines careen into one another, the hairs like tiny wheat sheafs, fascinates me.

Emily giggles. "Nicholas, you are so perfectly silly sitting there with that bemused look on your face. Anyone would think you'd just had a miscarriage."

I wonder if there is something wrong with our relationship; it seems as blank as my life as an orphan. Besides, "miscarriage" is not the appropriate logic leap to describe the look on my face. Granted, I cannot myself think of the appropriate hoop for this dog of syntax to leap through, but still…

We return to our separate apartments. All I can think about are dwarfs, hunchbacks, cripples. I sleep and dream of dwarfs, deformed and malicious, with sinister slits for smiles. But when I wake, I have the most curious of thoughts. I remember the weight of the dwarf woman's body against my side as she stuck the sliver into my palm. I remember the smell of her: sweet and sharp, like honeysuckle; the feel of her hand, the fingers lithe and slender; her body beneath the clothes, the way parts do not match and could never match, and yet have unity.

V.

A most peculiar assignment lies on my desk the next morning, so peculiar that I forget my damaged palm. I am to write a sentence about a dwarf. The Director has left a note that I am to complete this sentence A.S.A.P. He has also left me photographs, a series of newspaper articles, and Xeroxes from a diary. The lead paragraph of the top newspaper article, a sensational bit of work, reads:

> David "Midge" Jones, 27, a 4-foot-5 dwarf, lived for attention, whether he ate fire at a carnival, walked barefoot on glass for spectators, or allowed himself to be hurled across a room for a dwarf-throwing contest. Jones yearned for the spotlight. Sunday, he died in the dark. He drank himself to death. Tests showed his blood alcohol level at .43, or four times the level at which a motorist would be charged with driving under the influence of alcohol.

I pick up the glossy color print atop the pile of documentation. It shows Jones at the carnival, the film overexposed, his eyes forming red dots against the curling half-smile of his mouth. At either side stand flashy showgirls with tinsel-adorned bikini tops crammed against his face. Jones stares into the camera lens, but the showgirls stare at Jones as though he is some carnival god. The light on the photograph breaks around his curly brown hair, but not his body, as if a spotlight had been trained on him. He stands on a wooden box, his arms thrown around the show-girls.

The film's speed is not nearly fast enough to catch the ferris wheel seats spinning crazily behind him, so that light spills into the dazzle of showgirl tinsel, showgirl cleavage. Behind the ferris wheel, blurry sand dunes roll and beyond that, in the valley between dunes, the sea, like a squinting eye. The photograph has a sordid quality to it: when I look closer, I see the sheen of sweat on Jones' face, his flushed complexion. Sand clings to his gnarled arms and his forehead. The lines of his eyes, nose, and mouth seem charcoal pencil rough: a first, hurried sketch.

JEFF VANDERMEER

I turn the photograph over. In the upper right hand corner someone has written: "David Jones, September 19—. The Amazing Mango Brothers Seaside Circus and Carnival Extravaganza. He cleaned out animal cages and gave 50 cent blow jobs behind the Big Top."

Jones is a brutish man. I want nothing to do with him. Yet I must write a sentence about him, for a client I will never meet. I must capture David Jones in a single sentence.

I read the rest of the article, piecemeal.

> In his most controversial job, Jones ignored criticism, strapped on a modified dog harness, and allowed burly men to hurl him across a room in a highly publicized dwarf-throwing contest at the King's Head Pub.

> "I'm a welder, which can be dangerous. But welders are frequently laid off, so I also work in a circus. I eat fire, I walk on broken glass with bare feet. I climb a ladder made of swords, I lie on a bed of nails and have tall people stand on me. This job is easy compared to what I usually do."

I spend many hours trying to form a sentence, with sweat dripping down my neck despite the slow swish of fans. I work through lunch, distracted only by a dwarf juggler (plying his trade with six knives and a baby) who has wrested the traffic circle away from a group of guildless mimes and town players.

I begin simply.
> *The dwarf's life was tragic.*

No.
> *David Jones' life was tragic.*

No.
> *David's life was unnecessarily tragic.*

Unnecessarily tragic? Tragedy does not waste time with the extraneous. A man's life cannot be reduced to a Latinesque, one-line, 11-syllable haiku. How do I identify with David? Did he ever spend time in an orphanage? Did he ever find himself on a beach, his parents dead and never coming back? How hard can it have been to be an anomaly, a misfit, a mistake?

Then my imagination unlocks a phrase from some compartment of my brain:

> *David left the flesh in tragic fashion.*

LEARNING TO LEAVE THE FLESH

Again, my palm distracts me, but not as much. I see all the imperfections there and yet they do not seem as ugly as before. David may be ugly, but I am not ugly.

As I drive home in the sour, exhaust-choked light of dusk, I admire the oaks that line the boulevard, whorled and wind-scored and yet stronger and more soothing to the eye than the toothpick pines, the straight spruce.

VI.

By now the plants have conquered my apartment in the name of CO_2, compost, and photosynthesis. I let them wander like rejects from '50's B-grade vegetable movies, ensuring that Emily will never stay for long. The purple and green passion flowers, stinking of sex, love the couch with gentle tendrils. The splash-red bougainvillea cat cradles the kitchen table, then creeps toward the refrigerator and pulls on the door, thorns making a scratchy sound. Along with this invasion come the scavengers, the albino geckos that resemble swirls of mercury or white chocolate. I have no energy to evict them.

No, I sit in a chair, in underwear weathered pink by the whimsical permutations of the wash cycle, and read by the blue glow of the mute TV screen.

David grew up in Dalsohme, a bustling but inconsequential port town on the Gulf side of the Moth River Delta. His parents, Jemina and Simon Pultin, made their living by guiding tourists through the bayous in flat-bottom boats. Simon talked about installing a glass bottom to make business better, but Jemina argued that no one would want to see the murky waters of a swamp under a microscope, so to speak. Instead, they supplemented their income by netting catfish and prawns. David was good at catching catfish, but Jemina and Simon preferred to have him work the pole on the flat-bottom boat because the tourists often gawked at him as much as at the scenery. It was Jemina's way of improving business without giving in to Simon's glass bottom boat. Some of the documents the Director gave me suggested that Simon had adopted David precisely for the purpose of manning the boat. There is no record of what David thought of all of this, but at age fifteen he "ran away from home and joined a circus." He did whatever he had to on the carnival circuit, including male prostitution, but apparently never saved enough money to quit, though the schemes became grander and more complex.

> "Most little people think the world owes them something because they're little. Most little people got this idea they should be treated special. Well, the world doesn't owe us anything. God gave us a rough way to go, that's all."

Soon the words blur on the page. Under the flat, aqua glow, the wound in my palm seems smaller but denser, etched like a biological Rosetta Stone. The itch,

147

though, grows daily. It grows like the plants grow. It spreads into the marrow of my bones and I can feel it infiltrating whatever part of me functions as a soul.

That night, I dream that we are all "pure energy," like on those old future-imperfect cardboard-and-glue space journey episodes where the budget demanded pure energy as a substitute for make up and genuine costumes. Just golden spheres of light communing together, mind to mind, soul to soul. A world without prejudice because we have, none of us, a body that can lie to the world about our identity.

VII.

The day my parents left me for the sea, the winter sky gleamed bone-white against the gray-blue water. The cold chaffed my fingers and dried them out. My father took his calf's skin gloves off so my hand could touch his, still sweaty from the glove. His weight, solid and warm, anchored me against the wind as we walked down to the pier and the ship. Above the ship's masts, frigate birds with throbbing red throats let the wind buffet them until they no longer seemed to fly, but to sit, stationary, in the air.

My mother walked beside me as well, holding her hat tightly to her head. The hem of her sheepskin coat swished against my jacket. A curiously fresh, clean smell, like mint or vanilla, followed her and when I breathed it in, the cold retreated for a little while.

"It won't be for long," my father said, his voice descending to me through layers of cold and wind.

I shivered, but squeezed his hand. "I know."

"Good. Be brave."

"I will."

Then my mother said, "We love you. We love you and wish you could come with us. But it's a long journey and a hard one and no place for a little boy."

My mother leaned down and kissed me, a flare of cold against my cheek. My father knelt, held both my hands, and looked me up and down with his flinty gray eyes. He hugged me against him so I was lost in his windbreaker and his chest. I could feel him trembling just as I was trembling.

"I'm scared," I said.

"Don't be. We'll be back soon. We'll come back for you. I promise."

They never did. I watched them board the ship, a smile frozen to my face. It seems as though I waited so long on the pier, watching the huge sails catch the wind as the ship slid off into the wavery horizon, that snowflakes gathered on my eyes and my clothes, the cold air biting into my shoulder blades.

I do not remember who took me from that place, nor how long I really stood there, nor even if this represents a true memory, but I hold onto it with all my strength.

Later, when I found out my parents had died at sea, when I understood what that meant, I sought out the farthest place from the sea and I settled here.

LEARNING TO LEAVE THE FLESH

VIII.

At the store, I have so much work to do that I am able to forget my palm. I stare for long minutes at the sentence I have written on my notepad:

David was leaving the flesh.

What does it mean?

I throw away the sentence, but it lingers in my mind and distracts me from my other work. Finally, I break through with a sentence describing a woman's grief that her boyfriend has left her and she is growing old:

She sobs like the endless rain of late winter, without passion or the hope of relief, just a slow drone of tears.

As I write it, I begin to cry: wrenching sobs that make my throat ache and my eyes sting. My fellow workers glance at me, shrug, and continue at their work. But I am not crying because the sentence is too perfect. I am crying because I have encapsulated something that should not be encapsulated in a sentence. How can my client want me to write this?

IX.

Emily visits me at lunchtime. She visits me often during the day, but our nights have been crisscrossed, sometimes on purpose, I feel.

We go to the same park and now we feel out of place, in the minority. Everywhere I look dwarfs walk to lunch, drive cars, mend benches. All of them individual palmprints, each one so unique that next to them Emily appears plain.

"Something has happened to you." She looks into my eyes as she says this and I read a certain vulnerability into her words.

"Something has happened to me. I have a wound in my palm."

"It's not the wound. It's the plants out of control. It's the sex. It's everything. You know it as well as me."

Emily is always right, on the mark, on the money. I am beginning to tire of such perfection. I feel a part of me break inside.

"You don't understand," I say.

"I understand that you cannot handle responsibility. I understand that you are having problems with this relationship."

"I'll talk to you later," I say and I leave her, speechless, on the bench.

X.

After lunch, I think I know where my center lies: it lies in the sentence I must create for David Jones. It is in the sentence and in me. But I don't want to write anything perfect. I don't want to. I want to work without a net. I want to write rough, with emotion that stings, the words themselves dangling off into an abyss. I want to find my way back to the sea with the darkness coming down and the briny scent in my nostrils, before I knew my parents were dead. Before I was born.

David Jones found his way. If a person drinks too much alcohol, the body forces the stomach to vomit the alcohol before it can reach a lethal level. Jones never vomited. As he slept, the alcohol seeped into his bloodstream and killed him.

My shaking fingers want to perform ridiculous pratfalls, rolling over in complex loop-the-loops and cul-de-sacs of language. Or suicide sentences, mouthing sentiments from the almost-dead to the definitely-dead. Instead, I write:

From birth, David was learning ways to leave the flesh.

It is nothing close to layered prose. It has no subtlety to it. But now I can smell the slapping waves of the sea and the alluring stench of passion flower fruit.

Before I leave for my apartment, Emily calls me. I do not take the call. I am too busy wondering when my parents knew they might die, and if they thought of me as the wind and the water conspired to take them. I wish I had been with them, had gone down with them, in their arms, with the water in our mouths like ambrosia.

XI.

When I open my apartment door, I hear the scuttling of a hundred sticky toes. The refrigerator's surface writhes with milk-white movement against the dark green of leaves. In another second, I see that the white paint is instead the sinuous shimmer-dance of the geckos, their camouflage perfect as they scramble for cover. I open the refrigerator and take out a wine cooler; my feet crunch down on the hundred molting skins of the geckos, the sound like dead leaves, or brittle cicada chrysali.

I sit in my underwear and contemplate my wound by the TV's redemptive light. It has healed itself so completely that I can barely find it. The itching, however, has intensified, until I feel it all over, inside me. Nothing holds my interest on my palm except the exquisite imperfections: the gradations of colors, the rough-pliable feel of it, the scratches from Emily's cat.

LEARNING TO LEAVE THE FLESH

I walk into the bedroom and ease myself beneath the covers of my bed. I imagine I smell the sea, a salt breeze wafting through the window. The stars seem like pieces of jagged glass ready to fall onto me. I toss in my bed and cannot sleep. I lie on my stomach. I lie on my side. The covers are too hot, but when I strip them away, my body is too cold. The water I drank an hour ago has settled in my stomach like a smooth, aching stone.

Finally, the cold keeps me half-awake and I prop myself sleepily against the pillow. I hear voices outside and see flashes of light from the window, like a ferris wheel rising and falling. But I do not get up.

Then he stands at the foot of my bed, staring at me. A cold blue tint dyes his flesh, as if the TV's glow has sunburned him. The marble cast of his face is as perfect as the most perfect sentence I have ever written in my life. His eyes are so sad that I cannot meet his gaze; his face holds so many years of pain, of wanting to leave the flesh. He speaks to me and although I cannot hear him, I know what he is saying. I am crying again, but softly, softly. The voices on the street are louder and the tinkling of bells so very light.

And so I discard my big-body skin and my huge hands and my ungainly height and I walk out of my apartment with David Jones, to join the carnival under the moon, by the seashore, where none of us can hurt or be hurt anymore.

*Article excerpts taken from newspaper accounts in 1988 and 1989 by Michael Koretzky (*The Independent Florida Alligator*) and Ronald DuPont, Jr. (*The Gainesville Sun*).*

151

The Hoplite

PAUL FINCH

Charlie entered Worthington Park at roughly nine o'clock that evening.

He stopped for a moment just the other side of the wrought-iron gates, to adjust his gloves and get his bearings. Then he set off walking. It was February and a hard frost was forecast. His breath smoked thickly as he strolled. Not that Charlie was cold. He wore a heavy sweater under his cashmere coat, and beneath that a solid breastwork of covert ceramic plate. He didn't believe in taking chances, though he wasn't frightened as such. At this time of night, the park was filled with opaque shadows and icy mist, and he was already deep into it...but despite appearances, he wasn't alone. These days, he never went anywhere alone.

That was more than could be said for the solitary figure waiting ahead on the moon-lit bandstand. Once Charlie caught sight of him, he stopped. Then he smiled. It was a cunning, predatory smile, but it was also wary. When Charlie proceeded, he did so with caution. There was high potential for danger here, yet despite this, he hadn't armed himself. Charlie never armed himself. Partly because he didn't like getting his own hands dirty, but mainly because he didn't need to. Of course, this hadn't always been the case...

‿:‿

Charlie wasn't sure what first drew him to the figurine.

It wasn't in a prominent position—tucked away on a low shelf to the rear of the shop; it wasn't even an outstanding piece—about ten inches tall and fashioned crudely from dull red clay. It caught his attention all the same, and Charlie found himself staring at it in fascination.

It was a man, a warrior from some distant age of antiquity. It wore a plumed, full-head helm, knee-to-ankle greaves and corslet body armour, and it sported a spear and a huge convex shield.

Its base was inscribed:

> Elite Fighting Forces of History
> Spartan Hoplite
> Circa 480 B.C.

Charlie took it from the shelf and examined it. It wasn't exactly high art—probably one of a cheap line in fact, but the more he looked at it, the more he liked it. It was weighty, solid; it wouldn't be out of place on the mantle at home. He turned and considered, surveying the rest of the shop as he did. On the outside, it was one of a terraced row of narrow, gabled buildings; here on the inside, it was cramped and pokey, typical perhaps of the ornate but sleazy Amsterdam back streets. It didn't seem to sell anything in particular; assorted junk, collectibles, curiosities.

The shop's owner matched his eccentric wares, looking a little like something from Dickens. He was tall and sombre, with lank grey hair, grey sideburns and greying, yellowish skin. He wore a cravat and a green velvet frock-coat with leather patches on the elbows, and he rang up Charlie's purchase without a word, not even offering to wrap it and pack it, which was a big break from the norm where Dutch gift vendors were concerned. Charlie had to request that service, which to be fair to the shopkeeper, he then provided free of charge. Just before Charlie left the shop, however, the man gave him an odd, lop sided smile, just a faint glimpse of his teeth…it was almost feral.

As he strode around the Amstel harbour, looking at the brightly-coloured house boats, Charlie wondered what that smile had signified: probably that twenty identical sculptures all sat in the shop's back room, not worth a penny between them; or maybe that it was a rare one-off, but that Charlie could expect the Customs officers to break it open when he tried to go through. He might've laughed at the irony of that, had the thought not sent a chill through him.

He glanced at his watch. There was still two hours to go before he needed to board the ferry. It would probably be the longest two hours of his life.

᠁

Charlie was back in England, heading along the M62, by three o'clock the next afternoon. He'd been off the boat two hours, and he was still shaking.

THE HOPLITE

He'd never liked going through Customs even when he had nothing dodgy on him, so on this occasion he'd *really* been tested. Had anyone bothered to stop and search him, they'd have found nothing on his person. Had they glanced inside his Sierra, they'd have found a suitcase stuffed with second-hand clothes, and a briefcase filled with documents pertaining to various above-board but non-existent business transactions. If they'd checked underneath the car, however, that would have been a different matter.

That was where the heroin was, duct-taped behind the exhaust in eight water-proof sachets.

Now that he was through it though, Charlie wanted to laugh. To him, Customs and Excise always had that aura of being civil-servants playing at police. The cool, arrogant way they eyed you, the clipped, efficient manner they adopted when speaking; and yet there you were, bringing in drugs, bringing in contraband, bringing in firearms, explosives, porn, flooding the country with oodles of illicit materials, even smuggling refugees through, and they still stood at their barriers in their shades and crisp uniforms, staring you down like they were part of some secret higher order.

For all that, he was still sweating, still glancing into his rear-view mirror. He treated himself to a nervous cig. He was actually trying to quit, but on this occasion he felt he'd earned it. Yet again, he'd been a flyspeck beneath everyone's notice, though for once it had served him well.

He arrived at Roy Prendergast's house at half-past-seven that evening. It was a large semi-detached home in a quiet but slightly disheveled suburban backwater. A skip full of household rubbish sat on the drive, beside a Suzuki motorbike. The front garden was weedy and untended. Charlie parked on the road, then climbed out and rang the bell.

A moment later, Phil, Prendergast's eldest son, appeared at the door. He was a pugnacious twenty-two-year-old, with a mop of red hair and beady, suspicious little eyes. He was still wearing his oily, dirt-smeared overalls from work. "What do *you* want?" he asked curtly.

If one thing got on Charlie's wick, it was having to deal with the monkey rather than the organ-grinder. "What do you think?" he replied.

The lad considered this, then retreated into the house. "It's that loser, Stockton," Charlie heard him mumbling.

A moment later, Prendergast himself appeared, a balding, overweight version of his son, with a scraggy beard and borstal cross-and-star tattoos on his earlobes. He was every inch the slob. Beer stains were visible on his t-shirt and tracksuit pants. "Everything go okay?" he asked warily.

Charlie nodded.

Prendergast visibly relaxed...so much so that a cocky sneer now appeared on his fat lips. "So what've you brought it *here* for? I told you the garage."

"I've just been past the garage. There was nobody there."

Prendergast rolled his eyes as if this was somehow irrelevant, then he nudged his son. "Go with him."

Phil nodded obediently, but clearly regarded the duty as an odious one.

Charlie turned back to the car, but Prendergast stopped him with a searching look. "It would inconvenience me, pal, if I found out you'd taken a dip."

"It's all there," Charlie replied.

Roy Prendergast had made a career out of not taking people at face-value. "It had better be," he said.

A moment later, his son was seated beside Charlie and they were driving towards the garage and repair-shop. The lad hadn't bothered to change out of his dingy, oil-covered overalls, and made no apologies for that...regardless of Charlie's upholstery. Charlie didn't mind. It was hardly plush stuff, and in any case, he was still too relieved to have the job over and done with it.

"There was a minute when I thought they were going to nip me," he said conversationally.

Phil Prendergast didn't bother to reply.

"You know...bloke my age, travelling on his own?"

Still the younger man said nothing, just stared through the windscreen blank-faced. Once they reached the garage, he opened up, flicked a few lights on and briskly instructed Charlie to put the Sierra on the ramp. He then closed the doors behind them, cranked the vehicle up and jumped down into the pit.

"How many packets are there supposed to be?" he asked, immediately mistrustful.

Charlie felt a pang of fright. "Eight...why?"

Again, Phil Prendergast made no reply. Which evidently meant that all eight were there, though he didn't bother to acknowledge this. He unpeeled the tape, and took the sachets into his possession. Charlie watched in silence. He wondered if the lad was now going to cut one open and sample the goods on the tip of his tongue, the way they did in the movies. But no. Phil Prendergast wasn't *that* cute an operator. Instead, he took the stuff through to a side-office, and only re-appeared several minutes later. He made sure to lock its door behind him, then turned and faced Charlie.

Clearly, he now expected a ride home.

⚘

It was close on nine o'clock before Charlie got back to his own pad, a run-down council house in one of the town's less salubrious districts. When he entered, Lynn was still in the skirt and blouse she wore at the supermarket, but lazing on the couch in front of the television. Her kicked-off high heels lay on the floor in front of her.

"Hi," he said.

"Mmm," she muttered, hardly glancing at him.

He rubbed his hands together. "Any chance of a cuppa?"

"Kettle boiled half an hour ago. Help yourself."

THE HOPLITE

He'd expected this reaction, of course, so it was easy controlling his temper. In any case, after the few days *he'd* just had, he was too weary to get angry. "No welcome for the conquering hero?" he said.

She finally looked round at him. She was still plastered with the OTT make-up she was required to wear in order to serve at the perfume and cosmetics counter. With her plump cheeks and furrowed brow, it made her look false and gaudy, like a pantomime caricature. "What've you conquered this time?" she asked.

He sat down on the arm-rest. "Our debt problem for one thing."

Lynn snorted. "Hah…I wish! You may have conquered *your* debt. To what's-his-name. Not *our* debt. There's still the bank, the building society…"

She turned back to the inanities of late-evening TV, as if that was all that needed to be said.

Charlie slid down next to her. "Come on, love…give us a break. I could've got seriously pinched today."

"And whose fault would that've been?"

"Aren't you even glad I've not been?"

She gave him another long look. It was withering in its intensity. "What difference would it actually have made, Charlie?"

They sat there in silence for a moment. There was something on the telly about lives of the rich and famous. A Hollywood wife—all jewels and teeth and deep-tanned cleavage—was talking about the last uplift job she'd had. Charlie glanced sideways. The hem of Lynn's skirt had risen to the top of her chunky thighs. She wore tights these days, rather than the stockings and suspenders she'd endlessly teased him with when they'd first got married, but it still touched something inside him. He ran a hand up her nylon-clad leg…

"Don't even think about it," she warned.

There was a cold finality in her tone, which brooked no argument. Charlie withdrew his hand and sat back. "I've got you a present," he said after moment.

She glanced round again, this time with a flicker of interest. "What?"

Charlie stood and grabbed his jacket. "It's in the hall. Check it out."

"So where are *you* going?"

"The pub," he said, walking from the room.

"Oh, surprise surprise!" As usual, her disinterested tone had turned quickly to a whip-crack.

"There's nothing to keep me here, is there!"

"It's not *my* fault I'm on the rag!" she shouted after him.

He looked back from the now-open front door. "Tell the neighbours, why don't you?"

She made no reply to that, but he hesitated before going out. His eyes had come to rest on the figure of the hoplite. He'd unwrapped it and stood it on the hall table, next to the telephone. Away from the must and mystery of the Amsterdam shop though, in dull surroundings like these, it seemed incredibly ordinary. Minimal workmanship had gone into it. He'd seen clay sculptures in the past where the simplicity and crudeness of the artistry was part of the attraction—like they were a genuine effigy from some far-off heroic age. Not in this case. This one just looked basic. Whoever had molded it, had probably done so in ten seconds flat.

Well...sod Lynn, anyway. He hadn't really bought it for her. He might've had it in the back of his mind at the time that some kind of peace-offering would be needed on his return home, but in reality Charlie wasn't sure why he'd bought it. It had only cost twenty guilders...and what was that, about a fiver? Not a lot, but a fiver he now wouldn't have to spend on booze.

⚜

He didn't exactly get sozzled that night, but he stayed in the pub 'til closing-time and took his beer with whisky-chasers.

It was mid-week, so there was nobody in he knew: a couple of drunks at the bar, a loutish bunch of biker types around the pool-table. Charlie sat alone in a corner of the vault, ruminating on his life. What there was of it. He wasn't forty yet, but his hair was already shot with gray, his once-athletic physique now flabby and soft. Lynn had similarly deteriorated during the twelve years of their marriage. It was hard to associate the svelte, vivacious bar-maid with the long blonde hair and generous bust, who he'd first met all those years ago, with the irate, overweight gorgon he now felt chained to. Mind you, he could hardly blame her. It wasn't as if he'd delivered on the many promises he'd made on first hooking up with her.

And there lay the problem.

Charlie had first attracted his future wife *because* he was a jack-the-lad, not in spite of it. She'd been young and impressionable, and he, though strictly small time, had always put on a good show. It hadn't been difficult to convince her that shacking up with him would be dangerous and exciting, not to mention lucrative. He'd had big plans, had Charlie Stockton. Another Great Train Robbery was in the offing, he'd assured her; and in the meantime there were plenty of readies to go around from a variety of protection and gambling rackets he was involved with. In actual fact, though he was fully employed at the time in crime, he only ever got round to pulling off one really *major* job—a wages snatch, which he took a twenty-grand cut from, but which still landed him six years in jail. He served four, and then came out to find that he wasn't a face any more. A new generation of thieves and blaggers had grown up—younger, fitter, more prepared to target the weak and vulnerable, readier to batter and destroy; then, of course, there'd been the burgeoning drug-culture. All sorts of cowboys had come into the game on the back of that, Roy Prendergast and sons for example. Yes, it had provided work here and there, but it was an undeniably dirty business...and Charlie, an "honest thief" in his own earnest opinion, hadn't been able to throw himself into it with any real vigour.

And that had been the story ever since. While Lynn rode the nine 'til five drudge train, bringing in a paltry but regular wage, Charlie bummed his way around, ever hopeful the one big score was just around the corner, but steadily slowing down…both in terms of his physical powers and his enthusiasm. The little cash he earned these days, he tended to drink away or gamble…it was so insignificant that Lynn scarcely noticed it, anyway.

"Budge up, mate…budge up!" one of the bikers said, thrusting his leather-clad arse into Charlie's face, so that he could make a complicated shot.

Charlie moved his stool a foot or so, still deep in self-pity. The problem was that time had passed so quickly. He hadn't been bullshitting Lynn all those years ago; his schemes had been genuine—he *was* planning to do the overnight mail train, he *would* provide them with a swanky bar and palatial villa on the Costa del Crime. But where had the time gone?

"Budge up, mate!" he was asked again, the pool-playing biker edging Charlie yet further out of his way.

Charlie was already at the end of his tether. "Fuck's sake!" he snapped. "You're not the only ones in here, you know!"

Instantly, the bikers' ape-like jabbering ceased. As one, they stared round at him. Charlie felt his mouth go dry. He knew immediately that he'd said the wrong thing. There were six of them, and close up they were as rough as they came. Charlie saw tattoos, facial scars, long greasy hair and steel-studded belts. One of them, a bloke seated on the other side of the pool-table, stood up. He was tall, lean, with a hard, hatchet-like face and a goatee beard. Even though he wasn't participating in the game, he was now carrying a cue. Charlie saw the faded words 'Hell's Angels' on the back of his left hand.

"You speaking to us?" the bloke asked.

Charlie drained what was left of his drink, then placed the glass down. "Forget it…I'm moving."

He stood to go, but suddenly they were on all sides of him, hemming him into his corner.

"Look…I don't want any trouble," he said.

They glared all the harder. The one who had first spoken had now come round the table. He walked casually, the pool cue resting against his shoulder. "You probably don't," he replied, "but you don't fucking mouth off at my lads."

"Alright, I apologize…it was a mistake."

"Fucking right it was a mistake."

Charlie glanced through the door to the bar area, hoping to signal to the landlord that he was having trouble, but the landlord—a short, youngish guy—was looking the other way, perhaps deliberately. Charlie glanced back at his tormentors. They closed in steadily, purposefully.

Then someone intervened.

Like a whirlwind.

The first thing Charlie knew about it, a bottle had exploded on the head of the geezer standing to his immediate right. The jagged glass hilt was then thrust into the face of the one with the goatee beard. He gave a wild screech and yanked his head away, blood slicing down onto his oily Wrangler.

Charlie fell back on his stool in surprise. Events around him were suddenly a blur of motion. A tall man in a suit seemed to have come from nowhere. A biker aimed a hooking punch at him, but he blocked it with his forearm, then chopped the biker on the neck, savagely. A kick flew in at his groin; he caught the foot, then drove in a punch over the top of it, his fist slamming into genitals. In less than a second, four of the six hoodlums were already on the floor. The fifth one picked up a stool and swung it. The man ducked, then grabbed this new opponent by his collar, and head-butted him so fiercely that his nose and cheekbones audibly cracked.

Now only one biker was left on his feet. He grabbed up a pool-cue and threatened the tall man with it. The tall man advanced regardless. The biker, screaming in both rage and fear, lashed out with the pool-cue…only for the man to catch him by the wrist, yank it downwards and snap it over the edge of the table. The biker's screams became girlish shrieks of agony. The tall man then backhanded him across the mouth…with a full set of knuckles. The biker went staggering away, to fall over a table and vanish from sight.

The tall man turned slowly. Charlie caught a fleeting glimpse of hard angled features, a stiff mass of curly white hair…then the leader of the hoodlums was back in the action. His gouged face was a mass of blood and hanging flaps of skin, but he launched a flying-kick with his steel toe-caps. Again, the tall man caught his leg and violently twisted it, turning him in mid-air, dropping him onto his head. Frothing at the mouth with anger, the biker chieftain tried to get up again. The tall man helped him, taking him by the throat and, before he could even react, hurling him clear across the room, sweeping drinks and bottles from the various surfaces and bouncing him from the far wall, leaving a huge, cranial-shaped dent in its plaster.

Now that damage was actually being done, the timid landlord seemed to feel he had no option but to get involved. "I'm calling the police!" he said, appearing in the entrance to the vault. "If you don't all get out of here, I'm calling the police!"

Absurdly, he was mainly directing his comments at Charlie, who was still innocently sitting there, not having laid a finger on anyone. Charlie nodded dumbly, too bewildered to argue or even reply. He looked again at the scene of devastation. The various bikers lay broken and bruised in a wreckage of pub furniture, the air filled with their groans and whimpers.

But of the man who had done this, there was suddenly no sign…that was until Charlie happened to glance up, and saw a tall, white-haired figure leaving the premises by the front door.

"Hey…hey, wait," he said, scrambling to his feet and following.

When he burst out through the entrance onto the pavement, however, there was no trace of anybody. Charlie gazed along the street in both directions. Nothing moved. There wasn't even any traffic. Then he spied the entry opposite. At this time of night, it was a black recess between two grilled shop-fronts. He knew it led into a back-alley, and didn't, as far as he was aware, give access to anywhere in particular, but he crossed the road towards it all the same. Whoever his saviour had been, he must've gone down that way...it was the only possibility.

Charlie hesitated for a moment before entering the passage. He didn't know what the guy's motives had been in defending him. Perhaps he'd owed the bikers a kicking for something else? Perhaps he just liked a fight? Either way, it might not be safe to follow him. On the other hand, someone who could handle himself like that was someone you should thank. Charlie had always believed in making friends where possible.

A moment later, he was sidling between overflowing dustbins, wading through heaps of spilled trash. There was a squealing of rats around his feet, and a ripe stench of decay. It was also deep in shadow down there; no security lights flicked on, and only a thin sliver of star-lit sky was visible overhead. Charlie delved further in anyway, though he couldn't imagine what his quarry had been doing coming this way. Then he saw him.

Charlie stopped in his tracks. Just ahead, the alley came to a dead-end wall. And that's where the man was standing, perfectly still, his face to the bricks.

A chill ran down Charlie's spine. A voice told him to back up, to get the hell away from here. He stepped closer, however. It wasn't easy to tell, but now that his eyes were attuning to the darkness, the petty criminal was fascinated to see that his saviour was wearing the same shabby gray suit that *he* was. Now that he thought about it, from the brief glimpses he'd had of the guy during the fight, he'd also been wearing a shirt and a loose, flower-patterned tie. Unconsciously, Charlie groped at his own tie...it hung in a loose knot from his collar, and bore flower patterns. This was too much...

"Hey!" Charlie said. He was tense, wary of being attacked himself, but something drew him inexplicably closer. He was now only five yards away. "I wanted to thank you for helping me."

The figure by the dead-end wall didn't respond. Didn't even look round.

Charlie was now within touching distance, but he managed to refrain from actually doing that, though the impulse was intense. Sweat had broken from his brow. He felt as though he wasn't actually in control of himself here...he'd heard how opposites attract. The urge to tap the guy on the shoulder was intense. It was a struggle to resist.

"I said...thanks for protecting..."

The man turned. He was a head taller than Charlie. And such a head. The thief found himself gazing up into a face which in moonlight was as cold and pale as marble. Blank eyes stared without seeing into the darkness. The smooth lips didn't so much as quiver. For a mad moment, Charlie was staring up at the face of one of those ancient Greek statues...Achilles or Alexander the Great. It was abominable, nightmarish, and Charlie didn't wait around to see more.

With a choking scream, he fled.

The hoplites made up the elite core of the Spartan infantry, and the very heart of what for five-hundred years, leading up to the second century BC, was the most formidable war machine in the world. As individuals, the Spartan troops were characterized by their extreme toughness, and their extraordinarily high levels of training and battle-skill...

Charlie looked up from the dusty *Encyclopedia of the Ancient World.* Similar tomes stood on the library shelf in front of him: *The Dawn of Civilization; War and Poetry; The Helenic Era.*

He'd had to look all this up, because when it came down to it, he didn't know that much about the ancient Greeks. He'd heard of the Three-hundred Spartans of course, and Jason and the Argonauts, but that was because he'd seen the movies. He had vague memories of studying the Trojan War when he'd been at school. The fine detail however, the scholarly stuff, had eluded him. But even from the little information he possessed, he could recall a vivid impression of how they'd looked and lived, those Greeks—their temples and togas, their vineyards and olive groves, their rocky, sun-bleached homeland steeped in the myths of men and monsters. And, of course, their gods, who'd often seemed as real as normal people; who were petty and childlike; who, according to myth, would interfere in the affairs of mankind at a whim, granting favours here, passing curses there, setting one person up against another for their own amusement, like pieces on a chess board. Of course, Charlie didn't believe in any of that. No more than he believed in Santa Claus or the Easter Bunny. But he didn't dismiss it totally; he never dismissed anything totally...he was too much of an opportunist.

Charlie knew there was such a thing as fate, and the mysterious hand of fortune. A lot of the time in life you got dumped on. But now and then, there were occasions when chances came along, and it was down to you to exploit them, however bizarre they might seem. He supposed if he had any religion at all, it was Christianity. But there was nothing contradictory there. What was it the priests always said?...that the Lord moved in mysterious ways.

Even as he considered this, he sensed that he was being watched. He turned. He was alone in that particular aisle of books. But someone else, he knew, was close at hand. For once in his life, though, it wasn't a malign presence. Charlie crept to the end of the nearest book-case and sneaked a peek around it. There was nobody in that aisle either, or in the next one. He ventured furtively through them all, observing any fellow browsers with intense, scrutinising eyes, not concerned whether he unnerved them or not. At no stage, though, was he afraid or even alarmed; it was more like a game, a lark...so much so that one of the assistant-librarians—a stumpy, stuffy-looking gentlemen in steel-rimmed spectacles—spotted him and came suspiciously over. Before he could speak, though, Charlie cut him dead with a warning finger.

"Don't say a word to me. You understand? Not now. Not ever."

THE HOPLITE

The assistant-librarian clammed up before he'd even spoken. He could only gaze in wonderment as Charlie then sauntered out of the building, casually tossing the encyclopedia onto the desk on his way.

Back home, Charlie stood staring at the statuette. It now occupied a place of honour, over the gas-fire, where it looked a sight more impressive than it had out in the hall. He looked again at the figure's armour, imagined it burnished in the hot Greek sun, dust-coated, spattered with Persian blood. And he thought again about the bikers in the pub; mindless savages, who didn't care who got caught up in their path of violence...now lying beaten and dying in the wreckage of their pride; a clutch of primitive boy-men, to whom courage and prowess in combat really mattered...now on the wrong end of the most humiliating defeat in their history; their own Marathon or Salamis. Charlie couldn't contain a big, cat-like grin.

"You're really impressed with that, aren't you?" Lynn asked from her usual prone position on the couch.

Her husband nodded. "More than you realise."

"Well...it wouldn't be the first time you'd bought me a present that *you* wanted."

"This is for both of us," he said.

"It's alright," she replied. "While it matters so much to you, you can have it all."

He looked round at her, but her attention was fixed on the TV again. Despite the constant scorn and sarcasm, he still loved his wife. He remembered what she'd once been...and perhaps could be again. Nothing was impossible at the moment. Charlie gazed at the hoplite. He'd roll back the years. He was invincible.

⋌⋮⋋

The following day, he went to see Roy Prendergast.

He'd been trying to work out the value of the smack he'd brought in from Holland, and figured that it had to be worth at least three times the twenty-grand he'd owed the gang boss, because Prendergast was never happy with anything unless it left him well in profit.

Sixty grand, then. It was a nice round figure.

He smiled as he parked up opposite Prendergast's garage. A moment later, he was crossing the road, vaguely aware as he did that someone else had fallen into step beside him. Charlie was dressed in jeans, a sweat-top and trainers. So, he sensed, was his companion. It was odd, but it seemed to be the way of it. Charlie didn't mind. He'd always wondered what it would be like to have a twin.

Prendergast and his two sons, Phil and Dean, were working on a couple of cars. They were all three of them in overalls. Various engine-parts were scattered across the oily floor. They glanced at Charlie with only mild interest as he stood in the doorway. Evidently they couldn't see anybody else...at least, not yet. This also seemed to be the way of it.

163

"I've come for my cut," he said.

Prendergast himself finally came over, wiping his hands on a greasy rag. "What?"

"My share."

Prendergast glanced at his two sons, genuinely bemused. "Share of what?"

Charlie shrugged. "I didn't run those drugs over here for nothing, Roy. Fifty percent seems fair, considering the risk. Shall we say thirty grand?"

Prendergast gazed at him for a moment, amused, then his lip curled in a menacing sneer. "You're serious, aren't you?"

Charlie nodded. "I'm also serious about the other fifty percent."

"What other fifty percent?"

"The fifty percent I'll be taking of everything you make from now on."

The gangster was too stunned by this to reply.

"Call it protection," Charlie added cheerfully. "That should cover it."

"Protection?" Prendergast now spoke in a whisper. "I'll show you protection! Lads…show this mental bastard the way out!"

Charlie turned as the burly Prendergast juniors came across the garage towards him, their grimy hands clenched into fists. Phil Prendergast looked as if he was really about to enjoy himself. Charlie held his ground, however. Angered, they ran at him…and the intervention was so swift, they didn't even see it.

Phil Prendergast took a hay-making punch, which broke his nose clean across his face. He went down like a sack of spuds, dark blood flowing through his groping fingers. Confused, Dean Prendergast grabbed up a wrench and lurched towards this new assailant, but in a shimmering flash, a sword had appeared…a lethal half-yard of double-edged steel, the infamous *gladius* of the classical age. Blinded with rage, Dean Prendergast struck hard with the wrench, but the sword swept out faster, made good contact and clove…severing flesh and bone mid-way at the point between wrist and elbow.

The lopped-off hand spun through the air in a fine crimson mist, still clutching its grubby work-tool. Dean Prendergast could only gawk at his horrendous wound, but not for long…for the counter-strike then followed, a stunning blow to the skull with the weapon's pommel. The maimed man crashed heavily to the garage floor, his head smacking the concrete.

Phil Prendergast now came howling back into the action, only at the last moment to spot the gore pumping from his senseless brother's stump, and to throw himself down on his knees, where he tried to staunch it with his own hands. Even this vaguely chivalrous act bought him no time. A savage kick shattered his front teeth, and a second downward smash with the pommel, toppled him into unconsciousness as well.

Through it all, the two lads' father had stood there bug-eyed, as if he couldn't quite believe what was going on in front of him. When the triumphant intruders finally turned and faced him, he gave a wild, chicken-like squawk and scampered away through the adjoining door to his office.

THE HOPLITE

It was a cul-de-sac, of course. And small. Prendergast turned round and round in a sweat-sodden frenzy...then the big guy who'd come with Stockton, the psycho with the curly white hair, followed him in. Frantic, the gangster rummaged in a drawer and brought out his old Webley automatic. He aimed and fired at his enemy's chest, yet it had no discernible effect; the psycho just came on. A bullet-proof undershirt? But the bastard hadn't even flinched! Prendergast got a second round off, this one in the guy's face, and from point-blank range. He expected to *hear* the impact, to see the slug rip a hole the size of a saucer in the intruder's forehead. But he saw nothing of the sort.

The next thing the garage-owner knew, the gun had been slapped from his grasp, and an iron hand had clamped his throat and was forcing him back against the girlie-calendar on the wall, exerting choking pressure. Prendergast gasped as much in terror as he did in agony. The eyes boring into him were unimaginably awful; they were blank eyes, empty eyes...yet something at the very back of them denoted extreme horror and bewilderment.

"The price has now gone up to seventy percent," said Charlie from the doorway, "to cover my partner's trouble. In fact, on this occasion, we'll call it a neat one-hundred."

Prendergast—his mouth running with saliva, his neck-bones set to explode—glanced up and the saw the *gladius* hovering just over his head, bloodied and gleaming, like a guillotine blade. One blow from it would split him to the guts...he was sure.

"Well?" Charlie asked.

Desperately, the gangster nodded, and a moment later, he'd been manhandled across the office and was down on his knees in the corner in a panting, crumpled heap. He had to remove two panels from the plywood wall, to get to the safe, but he did it hurriedly, almost gratefully. He could still sense that blade at his back, that terrible, shearing blade. The moment the safe was open, he started handing over its contents in generous bundles...great wads of twenty-pound notes fastened with elastic bands.

Charlie produced a plastic shopping-sack from his pocket, and began stuffing it full. "I'll take the dope too," he said matter-of-factly. "A man's got to start out somewhere."

Prendergast made no objection. Once the money had gone, at least a hundred grand's worth, at Charlie's estimation, he dug out the sachets of heroin; there were eight more on top of the eight from the last delivery. Charlie bagged the lot of it.

Prendergast then flopped down onto his tearful, sweat-soaked face, exhausted by sheer terror.

Charlie liked that...he liked it so much, that he only stamped on the back of the gangster's head once, before he made his way out.

It was a joy, pouring the river of cash onto the carpet in front of his wife.

The look on her face was priceless. Naturally enough, she asked him where it had come from, and, naturally enough, he declined to say, telling her instead that if she didn't shut her yap and do exactly as he told her from now on, she wouldn't see a penny of the next consignment. A touch of her old fire returned at that, but Charlie had the last word. He informed her that he was going into business, and that it was going to be very profitable, but that there was only work for one. Her job was simply to be a good wife to him...which was easy. All it entailed was getting in shape and going regularly to the beautician. It didn't even mean spoiling her hands with cooking and cleaning. Once they'd gottten out of this crummy neighbourhood, and that would be soon, he'd employ a skivy to do that humdrum stuff. He intended to provide them with a beautiful new house, and he wanted Lynn to be its prime ornament.

His wife spent the rest of the evening counting and re-counting the loot, and he spent it making phone-calls. Charlie wasn't exactly what he'd call *connected,* but he knew a lot of people—not least those various suppliers, couriers and dealers he'd met while muling for the Prendergasts, so it wasn't difficult setting up his own network.

Of course it wasn't all going to be plain sailing. He'd only bruised the opposition, not slaughtered it. The retaliation came exactly one week later, in the form of a hose-pipe through his front letter-box at around three o'clock in the morning.

Charlie, who'd been lying awake expectantly, heard it, leaped from his bed and ran to the top of the stairs. But before the petrol had even started to gurgle through, the would-be arsonists were ambushed. Charlie chuckled as he descended, listening to the crashing and banging in his porch, to the grunting and squealing, to the heavy fists impacting on skin and bone. A moment later, he pulled the lounge curtain to one side, and saw that the melee had moved away from the house and onto the road. Two ski-masked men—one who by his shape was paunchy and middle-aged, and one who looked younger—were now staggering away from a tall, pursuing figure. As Charlie had expected, cracks of gunfire soon sounded, but the stalk went on. There was a glint of metal as the sword appeared, and with terrified shrieks the masked figures turned tail and fled.

He never saw Roy Prendergast again. In fact, three days after the incident with the petrol, Charlie drove past the fat guy's garage, and noticed that it was "Closed until further notice." The windows and doors were all locked. There was no sign of life on its forecourt.

From this point on, life was relatively easy for the Stocktons. Money, as they say, attracts money. The following year Charlie bought Lynn a four-bedroom detached house in one of the town's swisher suburbs. He got her her own car, and even set up a small print-business, to act as a front for his real operations. He no longer needed to make the delivery runs himself, but employed professionals to do it. Needless to say, a variety of precautions had been taken to ensure that if any one of them got pinched, the trail wouldn't lead back home. After years and years handling all the shittiest jobs, Charlie was now determined that he'd keep his own hands lily-white.

In enforcement terms, he anticipated no major problems. Charlie already had his own personal protection sewn up, but his wasn't a large town, and it wasn't as if it was swimming with rivals. If strong-arm stuff ever was called for, he could always hire wannabes, but as a rule Charlie preferred a quiet life. Treat people well and expect—and get—the same in return. That was his motto.

Except…it didn't *always* work out like that.

The phone call that took him to Worthington Park that fateful evening came on his mobile while he dozed in first-class on a business trip down to London. Charlie was puzzled when he picked the phone up…he didn't recognise the caller's number. He was even more puzzled when he heard the voice of Phil Prendergast. For once, however, the gangster's son was civil, even polite. There was no gloating, no aggression. They had to talk, he said. Charlie asked why. Phil Prendergast assured him it was to all their mutual advantage; could he please have a meet with Mr. Stockton and his albino friend? Charlie didn't trust the Prendergasts as far as he could throw them, but he was intrigued by this. They were outclassed, and they knew it—after all, when gunfire fails you, what else is there? Perhaps like all bullies, though, they'd sensed the power-shift and were resigned to shifting their allegiance? It happened.

So Charlie said okay. He agreed.

ᴗ:ᴕ

And that was how he found himself approaching the bandstand, on a cold February night.

It wasn't a bad place, in actual fact. Rhododendrons might hem the various footpaths in, but this central area of the park was more open…extensive lawns and flower beds swept away from the bandstand on all sides, so it would be difficult, if not impossible, for anyone to sneak up unseen, even in the darkness.

Phil Prendergast was waiting there. As he'd promised, alone.

Charlie paused before he went any further. The bandstand was a creaky old structure. It consisted of a raised circular platform with a diameter of about twenty feet, and a pagoda-type roof supported on four pillars. Basically though, it was wide open. Nobody could conceal themselves in or around it. Satisfied, Charlie proceeded, finally mounting the two steps onto the stand and confronting the son of his former arch-enemy.

Of the two of them, it was Phil Prendergast who seemed the more nervous. He was clad in jeans, a jumper and a heavy black donkey-jacket, but was hugging himself in the cold, and moving repeatedly from one sneakered foot to the other.

He still bore the visible scars of their last meeting. When he spoke, his voice sounded hollow, mushy. "You look well," he said.

Charlie didn't bother with small-talk. "I'm going to have to pat you down."

The younger man shrugged and held his arms out. Charlie approached and commenced a light body-search. It was routine more than anything else, a few careful fingers here and there to check for guns or knives. He didn't know for sure, but it was a near-certainty that modern bugging devices were smaller and more sophisticated than the old-fashioned wire-and-mike. Not that this worried him unduly. He had no intention of saying anything incriminating.

"Where's your partner?" Phil Prendergast asked, as Charlie turned him around.

"He's close," Charlie said. "Don't worry about him."

"I need to talk to *both* of you."

"My friend doesn't talk much. He leaves that to me."

"This wasn't the deal."

Charlie straightened up again. "We haven't got a deal. Say what you've got to say, or I'm off."

The lad considered, then: "I was thinking...I could do a job for you."

Charlie smiled and shook his head slowly. "No dice."

"Look...what's the point in us fighting?" Phil protested. "Why don't we pool our resources?"

"You haven't got any resources, you're out of the game."

The lad shook his head vehemently. "My dad may be, but *I'm* not."

Charlie still wasn't impressed. "You expect me to believe you'd side against your old man?"

"I'm not siding against him. I'm just branching out on my own."

"But I don't *need* you," Charlie said.

Phil Prendergast was starting to look desperate. "I bet you don't need me *against* you!"

"That's what this is, then, is it? A threat?"

The lad mopped sweat from his brow. "Take it anyway you want."

Charlie sighed. "It doesn't have to be this way, you know. You could just walk away."

"What...like you did, you mean? When my brother was bleeding to death." Now the lad took up a combative stance. "You know he died from that wound?"

Charlie shrugged. "Your brother died? I knew nothing about that."

Phil Prendergast curled his lip in contempt—just the way his father used to. "You'll bloody know about this!" And he spat something bright and flat into his hand.

It was a razor-blade. It had been taped to the roof of his mouth.

Charlie tensed and backed off. Phil Prendergast came swiftly towards him...but stopped dead in his tracks, as a giant hand grabbed him by the scruff of the neck. The hoodlum slashed round with the blade, but met only thin air. Then he was flung, hard...like a doll or dummy. He hurtled a good six feet across the bandstand, and crashed into a steel pillar with a colossal *clong!* The entire bandstand quivered. The hoodlum then collapsed in a heap, but he was still conscious enough to give a single choked command: *"Now...!"*

The gunfire was deafening on the cold night air, three massive reports, which rang around Charlie's ears as he dived to the floor. The stupid bastards hadn't learned anything, he thought feverishly, as he rolled towards the steps. But this time they'd pay for it.

This time they'd *really* pay.

"Kill 'em...kill 'em all!" he shouted, as he threw himself off the stand onto the park path, expecting to hear the instant rasp of steel as a sword was drawn from a hidden scabbard, expecting the hack and chop of the butcher's yard to follow...but all he heard was silence.

Perplexed, he glanced up. The first thing he saw was the looming shadow of his guardian...tottering, about to fall. Charlie watched with incredulity. On the other side of the stand, meanwhile, a pale patch of moonlight showed Phil Prendergast's disbelieving but delighted face, sweat gleaming silver on his brow.

"Again!" the hoodlum cried hoarsely.

Three more shots rang out, and with each one, the hoplite juddered, as though in response to awesome hammer-blows. The last one flung him violently from his feet. Charlie didn't wait to see any more. He leaped up and hared away along the path.

"Yeah...run, you chickenshit!" Phil Prendergast jeered after him. "Run!"

But Charlie didn't hear. He was too busy listening to something else... something that repeated itself over and over again in his mind's ear.

The smashing and shattering of glass, or porcelain...*or was it plaster?*

He drove home like a lunatic, screeched to a halt on his gravel drive, staggered to and crashed through the front door, and bounded into his spacious lounge. Lynn was in there, standing by the mantle, staring confusedly down at the corner of the stone hearth, where a scattering of fragments was all that remained of the figurine. The scream of rage built in Charlie's chest like a volcanic eruption, and finally tore itself from his throat. *"You stupid bitch...what have you done!"*

"I...I haven't done anything," she stammered.

"You haven't done anything! You've broken it!"

"It broke itself," she replied helplessly.

"Ornaments don't break themselves!" he thundered, grabbing up the plinth, which oddly still remained on the mantle-piece. *"Jesus H. Christ in a cartoon!"*

And before he knew what he was doing, he'd hit her with it...swung it round in a brutal arc and slammed it into her left temple. It was a shuddering blow, and Lynn slumped straight to the ground, her legs simply buckling beneath her, her head falling at a ninety-degree angle.

Charlie wasn't finished, however. *"Don't you realise what this means?"* he howled, kicking at her body over and over again, landing the boot perhaps ten or eleven times before he suddenly realised she was totally limp, totally unresponsive.

He gazed down at her, breathless. Her eyes were still open. But they were dull and glazed. The left one filled slowly with blood.

A sickly moment passed, then Charlie staggered backwards across the room, the weapon still stuck in his hand...like it was glued there. He fell onto his couch, and in that same instant there came a furious pounding at the front door. Zombie-like, he glanced sideways through the bay window, and saw a spinning blue beacon at the far end of the drive. Which surely wasn't impossible. Not in so short a time.

None of this was possible!

But then again, when the Lord moved in such mysterious ways...

In another part of town, in a smaller, less showy lounge, Roy Prendergast treated himself to a celebratory whisky. There was a good night ahead on the telly, his wife was busy cooking what smelled like a delicious supper, and by now his son Phil should be on his way back from the park.

Across the room from him, on the mantle...there was a plaster figurine. It wasn't especially fine, rather crude in fact. But it was clear what it depicted. On the plinth, it read:

Elite Fighting Forces of History
SS Panzergrenadier, sharpshooter unit
Circa 1942

Chained Melody

PATRICIA LEE MACOMBER

It was fall and a radiant burst of color had set the world on fire. Fall, glorious fall, small town America caught in the throes of last-gasp passion and bracing against the long slide into icy oblivion. Outside, young boys chased torrents of leaves along the sidewalk with a football for motivation. Dogs yapped at their heels and chilly winds dug sharp teeth into their backs.

Inside, Philip Singletary stared out the window, his face hidden from prying eyes by a large circle of breath-steam as he focused on the boys, tracking them in silent envy and praying, wishing with all his heart that he could be anything but what he was. A quick slam of his fist against the window sill and he was off, crossing the room in raging strides to plunk himself down on a stool which had long since passed its prime.

Slender fingers caressed the keys, testing the resilience and limbering themselves in a silent exercise. His eyes watched their movements, watched as someone else apparently controlled a part of his body. Having a gift was another way of saying you had nothing else, that your life was limited to that gift, bereft of normalcy. Philip hated the gift, he hated himself. All he wanted to be was somebody else…anybody else.

He was playing now; couldn't remember having started. The fact that he couldn't place the song annoyed him more. It was soft and lilting, tickled at his ears the same way his urge to play itched at the pit of his stomach. He was helpless in that state, forced to play through to the end, until his body was left

171

limp and dangling from the edge of the stool, eyes closed, mouth open, foaming as though he had gone mad.

Philip's eyes were closed. His skin danced with the electricity, danced in time with the music until he could no longer hear the melody. He played softly, his hands moving mechanically over the keys. Even lack of control over his hands could not break the mood, couldn't dull the sultry tone of that piano or the haunting tune which broke free from its strings and echoed through the frame house. He had played for her three times and three times she had come to him, wishing to be set free. But Philip had failed her. He had not been able to play well enough or long enough to bring her to that final stage.

He felt her arrival like fire in his blood. Instantly, his skin was on fire with the change in atmosphere. Still, he dared not look, couldn't risk that first glimpse of her half-formed body. It would take long moments, he knew, for her to come into full view. Until then, all he could do was play but as far as he could tell, his fingers were no longer on the keys. Control of the music had fallen to the piano itself rather than to him.

The soft eardrum pop of air being displaced made Philip jump. One long strand of golden hair cascaded before his eyes, brushing against his long lashes and teasing over his soft features, his skin chilled as a breeze rippled through the room. The window was open, yes, but the air outside was warm and fresh. This gust had been cold and stale, fetid as though it had been too-long held in a pair of misused lungs.

That veil of long dark lashes fluttered open on crystal blue eyes, two deep-set shining orbs that danced their way across the room and landed on the gently swaying vision before him. His full, almost feminine lips pushed his cheeks back into dimples and once more he was aware of the world.

"Hello, Sherese." He tossed back that errant strand of hair, revealing the full depth of those eyes and one nearly luminescent cheek. One more glance was spared for her, briefly and from the corner of his eye.

The woman before him feigned indifference. She was bright and soft, draped in a diaphanous gown and ethereal as she danced before him. Long dark hair drifted on an unseen wind as she moved, her lithe body seemingly fluid and trapped in the currents of the breeze. She was as helpless to resist the dance as Philip was to resist the music. Yin to his yang, she executed a perfect pirouette and targeted him with those dazzling green eyes.

"I thought you'd never play again, dear Philip. What took you so long to call me?" Her voice, harmony to his melody, rose and fell with the notes from the piano, blended with them and fell away into a soft hum.

Philip never missed a beat. His fingers rippled over the keys in a long wave of motion and then slowed to soft chords. "You know I have to rest between sessions. It isn't easy to do this, you know." He watched her movements, tracked her progress across the room as she swirled in and out of furniture, translucent and soft, like a cloud as she danced.

CHAINED MELODY

Sherese leaped through the air, one long leg stretched out behind her, one before, both elongating, forcing themselves to meet the demands of height and touching down on the floor. "I'm sorry. I don't mean to nag at you. I just need to be...free."

Philip watched her dance, his head swimming more with each movement, thoughts tangled in the sight of her, the thin fabric of her dress as it caressed her skin, seemed to dance of its own accord. He was only twelve but already he could feel the pull of those curves, the way her breasts thrust forward as she arched, the thrill as the fabric slid over one thigh, nearly revealing her charms. He felt a stirring deep in his soul and he looked away, drew his eyes from her and back to the piano. "I know."

Something about that song reminded Philip of his mother, something deep and sorrowful. He could almost see her sitting next to him, could nearly feel the touch of her soft hand as she stroked back his sodden hair and tried to calm him. He had been only four then, that day the first vision had appeared as he played. Without lesson or practice, he had simply climbed onto the stool and begun to play. What appeared before him was no less beautiful than Sherese was now, but it had frightened him just the same.

"You have been given a special gift, Philip," his mother had said in that soft lilting voice of hers. "When you play, even the Gods will listen."

Ever since that day, Philip had played in all sorts of places, traveling the back roads and playing in seedy bars, pleasing the crowds in revival tents and stunning the elite from concert halls. But wherever he played, spirits appeared and the crowds faded into small groups of fearful admirers, clutching at each other and staring in awe-struck silence as he gently freed them. The visions weren't always as lovely as Sherese. Sometimes they were horrible and vicious.

"Don't stop!" Sherese called suddenly, her voice trilling as she lost her tenuous hold on reality. "Please!"

Philip shook himself free of those memories, clawed his way back into the real world to realize that he had nearly quit playing entirely. What had previously been an autonomic function was now produced only by sheer force of will on his part. He had to concentrate to make his fingers move. They ached. His head throbbed. A quick glance at the clock told him that he had been playing not for minutes, but for hours.

Outside, the sun had set, obscured now by a thick blanket of murky sky. Lamps had come on in the houses across the street, casting small chessboards of light onto the lawn before them, and a long trail of headlights had begun winding its way up the hill, their numbers thinning as they dispersed to parts unknown. Philip watched that trail for a moment, fascinated by the twinkling of those lights as they wove in and out of streets and houses, behind trees and past signs. As he watched, he found his rhythm again, the notes flying free, floating from his fingertips once more. He straightened slowly, stretching out his back and easing the kinks at the base of his neck.

"You were thinking of your mother again, weren't you, Philip?" Sherese still danced, her voice devoid of that breathless quality by which mortals are usually affected.

"Yes." He rippled the keys in a long glissando, up and then back. "She's been gone nearly six years but I..."

The back door creaked open, slammed against the wall, a bass drum beat to the staccato snares of his father's boots. Thus ended all talk of his mother, at least for now. But the picture of her face as she looked on that last day was embedded in his mind. It tore at his heart and drew the sadness into the music.

"My God! He's playing again." Daniel Singletary's tone was soft, almost reverent. His eyes, locked on the middle of the room where Sherese danced, were blind to her. "Is there..."

Philip nodded curtly and continued to play. A deep ache traveled up his arm, settled into his joints. He sank his teeth into his lower lip to stave off that bit of agony. He still saw the sofa as he stared through Sherese. He would be playing for a long time to come.

"I'll leave ya be, boy. Just holler if ya need me." Daniel clapped one beefy hand on the boy's shoulder as he passed, nearly throwing him off balance and toppling him to the floor. He had never actually seen the visions, though he knew from his wife's telling of them that they were real, that his son's work was important. It was Philip's talent that worked the miracles but Daniel was the one who chose their destinations, arranged for the revivals, brought in the donations. And it was Daniel who never saw the spirits, never knew if he was selling absolution or snake oil.

Philip righted himself as best he could without the use of his hands and blew back a thin veil of hair that had fallen into his eyes. Crickets had joined the chorus. He focused to block out their song and continue his own.

"It has to be tonight, Philip. Please don't stop playing." Sherese's voice was fringed with worry, her words spat out quickly, as though she were in some kind of pain...or pleasure.

"Don't worry. I won't stop. Not till it's done." His bladder was full. He was hungry. He looked down to see that his hands had swollen, the skin drawn painfully tight and red from the heat of pain.

"And when it is?" Sherese cavorted with the breeze, dancing behind the drapes which now billowed in that cool wind and sailing through them unfettered.

"I'll go. We always move on, town to town, house to house. Anywhere but..."

"...home?" Sherese slowed her movements, drew alongside him for a brief moment before flitting away again.

"Yes." Philip picked up the tempo, trying to play his way out of the truth he couldn't fight on his own.

Sherese followed the lead of the music, let her body drift into Philip's pace. Her feet pounded the floor in a wild flurry of movement, her face drawn into a smile of pure ecstasy. He watched her, playing faster, marveling at her ability to keep up. She was so serene when she danced, he so enraptured. Suddenly, his face slid into a scowl, that smile dripping from his lips as he stared.

"Sherese, look!" He never missed a beat. Not one finger landed on a wrong key as he stared at her in awe.

Sherese slowed her movements, hesitated long enough to flash one hand before her face. Philip quickly adjusted, slowing the tempo and gazing at her form, now solid, tangible. She shifted slightly, arms reaching high, grasping at stars and then drizzling fingertips down over her chest.

"It's happening. Oh God! It's really happening." Her hips traced small circles in the air as she moved, slowly, inexorably drawn to him.

Philip watched, transfixed by the image of her now-solid body as it drifted away from him, her bare feet finally grazing the floor. The air had gone still. The night creatures were silent. Only the piano music remained, that and the hard beat of his heart.

"Philip, I'm scared." Her face was a study in grief, that deep longing to be free now eclipsed by the fear of what freedom itself would mean. A lone tear wound its way down her cheek, escaping from the tip of her chin and falling to the floor.

"It's okay, Sherese. It won't hurt. I promise." He had been playing since morning; his back and arms were numb from the pain. As his eyes trailed downward, his face paled. There was blood all over the keys, his blood. He shook himself free of that sight, tried to clear his head. The words were soft as he spoke, but they cut through the air and into Sherese's soul. "It's time."

Daniel had crept quietly into the doorway to stand and watch his son, his own face a mask of pain. Philip caught a brief glimpse of him as he shifted his gaze from keyboard to Sherese and back again. She had stopped dancing, stood dead-still in the center of the room with a backdrop of fall leaves as they gently cascaded past the window. Philip couldn't bear to look at her, couldn't watch what happened next. He never had any idea which way it would go, where they would end up.

His words were barely audible over the soft murmur of his father's prayers. "Godspeed, Sherese."

Carefully, each movement a study in agony, Philip shifted on the piano bench. His eyes grazed his father's morose face as they passed, then locked onto the keyboard and held for a moment before he closed them. He blocked out the sight of it all, shut out the music as it pounded in his ears. In one quick movement, he jerked his hands away from the keyboard, letting them hover inches above the keys, trembling and dripping blood onto the ivory. In an instant, the music was gone, the last of it rippling over the sounding board and dying away note by note.

At the piano, Philip was board-stiff. He was afraid to look, terrified of what he would see when he did. Suddenly, there was a hand on his shoulder. He sat up straighter, rolled that shoulder to dislodge his father's grasp. "Is she gone?"

"I can't tell." His voice was deep and resonant, filled with a mystical kind of awe. Philip felt him turn, incline toward the middle of the room, looking. "Yes."

Philip turned slowly, letting his eyes find what his father had seen. Nothing remained of the beautiful Sherese save for a small pile of dust on the floor. Slowly, each movement painful and unsteady, he stood from the piano bench and crossed the room. "I'll get an urn."

The boy moved away slowly, feet dragging across the wood floor, eyes glued to it. Each step took an eternity, a force of will that he thought impossible. When he returned, Daniel was kneeling on the floor, hands clasped in prayer, lips working silently. Philip watched him for a few moments, then bent to scoop what was left of Sherese into the urn.

Each time Philip performed one of these little miracles, he and his father moved. There was a new house to get used to, new friends and schools, new lives. And in every house, every place that he lived or played or studied, there was pain, the agony of a soul trapped and screaming to be set free. He never knew who or what these spirits were. He knew only that it was his job, his God-given duty to see that they were freed.

"How soon do we leave," Philip sighed as he sat back on his heels, suddenly aware that his father was watching him. "Shall I go pack my stuff?"

"Not just yet, son." He stood, placing one hand on the boy's shoulder for balance and squeezing a bit. "This here's a nice little town. I think we'll stay around for awhile. It's about time ya finished a school year in the same place ya started, hm?"

Philip's face lit up, his eyes danced with captured light and unbound joy. "Do you mean it?"

"'Course I do. It's getting late now. Go get some rest, boy." Daniel tousled the boy's hair and proffered a thin smile as Philip clutched the urn tightly to his chest and wandered off toward his room.

Philip stopped, thought better of it. Slowly, he turned to face Daniel again, a quizzical look shimmering in his eyes. "Dad, why can't we just go home? What are you afraid of?"

The question landed flat on Daniel's ears, forcing tears into his eyes before he could will them away. "That you'll conjure up your Mama, boy. And I won't even be able to see her." He swiped at his suddenly runny nose with the back of one hand, shuffled his feet and frowned at his son. "And what are you afraid of, Philip?"

"That I won't." He turned then and made for his room quickly, like the proverbial fox escaping the hound, hot on the scent of secrets.

Mindless of the exhaustion, of the blood-stained fingers which worked at his shirt buttons, Philip stripped off his clothes and stretched out on the bed. Fingers laced behind his head, ankles crossed, he lay there, staring at the wood ceiling and smiling as he remembered Sherese's dance. He knew nothing of most of the souls he freed, knew only that somehow his playing gave them form, made them tangible, and that stopping the music set their spirits free of that form. Not all of them were as beautiful as Sherese, nor as gracious. Sometimes, they fought for their freedom rather than begged for it and more than once Philip had been nearly destroyed in that fight, drawn down into the pain and almost driven mad by it.

But Sherese was different. He hadn't just happened onto her tragic existence, he had sought her out. Philip leaned over and pulled open the drawer of his nightstand, fingers fumbling over marbles and scraps of paper as he sought that one prized possession. Pinched between thumb and forefinger, the paper found its way into the jaundiced light cast from a street lamp and embedded in the blanket in small squares. He squinted to bring the picture into focus, that long hair, the dazzling green eyes. Philip smiled as he read the headline, shifting the bit of newspaper to bring each word into the light, reading slowly through the entire obituary for the umpteenth time.

"Sherese Morgan is survived by one daughter, Beth Singletary, a son-in-law, Daniel Singletary, and one grandson, Philip Singletary. She died peacefully in the same house in which she was born." Philip tucked the piece of paper neatly into the drawer and slid it shut gently.

Philip smiled as he rolled over and stared at the ceiling, imagining it invisible, a glittering curtain of stars above him. "Don't worry, Dad. Mama will come to us. She has to. It's my music that frees them but it's the place they were born that calls them back."

Works of Art

J. F. GONZALEZ

When I walked into our motel room that night I didn't expect to find my husband missing, his blood drenching the walls.

The sudden shock was immense; like being sucker-punched in the stomach. This was similar, yet magnified the feeling of dread to immense proportions. With such a wide feeling of darkness looming in front of you, there's not much chance for escape.

Out along the two lane main drag of the town we had holed up in, the hum of traffic was faint amid the background noise of neighboring tenants watching TV, talking and laughing, splashing in the swimming pool. It was that which snapped me back to the harsh realities of what had just happened.

I was out the door and down the steps to our little Volvo, taking them two at a time. The only clothes I had were the ones on my back, my only belongings stashed inside my purse. I peeled away from the motel, down Interstate 5, heading south. Putting the distance between Nick's obvious death and my sanity.

I drove non-stop, stopping only to refuel and head back out on the road. I drove for hours at a time, not caring that I was speeding. Distancing myself as far away from the nightmare as possible was the only thing on my mind.

As I drove I could feel the tattoo on my back itch and burn as it sought virgin territory.

I still haven't found the nerve to expose my back to a mirror and watch the designs taking shape. Just feeling it, *knowing* it's taking place, is driving me mad.

What happened back at the hotel is quite simple: Nick was alone in the room while I was out getting groceries when they broke in. We were planning on staying at the little dive for another week before heading further east, toward northern Nevada and points beyond. I don't know how they found us. We used every trick in the book to make sure nobody was on our tail; we didn't use our credit cards, we used false names, and most importantly, we saw nobody on our tail through the drive. Whatever happens in the end, though, all boils down to the same conclusion: they had found what they wanted.

From the amount of blood on the walls, the broken headboard of the bed, the overturned lamp on the floor, and the scattered clothes and other items on the floor, I surmised that Nick had fought hard. I was afraid they had taken what they wanted right then and there, judging by the amount of blood in the room. Fortunately for my sanity, they hadn't. I wouldn't have been able to stand seeing Nick in the state they would have left him in.

I can't stand to see it. His face is superimposed in my mind forever now. It's an image I can't banish no matter how hard I try.

❧

What started our life as fugitives on the run was a classified ad in the *LA Weekly* I saw almost two years ago. Before I get to that, though, perhaps I should tell you about Geraldo Montivaldi, the man who placed the ad.

Geraldo Montivaldi had been one of Italy's most prestigious artists to emerge in the last twenty years. Always controversial, always breaking the rules and setting new limits, Geraldo was this generation's answer to Goya or Rubens or Bosch, with perhaps a touch of Bok as well. He won a European Art Festival for a painting—"A Day in the Life Of…"—that depicted a young, pregnant Negro woman hanging clothes on a sagging clothesline in the backyard of a New York Brownstone. Pterodactyls swarmed overhead, dropping large, white eggs that exploded in what appeared to be a noxious, green gas whose mist trailed into a huge mushroom cloud exploding off in the distance. Long reptilian fingers with razor sharp claws parted their way through the opening between the woman's legs as she almost nonchalantly went about her chores. Clustered around her, and seemingly oblivious to her presence, are four children, presumably hers, screaming and crying with looks of pain, rage, and fear. The children's eyes are a deep, blood red, and the faint nubs of horns can be seen slightly beneath their fine, silken hair just shy of the hairline.

When we first saw the print at a gallery in Encino, Nick immediately said that it disturbed him. It didn't have the same effect on me; I've always thought it was a beautiful piece of work.

The themes in Montivaldi's art always centered on the images of pain and fear, sex and death, eternal destruction and chaos. Equally beautiful and terrifying, the emotions one felt while looking at one of his pieces would often move you to tears or provoke a feeling of utter revulsion, sometimes both rising

WORKS OF ART

from the same work. Despite the effect "A Day in the Life of..." had on Nick, he became enamored with Montivaldi's work.

While his work wasn't widely known, Montivaldi had a strong underground following. There were rumors about him that were as dark as his visions; that he dabbled in the occult; that the visions he received from his occult workings often drove him to madness; that the results of those rituals resulted in most of his works in paintings and sculptures. It was also rumored that Montivaldi was obsessed with his work, that he finished everything he started.

Our dream was to some day be the proud owners of a Montivaldi original.

One day, a little over two years ago, Nick discovered in an interview in *Modern Art* magazine that Geraldo Montivaldi had taken up body art and modification as a hobby.

A few weeks later, while scanning through the classifieds of the *LA Weekly*, I noticed the aforementioned advertisement:

> *Artist Geraldo Montivaldi seeks subject for the purpose of practicing body art, specifically tattooing. Male or female, must be over eighteen. Must be drug free, HIV negative (proof from board-certified testing center required). OK if subject already has a few tattoos. Artist is working on creating a 'human canvas' and the subject will be the end result of what will probably be a near full-body covering of intricate designs. Serious inquiries only. (818) 793-8055.*

Naturally, I showed Nick the ad immediately. He called and made an appointment to meet the artist for an interview.

The following week was spent getting the required HIV test, waiting for the results, and getting the certification. Nick was nervous. He hoped the interview would go well. I assured him that it would. "You'll be the perfect subject," I told him repeatedly. "Don't worry."

When I first met Nick he was already graced with seven gorgeously rendered tattoos that rippled across his taut skin. A bat silhouetted against a blood red moon on his upper left bicep was the first, followed by a black rose entangled in cobwebs with blood dripping off the thorns on his right bicep. A serpentine dragon circling around a mean looking dagger marked the underside of his left forearm, while a helter-skelter mirage of demons and skulls emblazed in fire occupied the underside of his right arm. A dozen ancient-looking keys with Celtic symbols sat on his right chest. His right ankle bore a heart and a rose with an old girlfriend's name. A pair of red lips were poised over his groin, as if some woman had given him a lingering kiss there. His most recent was a banner over the black rose on his right bicep with my name inside it. He got it four months after we met.

Unlike the black-inked dragons and scantily clad women that graced the skin of bikers and spike-haired punk rockers, Nick's markings were etched out of utmost care. The designs were rendered with precision and skill; not some back

181

alley tattoo parlor's work here. Nick demanded the best in everything, and that included the markings he chose to decorate his body with. I knew he wanted to decorate his flesh with more than what he had, but full body tattoos often come out looking both unattractive, and unnatural. Only the most exquisite of designs would be allowed on Nick's body. Of that I was certain.

If Montivaldi chose Nick as a suitable canvas as an outlet for his brilliant vision, the solution to our problems would be solved: owning a priceless Montivaldi original without the hefty price tag. Montivaldi was doing the honors for free for the benefit of practice (I know that sounded scary at first, but *Modern Art* had a photo journal of the work Montivaldi had performed on himself, and they were brilliant). Wearing it on his skin would be an added bonus for Nick.

Nick's appointment was on a Tuesday evening, at a home in Sherman Oaks.

We were both nervous when we pulled up in front of the house, which was on a quiet, tree-lined street in a cul-de-sac nestled far from the main thoroughfares of Van Nuys Boulevard. I clutched Nick's hand in a gesture of support as we walked up the lawn to the front porch and rang the doorbell.

The man that answered the door was tall, lanky, and very thin. He had a hard edge to him that sort of reminded me of Keith Richards, without the corpse-like appearance. His long black hair was speckled with gray, framing his sunken face. His eyes were encased in blackened pits of sockets. His skin was leathery, parched. His thin form was clothed in billowy slacks and a white, long-sleeved shirt; the sleeves were rolled up to the elbows, showing a multitude of gorgeous designs on his left forearm. A single gold ring adjourned the pinkie of his left hand. I think we knew immediately that this man was Montivaldi.

The man's kind, gray eyes rested on us, lingered longer on Nick. "Please. Come in." His voice was strong and commanding.

We sat together on a velvet sofa in the living room. Nick's hand reached out and found mine. Our eyes were fixed on Montivaldi; a god in our midst.

"Thank you for coming," the man said, fixing us with that stare. "I'm Geraldo Montivaldi."

Nick and I murmured introductions and we shook hands with the artist. His grip was firm, his skin felt leathery. "Let's get the first part of our business done, shall we? May I see your identification and HIV card?"

Nick handed the identification and papers over. Montivaldi looked at them carefully, nodding. He handed them back, then asked to see Nick's work. Nick rolled up his sleeves and unbuttoned his shirt, revealing the collection he had acquired over the past three years. It appeared to me that Montivaldi looked impressed by not only the work Nick already had, but by his muscle and skin tone and the general physique of his body. Nick's body was a work of art itself.

Montivaldi rose. "This way." We followed him to the rear of the house to a room that had been converted into a makeshift tattoo studio. Paintings hung on the walls. What resembled a dentist's chair occupied the middle of the room. Montivaldi motioned Nick toward the chair. "Please. Take off your shirt and sit." Nick peeled his shirt off and reclined on the chair.

WORKS OF ART

Montivaldi sat down on a stool and put on a pair of glasses. He leaned forward, and for the next ten minutes his eyes and hands explored Nick's body. His long, artist's fingers traced invisible patterns on Nick's muscular frame, moved along his abdomen, his chest, his shoulders and biceps. It was like watching a masseuse or a chiropracter running his hands along the muscles of a patient, familiarizing himself with the body before him. Montivaldi asked Nick to turn over and Nick complied. The artist's hands roamed over Nick's back, and I could tell from the expression on his face that he appeared pleased.

When Montivaldi was finished he asked Nick to put his shirt on and to join him in the living room. I know Nick must have been shaking because I certainly was. Once seated, Montivaldi leaned forward. "Let's talk. Get to know each other a little. Shall we?"

I didn't think Nick would speak. For a moment I was afraid that he had become so tongue-tied over the shock of being in the same room as his idol that he would remain frozen.

Montivaldi leaned forward, his gaze fixed on Nick. "You have an idea of what images you would like to carry on you permanently. I'd like to hear it. I'd also like to hear what inspired you to answer my ad, and why you think you would be a good candidate for this project. And then I'd like to tell you what I have in mind. Does that sound fair?"

Nick nodded, and began to speak. Montivaldi listened, slowly stroking his chin as Nick spun his dreams. Then Montivaldi shared his own visions, and as they talked I sat back and grinned. They were connecting: Montivaldi had found his subject.

～:～

The process in its entirety took almost eight months.

Montivaldi completed the first session in a little less than four hours that first night. Using a high quality tattoo needle, he worked while the strains of Puccini filtered through the speakers. Nick sat in the dentist's chair, nursing a ginger ale. He was shirtless, his right arm propped out for Montivaldi to work on. Nick kept quiet the first half hour, his face giving away the awe he still felt, but soon giving in to idle relaxation.

Nick remained calm throughout the first session. The night passed rather slowly. Normally, tattooing is a pretty fluid procedure. A simple rose takes less than thirty minutes to complete. But the scope of the detail of Montivaldi's work on himself, and on Nick, convinced me to believe that if Nick ever decided to go all the way—a full body covering with Montivaldi as the artist—it could take several years. Such fine detail in art demands time and precision.

When Montivaldi was finished for the evening he leaned back, surveyed his work with a smile. "Ahh, yes. Beautiful. And I can make you so much more beautiful, yes?"

"You got it, my friend," Nick said, rotating his arm, which now bore the elegant design of the Major Arcane of the Tarot covering his entire right shoulder and upper arm. Montivaldi had tattooed the design over my banner. A slight jolt of jealousy erupted within me for a moment until Montivaldi soothed me with his calm voice.

"Don't worry, my sweet," he said as he began to pack up his equipment. "For you, I have big things in store. Many big things."

Montivaldi patched the fresh tattoo in gauze and bandaged it up. "Saturday. You'll be here early, yes?"

"You can count on it." Nick held out his hand, his features firm and strong. More in control. Montivaldi smiled and they shook hands. He ushered Nick and I out into the night, chattering gaily as we said our good-byes.

The next few months were filled with careful trepidation as we returned to the studio. Montivaldi was always calm, always charming. During his sessions, as the electric hum of the tattoo needle stung the air, he would rattle on about his life, his work. The sights he had seen from extensive traveling. The people he had met, the experiences treasured. I know it held Nick in absolute fascination, for as Montivaldi's skilled hands wove their patterns of delicate artwork across Nick's arm, I couldn't detect a single flinch. Nick's face was devoid of pain. Even when work was begun on the fleshy underside of his bicep, an area that is always tender, I caught no sign of discomfort. Instead I saw what might be pleasure. The work that was blossoming along Nick's body was both a sight to behold and an intoxicant to the eye.

The days and weeks passed quickly into months. When the first part of the process was finally finished on a late September evening, Montivaldi stepped back, wiped his sweaty brow with the back of his thin hand, and beamed down admiringly at his work. A warm, pleasant sensation ebbed through me at the sight of it and I forced myself to erase the smile that wanted to erupt on my features. Some things are easier said than done.

Nick's right arm, from just above the bony ridge of the wrist, all the way to the uppermost part of his shoulder, and then snaking down and blending over the right section of his chest just above the nipple, sported the most glorious display of artwork I had ever seen. Carefully structured, blended, and color schemed, it was a never-ending river of pastels that portrayed the deepest of emotions: love, hate, mirth, pity, and fear. Save for the small circular area of bone at the elbow, there wasn't a trace of skin on Nick's right arm that had gone untouched. Everything was smooth and even. Wickedly beautiful.

Nick surveyed the final touches in a full-length mirror behind the dentist's chair. The look on his face was of absolute joy.

"I can't believe this," he whispered. "I can't believe this. It's so... beautiful."

Montivaldi clenched and unclenched his fingers, loosening the joints. His smile was one of content. "There is more where that came from, my friend. Much, much more."

WORKS OF ART

Nick turned to look at his idol. "You aren't finished yet?"

"Far from it." Montivaldi stepped toward Nick and laid a hand on his left shoulder. His untouched shoulder. "When I am finished with you, you will be a living masterpiece. A rarity in the world of art." His voice had reduced to a brittle whisper. It sounded like the rustling of drapes in a cold, empty room.

A look of rising excitement surged behind Nick's flecked green eyes. I'm sure the thought that was racing through his head was the same one that was making tracks in mine: *You will be a living masterpiece.*

Montivaldi looked like a shriveled, eccentric professor detailing the wonders of life. "Nobody really sees tattoos for what they are. And people don't seem to realize, or care for that matter, what they *could* be. After all, this is the twenty-first century now, is it not? Tattoos aren't just crude designs for sailors and bikers. They are no longer acquired to show masculinity the way they were when I was a young man. You aren't branded a thug, or a social deviant anymore, if you get tattooed. Tattooing has regressed back to its original state of being: an art form."

"Yes," Nick said, his voice low and smooth. "The ancient Egyptians used to tattoo each other, as well as the ancient people of the Pacific Islands. In some of those cultures, tattooing was a form of religious expression: paying homage to certain pagan gods. Some cultures even consider tattooing as marks of beauty."

"That is correct." Montivaldi walked over to a small sink set against the wall and washed his hands. "Japanese and certain Asian cultures have regarded it as an art form long before Western Civilization picked up on it. Some of the most elaborate tattooing was done, and is still being performed, by primitive cultures."

"And now it's close to a full circle," I said. I hugged Nick closer to me, feeling his hot skin on my cheek. "There's always a rebirth in everything, always a circle."

"Precisely!" Montivaldi began drying his hands on a fresh, white towel. He mopped his tired, strained face as he tidied up his workspace. "No longer is it a custom practiced by soldiers and derelicts. Tattooing has gone out of the back alley and into the main thoroughfare of Beverly Hills."

When he was finished, Montivaldi stepped forward and touched both of us. His bony, callused hands were smooth, yet strong. Reassuring. "I will resume my work with Nicholas in approximately six months. Your friends and acquaintances will notice your new tattoos, will marvel at them, admire them. Some will find it disgusting that one so young will want to mar his body in such a seemingly unhealthy way. But they will neither suspect that these markings are the work of a *real* artist. If you were to walk into this gallery with a sleeveless shirt on tomorrow, art aficionados wouldn't give you a second glance. I know what most people think of body art. If Munch were to come back from the dead and render *The Scream* across your chest in stunning detail, the elite in the art community would be unimpressed."

"You're right," Nick said. "Art elitists can be pretty snobby."

Montivaldi harrumphed. "Yes. Know-nothings who lack the talent to produce anything themselves but would rather choose to attack and ridicule anything they can't, or refuse to, understand. I know the type. They're *everywhere.* "

Nick and I nodded. We knew it too. When you lived in the real world you run across them every day of your life.

Montivaldi stepped to the light switch at the door. "Well, I think we should call it a night." Nick moved to the sofa where his shirt lay and put it on. We moved out silently, each of us absorbed in our own thoughts and personal joy. Outside we parted with hugs, handshakes, and good-byes, with promises of meeting again in six months. Montivaldi was off to New York for two months, then Paris, and then London. Most of his engagements were for art festivals and other artistic endeavors, but he was also traveling to Iran to follow up on his occult studies, something he had mentioned casually the week before. When he returned he would begin work on Nick's left arm. "By then," he said as we walked out to our cars, "I'll need to get back into the work. I would have spent the months meditating on what is left to complete on your body, and will be not only inspired to continue, I'll be obsessed with continuing where I left off." He told Nick to begin formulating ideas of what he wanted. He even told me that, if I wished, he could do one for me. Something small. "We could perhaps start with something on your back, or above your breast." The invitation sounded so alluring that I tucked it away in the back of my mind for future reference. Just in case.

When Montivaldi returned six months later it was like a family reunion. We dined at a small, but intimate, Italian restaurant on Ventura Boulevard that first night and talked aimlessly. Montivaldi shared his past month's travels and experiences, which I'm sure Nick soaked up. After the meal, when we were safe within the haven of the gallery, Montivaldi popped the question. "So, what will it be?"

Grinning, Nick unveiled his ideas. Montivaldi nodded, soaking it all in. When Nick was finished, Montivaldi clapped his hands together once. "Fantastic! I love it. I love it. What you want dovetails perfectly with the inspiration I got on my trip to Iran. You shall have that and more. Much more."

Nick and I turned to each other, excited.

The limits of our fantasy were endless.

The next evening Montivaldi let the dreams run wild.

☙

The news of Montivaldi's death from a heart attack came as a crushing blow to us. If he was sick, we surely didn't notice it. That first meeting after not seeing him for six months was a reunion of old friends. The next time we saw the artist was at the gallery, after hours, during Nick's first session. If he seemed unusually hurried I figured it was because he was feeling rushed. Nevertheless, he did a splendid job that first session on Nicholas's left bicep. He followed it up over the course of the following day by adding color, tint, and background.

Montivaldi appeared preoccupied, as if there was something on his mind, but I thought nothing of it.

Three weeks after starting on Nick's left arm he asked if he could temporarily abandon that and start a new piece on his back—he had a vision he wanted committed to skin, one that was within the cosmic spirit of his recent occult studies. Nick agreed; they talked about it, and Montivaldi gave him an idea of what he was trying to accomplish. Nicholas was excited at the possibility, and gave his go ahead.

Montivaldi began working on Nick's back. I watched as the design took shape. As it burst forth amid its vast array of dark colors, I felt a mixture of excitement and dread. The image Montivaldi was etching into Nick's back was the conjuration of dark nightmares from the abyss, punctuated by a section of parchment-like designs with some hieroglyphic writings. Between his sessions with Nick he turned to me, rendering a similar design over my right breast; Nick could only take so much pain per session.

Montivaldi's ramblings on the evening of what was to be our last session with him were startling to me. He seemed nervous, and kept muttering that his studies and his recent trip to Iran had given him visions that he did not desire. I only remember certain phrases that he kept repeating between other bits of conversation. One of them was, "I must write it down lest I forget, and I must do it quickly." Another phrase that leaps into mind is this: "But I am afraid that if I don't get it down right, if I don't get it down quickly, that they will come in and finish it for me."

Nick and I had looked at each other with worry. Montivaldi had been working on a very small portion of the small of Nick's back, and my first impression was that the man was drunk. I asked him if he was feeling okay and he finally stopped his work. "No," he said, his eyes fearful and haunted. "I am exhausted. Please forgive me..."

We both insisted that he stop the work immediately. Nick further insisted that Montivaldi get some much needed rest. The artist nodded, then said cryptically, "Perhaps if I get away they will leave me alone." Nick and I glanced at each other again, wondering of our newly found friend's mental stability.

We made tentative arrangements to continue our sessions a week later.

And then, Sunday morning we learned of Montivaldi's death.

For me, it started with a slight itch. It hit Nick at precisely the same time. It was so subtle that I wasn't even aware that Nick was afflicted with it. With me it started in the area immediately surrounding my new tattoo. The itch trickled down to my right nipple, then blossomed to the left in the valley between my breasts. At first I thought it might be the signs of a rash, but when none came and the itch died down, I forgot about it. It was around then that the phone calls started coming.

Most people get hang-up calls. We've gotten our share of them. These calls could be described as hang-up calls; once answered, whoever was on the other line said nothing. I would hear an audible double-clicking, as if someone was hitting the hang-up button on their phone, jiggling it, trying to get a connection. I kept saying "Hello?" into the receiver, finally hanging up. That night I got three of them, one right after the other. By the fourth one I let it ring into voice mail. When I checked the readout on my caller-ID box it told me that the caller's ID was blocked.

This was cause for concern. Prior to this, the few hang-up calls we'd gotten that were similar came with the ID "Unknown Caller," which denoted that they came from either a telemarketing firm or a machine. A blocked call meant it was coming from somebody who didn't want their name and number broadcasted on the caller ID system.

In the space of the next hour, I got twenty calls from somebody with the same blocked ID.

When I checked our voice mail I saw that whoever it was had left messages.

And they were all that same clicking sound.

I began to feel nervous. Then, Nick came home with phone call stories of his own.

"This is weird," Nick said as the phone rang.

I was beginning to get scared. "Do you think it might have something to do with…" I didn't know what to say.

"With what?"

"Our tattoos."

"What do you mean?" Nick looked nervous. I could tell the way his eyes darted around the room.

"Montivaldi was working on something related to his studies, whatever they were," I said, not really knowing what to say, just knowing that everything was connecting somehow. "He was implementing it in the work he was doing on us and he died before he could finish. We both know he was involved in occult rituals. Do you think…"

The phone kept ringing. It was driving me crazy.

"Let's pack up and get out of town for a few days." Nick began removing clothes from the closet, throwing them in a large suitcase he had brought down. I moved closer to him, unable to understand why all these horrible threats were being made toward us. How could anybody have found out?

"Nick, we can't just leave! We have to do *something!*"

Nick looked at me. "Don't you feel it? Your tattoo?"

My response stuck in my throat. It was happening to him, too. It was then that I went into the bathroom and looked at my tattoo.

The scream shattered my nerves. Nick burst in and tried to calm me down. By the time I regained control of my senses I realized that it was I who had been screaming.

The tattoo Montivaldi had inked over my right breast had started to inch its way outward, spreading down toward the nipple and reaching up toward my collarbone.

WORKS OF ART

We left. That's all I can say. We packed up a few days worth of clothes and we got the hell out of our apartment. I can't explain what drove us to flee; it was just an instinctual feeling that told us to get the hell out.

And we did. And we eventually wound up in northern California, in the small motel room off Interstate 5, where they finally caught up to us.

∾∶∾

Even now it's the same road it was when Nick and I originally fled Los Angeles. The only difference now is the scenery.

The Arizona desert bears the same scenic landscape in the winter as it does in the summer. Barren. Dry. Wind-blown tumbleweeds flutter across the bleak landscape like dry finger bones playing a daddy long-legs dance. Tall silhouettes of cacti stretch curved arms to the sky. The green foliage of sagebrush dots the landscape with the occasional beady eyes of a jackrabbit, or a badger, hiding beneath its shelter. Sometimes I felt that the eyes of the natural inhabitants of the desert were tracking me as I drove down the highway. Despite the buffeting howl of the wind creating a whistling cry through the desert floor, confirming my isolated state, the feeling that I wasn't alone continued to hound me. It got worse every time a car passed me on the highway, or when a vehicle materialized in my rearview mirror.

Our initial flight from Los Angeles took us to Mount Shasta, where we holed up in a little motel off the main drag of a sleepy little town called Oak Run. There we lived like convicts on the run, hardly venturing out of our room. We lived on cold cuts I bought from the local liquor store and water from the kitchen faucet. I OD'd on episodes of *Friends* and *Seinfeld* until I thought I was going to puke. When the cold cuts ran out, I ventured out once more to pick up some nourishment, preferably something different, along with some skin ointment to help cut down on the painful itching the tattoos were creating on our tender skin. I was gone no more than thirty minutes.

I came home to an empty, blood-splattered motel room.

I've tried to put the pieces together, arrange them systematically so they could make some kind of sense. At first I tried to tell myself that everything that was happening was logical—that we were being stalked by some fanatical collector who somehow found out about our newly acquired tattoos. But then when I thought about the phone calls we received, the feelings of being watched that overcame me at almost every moment, Montivaldi's obsession with the occult and the things he was hinting at toward the end, and the tattoos that were finishing themselves—

Whatever it was Montivaldi was working on, it must mean something. I remember looking at it one night while Nicholas lay in bed on his stomach in our motel room. I looked at the half-finished design on his back, marveling at the cosmic image. Starting from the top of his back was an array of wispy images merging with strange symbols that looked like they would have come straight

189

out of some mystical occult bible. These designs were not there when we first fled Los Angeles; they came later. When I first looked at this design—still not finished—my mind flashed on one of the things Montivaldi had muttered at that last session. *I must write it down lest I forget,* and *I must do it quickly.*

Somebody—or *something* knows this.

And whoever it is, they're pursuing it.

That's why I am always on the run.

I am afraid that if I don't get it down right, if I don't get it down quickly, that they will come in and finish it for me.

I watch the progress of the designs every night when I check into the next motel. I look in the mirror as they spread from my breast, to cover my upper back, to snake down both shoulders down my biceps. I try to make out the designs, the same hieroglyphics that had been etched into Nick's skin by Montivaldi as he attempted to deliver the messages he was receiving; messages they were now finishing themselves.

Messages somebody else wants, so they can act on them.

I think about Montivaldi, and know now why he had a heart attack. Had the strain been too much for him? Did he know that he was unwillingly being directed by great, cosmic forces, and as a result had gone into cardiac arrest because of it?

What will happen if whoever it is that is pursuing me gets what they want?

All I can do now is drive, gas up the car, and stop for food. Sometimes I stop at a motel for a night of restless sleep, and sometimes I even stay a couple of days or so. It's been this way for three weeks now, and it won't be long before the limit on my credit cards runs out, or my pursuer, whoever he or she may be, catches up to me. For now, all I can do is drive.

I'm sure my pursuer won't give up until he can slice the skin off my body, cut the unmarred sections away from the spots that Montivaldi graced, and put them together with what he took from Nick to complete whatever vision directed Montivaldi to etch into our skins.

I am afraid that if I don't get it down right, if I don't get it down quickly, that they will come in and finish it for me.

And that's exactly what I'm afraid of.

The Disinterment of Ophelia

MICHELLE SCALISE

I awoke with the sensation that someone was watching me. Even before I could acknowledge the suspicion, a paralyzing chill clenched my limbs so fiercely I almost screamed.

Elizabeth Siddal knelt next to my bed, long hair the color of a sunset cloaking her shoulders. Brittle leaves clung to the hem of her lace gown and dirt stained her hands and fingernails as if she'd dug her way out of the ground. Her feet were small and bare. An infant cradled in her arms gazed through me with haunted eyes. I recognized the child's fixed stare. It belonged to every corpse I'd buried in Highgate Cemetery.

I couldn't fail to place the identity of the image that graced Rossetti's studio walls. From simple sketches of her features to full length paintings highlighting her slender frame. It was as if the room were a shrine to his dead wife or a passion grown out of control. At the time, I'd thought, if ever a ghost were to return to earth, hers would find him.

I hadn't lied to the artist, she was still beautiful even after eight years in the grave.

When she spoke, her full lips seemed to trail after her voice, forming the sounds an instant after I heard them. *"Tell Dante I am looking in his eyes though my eyes are dim."*

I pushed my back against the headboard, wishing to burrow away until sunlight could find me.

"You must return the words."

191

Somehow I managed to moan loud enough to startle Pip from his soundless sleep. Like a match blown out in the dark, she was suddenly gone.

I swore under my breath. And I cursed Rossetti.

His haunting had become mine.

⌒⁚〜

Studying the elegant calling card, I rang the bell at 16 Cheyne Walk in Chelsea, a part of town I'd never traveled before. Straightening Pip's collar, I said, "Now you remember what I told you? These creative types are all a little mad, even Mister Dickens I suspect, so don't be surprised at what Rossetti might say. You've heard the man spouting poetry at his wife's grave enough times so it won't..." The boy scowled and I couldn't help laughing. "Okay, perhaps not Dickens, but surly the rest of them."

Dante Gabriel Rossetti answered his own door. "Mister Duggan, welcome."

We were ushered in with a gesture as he murmured endearments to a small white owl perched on his shoulder. He led us down an unlit hall to his studio at the back of the house. The room had a high ceiling that echoed voices like a cathedral. Two vast windows gave view to an ancient mulberry tree in the center of a wild, overgrown garden with untended grass trailing out to an embankment. A barge floated along the Thames in the distance. The artist leaned against a wooden easel that held an unfinished portrait. He was a slight man, immaculately groomed in a black waistcoat and matching trousers. Dark wavy hair, worn long, fell across his sad brown eyes. His owl watched us like a sentry.

I turned to admire a large painting hanging above the fireplace. In an ornate frame, a woman floated lifeless in a stream, her lips parted as if welcoming a kiss. Gold lace gown sinking in the water, a spray of flowers clutched in her hand. It was the woman's gaze, though, that unsettled me with its soulless, blank stare. I asked about the model.

"Elizabeth Siddal," he said with a faint smile. "She was my wife. And these are my memories." His hand circled the room. I was greeted with her likeness on every wall.

"This one here gives me the shivers," I said, then quickly realized my mistake. "Oh, I don't mean anything by it though, sir. I can see it's a fine piece of art."

Rossetti waved the apology away. "This isn't one of my creations. It's the work of my friend John Millais. He thought I should have it when Elizabeth died. He's painted her as Ophelia, driven to insanity and suicide by Hamlet."

"She killed herself?" I asked.

"They both did," he said, petting his bird.

It took me a moment to realize he was referring to the character and his wife. "Well...she was certainly a lovely woman."

THE DISINTERMENT OF OPHELIA

"Who's this young man, Mister Duggan?" Rossetti asked, releasing the owl onto the back of a chair. "I believe I've seen him digging graves with you. Is he your son?"

"No, sir. This here's Pip. He don't speak but he understands you just fine. I found him outside Highgate one day begging and, my Christian nature being what it is, I took him in. We've been keeping each other company at the gatehouse ever since. I call him Pip on account of my fondness for Charles Dickens' tales."

As I spoke, the boy stepped closer to the canvas resting on the artist's easel. In the portrait, Elizabeth Siddal appeared in a strange trance, her eyes whited out. Head tilted back, a bird at her wrist releasing red poppies like blood drops into her open palm. There was a sundial situated behind her and two shadowy figures floating in the background.

"Dickens once called my work 'repulsive' in that rag *All The Year Round,*" Rossetti said, examining his art as if he were seeing it for the first time. "I've made her Alligheri's Beatrice." He pointed to the silhouetted shapes. "This is the poet here, and this one represents Love."

"She looks like she's praying," I said. "But I don't understand that bird or the timepiece, begging your pardon."

"Time stops for us all, Mister Duggan. The dove is a messenger of death. I just need to finish her eyes." He cleared his throat, looking as if he might break into a sob. "I'm having trouble closing them. It seems so final...like saying goodbye." Turning away, he stared out at his garden. A fall breeze picked up handfuls of dead leaves, blowing them in a blaze of red and gold against the window. Three peacocks darted through the dead weeds, their blue tails disappearing behind a bush.

"Mister Duggan," Rossetti said, his gaze still fixed on the view. "I have a job to offer you and I'll pay well for the service."

Pip and I exchanged a glance. Some of the wealthier bereaved made it worth our time to plant flowers and keep up the resting places of their departed. Grave gardening, I liked to call it. I expected the artist to request a similar service.

"I wish to have..." Rossetti turned to me, then quickly looked away as if judging my reaction before he made the request. "Have you ever unearthed a grave?" He pointed to a small pouch on a side table. "It's all yours if you'll exhume something very important to me."

Pip grabbed the brown bag before I could stop him. It contained more money than I could earn in a year at Highgate.

I tried to speak, even opened my mouth but I couldn't think of a single thing to say.

Rossetti hurried to my side. "Here, you look quite pale." Leading me to a red satin divan, he poured a glass of wine and forced it into my hand. "Please, I think you misunderstand me."

Pip knelt at my side, rubbing my hand. "I'm fine, boy," I said.

Rossetti opened a small vial filled with a crystalline liquid, pouring its contents into his own glass. He swallowed the drink and took a deep breath.

"Before my wife was buried I placed a poetry manuscript in her coffin. Now my publisher is interested in it but I never made copies." His words were coming faster as if he feared I might leave before he could make his case. "Lizzie would have understood. If she could open the grave herself, no other hand would be needed. I just want back a reminder of the man I used to be. Can you understand that? I'm going to shrine her in verse." His hand shook as he ran it through his hair. "Perhaps then I'll find absolution."

I figured he'd spoken those words a hundred times to himself, but they hadn't given comfort. Grief threw shadows in his eyes.

Rossetti forgot about me as he muttered to the ceiling, gazing as if mesmerized by the dangling cobwebs. "Let all men note that in all years, they that would look on her must come to me." When he tried balancing his glass on the edge of a table, it tipped forward, shattering.

"God in Hell!" he shouted, falling to his knees. "See what the blasted spirits have done?"

I didn't know what to say. But I smiled at Pip as if it all made sense. The boy squeezed my fingers so tightly I feared for my circulation.

"Why must you haunt me?" Rossetti asked, burying his head in his hands.

I knew I should flee the house and let Rossetti wallow in his madness and drugs. But the bag of coins was a small fortune to a man like me. Pip and I could leave London. Live by the sea, perhaps. And I figured if I could make a grave, I could easily dig one up again.

Footsteps coming down the stairs interrupted my thoughts. A tall, slender man appeared from the shadows of the hall to observe us, casually leaning against the doorway. He tapped his walking stick against the floor to draw Rossetti's attention. "Blasphemous bastard," he said with a smirk, ducking slightly as the owl skimmed his long red hair. "Dante, must these creatures have free reign of the house? I believe your raccoon pilfered one of my silk slippers last night."

Rossetti looked up and sighed. "Mister Duggan, this is my friend Algernon Swinburne. Do what you can to ignore him, he's a demonic boy."

With a practiced, aristocratic air the man appraised me. Inhaling deeply from a fat cigar, he let the smoke cloud his face like a temporary mask. "Quite true," he said. "And Dante here is London's foremost martyred saint. At least that's the part he plays *ad nauseum*. But I don't fault him, it's the Mediterranean blood in his veins. Gives one a passion for melodrama. What is your profession, Mister…"

I rose, repeating our introduction. I was sure he'd forget my name again within minutes.

Rossetti gripped the table as he stood on shaking legs, shards of glass clutched in his hand. Blood trickled through his fingers, spotting the Persian rug. "Swinburne, I'm conducting business. If you'll be kind enough to close the door behind you."

THE DISINTERMENT OF OPHELIA

"This is the thanks I get for coming to your rescue?" His friend laughed. It was a bitter sound. "I distinctly heard you shouting about your ghost again...or was that just the melodic sounds of chloral echoing down the halls?"

Rossetti stumbled to a chair, sweat beading on his forehead. "I'm arranging the removal of my manuscript. And as you have made it abundantly clear how you feel on this subject, I suggest you leave us."

Swinburne glared at me so fiercely I backed away from him, placing my arm around Pip. The boy still held the bag of coins.

"Dante, you can't desecrate Lizzie's grave," Swinburne said. "For God's sake, leave her be and go paint something. Better yet, why don't we give a party. Browning's in town and you can invite Yeats, that Irish boy you've been making so much about."

"What honor do words bring her when they go unseen?" Rossetti cried. "My fame as a poet lies buried in the grave...you of all people should understand."

Reaching into his pocket, he drew out a wad of crumpled papers and handed them to me. "I've been given the lawful right by the Cemetery Authorities and the Church. But you must conduct this business at night...I couldn't bear to have people gossiping. And once you get the manuscript take it to this address. He'll be expecting you." Rossetti saw the questioning look on my face as I studied the card. "He's the doctor whom I've hired to...I'm told the journal must be disinfected and dried. Now, if you'll excuse me, Mister Duggan, I'm not feeling well. Swinburne, could you show them out?"

I shook Rossetti's hand. His grip held mine tightly as if he were hoping I might drag him out of the misery he was drowning in.

"You won't find Lizzie in the coffin." His eyes, strangely dilated, gazed somewhere far beyond me. "I and this love are one, and I am death."

"I don't understand you, sir," I said, pulling myself free with a shudder.

"My friend, in bad form, quotes his own poetry," Swinburne said, then continued in an exaggerated manner. "My master that was thrall to love is become thrall to death. Bow to him." With a flourish, he removed an imaginary hat, dipping low with a grin.

"I'll get the manuscript for you, sir." Pip was already heading outside and I quickly followed.

At the doorway, Swinburne caught me with an outstretched arm, the smell of whiskey fresh on his breath. "Dante feels that Lizzie's spirit is tormenting him," he said, casually tossing his cigar with a flick of his thin fingers. I watched it bounce down the steps, landing at the base of one of the lime trees that lined Cheyne Walk. "Every shadow in the corner, every creak on the stairs is his dead wife returned. Of course, if it's true, imagine her indignation if one were to unearth her grave...that is if you believe in such things. I'm not claiming it as fact but I have discovered that there's not enough chloral in all of London to make her go away. I'd hate for you to find out the hard way that my friend is haunted by more than memories and his conscience. Good evening to you, Mister Duggan."

་་

Hours after I'd latched the cemetery gates for the night, Pip and I lit torches at Elizabeth Siddal's grave site. I talked to the boy as we readied our spot, feeling as culpable as a thief in spite of the legal papers in my pocket. "Pip, you ever been to the sea? We could travel to the boarding house my sister runs in Portsmouth. Ever since her husband passed she's been after me to join her but I never had the money. It might be nice to be a fisherman. No more sooty air in our lungs. And we'll buy ourselves a little boat. I'd be willing to trade vultures for seagulls circling my head. How about you?"

Elizabeth Siddal Rossetti's tombstone was modest and unadorned. A handful of wilting roses lay on the marker, engraved with her name and the inscription: *We are lost like stars beyond dark trees.*

"Well, the sooner we get to work, the sooner we'll be done with it. What'd we guess your years to be, Pip? Fourteen? Fifteen? I'll bet you've never even seen the ocean. Oh, you're going to love it."

He grabbed a shovel, making a waving motion with his free hand.

"That's right, boy. I fancy we'll make an admirable pair of sailors."

Swinburne's parting words suddenly came back to me. At the time, his warning about Elizabeth Siddal's spirit had seemed like a hoax to scare me off. Now I wasn't so sure.

Clearing my throat, I took up an old song. Our breath clouded in the chilled air like foxfire as we dug.

"Head-over-heels in love with him was the Ratcatcher's Beautiful Daughter."

I couldn't carry a tune but Pip liked it just fine.

"But the Ratcatcher's Daughter had a funny dream that she wouldn't be alive come Sunday. Still she crossed once more for to sell her sprats and fell down into the water."

The ground was unyielding from an early frost but after a half hour of heavy labor, an abrupt thud let me know we'd succeeded. Pip held my shovel as I crawled down into the hole, still crooning.

"'Twas an accident, they all agreed, and nothing like self-slaughter. So not guilty of fell-in-the-sea, they brought in the Ratcatcher's Beautiful Daughter."

The casket was black metal with a silver coffin-cross affixed to its top. Using my tools, I unscrewed the sides of the lid. "Pip, bring a torch up close so I can see what I'm doing here." The bells of Saint Michael's church chimed midnight, sending a shiver up my spine. I wiped the sweat from my brow then raised the top. I could tell from the way the light above wavered, casting slashes of gold against the corpse, that Pip's hands shook. I didn't much blame him.

Expecting a decaying corpse, I was shocked to discover her spared image. Elizabeth Siddal had been dead eight years and yet looked so perfectly preserved she might have been sleeping, though the smell of grave rot told a different story. I gagged, covering my mouth with a kerchief as I pushed aside handfuls of her burnished auburn hair. Her skin was supple yet as frigid as the earth she inhabited.

Rossetti hadn't exaggerated the beauty he'd captured on canvas. Nor had the artist who'd painted her as the drowning Ophelia. It was almost as if he'd seen into the future how Elizabeth Siddal would appear once she was laid to rest.

Observing a book pressed to her breast, I swallowed hard, slowly sliding it out from under her hands. When I raised it to the light, I realized my mistake. It was a bible with her name engraved in gold lettering. Returning it as gently as I could, I apologized under my breath. Next to her head, twined in her hair like a fish trapped in a net, lay the rough, gray, calf-bound manuscript. I had to pull and tug to free it from her tresses. Once it came loose, I quickly slammed the lid, scrambling from her tomb back into the world of the living.

Pip clapped his hands as I laughed, waving Rossetti's poems in the air like a boat on the sea.

~:~

Wrapping the manuscript in an old cloth, I carried it back to the gatehouse. As Pip cleaned and stored our tools in the cemetery shed, I laid the book out on a table in front of the fireplace. Turning the fragile, damp pages, I was surprised to see the ink still sharp enough to decipher. I read Rossetti's verses, all of them a commemoration to Elizabeth Siddal's passion and mournful beauty. His words were new blood flowing through her veins, bringing her to life again. I knew what it was to be her lover, to hear her laughter. I could feel the soft touch of her auburn hair, see her gray eyes observing me from her bridal bed with all the sensuality that radiated from every portrait on Rossetti's walls. I could see her as clearly as the manuscript she now existed in. Suddenly, I longed for a woman I could only know in death.

I held my breath as I read the last poem, entitled *Secret Parting,* tears brimming in my eyes.

And as she kissed, her mouth became her soul.

Sara, my wife, had died ten years ago but we'd never lived in Rossetti's rose-petal world of art and poetry. I wanted what he had with a yearning I'd never felt for anything. Ripping the final verse from the book as cleanly as possible, I placed it atop a shelf next to my tea tins to dry. Rossetti hadn't seen the manuscript in eight years, he'd never miss what he probably wouldn't even recall in his drug-addled mind.

I covered the journal up again. When Pip returned, we delivered it across town to the doctor.

~:~

From that night on, Elizabeth Siddal appeared at my bedside. The dead baby in her arms seemed as soulless as a rag doll, but she liked to coo to it before addressing me. And it was the infant that frightened me even more than the woman's ghost. It was too still, too empty, as if it had died without ever living.

She knew I'd stolen her poem.

The thought of breaching her grave again, crawling down into that dark hollow with the knowledge she wasn't resting in peace, sickened me. But I was convinced that as long as I kept the page, she'd continue her visits until I went insane.

I left Pip one afternoon to care for the cemetery grounds while I made my way back to Rossetti's house.

This time Swinburne greeted me at the door with a look of disdain. "My God, what's Dante called on you for this time?"

"I'm not expected, sir," I explained. "But I've got business of a personal nature to discuss with him."

"This should be amusing," he said, leading me down the hall into the artist's studio.

Rossetti sat at a large round table littered with papers. I was startled to see how drastically his appearance had changed in the last week. The white linen shirt he wore was stained with his sweat and wrinkled. It was clear he hadn't shaved or bathed in days. Leaning precariously from his chair, he appeared to argue with the wall. "I did place you above art and you abandoned me."

A black and white Chihuahua sitting in his lap reared its little head to bark at my intrusion. The book I'd retrieved for him lay next to a bottle of ink. Dark circles under the artist's eyes told me I wasn't the only one finding it impossible to sleep.

Rossetti cradled the dog as he stood. "William, have you found Lizzie?" he asked me. "I can't think where she could have run off to."

"Dante," Swinburne said. "Get ahold of yourself. This isn't your brother, it's the man from the cemetery. Mister Dig…something."

"Duggan," I said, tightly pressing the stolen poem that rested in my coat pocket. "Mister Rossetti, I must speak to you regarding your wife."

"I knew it," Swinburne said. "He's come to blackmail you for more money, just as I warned you he would. If this debacle gets out you'll be ruined."

"I'm not a fine gentleman like you, sir," I said. "But I'm no criminal either and I resent your thinking low of me without cause."

"You killed me too, Lizzie!" Rossetti yelled at the Ophelia painting where his wife lay drowned yet less dead than he. Taking a long drink from his wine glass, he fell back into his seat, dropping the dog to the floor.

"Without cause?" Swinburne continued as if Rossetti's hallucinations were commonplace. "You and that boy are no better than a pair of bloody grave robbers. Highgate's own Burke and Hare for hire. You should be locked up." He nudged the yapping Chihuahua away with his walking stick. "Oh, good God, Dante, do something about this beast of yours."

Before I could speak, Rossetti's eyes cleared as if he'd just stepped out of a fog. "Aren't you the man who dug up my Lizzie's grave?"

"Yes, sir," I said, speaking slowly as if I were communicating with a child. "I got your poems back for you."

"I know what brings you here," Rossetti said. "My wife was not in her coffin, just as I told you. Correct?"

"No, sir," I said. "I saw the body."

He shook his head. "That's not possible. She's still as beautiful as the portraits."

"Yes, she is," I said, brushing the stiff page of poetry with my fingers. "I never saw anything like it, sir. She could have been sleeping, so little effect death's had upon her." I stepped over to the table but couldn't bring myself to glance at the book itself. Bending down, I whispered, "But she's haunting me too, sir. I fear closing my eyes."

"What's that, old man?" Swinburne asked. "What's that you say?"

My throat grew dry as the dust at the bottom of a grave. "You have to help me. Tell her I'm sorry."

"You?" Rossetti asked. "What have you to feel guilty about?"

"Explain how you paid me 'cause you wanted your words back."

Rossetti's mouth nearly broke into a smile as a guttural titter worked its way up his throat. He grabbed my arm. "Did you hear that, Swinburne? Did you? I'm not mad. I've been telling you for eight years that her spirit is still with me but you remained a skeptic. Now what do you think?"

"You both belong in Bedlam," Swinburne said. "I tried to unnerve this devil by threatening him with Lizzie's ghost. I never dreamed he'd actually go dig up her grave and then choose to believe me." He turned on me, sneering. "You were supposed to heed my warning before you committed the crime, Mister Duggan, not afterwards."

I knew then if I returned the poem, Swinburne would have me thrown in jail. Or worse, I'd have to face the look of triumph on his face once Rossetti discovered what I'd done.

Clutching the manuscript in his hands, Rossetti said, "Has my wife told you why she can't find peace? Tell me everything."

I glanced at Swinburne. He crossed his arms, smiling. "Yes, please do," he said. "I suppose she was surrounded in mist and you heard wolves howling in the distance."

I suddenly realized how foolish it all sounded. But I'd come this far and I knew Rossetti needed to hear his wife's message. "Well, sir," I said, clearing my throat. "She wears a lace gown with no shoes and appears like a vapor. And she has an infant in her arms, she hums to it."

Rossetti flinched as if I'd swung at him. The journal slid from his grasp, landing on the table with a thud. He didn't seem to notice.

Swinburne grabbed my shoulder. "Who told you that? About the baby?"

I shook his arm away. "I have a missive she wants me to pass on."

"Lizzie has our child?" Rossetti asked in a soft voice. "Then why can't she forgive me? Haven't I suffered enough?"

"Elizabeth Siddal, dead eight years," Swinburne said. "Is now taken to visiting you in your gatehouse?"

"I've been caring for Highgate Cemetery for twenty years," I told him. "Not many men would take my job for all the money in the Church's coffer on account of silly superstitions but it's never bothered me none. I always believed once I buried them, they were safe in God's hands. Now I'm telling you this as a sane man," I said, pointing to the portraits. "That woman's been to see me seven nights in a row."

Swinburne watched his friend's reaction, then turned to me, speaking under his breath. "Can't you see he's in no condition to hear these things? Please, come with me. We'll discuss this outside." With that, he led me towards the doorway.

"Your wife's message is, 'Tell Dante I am looking in his eyes though my eyes are dim,'" I said, pushing my way back into the studio. "Don't know what it means but she keeps…"

The look of arrogant satisfaction instantly died on Swinburne's face. He dropped his hand from my back. The astonishment in his eyes unnerved me more than his anger. But Rossetti's gaze was suddenly clear as a diamond and savage. "God in Hell! You read my unpublished work? How dare you do such a thing without my permission."

"Dante, have you completely lost your sanity?" Swinburne said.

Rossetti leaned over the table, pointing the book at my chest like a knife. "I am looking in his eyes though my eyes are dim? Those are my words! They're in this journal and you dare come here reciting them to me?"

"Dante, you haven't been able to open that book since it was returned," Swinburne said. "You don't know what it contains anymore. You just sit here day after day waiting for Lizzie to grant permission for its publication. Besides, the poem you speak of isn't in that cursed manuscript. And if it wasn't for the chloral, you'd realize that."

"I know it's here somewhere," Rossetti cried, turning pages until he reached the end. "Look at this! I can see where it's been torn out. Did you imagine you could sell it?"

I thought of throwing the stolen verse at him, humiliation be damned. I'd read it enough times to have memorized every line. I knew his wife's message wouldn't be found on the page. It was just an ode to love, filled with images of his bride.

Before I could act, Swinburne grabbed my arm, pulling me from the room.

Rossetti's mad ranting followed us down the steps and out into the street.

I stopped at the sidewalk to catch my breath, ready to strike the man if I had to.

"You must forgive him," Swinburne said. "He imagines odd things once the drug seeps into his thoughts. It's rather frightening to witness. I love Dante like a brother but…well, one must make exceptions for poets these days. Personally, I blame it on Keats. We all feel compelled to live a melancholy existence and die young. It's almost unseemly to be an old, happy bard."

THE DISINTERMENT OF OPHELIA

"But you believe me?" I asked. "Why?"

"I have no choice," he said, reaching into his pocket and pulling out a cigar. "If I knew of any way that you could have quoted that line, I'd call you a liar and a lunatic to your face. But I can't. Dante's partially correct, they are his words but it's a verse he composed two weeks ago. It's not in the manuscript." He stopped to ask a gentleman for a match, then continued. "Perhaps she'd find peace if Dante could just accept her death. But after all these years she's become a romantic ideal...and a drag chain around his neck."

As we walked past shop windows I told Swinburne all the details of Elizabeth Siddal's nightly visits. "Begging your pardon, sir, as I know this is none of my affair, but what reason does Mister Rossetti have for feeling guilty? Seems to me he held his wife in great esteem."

"Lizzie gave birth to a dead child," he said. "Her life probably ended on that day, we just didn't know it yet. I watched them both suffer but Dante had his art to give him solace. She had only laudanum. It took me two months before I could tear him away from his studio. The night she died, we dined at the Sabloniere. Dante sent Lizzie home early and remained with me until dawn. He was the one who discovered her body. She needed solace and he couldn't see beyond his own grief. At the inquest, her death, from the opiate, was declared an accident. Dante knew better, we all did."

I shook Swinburne's hand when it was offered to me. He returned to Rossetti's house as I slowly made my way back to the cemetery. Removing the poem from my pocket, I looked it over. It was damp now from my sweat. I almost crushed it in my fist. The thought of tossing it away seemed like my only recourse. But I quickly realized that Elizabeth Siddal wasn't going to leave me in peace that easily.

⌣⁚⌣

"I don't know what made me take it," I explained to Pip that night, leaving out any reference to the woman's ghost. "I've always been an honorable man but it won't surprise me none if you think less of me for what I've done. I'm going to make things right though. Seeing as how I can't give the poem back to Rossetti without retribution, I got no choice but to dig up her grave again."

Pip put his hand on mine and squeezed. It took all my strength not to weep with shame. He insisted on helping me and I was grateful for the company.

The wind swirled between the trees, slapping at my cheeks as we stood at Elizabeth Siddal's gravestone. I couldn't move. I kept picturing her down beneath the earth waiting for me.

Pip watched me for a minute then started digging. I followed his lead, repelled with every thrust of my shovel into the cold soil. When the boy tapped my shoulder, I jumped. He made a few awkward motions with his hands as if he were leading an orchestra. I smiled, "I know, I ain't singing. Most folks would be grateful for that, of course they don't appreciate my melodic sounds the way that you do." I started in with his favorite song, raising my voice to be heard above the din of the coming storm and my own frightening thoughts.

"Not long ago, near Westminster, there lived a Ratcatcher's Daughter."

I went on serenading the cemetery until I glimpsed metal peaking through the ground. Moving the torches to the edge of the grave, I looked down, grasping the poem in my hand.

More than anything, I wished I'd never heard of Elizabeth Siddal or her husband.

Pip saw my hesitation. He patted my arm gently as if I were as mad as Rossetti. Grabbing a heavy rock, he knelt, banging out the rhythm of the silly tune he loved against his shovel. "You gonna do that while I'm putting this page back?" I asked. The boy nodded. "You don't mind if I accompany you, do you?"

I crawled down on the coffin, singing loud enough to wake the vicar at Saint Michaels.

"So he cut his throat with a blade of grass and stabbed his donkey after. That was the end of Lillywhite Sam, the donkey and the Ratcatcher's Beautiful Daughter."

With an almost giddy sense of fear, I unscrewed the top, my tool repeatedly sliding out and scratching the dull black sides. I wiped the sweat from my palms and tried again. Pip banged his stone clear enough for me to recognize the chorus. Glancing up, I saw him wave. I held my breath, whispering a quick prayer, then lifted the lid.

Elizabeth Siddal wasn't sleeping anymore.

Her long auburn hair had grown dull as a shadow. And the face that had inspired poets and artists had changed drastically too. Her skin, brown and peeling, was rough as hide. Stretched back tight against her bones, her mouth gaped open in a frozen scream. Her eyelids were rotted away, revealing two sightless black holes. Watching me. I couldn't bear to look into them. It was like a view of hell.

Pip, God bless him, never stopped pounding. I choked on a sob, laying Rossetti's verse on the Bible that rested on her breast. "I'm so sorry," I said.

Pip battered his shovel repetitively to get my attention. "I'm coming," I said, closing the lid and crawling out of the grave. When I was back at his side, he pointed down at the coffin then ran his hands over his face.

I shook my head. "I don't know," I said, filling in the hole from a pile of dirt behind us. "Probably caused by the air getting into that metal coffin after eight years. Or maybe it wasn't our place to take that book. It belonged to her and she was the only one had rights to give it back. Could be those words preserved her beauty."

Pip rolled his eyes, patting down the earth until it looked like a fresh site.

Just as we finished, a strong gust of wind snuffed out the flames of our torches. "Nothing to worry about," I said, clutching my shovel. "We're all done here. Let's head home." My hand shook as I took his outstretched arm.

THE DISINTERMENT OF OPHELIA

The trees overhead swayed and twisted in the air, sending dead leaves scurrying like rats across our path. The smoke from our fireplace still burned up ahead. I stopped and listened.

I heard the faint sound of footsteps stalking us. Stumbling, I cried out. Pip smiled, wrapping his arm around my waist.

I wouldn't turn around. If I didn't see it then it couldn't possibly be there. "You know a storm can bring some odd noises with it." My voice seemed louder than the church bells. "Ain't nothing to us though, is it?" My heart beat so fast I feared I might die right there on the cemetery footpath. I couldn't pick up my feet. My legs were dragging underwater.

Bare soles slapped against the ground. Coming faster as it pursued us.

I hung onto Pip, breathing heavily. "Do you hear that?" I asked.

He looked at me strangely, shaking his head.

The hair on the back of my neck stood. It was so close I feared it would reach out and grab me. The scent of the grave filled my lungs, choking me. I pulled at the kerchief tied around my neck.

The gatehouse seemed so far away.

Using all my strength, I jerked the boy to my arms. We tumbled into the damp grass, my body shielding him as he struggled to free himself. Something bitterly cold brushed against my face. I bit my lip to keep from screaming, feeling sick from the touch.

When I raised my head, I saw a piece of paper fluttering in the night air above us.

⌒∴⌒

As the carriage pulled up to Rossetti's house, I told the driver to wait. I'd hoped to never see the place again but when we'd returned from purchasing Pip's clothes the church vicar informed me that Swinburne had been to the cemetery looking for me.

I rang the bell, adjusting Pip's new suit. "We look like a pair of fine gentlemen, don't we? I won't be surprised at all if we don't find ourselves an admirer or two once we get to Portsmouth."

Swinburne greeted us at the door. "Mister Duggan, I'm pleased you received my message in time. Come in."

We followed him back to the candlelit studio. The curtains were closed, casting the room in shadows. "How's Mister Rossetti doing, sir?" I asked, dropping my bag next to a chair.

"He feels a great deal of regret for disturbing Lizzie's grave," Swinburne said, pouring whiskey into a glass. "Dante had hoped to visit with you but last night he became quite ill. It's that bloody chloral, you know."

He offered me a drink and I shook my head, glancing down at my pocket watch. "Pip and I are going to dine at the Swan With Two Necks Inn before our coach leaves."

"Yes, of course, you're traveling," Swinburne said. "When I came to Highgate today the vicar, who, by the way, seems quite mad, informed me you were departing for Portsmouth. I thought everyone deserted London in the summer? What an eccentric action to take before the season's half over." He took a small package from the mantle, handing it to me. "Dante asked me to give this to you. He would have presented it himself but now I am duty-bound to convey his remorse for the abominable way he behaved."

"He didn't need to do this, sir," I said, removing the gold wrapping of the parcel. "I understand what grief can do to…" The words died on my lips. It was a framed etching of Elizabeth Siddal. She stood at a window with a bright smile on her face, her long auburn hair hung loose. My hands shook so badly, I almost dropped the picture. "I can't accept this."

Swinburne waved me away. "It's the least he can do, after all, you were accused of stealing a page out of that damn manuscript. Did I mention, we found the missing poem?"

I grabbed at the shrouded easel to my side, stars dancing before my eyes. Rossetti's gift felt as cold and heavy as a corpse. Pip gently pulled it from my grasp. Acting as if he were stuffing it into my bag, I watched him slide it under the chair then look up at me and wink.

"Sir, if I may ask, where did Mister Rossetti discover his verse?" I said.

"Out in the garden, at the bottom of the mulberry tree." Swinburne laughed. "I suspect that nasty Chihuahua got hold of it when he wasn't paying attention. Dante vaguely recalls leaving the book out there one day. Perhaps now he'll send all those blasted animals off to a zoo. Especially that dog. Damn little beast chewed up my second-best riding boots last night."

As he spoke, I noticed Pip peeking under the sheet that concealed the large portrait Rossetti had been working on when we'd first visited the house. Swinburne wasn't fast enough. Before he could move, the boy had pulled up the white cloth, revealing the finished picture of Elizabeth Siddal as Alligheri's Beatrice.

I shuddered, grabbing Pip's arm and dragging him back from the image.

"Good God!" Swinburne cried. "The child doesn't need to see that." He quickly covered the canvas but not before I got a good look at what Rossetti had done.

At last, he'd managed to paint his wife's eyes. The pale eyelids were rotted away. Beneath them two immeasurably black, sightless holes stared back at us.

"I can't bear to look at the bloody thing," Swinburne said. "Dante's always painted with a sense of romantic idealism and honesty, yet suddenly he does something vulgar like this. Even in his worst moments with the chloral, he's never defiled Lizzie's memory."

I'd confronted Elizabeth Siddal's blind gaze from the grave, seen a truth without poetry Swinburne would never be capable of understanding. A tangibility that blotted out ideals of beauty like roiling storm clouds.

Rossetti had finally created art from a reality that held no nobility.

If You Were Glass...

DAVID NIALL WILSON

Ice. It coated the shelves, dripped columns of crystalline light down from cabinet to counter, smooth and constant. Frigid air hissed into the room through small valves protruding from the wall. Light from the lamps flickered from surface to surface like will o' the wisps or dancing diamonds. Jacob watched through a fogged window, and smiled. His smile held no warmth.

The room where he sat was barely warmer than the icy palace beyond. The frost on the window showed the slight rise in temperature, but his breath, white puffs of frigid air, belied it. Jacob wore no gloves—no jacket. His black turtleneck sweater was thin, tucked tightly into black jeans that seemed too small to fit. The cuffs were frayed, and the frayed threads were frozen where they'd dragged across the rain-swept walk as he entered. Frost glistened on the smooth black of his ponytail. His lips were nearly blue, but there was no tremble to his hands. He held a glass—vodka—and ice.

Clay caked under his nails, dark now—hardened and flaking. Falling away. Dust to dust, ash to ash. Jacob lifted the glass to his lips and took a long swig of the clear liquor, letting it slide down his throat, ice—and fire. The flames from the kiln still danced before his eyes. The heat and the scent of baking clay permeated his lungs and lingered in his nostrils. He could never quite flush the fire from his mind, or spit the sour stench of the clay from his lungs. The icy vodka dampened the flame.

DAVID NIALL WILSON

In this outer room, the temperature was a steady 38 degrees Fahrenheit. Not quite freezing, though closer to the windows, the temperature dropped dramatically. The joining of two worlds.

Once, it had been a dining room. Now it was a gateway. There were three doors. One led to the world beyond, the other two doors leading inward. Two wardrobes, and two sets of tools in matched, black leather bags.

His numb fingers itched, but he steadied them and took another long sip from his drink. He couldn't hurry the process. If he began too soon; if his other world leaked beyond the frosted glass...

Jacob shook the thought from his mind. The ice clinked against the tumbler in his hand. Something in that sound jarred him deep inside. He stepped closer to the glass.

Directly across from the window, a long table stood against the wall, ice cascading down the front, water in static pseudo-motion, captured forever like a long-forgotten candle left to melt and puddle on the floor. He had designed the room so that the AC vents were placed high enough on the wall that the mist would not obscure his view of the table. Jacob stared intently at the object closest to him.

The gnomish creature glared back at him, eyes filled with malevolence, one hand raised behind itself, as if preparing to throw something in Jacob's face, or to slash with the claw-like nails of its too-small hand. Frozen. The sculpture glistened, brilliant and dancing with light from the cool overhead flourescent lighting.

Jacob studied the sculpture, but his mind was drifting. He felt the heat of the not-quite-frozen air at his back warming him, and he stepped closer to the glass. His memory resurrected soft words, whispered in his ear from far too close. Words riding warm breath and lingering on his throat. His cheeks reddened in a sudden blush. Heat invaded other parts of his body.

His drink sloshed as the tumbler hit the wall with a soft clink. Icy vodka dripped over his hand and left frost-trails running between his fingers. Jacob laid his cheek on the cold glass and closed his eyes, trying to clear his mind. He needed to work, but not like this.

It's lovely, she'd said. Too close. Too warm. *It's lovely, but wouldn't it be exquisite if you'd used glass? If it magnified? If each of those wonderful angles glittered like a diamond?*

Glass. The glass on the window in front of Jacob's face fogged, and the sculptures shimmered. He blinked. Focused. Everything faded. He saw her eyes reflected in the frost, felt her long, too-slender fingers teasing his hair. Felt transparent.

He pressed off from the window with a shudder. Just for a moment, his skin adhered, frozen in place. Joined to the glass—to the ice—to the frost.

"Not glass," he murmured. "Never glass. They could take that away. They could have it and hold it and..."

His mind whirled, and he pressed his hand flat on the window to steady himself as he let out a breath that nearly reached a growl.

It would be so COOL!

Her words echoed in Jacob's mind and he winced. Cool? Cool wasn't enough. Never enough. Cold. A moment frozen. That was art. Fragile, fluid and transient unless given one's full attention. Not timeless. Not to be hung in some huge, faceless building to be ogled by students and professors, would-be's and has-beens, critiquing what they didn't understand, judging experience that had never been their own by perception that could only, by definition, fall short. That was why Jacob had the clay. When he worked with the clay, it was for them. All the others. Let them stare. Let them wonder. God—let them stay away.

Glass.

Jacob shivered. His fingers itched to grip his tools. In the corner stood a small, faux-wood-grain refrigerator. Inside, he kept the chisels, the knives—a small and a large mallet. He kept them at 28 degrees. Any colder, and it would take time to be able to handle them. Some had metal handles. Any warmer, and he would have to stand with them, watching the ice, not *working,* until they reached a temperature where he could place them on the frozen surfaces of the room without fear of damage. Lessons learned.

Jacob gulped the remaining vodka and felt it burning its way down his throat. There was fire, but without the heat most fires elicited. Without the danger.

He staggered to the small refrigerator and slapped the now empty glass down on top. He opened the door, grabbed his tool bag, and spun toward the room beyond the frosted glass. The refrigerator swung shut behind him with a soft *snick!* And he hurried to beat the encroachment of the heat.

He pressed a black inset switch in the wall, and the door to the gallery slid open, allowing him just the amount of time he needed to step inside before it closed on an automatic timer. Forty-five seconds. The point beyond which Jacob couldn't guarantee integrity. Two entire degrees of heat would gain entrance in the vicinity of the door, but the room was kept at a very steady fifteen degrees. Nothing important was kept too-near the door. Nothing would be lost.

As he turned to his work, Jacob was suddenly very aware of the window at his back—and that the window was made of glass.

⌒⊹⌒

The gallery was quiet when Jacob pulled over to the curb. It was early. They weren't scheduled to open for a couple more hours, but he'd wanted to give himself plenty of time. In his mind, he could hear Michael already, strutting around the gallery with the single, too-long curl of auburn-tinted hair bobbing against his cheek. "Everything is *important* darling. Everything. The angle, the lighting—everything. You have got to give me time to work with things, Jacob." It was very early, and at that moment in time, Michael wouldn't be there to work his magic. Jacob would have to do his best—he tried never to leave anything to chance.

He was sweating. It was seventy-two degrees, and he stood in the shade of the gallery's low awning, a cool breeze tickling through his damp hair. Jacob had run the AC on high in his low-slung Mercury Cougar. The Freon had been recharged only a month prior, but he was considering taking it back in. The climate-control seemed unable to provide an environment much under 69 degrees. Too hot.

With a quick press of the remote in his pocket, the trunk lid popped up, and Jacob reached inside. All of the work slated to be shown was already inside. Jacob hadn't counted on this newest piece—hadn't even meant to work on anything new—but it had come upon him in a frenzy, and he'd worked through most of the night. It was rough—just the clay—this piece—but what he'd done after—what waited in his gallery he was excited about.

As he lifted the sculpture from the trunk, his hands shook. His palms were sweaty, and he wanted to wipe them on his pants, but it was too late. He gripped the piece so tightly his knuckles grew white from the strain, and he turned too quickly, nearly tripping on the curb.

The sculpture was wrapped in black canvas. Covering the work in cloth helped him to steady his nerves. It wouldn't slip. The sweat soaked in and left him feeling clammy, but not slick. His mind wouldn't quite accept the logic of it. His hands were like quicksilver, and at each step he felt things shifting, the impression that he was losing balance. Jacob leaned on the door frame of the gallery before entering, closing his eyes and trying to calm his nerves.

Closing his eyes was a mistake.

He could still smell the kiln. Metal so hot the scent of it permeated the air. Moist clay, baking, all liquid draining out into the air, shriveling from the heart out and hardening. The glaze had left a cloying, sticky coating in his nostrils. It itched, then ached—burned into his skin. His hands had formed the image so clear in his mind, wet clay gleaming, glistening—almost like red ice. Almost.

Jacob remembered the heat, and in that instant he felt it again, flowing over and around him. He imagined the liquid evaporating from his body. Imagined his eyes drying up and shriveling, sucked inward, skin pitted with the thousands of tiny imperfections the glaze could cover, but never truly heal.

Jacob clutched his package tighter and lurched through the door. He opened his eyes, just in time to see them reflect in the front window of the gallery. The image strobed through his mind. Captured. His eyes had been captured in that glass—not shriveling, or melting. Not dry empty husks.

Jacob shivered and was thankful for the air-conditioning. The sculpture in his arms seemed to pulse with heat, and the stench of baked clay caked in his nose sickened him. It was cloying, reeking of a world too mundane and static. As he walked under the jetted air of one of the air-conditioning vents, Jacob closed his eyes again and willed his mind back to his work room. To the ice.

If it hadn't been for the necessity to earn money, he never would have come to this place. It was like a mortuary to him, his dreams, his visions baked into clumsy bricks and lined up for the curious. The room was lined with pedestals, shelves—displays of all types. Each was designed to set apart a particular piece, or group, of his work.

"This is *my* art, honey," Michael said, each time the subject was broached. "You *are* you, I *sell* you."

Not quite true, Jacob thought, steadying his nerves. The clay wasn't Jacob. It was close, a "rough" imitation of his art, but nothing more. The images he allowed Michael to present were imperfect. They were solid, clunky shadows of what was to come.

He placed his burden on an empty pedestal and caught his breath, then unfastened the drawstrings and drew the black cloth downward. Slowly, the sculpture was revealed. Tall, slender, with long hair trailing behind in a pony tail, Jacob mocked himself. The glaze was a deep brown, fading across the contours of the clay, darkening to pitch in the crevasses and sharper angles. Portrait of the artist. Hot. Too-hot, too-dry. Not real.

Jacob didn't know what had come over him. He didn't do reality. He didn't put the world that surrounded him, the super-heated, dry-to-the-bone images that bombarded him each day, into his work. He worked from his mind, from some recess that reality had overlooked, spiny lizards and serpentine dragons, gnomes and fairies, angels—demons. Among the pieces surrounding him, their hard-clay eyes glaring from shadows and splotches of sunlight slipping in through the windows, the new work was out of place. Though he'd stylized the piece by adding long flowing robes and giving himself a beard he'd never been able to grow, it was too close to mundane. He stared at himself, and he felt his tongue drying out like a piece of crumbling sandstone. He wanted vodka.

He lifted the sculpture from the pedestal and slid the bag from beneath it, replacing it with a solid thump. *Club-footed, half-finished crap,* he thought. The eyes continued to stare back at him, eerie in their detail. Like staring into a mirror, reflected from glass. *Glass.*

At that precise moment, his mind registered that he'd heard another rhythm competing with the heavy back-beat of his heart. Footsteps? Fingers closed over his shoulder gently, and he felt hot breath on the back of his neck. Jacob froze, afraid he'd stumble and knock the statue from its base. Afraid he'd turn and find himself, staring back, an endless reflected hallway dragging him into an Escheresque nightmare.

"Perfect," she said softly. Her words brushed him physically, the air dancing over his clammy skin. "Who did you make yourself, Merlin? Moses? I like the beard."

Jacob didn't turn. He stared at the statue, acutely aware of each point where their skin touched. He hadn't thought about the source of the image in that way. He hadn't seen the wizard, or the prophet in the flowing robes—until that moment. He'd wanted the beard because it was a symbol. It was unattainable, like perfection in the clay, something he couldn't have, but that he could create. It was the *point* of it all.

"You don't think it would be better in glass?" he asked, his voice unsteady. There was something in her heat—the nearness of her flesh—that was unnerving. The sweat that coated his skin trickled in a thousand Chinese water torture rivulets, but he controlled the urge to shiver.

She hesitated, considering.

"If it were glass," she said at last, "I could see through you. Somehow," she turned him slowly, drawing him back and closer to her by her grip on his shoulder, "I don't think you'd like that very much. There's too much you don't show."

Jacob met her gaze, just for a moment, as he turned, then blushed and looked away. She reached out with one finger, long nail pressing up under his chin, and turned him back to face her.

"I don't want to see through you," she said softly. "I want to see inside. I would love to look out from there, to see what you see. If I looked through you, all I would see is something on the other side, and you wouldn't exist at all—or would you be my lens?"

Jacob heard the words, but he couldn't concentrate on them. She seemed to be talking for the sole purpose of blasting the sweet-hot scent of her breath across his face. He had the intense urge to spin and run, hit the door and never look back. The draw of his workshop was stronger than he'd ever felt it, the need to feel the soft hiss of Freon-cooled air washing over him near-overwhelming.

As if she sensed his thoughts, she tightened her grip slightly.

"Don't," she said softly. "I'm sorry. You don't even know me—not really. I'm Sylvia—Sylvia Mathers. I'm studying at the University, Visual Arts major. I've been to every show you've had in the last year."

Jacob's mind whirled back. January—at the beach. He vaguely remembered her, colored streaks in her hair, which had been braided then, but her eyes the same. He remembered. He'd put those eyes into a fairy, smoothed the shaved ice and diamond-bright chips away carefully. He'd molded them in clay and dried them for the world to see. He'd put the hair on an angel, as well, though the clay hid the colors.

Jacob's glance shifted to the right and she followed with her own bright eyes. The fairy stood in one corner, half-shadowed. Sylvia's lips curved upward in a smile. Did she know? How could she know? It was only her eyes.

"I...I've had a lot of shows, he mumbled," trying to draw her attention away from the corner. What had she said? *Would you be my lens?*

He couldn't be a lens. He couldn't be seen through. He was dry, caked and solid—glazed and fired. Flesh / clay / all the same. Static. As she watched him, trying to read his eyes, he felt as if he'd put himself on display—not the clay statue, but something more. Something solid and permanent that could be viewed, and judged, criticized and misinterpreted.

"I have to go," he said quickly, drawing free of her fingers.

"The show?" she asked, eyes showing a bit of the hurt his rebuff had spawned. "Your show will be starting."

IF YOU WERE GLASS...

She was right. Jacob heard movement in the back of the gallery, and the lights would be on soon. Perfect lights. The lights that made these clay mockeries of his work seem more than they were, that caught the perfect angles and showed just why each was placed as it was. Michael was not going to be pleased at seeing a new piece he hadn't had the chance to display properly. More reason to be absent.

"They don't come to see me," he mumbled, turning toward the door.

She called after him. "That is exactly what they—I—come to see. There is no separating it. The art is you."

Jacob heard her words trailing away behind him. Fading. Echoing.

"Not this art," he whispered.

Would you be my lens?

He slipped behind the wheel of his car, jammed the key into the ignition and fired the engine. Tepid air instantly poured from the AC vents, cooling slowly. Sweat ran freely down Jacob's arms, down his back and under his collar. His hands shook and he couldn't fix his mind on the act of putting the car in gear and pulling away from the curb. His head lolled onto the steering wheel, and he barely avoided setting off the horn.

The impossible sound of the passenger door opening brought him upright. Before he could speak, or act, she was sitting beside him. Her eyes were wide with fear—with the expectation of—what? Rejection? Anger? Jacob couldn't speak.

Then she had closed the door behind herself, leaned closer and slid her hand slowly up his thigh, one finger trailing along the inseam from knee to crotch. Her touch was hot, and as she pressed her lips suddenly to his ear, her tongue slipped out to tease his ear lobe.

"Show me," she whispered. "Take me where you work, the clay—the fire. Show me how you stole my eyes."

Jacob glanced to the latch of his own door, but he knew there was no way he could run. There was nowhere to go, and he couldn't leave her in his car.

Her hand pressed more firmly between his legs, palm rocking up and back, and he felt himself molded, felt her re-forming him with heat. Jacob shivered. There was nothing else to do but to pull into traffic and hope a shred of concentration would be left to keep them from plowing into the side of a building, or painting a still-life on a canvas of asphalt with the body of a passing jogger.

Jacob had never allowed a living soul into his workshop. Neither clay, nor ice. His payments were sent to a post office box at a post office miles from home. His utilities were in a dead cousin's name, and he had never had a phone. He had spent time with others, but never in his own space.

He had even known a few women—fans, mostly—rich older women with too much makeup, expensive clothes and leopard-skin heels—art students hoping something would rub off of his flesh—not many. Time was too precious. His art was a fever that burned brighter and more painfully if he denied it, and his art left little room for the world beyond his walls. Eat. Sleep. Work. Anything else was an intrusion.

She was different. "Sylvia," he whispered softly.

He felt the zipper of his jeans sliding down and held his breath, afraid of the biting metal teeth. Afraid, suddenly, at how far and fast he'd pressed down on the gas pedal. The Cougar lurched through traffic, speeding, slowing, and Sylvia began to laugh softly, her hand fully inside his pants now, cupping him as her thumbnail stroked up and down the length of his erection.

"I have to work," he gasped, trying not to hit the brake and the gas at the same time. "I …"

"I want to watch," she replied immediately, ignoring the panic in his voice. "I want to see how you do it—to see it *really* happen. Could you sculpt me? All of me, not just the eyes? Like you did with yourself—maybe an angel?"

Jacob closed his eyes and shuddered, despite the danger of driving blind. Then he forced them open and swerved, narrowly avoiding a parked Jeep.

He was panicked, and he hoped it wouldn't show in his eyes. He was too hot. The heat washed through him and burned in his cheeks. It rose to her touch. It seeped into the Cougar, battling the steady flow of cold air from the AC. Winning. He felt as if his skin would crackle and curl up.

Jacob gritted his teeth, not wanting to embarrass himself by releasing in her hand—in his pants. Not knowing how the fuck to react or to regain control. Not sure at all that he wanted to regain either as long as she kept her fingers working, slow and steady—as long as he didn't kill them both.

Miraculously he held on, pressing his spine so tightly into the seat back that he thought he'd warp the frame work, shifting side-to-side in his seat each time the pressure threatened to bring that final release.

He made the final turn down the alley behind his home and wondered what the hell he was doing. He couldn't take her here. No one came here. Her hand curled around him and slid slowly in, and out—and he gasped a sharp little bark, gritting his teeth and cutting the engine, hand sliding down to grip her wrist and pull her back.

"What?" she asked, watching him, half smiling, half-worried that she'd committed some horrible offense and ruined the moment.

"Wait," he said. "Not here."

Her smile widened, and she nodded.

With a deep breath, Jacob opened his door and climbed out. He hesitated a moment, then moved to the passenger side door and opened it. Sylvia slipped out and Jacob pushed the door closed behind her, leaning on it a second to try and regain control. He felt his erection pressing tightly through his jeans and the heat that pulsed through his veins. He pushed off the car and lurched past her to the door, still unsure what he was doing—what he would do once they were inside.

He found the key and forced it into the lock. Sylvia pressed tightly to his back, and he shivered. With a quick twist of his wrist he opened the door and pushed it open, nearly falling inside from the pressure of Sylvia's body against his back.

At that moment, Jacob panicked. No one had ever been inside. He'd kept this place sacred, kept the silent promise of secrecy with his work. Now she would know. She would see what no one else had seen, and he would truly be transparent. Glass.

Jacob was afraid he might shatter.

Regaining his sense of balance, he turned and pressed a hand against her eyes, wondering what she'd seen.

"Wait," he said. "You asked me to show you—let me do that." He hesitated for a moment, then added, "No one has ever been here. Ever. You are the first. Let me be your guide."

"My lens," she answered, her words barely a breath of too-warm air, sweet-scented and tempting. Misting in the air. She shivered at the room's cold. The slip from outside into the constant 38 degrees was a shock, even when you were used to it. Without a word, he turned her, and led her past the small refrigerator and through the second door.

It was hot. Stepping from the cool room to the heat, their clothing matted to their bodies within seconds. Jacob spun Sylvia slowly, hands on her shoulders, one turn for every four steps. He wanted to keep her off balance long enough to come to grips with what he'd done—what he was doing. Somehow she had not seen the window. The secret—the real secret—was safe. Still, here she was, and as she spun, Jacob's attention caught and hung on the swell of her breasts and the small "o" of her tentative smile. Sylvia had very full, red lips.

Jacob stopped her suddenly, slipping in closer and wrapping his arms around her to steady her if she stumbled. Sylvia gasped, and as she did, he covered her lips with his own, teasing his tongue over even, white teeth. He pulled his hand away from her eyes, and she met his gaze with hunger, pressing into his arms.

The kiln loomed to their left, and behind her was his bench. Bits and chunks of clay littered the surface. Below the bench and lining the walls were metal cabinets—damp and cool, they held the huge plastic-sheathed bricks of clay. No shape, just block upon block of his future, stacked in pyramids and palisades of grey gook.

Unlike the cold room, there was no work on the table. When work was finished here, he glazed and fired it as quickly as time permitted. This wasn't a gallery, it was where he created. Where he worked with heat and clay, molding the rough work that the world shared. Jacob's work was born in fire, and at the moment, the fire worked within him as well.

Letting his hands slide down the small of her back, Jacob lifted Sylvia easily and stepped forward, letting her come to rest on the edge of his bench. She leaned back for a moment and watched him. Sweeping the room in a gaze filled with wonder, curiosity, and desire, Sylvia's smile widened. The kiln in the corner beckoned like a great, silent beast. The air was so warm that breathing was a conscious act.

Jacob saw the sweat sliding down her neck and disappearing beneath her blouse, and very suddenly he wanted to know exactly how it would continue downward. He wanted to know the final destination of each drop. As if linked to his thoughts, Sylvia gripped the bottom of her blouse and lifted, sliding it up and over her head and tossing it away behind her, where it landed atop a small mountain of clay blocks.

Jacob moved closer, but she held up one hand, her eyes challenging.

With practiced ease, Sylvia slipped from the remainder of her clothing, tossing each piece away without releasing Jacob's gaze. He watched and waited. His eyes watered from the salty sweat that drenched his hair and slid hot droplets down his cheeks. He sensed the heat of her body, but he respected the moment. Something hung in the air, something he couldn't define.

Jacob stepped forward again. Sylvia didn't move at first, her gaze locked on his eyes. Then her hands rose, pressing into his chest—stopping him just before the bulge of his jeans brushed between her thighs.

"You promised," she said, holding him with the soft pressure of her hands. "You said you'd sculpt me."

"I will," Jacob said, breath ragged and eyes suddenly wild with the need she dragged from him so easily. "I will."

"Now," she said. Her eyes flashed. Jacob knew she wanted him, knew that she was as hot as he was—Jesus, as hot as the kiln—but her eyes told him she was also serious. She leaned back against the bench, hands pressing down to lift herself up and back. Her thighs dropped to each side, and she slowly collapsed back against the wall. With one hand, she reached out and grabbed a glob of grey clay, lifting it and squeezing, letting it slide through her fingers, her gaze locked on Jacob.

He moved to the bench, but not to Sylvia. There was a space just to the left of her, between her thigh and the door of the kiln. Jacob moved to that space as if in a trance, walking forward, but watching Sylvia. He found the bench by running into it with his hands outstretched, and he stopped.

Jacob took in her features slowly. He let his gaze slide down her form so that every contour of her naked flesh etched itself into his mind. Then he closed his eyes and the image remained. Taking a deep breath, Jacob leaned to the cabinet beneath the bench, opened it and grabbed one of the blocks of damp clay. He reached for a second, then a third, before he was satisfied.

Sylvia watched him, eyes wide, sliding her fingernails up and down her naked thighs, leaving damp clay trails. Jacob shook his head and turned away from her. The room was hot, the temperature ten degrees higher than it needed to be. That is how he worked. This was different.

Sylvia's proximity shifted the dynamics of his universe. Jacob's pulse undulated slowly through his throat and pounded against the inside of his temple. There was a loud roaring in his ears that distracted his thoughts. He plunged his hands into the damp clay. Clutching the slick mass, he lifted his hands upward, drawing the clay into shape. His fingers kneaded convulsively, matching the hammering of his heart, and he forced the control that usually came so easily. He had to be more gentle—had to remove all the bits and pieces of slimy gray clay that did not belong on the form. At the heart of every slab of clay his demons waited. If he didn't concentrate, they would not be freed, and the alternative was something Jacob didn't want to contemplate.

His thumb brushed down the center of the piece, forming the cleft between Sylvia's thighs and he started as she moaned. Jacob let his gaze flicker to Sylvia, then back, then again. He did not stare, not at her, and not at the clay. Jacob didn't work from models. He worked from memory—from his mind and vision. He knew if he looked too long and too hard he'd lose the piece completely, and it was already difficult to concentrate with so much of his blood draining below his waistline.

He felt the heat of the kiln. The moisture drained from him slowly, sweating out to run down his neck, his arms and legs, dampening his shirt. Sylvia was sweating as well. Jacob tried not to think of that sweat, trailing down the curves of her body. He grabbed a tool from the bench beside him, flicking a bit of clay loose, rolling it on the bench—returning it—rolled and smoothed, a tiny rivulet of sweat, the woman beside him taking form in miniature beneath his hands, the heat working its way into the mix as his nimble fingers formed flames that licked and tickled from the ends of the statue's hair. He worked hot coals into the base of the piece and more flames, sliding up her flesh, baking the liquid from her body. Hardening.

He was hardening.

Sweat burned his eyes and his pants, too tight to begin with, clung and chafed each time he moved. The burning in his eyes blurred the room around him and he couldn't shake the image of steam. Moisture escaping.

The basic form was complete, and Jacob's fingers moved in the rhythm that set them apart from the fingers of a thousand other men. Each flick of his wrist sent a bit of clay flying, or pressed a shape into another shape, all so rapidly it was difficult, even for Jacob himself, to understand how such exquisite precision was possible.

Sylvia watched. Her lips were parted in—what? Wonder? Awe? Anticipation? Maybe pure hunger. Jacob couldn't be certain in the strobed flicker of images that was her face, the clay, her torso, the clay, his fingers molding as his mind recorded, and shifting it—each bit of it—to fit the fiery, molten creature he was transforming her into. A demon. A succubus.

And it came to him—to his touch and his call. He watched the clay, no longer needing the quick glances to the side to bring forth the magic. Her image was supplanted by the image of his creation. It was Sylvia, and it was not. She might as well have not been present.

Everything in the room was surrounded by a prismatic, multi-colored aura to his sweat-stung eyes. The statue gleamed, clay still wet, though it was slowly drying, the moisture seeping into the heat, misting and rising. It was hardening, and as Jacob's fingers gently stroked the smooth thighs, the long tresses of delicate hair, his erection throbbed.

Then he felt her. Sylvia had moved, slipping down and off the bench to shadow him, pressing in from behind. She was careful. She didn't move in until his hands were back and up, away from the work, and only slowly.

"Hey," she whispered. "Where'd you go, genius?"

Jacob shook his head, trying futilely to maintain the concentration.

"I ..."

He couldn't speak, and her hands were working now, much as his own had been, drawing the heat to each touch. He felt her breasts brushing the damp back of his shirt, felt her hips grind into him and her hand sliding around his thigh to grip him as he pulsed and lifted into her touch.

"It's wonderful," she said. "But you were—I don't know—gone. You didn't even know when I stood up and moved."

Jacob closed his eyes and leaned back into her for a moment, then he pressed up and off, hands on her thighs as he drew away.

"I can't leave it here," he said. "It has to be fired."

"I have some fire for you," she replied. Jacob heard the light disappointment in her voice.

Stepping to the kiln, Jacob reached over and turned the valve that would release the natural gas to the burners beneath. There was a soft *whoof!* as flames blossomed inside. The heat swelled. Jacob spun, walking to the workbench and sliding a tray near to the statue.

This was one of the trickiest parts. He had to get the piece onto the tray so that it could be slid into the kiln, but if he tilted it too far, or moved too quickly—if the sweat dripped into his eye and he staggered, it would be gone. All of it. There would be nothing left of the inspiration but a ruined blob. Already, it was drying.

Jacob slid a plastic paddle carefully under the clay base, lifting very gently with his free hand and working slowly. There was a particular danger of shifting the hair, and the flames, the tips of which were rolled very thin.

He didn't notice the quick burst of cold air as the door opened, and closed.

⌒∴⌒

The heat was palpable, permeating the air as Jacob slid the paddle / shelf into the kiln. He took a last look at the work, nearly reached out to touch it through the searing heat, then pulled back. He slid the door closed and he closed his eyes as well, letting the last image of the un-fired clay linger.

It was quiet. So very quiet that it itched at his mind. Opening his eyes and spinning, Jacob realized with a start that he was alone. He vaguely remembered brushing Sylvia off before placing his work in the kiln. He'd been so engrossed in that work that he'd not noticed her leaving.

"No." That single word and he was moving, muscles aching from prolonged standing and work in the high heat. The sudden motion made him dizzy, but he managed to reach the door and tug it open, slipping into the room beyond.

She wasn't there. Jacob looked around frantically, but there was no sign of Sylvia, other than her purse, which lay on a small table just inside the door. Not gone—then where?

His heart sank. He glanced at the frosted glass, and he saw a flash of dark where there should have been only crystal and light. The door to the ice room was closed—but she was inside. The timer had sealed off the heat. His heart clogged his throat in a sudden spasm of disbelief.

"No," he said again, leaping toward the door to the gallery. He was too hot, he knew that, and the clammy sweat that clung to his limbs and clothing would freeze to his flesh within moments of entering, but no options remained. He had to get her out of that room, out of his home and his life. Had to compensate before her heat, and the heat of the room she'd unleashed, unwittingly damaged his work.

As he slipped through the door and pressed the button to close it, not waiting for the timer, he leaned back into its frigid surface to get his bearings. She turned. Her features glowed. Her eyes sparkled and her fingers, he saw at a glance, rested atop the head of the gnome at the end of the row. Hot fingers. Hot flesh. Melting—releasing the moisture. Drying it away.

He stepped away from the door, and she turned to him, clasping her arms about herself. For the first time, Jacob noticed that she was still naked. She'd not removed the clay that had clung to her thighs as she stroked herself, and her nipples were taut—frozen. Her skin had a bluish tinge, and her breath smoked through pale lips. She was trembling.

"We—you have to get out," Jacob said.

Sylvia shook her head slowly, either in negation or disbelief. She stared at him, but she didn't really seem to be seeing him at all. Her movements were slow, and Jacob realized with sudden clarity that she'd been in the room too long. Hypothermia was setting in.

"You have to get warm," he said. *You have to get OUT!* he thought.

He stepped toward her and she turned away. Her limbs were clumsy, stiff from the cold, and her feet had frozen to the floor where her flesh momentarily melted the ice, then held still long enough for it to harden.

Jacob realized with sudden clarity that he was still hard. Throbbing. She was more like ice than any warm flesh he'd seen. She was turning to ice for him, heat, clay—then ice. His art, hard, cold and smooth. Enticing.

Then she was falling. It was very sudden in contrast to her sluggish motion. She tripped, tilted forward and staggered a single step before giving up hope and raising her arms to protect her face.

The long display bench stood directly before her, lined with his work. Lined in ice and sculpted carefully. Beside the gnome, the crystalline image of Jacob, beared and frigid, gleamed, its arm outstretched to her toppling form. Jacob was moving too slowly.

Sylvia's arms struck the bench sharply, twisting her and she fell with a dull thud, the sound dulled by the heavy mist in the air. As she struck, her head whipped back, striking the bench with a sickening thunk.

Jacob slid to his knees at her side, crashing into the table in his haste. There was a crash, like thunder, and Jacob felt his own head crack into the ice-coated wood of the display table.

Cold misting air hissed through the vents on the wall.

The wizard-Jacob toppled.

Jacob reached out to try and catch it, to right it on the bench, but other works were falling as well, and he twisted, confused and disoriented. The ice sculpture toppled over the edge and down, its outstretched arm striking directly between Sylvia's naked breasts.

Jacob's question was answered, then, as the ice pierced her skin, and she screamed. She was alive. The statue leaned, caught now in her flesh, base tilted at an angle against the table behind. Sylvia arched, trying to rise, to push away, to move. Failing.

The room spun. Blood dripped down the side of his head where he'd struck the table. The tinkling crash of ice breaking echoed in his mind. Fallen, all but the gnome had fallen, some breaking, some shattering completely, others canted at odd angles.

Jacob staggered to his feet, gripping the edge of the table for support. He wanted to help her, but his mind reeled. Blood dripped into one eye now, and the room shimmered as the warmer air of the room beyond dragged mist from the slowly heating ice. His work was a wasteland, and his breath came in shallow gulps.

Out. He had to get her, get out.

Jacob turned, too quickly, and his foot slipped. Again. His knees struck hard and pain shot up through his body—paralyzing him before he could brace himself against the fall. His face struck the back of the wizard. His weight forced it down, deeper into Sylvia's arched, too-still form. Through skin gone blue and cold. The second impact on his head was too much, and his knees felt as if they'd been shattered.

Jacob tried to rise, but he found that his arms would not move. Nothing would move. Nothing. He stared.

The statue was clear and brilliant, stained in red below but pure and glistening between them. He saw Sylvia, her face drawn back as if to continue her long-silent scream. He saw her through the ice, through the image of his own body—the blue of her lips magnified—the clear depths of her eyes gone pale and empty.

"Be my lens."

The words whispered through his mind as thought faded and the numbing cold stole through him.

IF YOU WERE GLASS...

In the room beyond, the fire burned bright and hot. The moisture melted and boiled from the clay. Earthy and hard. Drained.

Lips, cracking with cold, froze in a smile.

A Splash of Color

MICHAEL OLIVERI

"Ma'am, we closed ten minutes ago," the curator said impatiently. "I'm going to have to ask you to leave. *Now.*"

"They're breathtaking," Lenore said, ignoring him. She twisted her silver ankh necklace in her left thumb and forefinger as she stepped over to the next painting. "So dark, so brooding. So…" She paused and considered the nude blonde kneeling before a shadowy figure, her back to the viewer. "…erotic."

"Are you planning on purchasing a painting?"

She glanced down at the fifteen-hundred dollar price tag and rolled her eyes. "I wish."

"Then please be on your way so I can lock up."

"Is it true they're all self-portraits?"

"Yes, they are. Now—"

"Casper Michaels," she recited as she eyed his signature. "Handsome devil. And the women?" She gestured vaguely toward a row of paintings featuring a pale redhead, a sleek brunette, and an athletic black woman.

The curator sighed heavily and pinched the bridge of his nose, then crossed his arms and glared at her. "Models. Women he finds in various places."

She nodded and smiled to herself, surprised at how easy it was to dissuade him. She let her ankh dangle and made a show of walking up and down the narrow corridor to inspect the paintings. In truth, she already knew their every line and brushstroke after spending the past several hours with them.

"His eye for detail is amazing. His light and shadow, his textures…"

221

The curator finally cracked a smile. "He's among the best I've ever seen. I'm very lucky to have him."

"Just how did you get him? I would think he would be able to nail one of the big city galleries, not a back-alley vendor." She gasped and placed a hand over her mouth. "I mean no offense, it's just that it seems like he could be a real success, you know?"

He frowned long enough that she feared she blew it. "Mr. Michaels doesn't want to attract the wrong kind of attention," he said at last. "And he still makes a good buck off what he sells. At least from his *paying* customers, anyway."

She chuckled politely.

"Look, Miss…"

"Call me Lenore." Her eyes wandered up and down a long splash of red in one painting, the only color in a field of charcoal and muted gray.

"What is it you really want here, Lenore?"

"I just—"

"Come now, no more bullshit. You've been staring at the paintings for hours. If you only wanted to admire them, you'd come back another time. I've got work to do before I go home. How 'bout you tell me what you really want so we can both get out of here?"

She crossed her arms and swallowed a snide comment, then nodded toward the paintings. "I want to meet him."

"Let me guess. You want to be the model in his next masterpiece?"

"That'd be great," she said with a shrug. "But I mostly want to meet him."

"Uh-huh. That's what they all say. Do yourself a favor, Lenore. Get out of here and don't come back until you've robbed a bank or stolen Daddy's credit card. Got it?"

"Hey, come on, man." She stepped in close and caressed his crotch. "Maybe we can work something out?"

He moved out of her reach, but not before she felt a twitch.

"What makes you think I'm not gay?"

"Because you've been eyeing my cleavage through our whole conversation," she replied with a sly grin. She thrust out her chest for emphasis, threatening to burst her bustier.

His eyes widened slightly. "Maybe I'm bi."

"Hate to break it to you, but that means you might still be interested. You're going to need a better blow-off than that."

He sneered and his face burned red. Before he could say a word, his pocket started ringing.

Saved by the bell, she thought as he pulled a slender phone out of an inside breast pocket.

"By the time I finish this conversation, you're gone." He thumbed a button and turned around as he raised the phone to his ear. "Yeah?"

Her heart leapt as she made a split-second decision. Before she could think better of it, she snatched the phone and ran.

"Hello?" she asked breathlessly as she hurried down the stairs in little more than a controlled fall. The curator pounded after her.

"Who's this?" a rich voice asked.

"Lenore."

"Are you running, Lenore?"

"Yes, I'm afraid so," she huffed. She hit the ground floor running and sprinted for the door. "Is this Mr. Michaels?"

"The same."

"I knew it!" she proclaimed. She started to pull the door open, giving the curator enough time to catch up with her.

"Give me the phone!" he shouted as he shoved the door closed with one hand and reached for the phone with the other.

"Let go, asshole!" She held the phone to her ear with both hands and wrenched it away from him.

"Stop it," the artist told her over the phone. "Give the phone back to Christie."

"But—" She sagged to the floor and batted the curator's hand away.

"Please, Lenore."

"He wants to talk to you, *Christie,*" she said with a sneer. She stopped struggling and held up the phone.

He snatched it roughly. "The name's *John* Christie, bitch." He put the phone to his ear but did not turn his back on her this time, nor did he make any move to help her up. "Sorry about that... Uh-huh... Well, sure, but... Right... Right... Are you sure that's wise?... No! No, I just... Yeah... Yeah, I got it."

She got back to her feet as he spoke, then straightened her miniskirt and adjusted her top. After he finished his side of the conversation, Christie listened for another moment before killing the phone and slipping it back into his pocket.

"You have something to write on?" he asked her.

"What for?"

"Because he wants me to give you an address."

⌒⋮⌒

She could have used directions with the address, and Christie wasn't very forthcoming when she asked. Still, she found the place without a great deal of trouble and parked in front of a vacant meter halfway down the block. Her rusted black Pacer blended in easily with the old Buicks and decrepit Cadillacs lining the streets.

She rarely frequented this part of the city, not necessarily due to any fear or real danger, but because there was nothing here for her. Simple shops like a grocer, a plus-size clothier, and an appliance dealer filled most of the storefronts, and most of the residents living above them retired years—in some cases, decades—ago. The singles bar hadn't changed since the fifties, and neither had most of its patrons.

Lenore found herself nearly alone as she walked down the street and compared the addresses over the doors to the numbers on the small scrap of paper in her hand. She stopped in front of a store called Ye Bookshoppe, and not surprisingly three rows of books filled the display case beyond the gold script painted on the glass. The door was closed and the store dark, but the green metal security gate stood open about a foot.

She took a deep breath and let it out slowly to calm her trembling. "Well, this is it," she told herself. She reached through the gap and knocked sharply on the door frame. The pane rattled noisily with each impact, and a second later a shadow eclipsed the dim light streaming through a small window on the opposite side of the store.

A reading lamp over a worn leather chair flicked on, illuminating a tall, slender man standing in the first aisle. He wore black pants and an untucked black shirt, and he padded to the door on bare feet. The streetlamps lit up his face as he unlocked the door with a dashing smile that melted her knees.

"Good evening," he said as he pulled the door open and stepped aside. "You must be Lenore."

"You're Mr. Michaels, then?" she asked as she stepped across the threshold.

"Call me Casper." He reached past her and slammed the gate shut. She winced as she noted there was no latch on this side, only a keyhole. She won't be going anywhere until he was ready to let her out.

Of course, if all went well, she wouldn't be leaving until morning anyway...

"Pleased to meet you, Casper," she said, offering her hand.

"The pleasure is all mine." He took her hand gently and lifted it to kiss her knuckles.

He's layin' it on a bit thick, she thought as she forced a smile. *May as well return the favor.*

"Oh, I don't know about that. Your paintings really don't do you justice."

The corner of his mouth turned up into a sly smile. "Let's go upstairs and get comfortable, shall we?"

Another wave of heat washed over her, and she mirrored his expression. "Yes, let's."

She eyed the row of books as he led her down the aisle toward the back of the store. She saw several frayed edges, leather bindings, fading scripts, and a handful of gilt edges before he killed the reading lamp.

"Watch your step," he cautioned her as they reached the stairway in the back.

"So you own the bookstore, then?" she asked as they climbed.

"I own the whole building. The bookstore downstairs, my studio on the second floor, and my apartment on top."

"Those books looked pretty old."

"Most of them are," he said as they turned a landing in front of a closed door and started up a second set of steps. "But those are not particularly valuable. The really old books worth some money are kept in an environmentally-controlled room at the back of the store."

Lenore looked the door up and down as they passed, and resisted the temptation to try the doorknob. Who cares about books? She wanted to see his works-in-progress, maybe even see him paint. Hell, to even just stand in the studio would be incredible.

"I've got Dickens, a Twain, a couple Longfellows, a first-edition Stephen Crane, some real classics. Fortunately street thugs don't know their books from their buttholes, otherwise I'd probably have more trouble with theft. There's so little cash involved with what I do that I'm not even worth holding up." At the top of the stairs he pushed the door open and gestured for her to enter first. "But I imagine you're not here to talk about books."

"No no, it's fine! Do you, ah, make a living off the store?" she asked, trying to sound interested. She stood to one side in the darkened room and waited.

He shrugged and hit a wall switch. Lights came on around what must have been his living room. "Make yourself comfortable," he told her as he walked into an open kitchen on the left. "The books pay the big bills, but the paintings keep me comfortable."

"I see." She found the place surprisingly quaint and Spartan. A battered coffee table stood in front of a brown love seat and beside a faded leather recliner. Two tall reading lamps flanked the love seat, and a 27" television sat atop a low chipboard TV stand across from the seating arrangement. On the next shelf down she saw a VCR and a handful of tapes, and below that a CD player and a twin stack of colorful jewel cases. The walls were all bare, and unless he put a rug under the furniture soon, the hardwood floor would need to be refinished.

She sighed as she listened to him rummage around in a cupboard and ramble on about his books some more. He talked about where he got them, which publishers were worth the most, his efforts at preservation, blah blah blah. Finally he came back into the room carrying two glasses of red wine.

"I'm sorry, I'm boring you." He held a glass out to her.

"Not at all!" she said with a weak smile. She took a sip and tried to read the titles off the stack of CD's.

"Perhaps my Poe collection would interest you more."

Her eyebrows shot up. "Now you're speaking my language!"

"I figured as much." He gestured to the couch and they sat down together. "So…" A pause for a sip of wine. "What's your real name?"

"What?"

"Come now. Lenore's not your real name."

She tried not to glare, and hid her expression behind her wine glass. "Why?"

"I like to get a feel for my subjects. It helps me decide how best to depict them."

Well, in that case...

"Elizabeth," she said quietly. "My mother called me Liz."

"Called? Past tense?"

"We don't talk much anymore. Not since Dad left us."

"What happened?" He set his wine down long enough to unbutton his cuffs and roll his sleeves partway to his elbow.

She sighed and thought about that for a moment, swirling her wine around her glass as she did so. "Mom drinks like a fish. She drove him off."

"You sure about that?"

She shrugged. "I woke up one morning and found Mom passed out in the tub, curled around a bottle of Jim Beam. Dad was nowhere to be found, some of his things were missing... His razor, several shirts, that sort of thing. It didn't take long to figure it out."

"How long ago was this?"

"Two-and-a-half years. Haven't heard a peep out of him since. Mom bitches about there being no money, yet her first stop after cashing her check is always the liquor store." She shook her head and took another sip, then glanced at him and chuckled. "Sorry, you don't really want to hear about my problems."

"On the contrary. I'm getting a few ideas here."

"Really?" She grinned sheepishly, and felt like an idiot.

"Yeah. So what do you do for a living?"

"This and that. I've flipped burgers, stocked shelves, delivered pizzas, you know, quick stuff. Mostly, though, I fight off the eviction notices."

"No school?"

"Can't afford it. And there aren't many scholarships for kids who drop out their junior year."

"Was that when your dad left?"

"Yeah." She blinked rapidly to stall the formation of tears. "I really don't know why I bother sometimes. I should just find my own place and let Mom fend for her fucking self, but most places I can afford are roach-infested shitholes that make our apartment look like a palace."

"I'm sorry. You're my guest and I'm upsetting you."

"Look at me. I'm acting like a little girl." She giggled and wiped her eyes with her fingertips. They came away stained with mascara. "I must look awful."

Casper drained his wine glass and turned to face her. He set his hand high on her thigh. His fingertips found the quarter-sized hole in her black stocking and caressed the smooth skin it revealed.

"The bedroom's dark. It won't matter what you look like."

She sniffled and looked from his eyes to his hand and back again. She drained her glass and set it next to his.

"Let's go."

A SPLASH OF COLOR

She finished stuffing her nylons into her bag as she followed him into the living room. He never turned the light on, so she quickly gave up trying to find her panties in the dark. She figured maybe he wanted to add them to a collection. If so, that was just fine with her. He went long and hard and didn't ask her to do anything freaky like most of her club pick-ups.

"I'll pour us some more wine, then we'll head downstairs," he said. He finished buttoning his shirt and tucked it in as he stepped into the kitchen.

"That would be great."

She took a deep breath and blew it out through her cheeks as she stood waiting in the center of the room. She wondered if he had decided how he would depict her, and somewhat feared the results after her embarrassing performance earlier. No matter, it would make for some great bragging rights at the club.

"You mind if I step into the bathroom to wash my face?"

"No, don't!" he said. She heard a spoon clinking around a glass, then a clank in the sink. He emerged with two new glasses a second later. "Stay as you are."

"If you say so…" She accepted a glass and tried to see her reflection in the side as he turned away. She caught a hint of disheveled hair and runny mascara. She frowned and followed him through the door and down the stairs.

Bragging rights, she reminded herself. And who knows? Maybe she'd love it. It could turn out wonderfully dark, making her friends all the more jealous.

Casper pulled a key out of his pocket, unlocked the door, and pushed it open. He allowed her to walk in first, then turned on the lights behind her. He closed and locked the door behind them.

The apartment followed the same layout as the upstairs apartment, though he cleared everything out for his studio. Dropcloths and lamps of various sizes filled the living area, and an easel leaned against one wall. He removed all the counters from the kitchen except the one holding the sink. The cupboards still hung from the walls, the doors and frame blotched with a rainbow of colors. The bedroom and bathroom doors were closed.

"You look disappointed."

"Not at all! It's a nice place."

"What'd you expect, something out of a Marilyn Manson video?"

She laughed politely. To be honest, she did expect quite a few props judging by what she saw in the paintings. Maybe that's what he kept in the bedroom.

"Drink your wine. It'll just take a minute for me to get set up."

Casper crossed the room and removed a dust cover from a table, revealing a computer and a bookshelf stereo. He flicked the switch on a surge protector mounted to the table alongside the wall. The computer, an iMac he had spray-painted black, whirred to life and the screen lit up. He pressed the power button on the stereo and light jazz gently wafted from the speakers.

She winced at his choice of music and told herself to endure it as she drank her wine. A shudder ran down her spine at the bitter taste. Thankfully, Casper wasn't paying attention.

He pulled a tripod out from under the table and telescoped the legs before setting it up in front of the computer. He then opened a drawer on the right side and removed a digital camera and a long cable. He screwed the camera onto the tripod and plugged the cable into the side of the computer.

"What's that for?" she asked. "I thought you were a painter."

He froze and glared at her. "I take several stills, then pick the best and paint from there."

"Sorry, I didn't mean any offense…"

He snatched an easel roughly off the wall and erected it near the workstation. He set a canvas on it, then walked into the kitchen and started rummaging through the cupboards.

"Finish your wine. I'm almost ready."

She took a long gulp and wondered what his problem was all of a sudden. Was she a lousy lay? Maybe he expected her to do something freaky after all. Or then again, maybe he expected her to fawn over him more, or gush about being in the studio.

Fat chance of that happening. He already got laid. What more did he want?

She just hoped he didn't shoot his pictures and kick her out. She'd love to see the painting as he created it. It would suck if she had to wait for it to appear in the gallery. Or, worse yet, if someone bought it before she had a chance to see it.

"Where do you want this?" she asked, holding up the glass after she finished off the wine.

"Set it by the sink." He stood behind the camera and fiddled with its settings.

Okay, fuck you, too, she thought as she did as he said. She turned away from the sink quickly and a dizzy spell washed over her. She stumbled and leaned on the wall, and suddenly he came to her side.

"Over here," he told her. He led her to the center of the room and abruptly let go of her. Her legs shook for a second, then gave out completely. She caught herself on her hands and knees, then rocked back to sit on her haunches.

"What's happening?" she asked. "I feel so woozy."

"Don't worry about it." He slid something across the room and propped her against it, but she couldn't bring herself to turn around and find out what it was. "Lean on this."

"I can hardly move," she said, her words growing slurred. She suddenly felt scared and wanted to get up, but her limbs would not respond. She hardly felt her legs. "What did you do to me?"

He arranged her arms to hang down the front of her body, her palms at her lap, wrists out. He then walked over to the camera and pressed a button, then quickly walked behind her. The camera started to flash periodically, and she watched the pictures scroll across the monitor. He struck a new pose for each flash, alternately looking mournful, angry, or frightened. Finally he turned off the camera and leaned over the computer to examine the results, one shot at a time.

Meanwhile she struggled just to keep her eyes open.

"Perfect," he said at last. He pulled the key out of his pocket again and unlocked one of the back rooms. He disappeared into the darkness for a few seconds, then re-emerged carrying a switchblade. The blade snicked into place as he approached and crouched down in front of her.

She tried to stop him, to voice a protest, but could not bring herself to move or even form the words. He cut away her clothes and tossed them aside, then leaned close to her ear.

"'From grief and groan, to a golden throne, beside the King of Heaven,'" he whispered, his breath hot on her ear.

She gasped as he drew the blade across her wrists.

Gushes of red punctuated by white flashes of light accompanied her into darkness.

⌇⁚∿

Christie eyed the leggy blonde from down the corridor and decided she must need some help. As he approached he took in the graceful curves of her calves as she shifted her weight from foot to foot. The fur coat she wore only reached slightly below her ass and the hem of her skirt just barely peeked out beneath the fur. He licked his lips when he saw the red-painted toenails poking through the open toe of her golden stiletto heels.

"Can I help you, ma'am?" He clasped his hands in front of his crotch just in case.

She casually looked him up and down. She had sharp, angular features, and the rosy tint to the lenses of her glasses made it tough for him to discern her eye color. When she turned back to the paintings he noticed she did not have much of a chest, but her pouty lips boasted worlds of possibilities.

"So this is the work of the legendary Casper Michaels," she said softly. She leaned in for a closer look at "Venus Impaled", a work depicting a blonde woman kneeling before Casper's crotch, a bloodied silver spike protruding from the base of her skull.

"Yes, ma'am. He's one of my more popular attractions."

She wrinkled her nose at "Enshrined", in which an athletic black woman hung crucified from a metallic cross. It was one of Christie's favorites due to the exquisite detail of the woman's Nefertiti curls and Casper's incredibly reverent expression as he knelt and looked up at her, his hands pressed together as if in prayer.

"I don't know," she said a moment later. "They say he has a way with capturing emotion, but it looks to me like he's obsessed with gore and perversion. Take this one for example." She gestured to "Red Fury", in which a redhead threw her head back in a scream, her fists raised high, as Casper cringed before

229

her, his arms held up as if in defense. "I mean, what's the point? If he painted chainmail on her tits and a sword in her hand, it would make a great cover for one of those cheesy fantasy novels."

Christie frowned. That incident was almost the end of Casper's career.

"Well, ma'am, I do have one more that you might like. The artist just dropped it off this afternoon."

She shrugged. "Why not? Can't hurt to take a look."

"I'll be right back." He retreated to the back room and retrieved the new painting from its case. He inspected it carefully, making sure it had dried completely, then carried it out to her.

As soon as she saw it she took her glasses off to get a better look. He pointed out the little details, like the contrast of her slit wrists and their wash of red against her pale thighs and the way the walnut patch of hair between her legs did not match the jet black of her hair. He showed her how the tiny silver ankh representing life twinkled between her breasts while the tool of her death, the switchblade resting between her knees, displayed a matching twinkle. He noted how one could easily see the depth of her anguish and futility by the streaks of mascara down her cheeks.

Rendered in deep blacks and pale grays, Casper stood behind her with one arm crossed over his chest, his face dropped into the opposite hand, his fathomless sorrow evident.

"This is a little better," the woman said. "What's it called?"

"'Lost Lenore'."

The Mist Machine

CHARLEE JACOB

Theo Nieblo's machines for the movies were legendary. In the days before computer generation made special effects a modern wonder, his devices did things in the horror films that no one else could match—much less explain.

It was Nieblo's mysterious clockwork which pulsed throughout the staging in *Tell-Tale Heart,* causing it to appear thunderously elastic, rippling concentrically outward with each footfall John Barrymore took in the maddening conclusion to the old silent classic. It had been Nieblo's first film, back when he was just a young wunderkind.

Gloria Holden, best known for 1936's *Dracula's Daughter,* leaning against the pillar of bones in *Reborn,* underwent that chilling metamorphosis—mauve-gray serpents twining through her black hair, slithering sensuously up her nostrils, into her ears, funneling down into her mouth, gimleting her eyes until even in black and white they changed color—due to Nieblo's hidden censors. These had burned a powder, producing a smoke drawn to the dampest regions—also making it necessary to film Miss Holden only from the waist up.

And who could forget Vincent Price in *Red Tears,* the moisture seemingly bursting from every pore of his body, thousands, millions perhaps of scarlet drops effusing as his character turned to blood? Nieblo claimed condensation and hocus pocus, never one to share an entire trade secret. Admitting only to a machine which hyperactivated sweat glands after the actor's body had been entirely smeared with a thin jelly which was clear only when dry and cool, but which reddened as soon as the conditions became hot and moist.

These were mythic in the movie world. Not to mention Nieblo's fire contraptions, cloud works, rain gadgets, dust engines, creepy crawly hydromatics, and contrivances part camera obscura-part kaleidoscope.

So Nash wasn't surprised to find a gizmo packed up among his grandfather's effects labeled the Mist Machine. He was only puzzled because he didn't think it had ever been used. All the other crated machines had filmography listed on their labels. This one had no filmography.

Of course, there were plenty of mechanisms on the stagecraft market that produced fog. Fog and mist were only marginally different. That is to say, fog could be exceedingly dense, so much so that a person couldn't see his hand in front of his face. Yet mist was only a very thin fog in which horizontal visibility was no more than a bit over the standard mile. Maybe there simply had been no interest from directors and producers in such a device.

Perhaps it hadn't worked.

Nash knew that was ridiculous. The man was famous in the business for spooky dependability and eccentricity. All of Theo Nieblo's machines must have worked.

He checked over the packaging carefully. Had he missed any notations? Were there chemicals to be mixed and then introduced into the appliance? Wasn't at least water necessary? And were there no fans to propel this vapor along?

It was only a very small, quite simple-looking motor, shaped like some pre-Columbian water jug or something. But, then, Nieblo had enjoyed housing his engines in casings that resembled antiquities and *objects d'art:* Egyptian sarcophagi, Greek funerary urns, wicker men and so on.

Nash located a switch and flicked it. Stepped back. Waited.

Faint haze began to rise from the pour spouts. The humidity in the room rose abruptly, making his skin clammy. It flowed up and out until the other crated machines beaded up, and Nash's hair and clothes went limp. It was faintly pink, a nice touch.

Satisfied, he turned it off. It was late. Tomorrow he'd call an acquaintance who was making a film.

⤙∶⤚

Immersion.
Someone else's memories.
Dreams of death, of the dead, everywhere.
An entire world of them.
True, wasn't it? The planet was made up of corpses.
Every square inch around us, from death of one sort or another.
How could you ever hope to escape the taint?
Well, you couldn't.
You wore it, slept in it, ate it.

THE MIST MACHINE

The earth was a ball of compact carrion.
No wonder people were obsessed with it.

Nash tossed in his sleep, night after night, watching the quicksilver remains reveal themselves in everything. From the dust in his bed sheets to the supper digesting inside him to the crud under his nails. It was as close as crowbait breath, walled in with microscopic fossils and decomposed larger beings within the substance that made up those walls.

He'd wake, screaming, wanting to hurl himself into the air to hang there, suspended like the clean mist. He'd start to run for the bathroom to wash off the sensation of filmy deteriorations. But even water suffered an infinite number of things dying in it.

He'd happen to look down and see the drying (dying?) white glob that had come out of him. And that scared him worse, knowing full well what it was he feared but not sure at all what that part of him wanted.

⌣∴∾

There were *parties* in those days...

Hollywood had always been rumored to have orgies. Most such claims were bullshit; some were true. Like the factual one where Fatty Arbuckle fucked a starlet to death with a Magnum champagne bottle. Or those held at Errol Flynn's house, spy holes into all the rooms, including the bathrooms.

But the people who attended Nieblo's affairs didn't talk about them after. It must take something formidably esoteric to keep a group so addicted to gossip silent on any subject.

Want to know what it's really like to sink fangs into flesh and gulp blood? (A kink only the novices were into. And that but briefly. The thrill passed and was passed on. There really were much more interesting taboos to break. Vampirism was childish, really, brought on by no greater a fascination than a child sucking its thumb while yearning for mother's nipple.)

Want to savor what the cannibals do? Sweet-salty, tastes like chicken or oysters, depending upon the body part and its degree of freshness. (Honestly, people thought this was so bizarre. But it lay strapped to the tongue like a slightly sour oil which mouthwash cleansed or kissing passed on, still digesting as any other meat. And straining, sickened, at the toilet bowl, staring at the turd afterward revealed it to be just another piece of shit. Just wait.)

Sleep in a grave? (This one was heavier than you might initially imagine. There was a pipe supplied for air so you wouldn't suffocate underground. There was a camera fitted to the box so everyone could watch you all night, as they took breaks from their own pursuits. And, of course, you weren't sleeping alone. There was a genuine corpse with you. Suitably ripe. Oh, your naked body was covered with insect repellent. But, you know, it's a funny thing. Worms and maggots aren't easily repulsed. Especially when you're so close to the cadaver you can't

233

help but feel them as they go about their pursuits. The worms crawl in, the worms crawl out...how does the song go? Emetics, enemas, and douches were supplied in the morning, along with delousing showers.)

Fuck the dead? (Age and sex according to your preference. Not so decayed that one good pelvic thrust and their bones crumbled under you, but enough that the pube flesh was like sticking your dick in a chilly jiggly gelatin dessert. Or the teeth could be palpably felt loosening in the mouth as the tongue rasped like sandpaper. Or the rectum might gurgle, then slip free of its moorings with a glug, colon coming out as you withdraw, adorning you like a moldy sausage casing.)

Be fucked by the dead? (Taxidermy rendering eternal the erection men were rumored to die with. No artificial lubrications supplied though. Part of the charm of this activity was the dry hump. Especially if the guest bounced so hard a seam popped and the penis ejaculated out plumes of grumy sawdust.)

No, nobody ever talked. To admit to average carnal indulgence outside of legally-wedded, happily-ever-aftered bliss might produce a scandal. But to say you'd ever been anywhere near this sort of depravity? It made the infamous Hollywood homosexuals, pedophiles, and champagne-bottle date-rapists look like apostles. Your career would be over in the worst way. Might as well be a leper with open sores and missing digits. Might as well have aborted fetuses tied with string to your genitals, angels pursuing you down the street, hurling fistfuls of the shit of saints onto your head.

Nash's father had seen some of these party games. Growing up in old Theo's house. Straggling downstairs in his bottom-trap pajamas, rubbing his sleepy eyes. He'd peeked through the library doorway and watched as the softening corpse of a curly blond-headed, fully-pregnant teenager was fisted by a man in a top hat. Little Lar backed away in shock, practically bumping into a man and woman sitting on the floor in the foyer. They were just sitting there, expensive evening clothes soiled, eyes staring into space. They each bore a look of frightened surprise on their perfect faces, as if they'd discovered (or rediscovered) a profundity so immense that it shook every tenet they'd ever believed or been taught.

"There is no heaven," the woman whispered to Lar, her lipstick smeared halfway across her face with what looked like (but didn't smell like) butter. "There is no hell. Being alive is only an intermission between death and death. We're only afraid because we don't remember."

But if that was true and she'd remembered, why did she still look terrified?

The man murmured, slack-jawed, "When you fuck the dead, you fuck your ancestors, your children, and yourself. Time has no meaning. It's really just an attempt at crawling back into the womb. Not the one this body of yours squeezed out of. No, the other one."

The gentleman then began to tremble, so hard the stiff bib on his tuxedo front popped. Lar noticed with dismay that there was a blond ringlet caught in the fly of the man's trousers.

"Lar, you shouldn't be down here. It's far too soon for you to glimpse the mysteries," said Nieblo himself, having just left the drawing room. "Adults only, in free will."

Theo scooped his son into his arms and carried him back up the winding staircase. After that the boy was locked in the nursery on party nights.

"I tell you these things only so you'll see evil for what it is. Stay clean, boy! Go to church and prostrate yourself before God's altar; beg forgiveness for even having that devil's blood in your veins! Pray for your immortal soul!" Lar Nieblo's teeth would chatter with every word, eyes bulging bloodshot, as he preached to his own son later.

And Lar would then scourge himself, metal tips of the nine tails opening up old self-inflicted scars on his back and legs, creating new ones. While Nash as a child cringed, hearing the leather crackle in the air, split his father's skin like a wet sheet, iron singing the sweet curses of seraphim. He'd hear only grunts from Lar, teeth grinding together, heart hammering.

Then, exhausted, his father would crawl to his own room, curling up on the bed which he shared with no one. Because Lar's wife, Nash's mother, Shiree, had left them to move in with Theo, who was fifty years her senior. Lar would then take a single tiny grain of poison from the special stash where he kept it, not enough to kill him, only sufficient to grant him spine-rattling seizures and the hallucinations of Judgement he so craved.

Nash still shivered as he recalled the night his father went through his jeans pockets. Nash was about seven at the time. He'd found a dead mouse, decapitated and partially devoured by a cat. It was the first dead thing he'd ever seen. He'd carried it with him for days, wrapped in a piece of wax paper, marveling at how its gradual disintegration felt moving against his thigh. He was mystified by what changes it underwent as hours passed. He'd even taken it out when he was alone in his room, holding it by the little bit of tail left and swinging it, the way he imagined the cat might have. He'd fancied he could actually sense it behind a wall, wriggling whiskers at the musty odors and cockroaches, next outside nosing through rusty iron-hued chrysanthemums, then actually fleeing from the feline, heart beating like a cheap watch. The boy'd even toyed with the idea of ingesting a tiny piece. If a cat could eat it, why not he? People ate dead things all the time; they just usually cooked them first.

He hadn't even considered the smell. But Lar must have recognized it, having a sense-memory of it down to his very neurons. Lar found it, shrieked inarticulately, and used the scourge on Nash for the first time.

"Just like your Babylon mother!"

And then there was the second instance, five or six years later. A girl from his middle school disappeared from the neighborhood. The police had been out searching, but to no avail. Nash found her in the park on his way home from that school. Stuffed mostly into the earth among heavy kudzu (immersed, as in dreams), only one stump-knuckled hand sticking out. He'd dug down a bit and found a finger. He put it in his pocket, intent on being more careful with this treasure. He hid it on the window ledge, just outside his room, so the fresh air would steal the odor away. He took it in every night to examine it, to sniff at it and make sure it wasn't so rank it might draw unwanted attention. One night he even kept it under his pillow, to see if her ghost would appear to him. The subsequent nightmares had been horrible. In them the rest of her body came jangling in, naked pieces hopping across the floor. He assumed they were there to collect the finger but they assembled themselves into a jigsaw of her which lay across him in hideous splendor, still jerking until that part of him that fearlessly wanted the secret something spasmed out another spoonful of cream.

As it decomposed, he began keeping the finger in a jar of vinegar to control the stench. Took it out every night, fascinated but not sure why. Holding onto it, he seemed to picture her in his head: selling choir candy, climbing the stairs at school until he could see her pastel underwear beneath the short skirts, copying off his paper once during a history test. He even saw a shadow, bearded and dirty, as it leapt upon her in the park, raping, murdering, and dismembering her. Nash wept, sniffing at the finger, smelling her wildflower shampoo, the mints she used to keep under her tongue, her musky sex. Then he put it back in the jar, taking it out again in the morning, holding it up to the light from dawn streaming in through his bedroom window, trying mentally to exorcise its intrigue. Failing.

His father found the jar under the bed and beat him again, nine tails snapping out sermons with each strike.

"Filth!" Lar exorted, a vein in his forehead like a big crimson Z. "Those who would lie down with the dead are damned to eternal death!"

Then he staggered to his own room and took another grain of the poison. Nash could hear him thrashing, the bed springs loud, headboard slamming the wall as if an act of passion was going on in there.

If it hadn't been that the authorities finally found her body and also the maniac who did it, Lar might have thought Nash was the killer. But to him perhaps this perversion was just as bad.

The third incident happened when Nash was a senior in high school. He'd gone to the library and checked out a book on death. It was filled with statistics of murders: stranger killings, crimes of passion, suicides, vehicular homicides, terrorism, state-sponsored executions, battle dead and nationally-perpetrated genocides. It was also replete with vivid photographs of the dead: single deaths in ripper alleys, multiples from a would-be reaper on a spree, and deaths so superfluous a clean-up crew had to use a bulldozer. He'd poured over it in detail, trying to put together a reason for how it could both disgust and fascinate him.

It couldn't be just him. The stamp card in the back of the book was full. Many checked this volume out. The page ends were worn from turning after turning. The text wore tear stains, coffee stains, snot stains, even semen stains.

Lar found it under the mattress. Took out the scourge to punish him. This time Nash snatched it away and beat his father instead. One snap of the leather. Another. Lar shuddered, moaned, arched his spine, made no move to run or fight back, his sour body reeking of that poison he shattered himself to sleep with on his worst nights.

It was: punishment for the sin of being Theo's child atonement witnessing iniquity.

༜༚

Disgusted with his father and himself, Nash took the whip outside and stuffed it down into the trash. He came back in, rapping lightly at the door, calling softly, "Dad? Are you okay? I'm sorry I hit you. I never have before and never will again. Dad? Can we talk? We can't go on like this. I suspect most other people don't live this way."

But his father had already taken his dose of poison. Nash heard the man's gargly-chokes and the click of his vertebrae.

༜༚

Chimeras.
Must be the Rapture.
The dead were coming out of the earth.
Out of everything that contained a part of them.
Walls, furniture, roads, paper, clothes.
Sliding from the refrigerator.
Rising from the toilet bowl.
Assembling from the dirt on his shoes.
They were tired of being used.
They were there to do the using this time.
Capable of every foul thing and more.
The worst sins of Hell were sexual.
It was small wonder it was called the Nether Regions.

Nash woke up, screaming, icy raw down his throat and up his ass where extermination's specters had stood in line for a peck (and pecker) at him. Maggots did a mambo through the sunken sickles between his ribs. His penis was erect but dead, flesh wet and gleaming Abaddon gray, trickle of sawdust around the head. And something female, by the scent of blighted rose petals and wasted mackerel, was slowly rolling from the shadows, bloatedly voluptuous, the smell damp in nubilation as from a perfume just released from an atomizer spray.

Then he woke up again, sweat cold on his face, living hands clutching his living erection. But he hadn't had an emission. No, the wet dream would only have been completed had he been able to see her face.

"Corruption," someone had whispered in the first or second dream. Or in both. Then they'd laughed with a rattle.

CHARLEE JACOB

Leaving Nash wondering if the word referred to the condition of the dead or to the carnal act with them.

⌣⠆⠆

Nash was never allowed to go to movies. But once he was in college, what could his father say? He'd managed to get a full scholarship and when he left Lar's house, he seldom went back, only returning now and then at night to make sure Lar hadn't finally taken too much poison. He doubted his father even knew he was gone as he spent his days and nights kneeling in broken glass and watching the biblical channels on the set. All other channels had been blocked.

There was a television set in the student union. And there was a cable channel that at four o'clock in the afternoons showed classic horror movies. Like *Reborn* and *Red Tears*. They even showed one called *The Accursed*—starring Shiree Nieblo. Made almost twenty years ago, in the seventies when horror films began to use a lot of explicit sex.

Nash stared at the screen, his mouth hanging open. He wouldn't have recognized her if he hadn't seen the credits. She'd left when he was only two years old. Lar had destroyed all her photographs.

Scenes showed her walking along the beach, long red hair blowing in the wind, watching for her lover to come to her out of the ocean when the waxing moon made the tide high. He was a grim lord of the deep, shadowplay alone at first hinting that his handsome form wasn't as human as it seemed. The way the god made love to her, the audience saw his muscled arms loosening into boneless appendages which folded perfectly to fit her curves. The way his broad back, exquisitely bisected by the long straight spine, snapped to produce pronounced dorsal cartilage. And then the small schools of things that separated from between the scales on his flexing buttocks to flutter across them both, a myriad of semi-shapeless sea anomalies as active as sperm.

In the end the coastal villagers discovered she was mistress to the monster that was wrecking the fishing boats and devouring the crews. They built a bonfire on the sand and burned her. But she got out, running into the surf, her red hair all burnt off. Except it wasn't a full moon and he didn't answer to her screams. She was washed out into the ocean or perhaps she swam out, drowning willingly. Opening her arms and legs without reservation as all sorts of eels and mantas and stinger-tentacled jellyfish zeroed in on her.

Nash was shaking by the time it was over.

"You okay, man?" asked a fellow who'd been watching from another corner of the room.

"That was my mother," Nash replied, words thick in his mouth.

The guy's eyes widened only slightly. After all, this was L.A. Lots of stars and the progeny of stars. "For real?"

Nash nodded. "I haven't seen her since I was a kid."

238

"Nor could you have. Sorry, man, but surely you know she's been dead since right after that film was made. And it was the last one Nieblo did. Great effects with those wriggly things coming out of the crack of the sea god's ass, huh? One of Nieblo's machines. He also did the spirits-of-the-damned fire at the end. And the bath water with how it came alive in the tub and got her all turned on," the young man told him, rattling it off with a grin of true respect. Then he stopped and shrugged. "Sorry. Can't help it. I'm a film student. Name's Vince Cooper."

"I'm Nash Nieblo. You said she died right after this movie was made?"

"Yeah, she walked right out onto Hollywood Boulevard, her clothes doused with gasoline, and flicked a lighter. The fire department came to hose her down, also the two Porsches and the Rolls Royce she managed to ignite as well. It's famous. Even more than that dwarf actor who tried to hang himself from the Hollywood sign. You didn't know that?" Vince gave him a sideways look that suggested he found it hard to believe a person wouldn't know how his own mother died, especially when it was on T.V. and in every newspaper tabloid in the world.

"Is Theo still alive?" Nash asked in a scratchy voice, feeling as if those creatures who'd manifested from the sea lord's backside were now crawling down his throat, or using his tonsils for trapezes.

"Yeah, lives in the Valley I think. I saw him give a lecture on horror in silent film a few weeks ago. Wouldn't believe how good a shape he's in for his age. He's in his nineties but he can walk and talk strong, and I'll wager he can still even get it up and keep it up."

Vince stood and walked across the room. Handed him a card.

"I'm making a film with some other students. Not for class. We're trying to make a few bucks, know what I mean? It's called *Nekker*. Two K's. Come by and watch if you want to."

"Thanks," Nash said, putting the card in his shirt pocket.

⌁

Mort T. Nieblo was in the phone book. Nash took a chance the T. stood for Theodore.

"Hello?" answered the voice from the other end.

"Is this the Nieblo that used to make the machines for movies?" Nash asked, holding the receiver in both hands because just one didn't seem strong enough. The man's voice sounded as if it were coming from the other side of a grave. Just because Nash had never known him and because of the ghastly things Lar had told him.

There was a pause. "Yes," the man finally admitted.

"I'm your grandson, Nash."

And they'd set up a time to meet. Theo's limo picked him up in front of the dorms to drive him back to the house in the valley.

239

"You don't look anything like Lar," Nash said, unable to help staring as the distinguished-looking man and he sat in the back. Vince was right. This guy didn't look like he was almost a hundred. But that was showbiz. Plastic surgery and spas, magic Swiss collagen injections and (what? good, clean living?) maybe Frankensteinian implants from dead people.

"No, your father and I haven't any resemblances: physical or mental."

No *how is Lar doing?* No *I think about my son often.*

Theo turned slightly and looked him over, finally smiling faintly. "You don't look like him either. You look like your mother. Same auburn hair, green eyes. Soft lips. Those are lover's lips you know. Valentino had lips like that. Do you have a lot of girl friends?"

Nash blushed furiously and glanced away.

Theo chuckled. "Oops…that looks like your father."

Nash looked back at him and met his eyes directly. "Why did my mother leave us and move in with you?"

The old man sighed wistfully. "She was bored and wanted me to show her things."

"Why d-did she k-kill herself?" Nash stammered, thinking back on how Vince said she'd died.

"Shiree was a goddess. I suppose her time here was up."

Nash gasped, flustered. "What kind of answer is that?"

Theo put a withered hand on the younger man's shoulder. "An honest one. Such creatures cannot simply grow old and die. Having lived with death so—intimately—she knew she had to have it on her own terms. Don't look vacant, boy. Your father must have babbled what he'd seen as a child. Shiree leaving him for me was the last break with his sanity. For which, naturally, I feel sincere guilt."

Nash desperately wanted to shout at him. To tell how Lar took poison almost every night, tortured himself, died a little more. He tried to feel something from that firm but liver-spotted hand resting on his shoulder. A sense of crawling flesh. Of apocalyptic disease. The gelid temperature of death. He sniffed the air. Surely evil would have a distinct odor. But there was no trace of sulphur or excrement or rot. Only leather, French-milled soap, Italian designer cologne. And the evidence of his eyes was that Theo Nieblo hadn't suffered the ravages of sin, hadn't been struck down by God, body deteriorated crime by crime into puling tertiary-syphilitic pink-bubblegum-snotted palsied incontinent-pantsed shit-bagged slime.

"But Lar never understood. Running from life isn't marginally any better than running from death," Theo said. "I don't know which appealed to your mother more about how I was so close to death: the advancement of my years or my profession. But it wasn't really me she loved, it was the state of death which I represented. Lord knows, I loved her. Still do. More than any other woman I've ever known, living or dead."

THE MIST MACHINE

Nash's voice cracked as he asked, "Are you telling me that she left us, left me for oblivion?"

Theo sighed and replied, "Never think oblivion isn't hungry. There is no futility; only mutability. And a caress of atoms like motes which goes on forever."

"What's that gibberish supposed to mean?" Nash demanded, knowing he was sounding completely judgmental, as his father always had. He was raising his voice and for that he felt ashamed. But he'd come to see his grandfather hoping for answers to the pain of his life. And instead he was getting only some debauched and incomprehensible philosophy lesson.

Theo Nieblo narrowed his eyes and pursed his lips. "You're a college boy. You should know your physics. Energy cannot be destroyed, only changed. Yet that flies in the face of every accepted definition of death, doesn't it? Everything dies but nothing leaves. See? Everything which has ever died is still in the earth. And we're there with them in every incarnation we've had before. Linked to the dust with bits of hair gone to cemetery silk and skin powdered into crystalline salt. Each of us has an unconscious sense that one day we'll again be a part of the decayed tabula rasa, intermingling the grams of selves and dreams. It's arousing in the manner in which things always are to highly charged beings like Shiree: sexually. Most of us fear it because—in our separate shells—it's such an alien concept, this complete mixture without vanity or privacy. But we crave it, too, on some level realizing that it's the one state that makes sense."

Nash recalled Lar relating what one female party guest had told him when he was a little boy. "Being alive is just an intermission between death and death."

He felt nauseous, listening to this nonsense. His grandfather was crazier than his father was. But hearing it stated so matter-of-factly, unlike Lar's fanatic rants, chilled Nash's blood even more.

The limo slowed to a stop. Flares dotted the highway as emergency vehicle lights pulsed. But the accident was on the other side of the median. There was no reason for the traffic on this side to be stopped but, of course, it was—as people paused to see what had happened, unwilling to drive another few feet until they'd had their eyes filled.

Theo turned to the window, his fingers coming up to settle on the glass like moths seeking burning light. Nash heard his breathing deepen.

There had been several cars in collision. It was impossible to tell from the shapes how many were involved as steel jaggedly interlaced with steel, crumpling here and there into fancy Celtic knotwork. Only by counting how many colors there were was it possible to assume the number of vehicles crushed together. Blue car, black car, red car, two-toned classic fifties number in green and white. Maybe two red cars. There was a lot of red.

Here and there a half-peeled arm or leg stuck out like an indifferent piece of modern sculpture. A body had catapulted through a windshield to have its top half lost in the wreckage of the auto in front of it. An occasional face pressed to a shattered window, pulped until it might have only been a latex mask, or

241

one excised by an Aztec priest in a rite to Xipe Totec. A body had been thrown completely clear...Half of it, rather. (Was it the front half of the juggernaut through the windshield? No, that had a woman's legs, pantyhose and thigh meat in bloody ribbons.) This was of a man, severed spine visible along with organs unraveling, fingers still twitching, an expression stamped indelibly on the face of a horror that seemed to have transcended even his extreme agony.

Nash heard Theo sob. "Hideous and grand. God's creations—and man's."

"Grandfather?"

"Look at it, youngster. Marvel at it. See all these other cars? The drivers and passengers gawking? Can't bear to see—can't bear not to? When something is really, genuinely, repugnant to you, you can't look. If you're afraid of snakes, you can't look at them. If you're afraid of open spaces, you remain a shut-in, your curtains drawn so you'll never glimpse the ugly, threatening outside. If you loathe heights, you don't go up sightseeing in tall buildings or vacation in the mountains. But death like this? Why do people stare if not because, deep down, they identify the beauty in it, the majesty that is exquisite creation unmade. The same thing that makes a flower's bloom, dissected, still lovely in the separated petals. And knowing, recognizing, how it's part of them and they're part of it."

Nash did look into the other cars. Could make out the cheesy pallor and the shining of the eyes. Could see them tilting their heads and craning their necks to perceive extra nuances. Watched them turn their faces away to stifle the rising bile, then turn back to the scene in queasy revelation.

He heard the limo's door open and saw that his grandfather was getting out. Theo made his way between the stopped cars and climbed across the median. The police and ambulance attendants didn't even see him at first as he walked over to a woman's arm protruding limply from mangled metal, took the hand in his and kissed it tenderly.

respond to me = give me a fraction

I respond to you of this sudden power.

"Hey, you! What do you think you're doing? Get the hell away from there!" A cop grabbed him by the shoulder and spun him around, then visibly did a double take at the smear of blood on the old man's lips and the smile curving itself at the corners of that mouth. "You old freak!"

Suddenly Nieblo's tall, lean form went rigid, except for a series of little tremors that rumbled along one side of the body. The old man collapsed as both Nash and the chauffeur hurried out of the limo, darting between the stalled traffic to vault the median.

"Grandfather!" Nash shouted, stunned at losing him so quickly after having only just found him.

"Hey! Come here!" The cop called to a couple of emergency personnel. "I think's this geezer's having a stroke..."

But Theo Nieblo was already dead, collapsed into the gory wreckage, half a grin on his face like a tweak at a fault line.

THE MIST MACHINE

✧⁖∾

"Thought you might be interested in using this for your film, since it was one of Nieblo's…" Nash told Vince Cooper at the ratty little bungalow where the students where shooting *Nekker,* two K's. Three young women made-up as fresh, lusty cadavers and a guy with gravedigger dungarees down around his ankles were engaged in several tangled sex acts when Nash was ushered in.

"You got to be kidding! Of course, we want to use it!" Vince babbled as he excitedly looked over the curious machine. "By the way, man, sorry to hear about your grandfather. One of the greats."

"…that is, if you have any scenes requiring mist," Nash continued, struggling not to accept the picture trying to bludgeon itself to the forefront of his thoughts. Of the "great" man sprawled into the carnage of a grisly tragedy on the freeway, after taking his final bow kissing one of the mutilated victims.

"We'll write them in if we don't. What am I saying, this is a cemetery love story. Of course, we need mist for atmosphere," Vince replied, practically jumping up and down with delight. "Wow. A real Nieblo. The special effects for our script we're having to do the old-fashioned way, with cosmetics and raw chicken. Can't afford any computer stuff. But using this will be an honor."

"Super. Switch is down here. No need to add water or chemicals or anything. Just turn it on. I'll leave it with you and…"

"Don't you want to stay for a while? Maybe you'd like to be one of the corpses."

"No thanks. I've got a class. But I'll come back later if it's okay."

"Sure, sure! We'll be here till the wee hours, people coming and going all the time when they have classes, too," Vince told him enthusiastically. But Nash could see the film student was distracted. Obviously the young man was anxious to try the machine out.

Nash left, trying not to look at the three "dead" actresses, mossy vaginas spread for the cameras and black lips pouty. Nor did he want to see what the necrophiliac lead was doing to them.

> Orifices tight with rigor.
> Shouldn't they be flaccid?
> Flabby and dry?
> Pots of petroleum jelly and strawberry jam.
> KY and bacon fat.
> Nipples simply wouldn't erect.
> They would twist off like apple stems.
> And would be filled with what commonly lives in apples.

Nash shivered, it reminding him too much of what his father had described from Theo's parties. And they were images straight from his dreams. He felt

243

a bulge beginning to strain at the crotch of his jeans. Doubtless filled with sawdust.

⌣⁚~

Nash drove back to the bungalow at day's end. On the seat next to him was an urn with Theo Nieblo's ashes in it. His grandfather had been cremated that afternoon as Nash sat in English Lit, puzzling over the rants of a graveyard poet named Robert Blair.

> The sickly Taper
> By glimmering thro' thy low-brow'd misty Vaults,
> (Furred round with mouldy damps, and ropy Slime,)
> Lets fall a supernumerary Horror…

Nash had swung by the mortuary to pick the ashes up, wondering what he should do with them now.

> Scatter them on the bed,
> roll naked in them,
> jerk off in them!
> The old man wouldn't mind.
> Hell, he'd applaud.
> He'd join in if he only could!

Nash moaned, wishing it was as easy for him as it was for his father. If he could simply lose himself in religious mania, crawl in broken glass, whip himself, masturbate the bestial erections with a raw handful of penny nails, poison himself as he shut out the temptations with a hoarsely cackled, "Yea, though I walk through the Valley of the Shadow of Death, I will fear no Evil…"

> because I carry its finger in my pocket

He was considering opening a museum of Nieblo's machines. If he had the guts he'd try writing a book on the man's secret soirees for the glitz set. But he couldn't prove any of it. And no one would admit to anything. He'd be sued clear through to doomsday. Besides, he didn't really want that to be Theo's final legacy. A museum would be more respectful.

He turned off the ignition, bowed his head, tears rolling down his cheeks. He hadn't even told Lar the old man was dead. Afraid he couldn't handle it if his father went off on a tirade about how the Devil must have carried him off and how Sodom had lost a general. But, then, Lar had never told him that his mother was dead.

THE MIST MACHINE

He wiped his face with the back of his hand, saw a young couple just down the street, knocking at the front door to a small yellow house, knocking again when they received no answer. The man shrugged and the woman said something like, "Guess Mom isn't home." They walked away.

Nash then noticed that Vince was sitting outside on the curb, his own cheeks bathed in the bloody glow of the sunset, eyes bulging. He had his knees up and his arms wrapped around them, rocking back and forth, singing to himself in a tiny voice.

"Vince?" Nash got out of the car and went up to him, kneeling beside the film student. "Are you okay? What's the matter? What happened?"

"I had to go to the bathroom. When a man's gotta go. I managed to turn off the machine when I got back. A man's gotta go. Bladder should've been empty by then except I wet myself anyway. But I turned it off."

Vince rubbed his grossly-flecked chin. "Hurled, too, didn't I? Something in the bug juice."

Nash glanced at the bungalow. The front door was open. He could see a few lights on. He got up and went inside slowly, hesitating at the doorway.

"Hello?"

There was no answer. But there was a smell. A stench. Of spoiled shellfish and something like rancid buttermilk. Of sweat and brine.

The camera was knocked over. What few pieces of furniture had been in the room were demolished into kindling and toothpicks and suggestively ripped wounds of upholstery.

There was a sheen over it all and stringy bundles of puke here and there. No people. No dead bodies. Not even people made-up as bodies. But it did look as if several had been vomiting recently, violently ill. Too much for it just to have been Vince.

What had Vince been ranting about? Turning off the machine.

There was no one here.

The crew had probably gone off to supper. And Vince was probably on drugs. That's what movie people did a lot of, go on binges with alcohol and brain candies. According to Lar anyway.

Nash hoped they hadn't damaged his grandfather's machine. He'd left it with them in good faith.

"Hey, what did I expect? Those movie types are all cruds."

He turned the machine on to make sure it worked. The mist began to pearl in the air, making the humidity cloying. Satisfied it was still operating, he started to switch it off again. Until he heard the voices. Distant, calling, almost as loud of a roar as surf. Except they weren't close enough to hear the Pacific from the bungalow.

He must be hearing a party or something going on further down the block. Still he paused, finger above the on/off switch. Mist still pouring from the strange bottle-casing's spouts. The voices may have seemed far away but they rose and fell like a chorus, like a very great number of voices indeed.

Nash went back to the doorway and stuck his head outside. There must be a stadium nearby and he was hearing the thunder of the crowds, shouting, cheering. But there was nothing but the all pervasive traffic noises, warbling sirens, and, of course, Vince crooning to himself over on the curb.

Nash walked back into the room, mist gathering, thickening like the ripples of mirage on a desert. The voices were in here.

Realizing that raised the hairs up along the back of his neck, even as the moisture slicked them down again.

Then he saw the baggie on the floor, white powder. He brought it up to his nose curiously and could detect a slightly bitter undercurrent.

Something in the bug juice.

He knew that smell. It was the poison Lar took to give himself seizures.

Was this what made Vince sick? Had they all shared it? He'd heard that sometimes poison-laced drugs ended up on the streets. That sometimes maybe a boyfriend was getting even or a dealer had gone wacko. It didn't really matter who had spiked the powder. Only that people had used it. More than the single grain Lar used.

Nash quickly checked the other rooms to see if anyone had crawled into them. Finding no one, he hurried back to the doorway. Vince wasn't perched on the curb anymore. The kid was foaming at the mouth, eyes rolled up and reflecting the silver from street lights which had come on down the block. His spine was bowed until the back of his head rocked against his boot heels. Nash either had to go help him or find a phone in this mess to call for an ambulance.

Then above the din of voices he heard just one voice.

It made him turn slowly back around.

She came together, made of moisture the way a cloud can seem to possess living form. The state of light penetrating the pearls of wetness created colors in prisms.

Rainbow limbs like oil on top of blood on top of charred, black death.

(Nash...) her one voice said.

He knew right away who she was. From the blackened meat of her and the dripping water. As she'd died in *The Accursed*. As she'd really died, setting herself afire and then being hosed down in the middle of Hollywood Boulevard. Red hair burned down to the skull, hands coming up melted into flippers the lord of the deep might have envied—or bestowed.

Beauty. Nightmare.
Love.
Illusion of careening mortality.
Darkness risen out of light.

(Nash...)

Behind and around her he could hear that pandemonic rumble and grind. Building to ear-splitting. His bones shaking with it, walls of the bungalow shaking with it. Only the mist was unperturbed, faintly pink from all the moisture gathered from living bodies—of which each was mostly water, even as the earth was mostly water—all the blood, all the flesh turned to particles of dust, dazzling as no other dust ever had.

He could see faintly the bodies of the other students who'd been making their film here. Who must have taken that poisoned drug together and died. With the machine running so they could go into this mist. They were fading away, however, smiling as they went to soft silt, like screen images gone to static. How Theo had done it, making this hazy grist mill which was some sort of bridge, he'd never know. Nobody would. The old man might not even have done it on purpose or else surely he'd have kept it running, waiting for Shiree.

Nash didn't know why she was whole and nothing else seemed to be.

Then he looked again, at the quartz-sheer shape. She was just a cloud, an exhale of frost, smoke that spoke his name.

(Nash...Nash...) a soft echo sparkling like the cracks in diamonds.

"Mother," Nash began, arms frozen at his sides. Trying to close his eyes so he wouldn't see the burned steaks of her breasts surmounted by the dark sapphires of her nipples, the slick black peeling stomach, the thighs that met where pelvic bone-burned-blue showed through.

And he had an erection, a vile despicable prodigal boner. He ought to turn and run but he couldn't, self-preservation abandoned for debased enchantment. He had to look, wanted to see her, third degree-ruin madonna, murmuring to him out of a lipless palate scalloped by flame. Gliding to him like the goddess of fuel and near-rain. And around her, shapes came together, pulled apart, nebulous caresses and vague Kama Sutra gauze, Tantric acts effervescing in a coital spume. And all along the floorboards and into the hall and out on the porch as the heavy moisture gathered, were those souls popping up as mushrooms, faces leering from agaric pulp, or their gills or stems unfolding fungal cunts and dicks?

All of a sudden, the things his grandfather had said made sense, the dreams which had haunted Nash finally computed. About the great universal deathwish, elementally sensual, exotically psychotically erotic. If a person was totally honest with the obsession to gawk and be jaded by gross visions, the admission would have to come that this was what everyone prepared for.

As the small child prepared for becoming an adult and having sex, so the adult prepared to die, the two acts becoming one and the same sometimes. In people like Theo and Shiree.

Shiree was reaching out for Nash, fused fingers steaming. She'd come back for him, after having deserted him when he was a baby. Should he go with her? Damn, he was so afraid. Finding her repulsive; finding her gorgeous. Almost close enough to him to rub that blue pelvic bone against the aching bulge in his jeans.

(Nash....ash....ashes....)

"What?" he mumbled, realizing she wasn't necessarily saying his name.

(Ashes...Theo's ashes...)

And he didn't know whether to be relieved as his heart skipped a beat or finally crushed beyond repair.

She wanted him to bring Theo's ashes to her.

Nash backed away, chewing his lip, erection shrinking with humiliation. He slid through the fogged doorway, saw Vince's body on the lawn, now quite dead. Now enveloped in the pink mist. The film student seemed to be getting up, smiling, fuzzing out like bad reception, his shape turning to infinitesimal scales like floating dandruff and dandelion fluff.

Not fair, not fair, Nash was thinking, hating himself for sulking, for being refused, for going solidly through the mist to his car, retrieving the urn from the mortuary.

Then for bending his mouth close to the urn's top and whispering, "You were wrong, Grandfather. Shiree does love you."

He could see the mist starting to filter down the street. Those horrible little sex-toy mushrooms were sprouting wherever it touched ground. Some old lady came out of the yellow house, gazed about her in awe at the occasional libidinous bodies in vapor, pulled up her shapeless dress, and gleefully sat down on one of the fungal pricks. Nash wondered absently if she had been lying dead inside that house, undiscovered by the couple who'd knocked at the door, risen only when the mist crept through the windows. Glancing back he saw her starting to powder, like a flower seeding in a breeze.

He brought the urn inside the bungalow.

"What do you want me to do with it?" he asked Shiree.

Her burned hands mimed a twisting. He understood and opened it. The contents began to swirl out. The beautiful, heinous image of her disintegrated, mixing with the ash. This took on the sensual ghostly shapes of lovers twining. Nash realized the voices he was hearing so *en masse,* by the billions, trillions and beyond weren't cheering or shouting after all. They were sighing, moaning, gasping in the throes of pleasure.

He reached down to turn off the machine and hesitated. Obviously the pink mist hadn't harmed him. He knew Vince had been dead and he suspected the old woman, too. So he didn't really believe it would hurt anyone if he left it running. It would shake a lot of people up though. At least at first.

Then maybe they would come to understand, as he (hoped he) did, about the nature of death and closeness. About what they were afraid of and about what was really out there.

Nothing to fear.

Scratching the Surface

MICHAEL KELLY

My time with Silva was short, but memorable. I remember it, all of it, like it was yesterday. I remember it with a sharp clarity that never existed in his photographs. Though, upon reflection, one could clearly see the real world swirling beneath the surface of his nightmarish portraits. It was an irony not lost on Silva, I'm sure.

He arrived one rainy, windy night in the Spring. It was a damp, miserable May and my twelve-year-old hands were already experiencing throbbing bouts of arthritic pain that plague me to this day.

Where he came from, I still don't know.

I was in the living room reading an Aquaman comic book, sitting close to the radiator for warmth, when I heard a muffled clumping sound from the front porch. It wasn't a knock on the door, just a slight shuffle and stamp, as if an impatient stallion were outside waiting to get in. I put the comic down and cocked an ear, waiting for the sound to return, but it didn't. So I waited and waited for what seemed an interminable amount of time, leaning forward, listening as the clock on the mantle ticked...ticked... as the water hissed and steamed through the radiator, then, THUMP-THUMP on the wooden door and I nearly jumped out of my skin.

I stood, my heart beating inexplicably fast. Mum and Dad were in the kitchen, their voices oddly muted. I stepped lightly to the door, bent to press an ear to the old warped wood.

THUMP!

I shrank back, then laughed. What was I afraid of? Mum and Dad were home.

I grasped the brass doorknob, gave it a quick twist and pulled the door open. It was dark and wet outside, the kind of darkness that is somehow thicker, more solid than it ought to be; a deep black darkness that suggests damp mystery. Of course, I was but twelve years of age, and given to fits of imaginative fancy. Perhaps it was just another wet night like any other.

At any rate, I peered into the void. At first I saw nothing at all but the rain washing by in cool sheets. The porch light was obviously out. Then, slowly, as my eyes adjusted to the gloom, I glimpsed a form take shape. The figure stepped forward, and I took an involuntary step back. It was a man, tall as the day is long. Of his physical features I could discern nothing. He wore a dingy gray slicker (what Mum would have called a mackintosh), one of those wide fisherman's hats that neatly deflected the rain, and dungarees tucked into black rubber boots.

The strange man—and even before I got to know him, just looking at him then and there, my adolescent mind knew Silva was a strange man—leaned into the doorway, doffed his fisherman's hat and bent regally, sweeping his arm before him, as if presenting himself to royalty.

"Silva," was all he said.

I squinted up at him. The man's coal black hair was stuck to his head in a pointy, barbwire tangle. It didn't look so much wet as it did greasy. One large dark eyebrow cut a line across his forehead. His face was round, almost cherubic, with puffy pale cheeks and, yes, a button nose. The whole effect was oddly incongruent on such a tall person. You come to expect a certain gauntness to tall, thin people. And under his slicker I could tell that Silva was thin. You expect sunken bony cheeks, deep-set eyes. You don't expect a face that would be more at home on a toddler, the eyebrow not withstanding.

And his eyes were a rich raven black, strangely iridescent. I couldn't differentiate the pupil from the iris. They shimmered and wavered like an oil slick. I remember feeling faintly sick to my stomach as I gazed at Silva's eyes. A warm wave of dizziness passed through me.

Silva stepped forward, into the house. He stared down at me, a thin dark shadow. Of course, at the time, I didn't know him. He was just a strange wet man standing in our doorway.

I stood, looking up at Silva, trying not to look into those swirling eyes, but unable to look away. His face shone waxy in the wan light, and patches of dry skin peeled off in tiny flakes. My hands were bunching in the front folds of my shirt. I recall this because my fingers were stiff and sore from the damp.

Finally, after what seemed minutes but was likely only seconds, I tried to speak. "D-Dad? D-Dad?"

Then Dad was there, behind me, his hands on my shoulders. "Well, Nate, I see you've met Mister Silva." Dad grinned. "Go on, then, Nate. Introduce yourself proper."

I relaxed my hands, stuck one out. "Pleased to meet you, Mr. Silva."

SCRATCHING THE SURFACE

Silva looked at my hand, gripped it gently, as if he knew it was aching. His palm was moist and damp and cool all at once.

"Likewise, Nathaniel." He rubbed the top of my hand, stared at it curiously. "Your tiny hand is frozen."

"Bad circulation," I said.

"Yes, well, I'm very pleased to make your acquaintance," he said. "I'm Silva."

His voice, like his appearance, was a strange contrast. It was soft rain and a scratchy jangle. And he'd called me Nathaniel. No one ever called me Nathaniel. To Dad I was Nate. To Mum, Nathan.

And he was Silva. Just Silva.

Dad had stepped around and was shaking Silva's hand. "Welcome Mr. Silva. With the weather like it is, wasn't sure if you'd be delayed."

"Bus was right on time," Silva said.

Mum was behind me, hovering, keeping well back. Silva looked past me, in Mum's direction.

"Good evening, Mrs. Swann," Silva said.

Mum nodded, almost imperceptibly.

"Nate," Dad said, "Mr. Silva has let the room."

Our house, like many in the neighborhood, had a room at the side accessible from doors inside and outside the house. Just a room with a bed, a desk, a small closet, a tiny ice chest and a small bathroom. Dad had been trying to rent the room for some time now. There had been a baby boom, sure, but the economic boom hadn't come to fruition. We weren't in a bad way, Dad could still buy me the occasional comic book and soda (his idea of love), but the extra money would surely come in handy. At least Dad thought so.

So now we had a stranger in the house.

Mum, I could see, was none too pleased.

~:~

After that first night, Silva quickly settled in. Mum was distrustful of him at first, peering at him surreptitiously whenever they crossed paths. But she soon relaxed, paying him no heed. Dad was happy and exuberant to have him around, chatting amiably on the rare occasions he saw Silva.

And me? Well, I was pleased to have someone else around, quite frankly. I was a bit of a loner, with no real friends, and no prospects of ever being part of the mainstream crowd. My parents paid me about as much attention as they did a house plant; a little water, a little sun, the occasional kind word. Here, in Silva, was another person, a man no less, alone with no friends or family to speak of.

Yet the fact was, Silva was somewhat reclusive. Which, to an inquisitive twelve-year-old, was tantamount to an invitation to pry. And he had people, mostly local people of mildly passing acquaintance, and some strangers, coming to his side door at odd hours. Perhaps, I thought, he wasn't so lonely as me.

251

Maybe he had many friends. But I dismissed that. Silva didn't seem the type. He was just too...odd. Whenever people would come by his place, I would tip-toe over to his door on the inside of our house and gently press a glass to the wood, my ear fixed to the base, and listen for any tell-tale sign of...well, anything my twelve-year-old mind could fathom. And it could fathom a lot. Each time I did this, and I have to admit it was quite often, odd lilting sounds and toneless conversations would filter back to me, as if I were underwater.

So, upon constantly hearing strange noises from the rented room—muted whirrs and thumps and the sound of liquid sloshing—I naturally had to snoop.

One weekend morning, with Mum and Dad downtown, I sat in our kitchen, waiting, knowing Silva's Saturday schedule. Soon enough I witnessed Silva swoosh by the window like a black wraith, his dark coat flapping bat-like. His pale, blurry, round face turned my way, fixed me with a strange grin, then he was gone, down the sidewalk and out of sight.

I stood, crept to the inside door and tried the handle. It was locked, as I knew it would be, so I went out our front door and around the side to Silva's exterior door. This door, to my surprise, was unlocked. Letting myself in, I stood in the small room and let my eyes adjust to the gloom. A faintly unpleasant scent of ammonia filled the dank room.

Silva had tacked up a large burlap canvas sheet, essentially cutting the room in two. His bed was shoved into a far dark corner, seemingly forgotten. A camera (a Hasselblad I would later learn) sat on a tripod near the bed. The wall behind his bed was covered in black and white photographs, tacked at curiously odd angles. The photos fluttered, waved in some illusive breeze.

A chill ran through me, sparking gooseflesh, but I didn't leave, couldn't leave. I felt compelled to stay, even though some distant part of my young mind knew that what I was doing was wrong. My hands throbbed in pain. Turning, I studied the canvas wall which also seemed to shimmer of its own accord. I noticed a small breach at one end of the canvas and slipped through it. I gasped. Sallow amber light flooded the makeshift room like some nightmare Dali vista. That strange scent of ammonia was almost overpowering. A long table had been set up, holding shiny metal canisters and trays of liquid from which emanated that smell. Alongside the trays was what looked like an inverted camera on two rails that ran from the tabletop.

Silva, it seemed, was a photographer. This was his darkroom.

I poked around a bit then carefully backed out of the darkroom and promptly bumped into Silva, who was standing expectantly, hands on hips, staring down at me.

I looked into Silva's face and felt a peculiar calm wash over me. His face seemed to pulse, and the dry flaky patches that interspersed the waxy areas peeled and fell off, drifting like snowflakes to the bare floorboards. My fingers bent and twisted in the folds of my shirt. I had a sudden urge to reach up and touch Silva's queer face. I had the feeling that it throbbed with the same pain that coursed through my hands.

SCRATCHING THE SURFACE

"Hello, Nathaniel Swann."

"Hello," I answered, unafraid.

"Do you like it?"

"What?"

"My studio," Silva said.

I glanced around. Yes, of course, the canvas acted as both a darkroom and a backdrop for Silva's photographs. It was quite clever.

"Yes," I said.

"Good. And your curiosity has been satiated?"

"Um, yes, I, you see the door was not locked."

Silva fixed me with his black shiny eyes. His one long eyebrow furrowed. "But it was closed," he said.

I had no answer for that, so I just nodded weakly.

Silva smiled. "No harm. You're a boy, and boys as a rule are curious. It's good to have an inquisitive nature, Nathaniel. Don't you agree?"

"Yes, sir."

"Silva, Mr. Swann." He grinned. "Call me Silva."

"You're a photographer?" I asked.

"No more. I'm getting out of the business."

"Why?"

Silva chuckled, but there was no mirth in it. His face twitched and he winced. "I'm tired, Nathaniel. That's all. It's time."

I rubbed my hands, tried to get the blood circulating in them. "But what will you do?"

This time Silva smiled. "So many questions. Nothing. I'll do nothing."

Silva turned abruptly, strode over to the wall tacked with photographs. "My art," he said winsomely, and it seemed he was talking to himself.

I took that as an invitation and went over to stand beside the tall man. I gazed up at him. His face pulsed red. His hands reached up for his face, stopped at his shoulders and reached out to the wall. His fingertips brushed the photographs lightly, reverentially.

Turning, I studied the photographs. They were portraits of people, individuals and families, but like no portraits I'd ever seen. I stepped closer, squinted up at the pictures. All the images were distorted, the corners of the photos seemingly pulling taut, the middles round, bulbous, beating like a heart. Of course it couldn't be real, I told myself then. It's just trick photography, a certain treatment of light and shadow, black and white, a dozen different shades of gray.

But that wasn't the worst part, no. The faces on the subjects were all slightly misshapen, their eyes stretched sideways, their noses askew, and their mouths a long oblong rictus. I blanched, tottered backward.

Silva caught me by the elbow. "It's okay, Nathaniel. Don't be afraid. It's my gift."

My hands burned with pain. I wanted to scream but couldn't. My mouth worked wordlessly like a fish out of water. My stomach fluttered and I spun, ran out the door and back to my house, to our bathroom, where I slumped beside the toilet and retched into the porcelain bowl.

꒰꒱

The very next day, Sunday, I returned to Silva's room. He answered the door before I even finished knocking, as if he were waiting for me. I believe he was. His face twitched, spasmed. His eyes were like shiny black stones on the bottom of a cool riverbed.

Silva stood aside. "Come in, Nathaniel."

I stepped into the small room, walked gingerly to the wavering wall of photographs.

"How?" I asked, though I didn't really know what I was asking.

Silva sighed, though he didn't sound close by. "My art. My gift, my curse. I don't know."

"Wh-Who would buy these...pictures?"

Silva's voice floated on the air. "Oh, no one would want these, Nathaniel. I give them what they want. I give them what they pay for. And I take what I need."

A silence ensued as I studied the malformed and distorted faces that leered grotesquely from the wall.

Then, "Come, Nathaniel, I'll show you."

Silva disappeared behind the canvas. I followed him into the makeshift room. The amber-colored safe light hanging in one corner gave the room an otherworldly glow.

Silva opened a drawer under the table, pulled out sheets of negatives. He fed a single strip of negative into a holder, then inserted it into the enlarger, between the bellows and the body. Silva flipped a switch and the enlarger hummed to life, projecting a blurry image onto an easel on the table. He reached up, turned a knob and the image came into sharp focus. Then Silva switched the enlarger off.

"Are you watching, Nathaniel?" Silva turned, stared at me, his face flowing, dripping like warm putty in the wan sallow light of the darkroom. "Some day this may be you. You will be the creator, the artist."

I smiled weakly, brought my hands up, studied them. "Not with these hands."

Silva slipped a sheet of paper from a black box and slid it into the easel. He turned on the enlarger, tapped the tabletop ten times, then turned it off. He pulled the paper from the easel, slid it into the first tray and proceeded to lift and tilt the tray, letting the liquid cover the surface of the paper.

"Developer," Silva said.

I stepped closer, peered into the tray. Slowly, an image took shape, a portrait of a man. After a while, when the image had fully formed, Silva lifted the sheet of paper from the tray with wooden tongs and deposited it into the next liquid-filled tray.

"Fixer," Silva intoned.

A few minutes later Silva was putting the photo into the final tray.

"A stop-bath and a wash," Silva told me.

Done, Silva pulled the wet photo from the tray and dried it with a simple hair dryer lying on the table. He handed the portrait to me. His face, I saw, had stopped fluttering.

"Well, Nathaniel, what do you think?"

I gazed at the picture. It was unremarkable. Even in the half-light I could see it was a simple, smiling portrait of a simple man. No curious eddies or swirls flecked the picture.

I shrugged.

Silva laughed, his voice a harsh bark, a cool wind. He snatched the photo from my hands and quickly ripped it in two, letting the halves fall to the floor.

"A simple man, Nathaniel. A dullard, wasting his life. So why not take some of it? Why not use it if he isn't? It's wasted on him."

Silva leaned in close. His face was flush and heat radiated from it. He smelled of acidic photographic chemicals and I feared a caustic reaction should I accidentally touch him. And I feared something else.

He smiled strangely. "Everyone's afraid to die, Nathaniel. Even me. Especially me." Silva paused. His voice grew faint. "At least I was at one time. Now I'm just weary." He shook his head, continued. "It's okay to be afraid. At least you have feelings. At least you're alive. I don't trouble those people." Silva straightened. His face drooped and he stared past me, blankly, as if I wasn't there. I didn't care for the tone of his last sentence. Didn't care for the way he said *trouble.*

"But some, Nathaniel, are afraid to *live.* They wake each day in drudgery, trudging off to work, blindly performing their menial tasks by rote. Then they return, to sit and stare at the television as their dinners congeal in their laps, no words issuing from their closed mouths." Silva trembled. "They are blind, Nathaniel, their staring eyes flitting over the wondrous minutiae of everyday life, just barely scratching the surface."

I thought of my parents.

"Don't be afraid to live your life, Nathaniel."

Silva shook his head, grinned, stared down at me with his oil slick eyes. "Those people are just taking up space. They are already dead."

I gulped.

Silva turned back to the table. "Okay, Nathaniel, watch. *Really* watch."

Again he grabbed a sheet of paper from the box and stuck it in the easel. Before he turned on the enlarger he placed his fingers on the smooth sheet.

"This is my art, Nathaniel."

Silva smoothed and polished the paper with his fingertips. His hands moved with a liquid grace. He prodded and probed the picture.

"You have to work the skin, the emulsion, make it malleable."

He switched on the enlarger, tapped off ten seconds, then placed the paper into the first tray. The image began to form. Silva dipped his fingers in the tray, worked them over the photograph like a baker kneading bread. He removed the soaking sheet of paper, dropped it into the next tray. Again he worked the image with his bare hands, employing his knuckles and nails, his palms and the heels of his hands, rolling them over and pushing them through the sticky emulsion. Silva dropped the photograph into the final tray, letting it rest several minutes, then pulled it out and placed the sopping image onto the tabletop.

Silva bent over the portrait. The air in the room wavered. Once again the sickly glow made Silva's head appear to shimmer and pulse. His frenzied fingers danced and skipped atop the wet photo, rubbing, smoothing, polishing the emulsion. He was scratching the surface, peeling away tiny flecks of what looked like skin.

Quickly, Silva dried the print and scurried out of the room. I followed. He stood at his wall, looking at his work, clutching his new piece of art. As I approached he turned to me. His face was crimson and bloated. Heat radiated from it in sickening waves. I reached up and Silva flinched, drew back.

"So very tired, Nathaniel." His cheeks vibrated. "There's no pleasure, no peace in the work anymore."

He handed me the photograph. "This is the real portrait," Silva said. "The deceit unmasked."

I stared at it. It was no longer a simple portrait of a simple man. The photo appeared to glow with its own light. The black shadows slithered, the highlights sparkled, graduating shades of gray quivered. The man's eyes bulged bug-eyed, his nose was splayed to ribbons. The mouth stretched sideways, lips cracked, revealing tiny pointy teeth. Something moved deep in the man's maw.

Silva's hot hand on my shoulder made me start. I dropped the photograph.

"It's all a facade, Nathaniel. The faces aren't real. It's just a skin, hiding what's underneath. And underneath we are all mostly the same; blood and bone and gristle."

Silva leaned in. His face was pulsating and peeling. "Can you see the real me?"

I took my leave then, scared of what I would do. Scared of what might happen.

It was the last time I saw Silva alive.

⌒∶∽

All the next week I busied myself with school and chores, trying to put Silva out of my mind. There came no noises from his room. No visitors came to his door. Curious, I thought. But he did say he was retiring.

My parents continued living their sedate lives, wearing their comfortable masks.

SCRATCHING THE SURFACE

Come Saturday I sat in the kitchen and waited for Silva to go bustling by the window. He didn't, and a queer dread flooded me.

With mounting trepidation I stood and went out to Silva's door. I knocked, but got no answer. Turning the doorknob, I pushed the door inward and stepped into his gloomy room.

Silva was prone, face up, in the middle of his tiny room. I stumbled over to him. Gazing down at Silva, I wept. Great sobs racked my body. It was the first time I'd ever cried and it felt good. It was real. I was *alive.*

Composing myself, I knelt beside Silva, gazed down at his grim countenance. His eyes shone blackly. His lips were pulled back in a smile or a grimace. On his chest, gripped in one clawed hand, was a photograph. I plucked the photo from his fingers, brought it up to eye level. It was a picture of himself, of Silva. His face was calm, his skin clear, unmarked, almost luminous. A remarkable portrait.

I turned the photo over. Written on the back was *Can you see the real me?*

I tucked the photograph into my waistband.

My fingers clenched. My hands screamed in agony, throbbed with deep pain. I knew what I had to do.

I bent, placed my fingers on his waxy face. I brushed my fingertips along his patchwork skin, skimming the surface. My fingers swirled, danced, probed. I rubbed, lightly at first, then harder, digging my nails into the spongy, dead skin and peeled back, bit by bit, long strips of parchment-like skin. I scratched, pulled, peeled. I dug at the flesh with nubby bloody fingers, raking them across his face over and over until I hit muscle and tissue, sinew and bone. Scratching until I saw Silva, the real Silva, all blood and bone gristle, behind the facade.

Smiling, I went home to wash my hands.

⌣∶~

I still have all of Silva's equipment. As I suspected, there was no family, no persons who came forward to make any claim to what little Silva possessed. It was given to my parents, who originally had wanted to sell it off to make a quick buck. But after some gentle pleading, convincing them I'd never want for anything else, I eventually coerced them into letting me have it. His camera, the trays, the canvas sheet, the enlarger, all sit in a dusty closet in my modest apartment.

And I still have his self-portrait. It is tacked to the wall where I can see it. Lately it has begun to fade and crack, the emulsion flaking and peeling.

I've begun to think that I might take up photography. My hands still pain me, giving me pause to those thoughts, but something else compels me.

You see, it's my face. I study it in the mirror. If I look close enough I can see tiny ripples, little pockets of flesh that pulse and move beneath the surface. And it hurts. How it hurts. It burns with an intense fever-heat. I want to reach up, rip the skin from the bone, rid myself of this false mask. But I don't. The pain reminds me that I'm alive.

So, I stay my hand. I sit and stare at the closet, my face and hands in agony. Perhaps, like my friend Silva, if I dig below the surface I can seek some succor in the lives of ordinary men.

Kodachrome

LORELEI SHANNON

The first corpse I ever photographed was my father's. It was on my seventh birthday. The whole family was over; kids running wild in the summer sunshine, women gossiping in the kitchen, men sitting in lawn chairs on the scrubby grass drinking beer.

My father downed his latest Bud and decided it was time to hang up the basketball hoop he'd bought me, hang it up over the garage.

It wasn't far to fall, really. The ladder wasn't that tall. But he lost his balance, pitched over backwards, and hit his head on the concrete driveway. It cracked open like an egg; his head, I mean. There was a terrible sound, like when my mother dropped a watermelon on the patio bricks the summer before. What was in came out, in a spill of gray Jello and a spreading pool of red.

I was standing there, holding the new Brownie Instamatic my Uncle Nick had given me. I'd been taking pictures of my cousins playing Cowboys and Indians. My dog taking a whiz. Stuff like that. I stared at my father, at his wide, surprised eyes, at his brains on the concrete. I knew my mother was screaming, shrieking, but I didn't really hear her. I raised the camera, boxed my father off in that safe little frame. He looked different through the lens somehow, like someone else. I know now that he looked like a stranger because he was already dead. Anyway, I pressed the button, and the camera went snap. I wound the little dial and advanced the film, and snap, I shot again. My father looked the same, but the blood halo around him was bigger. I snapped again, and again. I still really don't know why I did that. Maybe I was trying to catch him, to keep his spirit

259

with me on film. Maybe I was just in shock. Maybe there was something wrong with me, really badly wrong.

I never saw those pictures. My Uncle Nick, sobbing and yelling, slapped the camera from my hand, and it smashed on the concrete, just like my father's skull. Loopy film everywhere, like the flat intestines of a starving animal. Uncle Nick snatching me up in his arms, hugging me so hard, crying *oh God, Ben, oh God.*

Nick bought me another camera a few days later. He didn't say anything about it, he just pushed it into my hand at my father's funeral. He had his arm around my shoulders tight, or I would have taken a picture of my father in his coffin.

I took pictures of my mother; her puffy, grief-stained face and unwashed hair. I took pictures of my dog when he was asleep, and I pretended he was dead. I went walking through the neighborhood, a happy, bustling, multicultural slice of Los Angeles suburb, and I found a cat that had been hit by a car.

It lay in the gutter, sun-bloated and stinking. Black blood caked its fur; its mouth was a gaping scream. I took up the rest of the roll, shooting the cat from every angle. I even lay on my belly in the gutter to get a good shot of its face.

When the pictures came back, my mother took my camera away, and took me to a psychologist.

It was 1958, and thank God, the shrink was an aging beatnik. He had longish blond hair and a greasy nose and kind eyes, and he asked me, in every way he could think of, why I took pictures of the cat. I didn't know. I didn't have anything to say. I just watched him. He had me do some drawings. I drew my father in his coffin.

The shrink told my mother that I was just working it out for myself, trying to figure out what death really was. He said I was looking for answers in the form of the dead cat. He told her to give the camera back, to let me express myself. I'll always be grateful to him for that, because my mother did what he asked her to.

She never looked at my pictures again.

I took pictures of dead things. Bugs, birds, cats, dogs, the occasional snake or lizard. I kept them in metal fileboxes. I grew older. My mother died of grief and alcoholism, choked on her own vomit in bed when I was a senior in high school. I took an entire roll of film of her before I called the police.

I graduated high school, and got a job at the county morgue. I got fired for taking pictures of corpses.

I started working as a police photographer. In no time at all, I was the best. I got more detail, they said, than anybody else in town. It was true. I got the big picture, of course I did. But they say God is in the details. I got a close-up of every shattered tooth, every shred of skin, every splash of blood. I got it all.

You're probably wondering, by now, why I did that. No, I'm not a pervert. I'm not a sadist or a serial killer. The beatnik shrink was right. I was searching. Looking for something profound, something transcendent, in every death.

Did I find it?

KODACHROME

No. But I kept looking. I took so many pictures, just so many. And I collected the work of other crime photographers. I studied them, stared at them for hours at a time. I still kept them in little metal file boxes, like when I was a kid. I don't like change much, I guess.

That's why the cops eventually stopped using my services. Everyone started using color film, and I couldn't stand to. I'd never taken a color picture in my life, and I wasn't about to start. I took a job as a janitor at the hospital. Sometimes I managed to get pictures. It didn't pay much.

Some German publishing company saw my police photos; how, I don't know. They collected quite a few of them in a book, a handsome coffee table book filled with road accidents and suicides and bloody murder. I got royalties; enough to buy film with, enough to keep my darkroom stocked with chemicals. But eventually, they petered out. I was living in my mother's old house, eating dried Ramen noodles, and circling the halls of the hospital like a vulture, waiting for the next death.

The neighborhood had changed since I was a kid. It was no longer lower-middle-class suburbia. The houses were run-down, the streets plagued with drugs and gangs and random shootings. The people who lived here were poor. Some took care of their houses, mowed their lawns, washed their 70's sedans with pride. Others gave up, let their paint peel and the weeds grow and left broken bicycles and junker cars on the lawn. I was somewhere in between, I guess.

I was poor.

That's why, when the kid who called himself Byron came to my door and asked me to do it, I agreed. I agreed to photograph Byron as a corpse.

He was a handsome kid, in his early twenties. He was what you'd call a goth, I guess, with long, black hair and black clothes that seemed cut for another century. He had a slender redhaired boy with him, whom he referred to only as Rat. I'd taken quite a few pictures of dead rats in my time, I thought, as I let them into my living room.

"I love your work," said Byron, looking at the framed photographs on the walls. Yes, I'm a little vain, I suppose. I put my favorites up where I can see them.

"Thank you," I said. I've always been curious about the people who like my photos. I used to get letters, lots of them. Lots of people hate my work, think it's morbid and sick. And then there are the ones who love it. I don't judge them; at least I try not to. But the ones who sign their names in blood, who send clippings of their hair, who send me pictures of their own...well, they scare me.

Byron didn't, though. He was open, smiling. All he wanted, he said, was for me to photograph him in a coffin, as a corpse.

I didn't know what to say, at first. I didn't have indoor lights or reflective umbrellas or any of that. I certainly didn't have a coffin.

"I have all that," said Byron, his dark eyes sparkling. "Rat will do the make-up." He patted the silent boy on the shoulder. Rat blinked wide blue eyes, and smiled a little.

"I don't know…" I said.
"I'll give you five hundred dollars."
"Okay."
Byron said he'd be back that Friday, my day off. Sure, I said to him, see you then.

⌣∴⌣

You know that Paul Simon song? The one where he says "Everything looks worse in black and white?" It's true, in a way. It's also completely wrong.

When you photograph a road accident in black and white, it's easier to see the details. The blood is black, not red. The image is stark. Real. Details are crisp and true. A corpse has no color, after all, not really. What is a corpse but a black-and-white human, a shell of flesh with the color of life drained away?

A color photo of that same road accident…well, it's garish. That's the word for it. Red, red, red everywhere. You can't make anything out in that sea of red. It just looks like somebody dropped a jar of strawberry jam. And it's false. There may be every color of the rainbow; red blood, white bone, purple and pink loops of intestine, blue lips, milky eyes of green or blue or brown. But it's a lie. The person is gone; the color is like a mask. It isn't real. It isn't real.

⌣∴⌣

The days went by quickly. They always do. Time is slippery for me. I don't sleep, you see. Not for more than two hours at a time. I wake up with my mind racing, and my arthritic neck aching. Then I have to get up for awhile, to walk and to think. Think about death, and life, and death some more. I don't exactly get my beauty sleep. I look older than my fifty-one years. When I look in the mirror, I see the face of a tired old hound dog. But who cares? It's not like anybody ever looks at me.

Soon it was Friday.

Byron and Rat came by, right on time, eight p.m. They smiled, Byron shook my hand warmly and said he was glad to see me. Rat nodded and grinned. Then they went to get the equipment.

I had to smile. I don't do that very often, but they were driving a hearse. It was parked right in front of my house; a huge, long, black shiny beast with fins, and purple flames painted on the hood.

They took the coffin out on a gurney. It was really lovely; carved layers of buttery hardwood with a silver crucifix on top. Something from an old vampire movie. A black-and-white movie.

They set the coffin up in my living room, and put up black drapes behind it. They brought in big lights and silver umbrellas and arranged them, fussed over them. We decided that a row of candles next to the coffin would look nice. I got some from the kitchen. Then Rat put a cloth around Byron's neck and put on his make-up.

He didn't rouge his cheeks or his lips like so many funeral homes do. Rat powdered Byron down, paler than he already was. He put a faint purple tinge on his lips, which I knew would turn up as a satiny gray in the pictures. He did the same to Byron's eyelids.

Lying in the coffin, Byron looked beautiful. He looked like a dead angel. I'm not gay, mind you, but the boy was perfect, a work of art, in his ruffles and velvet and corpse-pallor. I was honored to take his picture.

We took several rolls. Byron was quiet and still throughout. Rat sat in my mother's old threadbare recliner, watching intently. When it was done, Byron pressed my hand in his, and gave me five hundred dollars in cash.

I was sorry to see him leave.

I ran myself a bath, to warm the stiffness in my neck.

⌇⁚⁚⁓

You may be wondering why I can't sleep. The answer is simple, really. I'm obsessed. Death is with me, night and day. When I meet someone, I start to worry immediately. There are so many, so very many ways for a person to die. When I meet someone, I start thinking of the possibilities. Take Byron, for instance. I wondered if he and Rat would die in a head-on collision on the way home, their old hearse a tangle of shredded metal and pulverized flesh. I wondered if he were sick, dying of AIDS, using me to confront his own mortality. I wondered if he would die of an overdose, like so many kids in my neighborhood. Or be shot dead on my front lawn by one of the local gang bangers.

This kind of thinking doesn't make for restful nights.

It doesn't make for good relationships, either.

I've been with women before. Of course I have. I'm half a century old, for heaven's sake...But never one that lasted. I couldn't commit.

How could I? How could I marry a woman, love her, and immediately start wondering when she'll die? Worry about her every second, every moment she's away from me? And even when she's with me, she could choke to death on her dinner, or electrocute herself with her hair dryer, or break her neck changing a light bulb. And children...well, it would be worse with them, so much worse. If I had children, I knew I'd never sleep again, even if I kept them locked in a padded room. I was lonely. But what choice did I have?

⌇⁚⁚⁓

When Byron knocked on my door again, I was happy, surprisingly happy. I was glad to see him again. I was even glad to see the silent Rat. This time, Byron told me, he wanted to be photographed in my bathtub, as if he'd drowned. I agreed. I only wished that it weren't so many days until Friday.

263

⌒:∾

I went to work, of course, like always. I had no friends at the hospital. People thought I was a nice old guy, I guess, but I couldn't let anyone get close. You know why. I was just Ben, the eccentric janitor. That was fine.

I was mopping up a puddle of urine in the hallway when Zack, a new young security guard, walked past and said hello to me. I glanced up and said hello. Then my throat constricted, and I couldn't say anything at all. Because just for a second, like a flash of lightening, I saw Zack dead. I saw his shattered cheekbones, his blood-soaked hair, glass embedded in his skin and sparkling like Christmas. And then it was gone. Zack laughed, and patted me on the shoulder. He said I should take a break.

⌒:∾

Friday night came, and Byron and Rat came to see me. I showed them the proofs from our last photo session, and they were delighted. I have to admit, they were fantastic. Byron looked perfect, almost transcendently beautiful, in his coffin. He looked dead; there was nothing to give away the fact that he wasn't. But he shone like a star. No corpse can look like that, because corpses are empty. It was an extraordinary effect. Byron asked for large prints of seven of the best photos, at eighty dollars apiece. Then we moved on to the bathroom.

They set up the lights, and Byron laughed and joked, saying he hoped that none of them fell into the tub and fried him. I shuddered at the thought, wrapped my arms around myself and shook. Byron cocked his head and looked at me, eagle-bright, as if he knew what I was thinking. Then he ran the water into the tub.

Rat used greasepaint this time, so it wouldn't come off in the water. He made the skin of Byron's face a delicate shade of blue; pale as milk, translucent and fragile. Byron's body, slender and muscular, was already as pale as the moon. He was unashamed of his nakedness, and he folded his clothes as he removed them with care and precision.

He insisted that the water in the tub should be cold. "It just wouldn't feel right," he said with a smile, "if it were warm. Besides, it might melt my make-up." Rat nodded emphatically.

I was a little ashamed of my bathroom, of the old porcelain tub. It was an unpleasant color of pale green, cracked and chipped in places. I'd just cleaned the room, but the tile was old and worn, the paint on the walls discolored with age and moisture and mildew stains. But Byron said it was perfect.

He slipped under the water like a seal, like he belonged there. His eyes were open, and his mouth, lips slightly parted. His long hair drifted around his face in wavy clouds, like water plants in a mountain stream. He didn't look at all like he was holding his breath. He looked dead.

KODACHROME

I took pictures quickly. I knew Byron couldn't hold his breath forever. But he did. Not forever, of course, but two minutes, three minutes, five. I began to panic; my heart pounded, and I turned to Rat, but he was calm and smiling. I was about to grab Byron, to pull his face out of the water, when he did it himself. Slowly, like he'd gone under. He breathed in deeply, but didn't gasp for air. He rested his head on the back of the tub for a moment, then went down again.

The second time he came up, he turned his head and smiled at me. "Let's try something new," he said. Rat knelt down next to the tub, and Byron spoke to him softly. Rat took out his make-up kit, and began to create deep gashes in Byron's forearms.

They looked real, so incredibly real. Just putty and paint, but it looked for all the world like Byron had slashed his wrists. I began to worry about that, worry that he would really do it. What kind of person wants pictures of himself as a corpse, if he doesn't want to be a corpse?

Then Rat went out to the hearse for a moment, leaving me alone with Byron. "Don't worry, Ben," he said. "I wouldn't really do it."

A feeling like electric shock went up my spine. But Byron hadn't read my mind, had he? No, of course not. He looked at my worried face, and he guessed what I was thinking. That's what I told myself.

"Good," was all I managed to say. I massaged the back of my neck.

Rat returned with two big jugs of something red. He uncorked one, and poured it into the tub with Byron.

Blood. I'm sure it was fake blood, movie blood, but it looked just like the real thing. It swirled through the water, around Byron's long, slim body. He slipped beneath the surface once more. I raised my camera.

When it was done, Rat took down the lights, and we left Byron in the bathroom to dress. Rat sat in my mother's chair, smiling at me pleasantly. I thought about speaking to him, asking him about himself, but I knew he wouldn't answer. Somehow, I knew he couldn't, and I didn't want to make him uncomfortable. So I just smiled at him, and brought out a plate of cookies. Rat nibbled one quickly, like his namesake.

Byron took quite a while in the bathroom. When he came out, he was perfectly dressed, as before. His hair hung damp around his collar. "I scrubbed your tub out," he said pleasantly. "Nothing worse than a bloody bathtub ring."

I started to protest, but he waved it away. "I always clean up my messes," he said. "See you next Friday?"

I was indescribably happy to agree.

⋌∶⋋

Of course, I had to worry that night. I worried, just a little bit, about what Byron meant. *I always clean up my messes.* Was he a sadist? A serial killer? Was I helping him, somehow, with his crimes?

No. No, of course not. There was something about Byron, about his warm eyes and gentle humor. He wasn't capable of such things.

But he still might die. He might slip, and hit his head, and drown in his own bathtub. He might get sick from spending so long in cold water, and die of pneumonia. He might cut himself in his kitchen and die of blood poisoning. Every two hours, my brain sang to me, sang the songs of death.

～:～

I went to the corner store, to buy a loaf of bread and some eggs. That store had been there since I was a kid. The owner, Mrs. Jiminez, was the daughter of the man who opened it in 1947. About ten years older than me, she was a laughing, round woman who wore flowered dresses and smelled like fry bread. She treated me like a little boy, like the kid I was when she first started working for her daddy. She called me Benji, which would have driven me crazy if she hadn't been so sweet.

"Good evening, Benji," she said to me as I walked in.

"Hello—" I glanced up at her, and my heart froze. There was the flash, like the pop of a camera's flashbulb, and I saw Mrs. Jiminez, dead in her coffin. She looked much older—she was thinner, and her thick, gray hair had gone pure white. But she was dead, cheeks rouged, lips painted, stiff and dead on a pillow of silk. I let out a little cry.

"Benji! Ju okay, *mijo?*" She bustled around the counter and patted me on the shoulder.

I looked into her eyes. They were warm and living. "I—I'm okay. Just my neck. It's giving me, uh, it hurts a lot today."

She nodded, and went to the aisle where she kept the aspirin, cold medicine, and herbal cures. "Ju take this," she said, holding up a tube of Aspercream. "Ju don't have to pay for it. Rub it on jour neck, *mijo,* and ju will feel better."

"Thank you," I smiled, and bought my bread and eggs. I blamed what I had seen on my lack of sleep.

But I went to work the next day, and I found out I was wrong.

Jamie Rabbin, one of the night nurses, said hi to me. That's all, just hi. And then she turned into a corpse. Lying in a hospital bed, skin like yellow parchment. Breathing tube down her throat, held to her dead face with white tape, blue showing around her mouth. I thought of all her cigarette breaks, and shuddered. I took a step back, and ran into the wall. Hot pain flared through the base of my neck.

"You okay, Ben?" she asked me, and she was alive again. How many years, I wondered? How many years until lung cancer eats her alive? I tried not to look at Dr. Roberts, but I saw him anyway, pulverized behind the wheel of his sports car. Then, on the third floor, I walked past an open door, and there was a new patient, a little girl in there, and she was coughing, coughing, and I couldn't look in. I ran. I ran outside and leaned against the wall, panting and crying.

KODACHROME

☙

Byron's photos were beautiful. He looked like an angel, a drowned angel, something too beautiful for the Earth. His dusky eyelids, alabaster limbs like the dead Christ of Michaelangelo's *Pietá*, the blood swirling around him in black clouds.

He was so pleased with the pictures, he laughed out loud. He had a great laugh, the kind that made you want to laugh along. I looked at him, and felt a pang, a lot like grief. I could have a son his age, if I'd ever married.

This time he wanted to be a gunshot victim. He wanted to lie on my kitchen floor.

Rat put on the bullet holes. They were amazing; the kid really was an artist. Three shots to the chest, one to the belly. One to the forehead. They looked stunningly real. Believe me, I've seen enough of the genuine article to know.

Rat came in with a big bottle of blood. Byron, already lying on the floor, shirt open, asked "Do you mind?"

I shook my head. I wasn't talking much that night. I didn't trust myself not to say something, something about the things I'd seen. And hell, the fake blood couldn't make the lime-green linoleum look any worse than it already did.

Rat painted it onto Byron, running down his face, his sides, and poured it around him in a shining pool. It soaked into his hair, crept up the fabric of his dove-gray silk shirt. The effect was fantastic.

Byron looked dead in my lens, dead, but glowing from within. I realized, as I snapped picture after picture, that this was what I had been looking for, year after year. What I had hoped to see in faces of the legions of the dead I had held in the lens of my camera. A sign that death meant something, that it wasn't all just an ugly waste. As I took the pictures of Byron, I was happy.

But it wasn't real, of course, because Byron was alive. He stood up when it was all done, stretched and yawned. He excused himself to the bathroom to take off his make-up while Rat cleaned the kitchen.

It didn't all come out. The fake blood left a faint pink shadow in the middle of the kitchen floor.

Byron was mortified. He apologized over and over, and wanted to pay for new tile. No, I told him, you don't have to do that. It's hideous anyway. And I started to cry.

"What is it?" Byron asked me quietly. "Tell me what's wrong, Ben."

"I can't," I said. And it was true. The words were stuck in my throat like broken glass.

"Whenever you're ready," Byron said. "Okay?"

I nodded, feeling like a fool.

LORELEI SHANNON

⌣∴∿

It was so stupid, the way my Uncle Nick died. I was nineteen years old. My mother had been dead for a little over a year. Nick worked in an appliance warehouse. He'd operated a forklift for twenty years. He was loading washers onto the top shelf, one after another. He parked the last one, neat as you please, and backed the forklift up.

Maybe he was tired. Maybe his foot slipped. But he backed into the towering shelves behind him. A kitchen stove, still in the box, toppled down and smashed Nick, smashed him like a bug beneath a flyswatter.

I didn't take pictures of him; they wouldn't let me in. But I saw them. I saw Nick, still sitting in the forklift, torso crushed, arms and legs sticking out at weird, unnatural angles. Head hanging on his broken neck like a sack of oatmeal. Blood everywhere, on the forklift, on the stovebox, on the cement floor. I stared and stared at the pictures, and I asked why, why, why, why. I don't know who I was asking, or what. There were no answers in Uncle Nick's remaining, blood-rimmed eye.

It was Uncle Nick who kept me up that night. Uncle Nick, and my mother, and my father, and the little girl in the hospital. I woke up, over and over, sweating and shaking. It was a terrible night, even for me.

⌣∴∿

Then I went to work, and learned that Zack had been killed, had smashed his old Camaro into the back end of a semi.

I tried not to look at anyone. I kept my face down. But by accident, I saw the little girl's mother. She looked about seventy when I saw her, eyes closed, book open on her chest. A heart attack, I guessed. I started shaking uncontrollably, so I went to the breakroom for a cup of cold water.

It was there that I saw Nick, a young intern. Wasted away in a narrow bed with metal railings. Kaposi's sores on his sunken cheeks.

I backed out of the room, trembling. I went home. I went home and got into bed, and tried not to sleep.

I called in sick for the rest of the week. I didn't care if they fired me. I'd made more money working with Byron than I made in three months at the hospital. And I couldn't look at anyone. I couldn't.

My neck hurt. I rubbed it with Aspercream, and that made it a little better, but it was a bone-deep ache. Like the one in my chest. Like the one in my heart.

⌣∴∿

Byron was worried about me. He touched my thin, unshaven cheek, and asked me if I'd been sick. Yes, I said, but I was better now. A lie. I showed him the

268

photos from last week. They were perfect, of course. A beautiful boy, tragically dead, a victim of senseless violence. His flesh stark white against the black blood that striped his skin, surrounded his head in a dark halo. He bought them all.

This time, Byron wanted to be hung. He asked if Rat could screw a big, heavy hook into a ceiling beam in my bedroom. Sure, I said, why not.

They put a harness on Byron, under his clothes. He hung from the ceiling by a leather strap. He kicked his legs and laughed, *Look, Ma, I'm Peter Pan.* They put a rough hemp noose around his neck, and passed it through the hook. By God if it didn't look real.

Rat had, of course, done an excellent job with the make-up. It was purple this time, a dusky, pale plum. Blue lips, bruised eyelids.

First, Byron hung limp, eyes closed. I shot, numb. I had trouble keeping my hands from shaking. Then he opened his eyes.

I don't know how he did it, but his eyes were bulging. His mouth hung slack, his tongue protruded, and he was dead, so completely dead, that I fell to my knees and began to sob.

"Hey," Byron said, hanging from my ceiling, feet dangling above my bed. "Hey."

Rat got him down. He sat on my bed, held my hand like I was a little child, and I told him everything. Everything I had seen since I first took his picture.

I looked up at Rat, and he was smiling. Not meanly, not mockingly. It was more like the smile of a proud parent, who had just taught his child something clever.

"You're ready," said Byron.

"Ready for what?"

"You're ready to know."

"I don't understand…"

"Look at your photos," he said. "Not the ones you took yourself. The others. The ones you've collected."

"But why?"

He smiled, like a man with a happy secret. "You'll see."

⌇⁚⌁

I called in sick to the hospital, and I sat on my bed, looking at pictures of death. I started with the most recent, and worked my way back. Men, women, children, infants. Hollow, empty shells, not horrible, just sad, so sad. For the first time, it hurt me to look at them. It hurt so much. But I did it, I looked, because I trusted Byron. I trusted him, and I think I loved him a little bit, like the son I never had.

On the third day, I found it. I very nearly missed it; the photo was grainy, a black-and-white snapped by some anonymous ghoul, turned in later to the police.

A hit-and-run, in 1979. A pedestrian killed on a night time street. It was in my neighborhood, not far from Mrs. Jiminez's store. The victim lay on his back on the asphalt. Blood trickled from his mouth, and his neck was twisted at an awful angle, bone protruding beneath the skin. His eyes were open, surprised. He had kind of a dopey look on his face, like he couldn't believe what had just happened to him.

My face.

I had a dopey look on my face.

Because it was me lying there, arms flung wide, one shoe in the middle of the road. It was me lying there. Me. Dead.

I laughed. Not because I was going crazy, not because I was hysterical. It was just funny, that's all. Me, splattered. With a dopey look on my face.

What the hell was I doing walking around, then?

There was a knock on the door. It was Byron, of course.

"You found it!" he said, with a grin.

"Yes." He came in, Rat behind him.

"May I see?"

I handed him the photo. He looked at it, and smiled. "Yes, I remember this. You had just come from a crime scene, a particularly nasty shooting. You wanted some air on your way home."

I looked into his dark eyes. "How do you know that?"

"I was there."

"You took the picture?"

"Yes. I'd been keeping an eye on you for quite some time by then."

"But you're not old enough..."

Rat laughed, the first sound I'd ever heard him make.

I grabbed Byron's hand. It was warm and strong as he squeezed my fingers. "Who are you?" I asked.

"Oh, you know."

I did know. Of course I did.

"Tell me what happened," I asked him.

"The damnedest thing. You lay there, on the road, for two hours. Then you reached up and straightened your head, pushed the bones of your neck back into place. You got up and walked away."

I laughed. "I never could sleep for more than two hours at a time."

Byron laughed with me. "You need some rest," he said.

I stopped laughing. I was still, inside and out. "What now? Do I...do I go with you? Will you take me...somewhere?"

Byron shook his head. "Nah, I don't do that. Can you imagine how busy I'd be? Worse than Santa Claus! People come to me. They come when they're called. Sometimes, they come when they're ready."

Rat grinned. Byron patted him on the back. "Rat here, he wasn't ready. So he's hanging out with me for awhile, as my assistant."

Rat opened his mouth wide. He had no tongue.

KODACHROME

"Throat cancer," said Byron. "Chewing tobacco is such a gruesome habit. Bet you never do that again, huh, Rat."

Rat shook his head ruefully, with a sheepish grin.

Byron stood up, and stretched. "So, Ben. Whenever you're ready. No rush."

I frowned. "What about the, uh, the things I've been seeing? The people..."

Byron sighed. "I'm afraid that'll stay. You've got one foot on the other side, pal. It's just part of the bargain. It's better to know, in some ways. You'll get used to it." He grinned. "Use it to your advantage."

I stood up, my eyes filling with tears. Tears of gratitude. Byron hugged me, a tight, quick squeeze. He smelled like jasmine.

"Later, Ben," he said. I watched as he and Rat got into the hearse and roared away.

⌣∶∾

I went to the hospital that night, and peeked in at the little girl. The flash showed her to me, an old woman in a cherrywood coffin, face lined with character and love and laughter. I went home, and slept like an exhausted child.

⌣∶∾

So, what now? I'll tell you what now. I think I'll drive up to the Angeles forest, and take a few pictures of birds. Maybe a raccoon or a squirrel or two.

Live ones.

Maybe I'll go back to school. I'd love to be a high school art teacher.

Maybe I'll meet a lady. A nice lady with a nice, long life ahead of her, and a peaceful death waiting at the end of it. And when she's ready to go, I'll go with her.

I miss Byron. But I know I'll see him again. Whenever I start to doubt that, I look at the pink stain on my kitchen floor, and I laugh a little.

Maybe, just maybe, I'll buy some color film.

271

Nightmares, Imported and Domestic

MATT CARDIN & MARK MCLAUGHLIN

His name was Lafcadio, and he was an artist, a creator of lavish and colorful landscapes. Or at least, this accounted for part of his life: the part lived by the conscious, waking, sensing self that opened eyes on the external world and breathed in the scents and sights of sun-filled skies and rain-wet streets. Lafcadio the artist spent endless hours reading Zen literature and attempting to incorporate esoteric ideas into his own paintings. Lafcadio the artist thrived on the sensuous impressions of the outer world and the intricate thoughts to which they inspired his overheated imagination.

But he was a man divided, and the other part of his life was not nearly so vibrant. For approximately eight hours out of every twenty-four, he assumed the identity of Brian, an accountant, a creator of neatly filled-out forms, who spent his days locked within the taupe walls of an aging suburban office. Lafcadio's life as Brian was uncommonly realistic for a nocturnal vision. As Brian, he felt pain, hunger, all the usual sensations, and in all their day-to-day, five-sensory vividity. But he did not see his Brian-self through the twin windows of his own eyes. Rather, he watched himself from a distance, as one might watch a character in a television show. Appropriately, this dream-life, Brian's life, took place in a world of black-and-white, like an old episode of *The Andy Griffith Show* or *I Love Lucy*. And the tenor of this dream-existence was entirely in keeping with its grayscaled hues.

The tension between the two selves—the glorious sensuality of the artist and the drab conventionality of the accountant—expressed itself in every habit and more of Lafcadio's life. One of his most oft-indulged amusements was to sample exotic coffees with his eyes closed and try to guess the precise blend and origin of the beans. By contrast, one of Brian's favorite drinks was instant coffee, mixed with one package of artificial sweetener and one teaspoon of nondairy creamer. He preferred Folgers, but he usually couldn't detect it when somebody substituted Maxwell House or Sanka.

The only person who had ever slept more than once in Lafcadio's bed was Lafcadio himself. The right half of Brian's bed had never held anyone but Susan, his wife for as many years as he could remember.

Lafcadio was high-strung and temperamental. Brian was even-tempered and meek.

The line of contrasts ran right down to physical appearance. Lafcadio was tall and thin, with a vaguely catlike appearance to his bony, bald head. Brian was of average height and weight, with a blandly amiable, slightly rounded face, and a six-dollar haircut.

Some mornings, Lafcadio awoke to a momentary disorientation, brought about by trying to decide whose bed he was lying in. The feeling lasted until after his shower, when the first sip of coffee hit his tongue and he discovered with relief that it was not Folgers, but Jamaica Blue Mountain. The bitter hot tang of the black liquid always confirmed that he was indeed the effervescent artist and not the unexciting accountant. But as time went by—months running into years, years into more than a decade, and all the while the nocturnal life of Brian playing like a classic TV show on the screen of his eyelids at night—he found that he slowly came to look forward to his nightly ramblings in a world of white-bread banality.

True, the morning disorientation sometimes left him with a lingering fear that one day, he might wake up to find himself in a two-tone world with Susan beside him in bed and his life as Lafcadio the Magnificent receding like foam from the shore of a dream ocean. But in the end he discovered that it was really quite easy to convince himself that a life as Brian the Maudlin wouldn't be all that bad. Not if Brian were able to spend at least eight hours out of every twenty-four dreaming that he was Lafcadio the Magnificent.

❧

"So this Brian," said Cornelia, Lafcadio's best friend, over steaming mugs one day at their favorite coffee house, Mondo Mocha. "Your dream buddy. What's he up to these days? You haven't mentioned him in a while."

Lafcadio reflected for a moment before answering. "He's not really my buddy," he said at last. "He's me. And Susan has been talking about flowers."

"Flowers?" Cornelia looked at him blankly over a Café Corretto.

"She thinks the house looks too plain on the outside," he explained. "All the other houses on the block have tons of flowers. We have to keep up with the Joneses, you know." He smiled privately to himself and turned his attention to

274

the steam rising from his Espresso Macchiato. The swirling vapor hinted at a snow-covered landscape, mottled by bizarre seismic convulsions. He allowed the image to take its course in his imagination, hoping it might lead him to his next artistic project.

Cornelia gave him a hard little smile. But then, practically everything about her was hard, though admirably so. She was into boxing and weightlifting, and it showed on her arms and shoulders. Her abs were like a rippled brick wall (as he had discovered once, long ago, on the sole occasion when they had become physically intimate and he had been able to indulge his long-held desire of placing the flat of his palm upon her stomach). Years ago she had served on the police force, before she decided to open a beauty and exercise spa for women only. "This Susan sounds like a perfectly hideous *frau,*" she was saying, as his snow-swept reverie became transmogrified by her chiseled physique into a Dali-esque scene of powder-and-ice piled into abdominal ripples on an arctic tundra. "Brian has to play gardener now? Tell me everything!"

"Oh, but I like it. I mean, he likes it." He could tell she didn't believe him, so he tapped his manicured nails on the tile tabletop in syncopation with his words to emphasize his sincerity. "No, really! All that housey-spousey stuff is actually kind of fun in Brian-world."

Cornelia tapped her chin with a long maroon-lacquered fingernail. "So, do they ever do it? Or is life all just chores and church socials?"

"Oh sure, they have sex," he said. "But I never get to see—" He twirled his forefingers in the direction of his crotch. "—the works in action. It's like watching a soft-core porn channel in a hotel room. No close-ups allowed, in case a kid enters the room. The camera moves toward them, then it veers off toward a fireplace or an open window with a pretty sky outside."

Cornelia's smile dipped down into a smirk. "How dreary. Must be terribly boring for you."

"Nooo…" Lafcadio thought for a moment. "In a way, it's rather sweet. And the lack of visuals isn't a total loss. I mean, I do still feel every sensation that Brian is feeling." He looked into Cornelia's eyes. "I think sometimes Susan is supposed to be you."

Her eyes hardened into a stare that clearly said, *Don't go there.* "You will recall," she said, "that we only slept together once. Before I'd figured myself out. I'm Susan? That hardly seems likely."

"Is it likely that I should be Brian?" he countered. To lighten the mood, he cocked his head and widened his eyes in a mock posture of exaggerated artsy-fartsy pretension, and she laughed. Her teeth were whiter than the foam on his Macchiato, whiter than arctic ice, and they transfixed him in a momentary flash of near-revelation.

"It's so like you," she said, "to have such complicated relationship issues even in your dreams." She was still laughing when she glanced at the clock on the wall. "Whoops, I'd better get going. I've got a class coming up. Keep me posted on all the exciting developments in Brian-land." She leaned over and pecked him on the cheek, then gathered her purse (more like a suitcase, he thought) and headed for the door.

He watched as her long, lanky strides carried her away from him. The rippled muscles of the arctic waste were still taking shape in his imagination, and for the millionth time in his high-strung life, he silently thanked the gods—any gods, whatever gods there might be, he didn't care who they were—for gifting him with a dreary dream life of almost archetypal normality, since it freed him from the fetters of psyche-bound inspiration and allowed him to take in, as if by osmosis, every subtle sensation of the world around him. Without anything of equal vibrancy buzzing in his subconscious to compete with the splendor of the outside world, he could work in complete inner freedom, allowing the obscure workings of his own creative faculty to transform scattered sense perceptions into magnificent paintings that made him the awe of the arthouse community.

The gods bless you, Brian, he said to his alter ego. Through the plate glass storefront, he could see Cornelia standing on the sidewalk, squinting up at the sun. After a moment she pulled out her flaming-orange sunglasses and slipped them on. As she loped down the sidewalk and out of sight, he found that he still couldn't decide whether or not he loved her.

But then he reasoned, if he couldn't decide, that probably meant he didn't.

ᴠᴉᴠ

The dream, as always, was in black-and-white, except for the part with the startling new addition of blood, which fountained and sprayed in gouts like bright red finger-paint. The color shocked him, but not into full consciousness. He soon discovered another fact about this remarkable dream: it could get amazingly tactile, almost more so than real life. Brian's world had always been pinch-yourself-and-wake-up solid, but never like this. The blood was warm and sticky as maple syrup, and the pain was like a white-hot pocket of concentrated agony searing into the socket of his right eye.

What had happened was that Susan had asked Brian to unload a pickup bed full of potted flowers. He had backed the vehicle up to the front porch like the dutiful dream-husband he was, and had lowered the tailgate and climbed into the bed to unstack the dull plastic pots with their colorless floral occupants.

(Lafcadio, watching from a nonlocalized point some distance away, while simultaneously identifying with his dream-self, had thought the grayish blooms most distasteful.)

It happened on the first jump. He realized it would be much easier to hop down than to squat and climb, so he steadied the pot in his hands and stepped off the edge of the tailgate, intending to drop lightly onto the balls of his feet. Susan's scream burst out with an impossible loudness, and hung in the air with a ringing reverberation that could only happen in a dream. He hadn't noticed the hook projecting from the porch ceiling, right near the edge under which he had opened the tailgate. It was meant for hanging a plant on, obviously. Susan must have mounted it there without telling him. The gray-silver point extended an absurd length past the overhang, maybe three inches or more, and was located precisely at eye-level from his standing position in the pickup bed.

The curved end was vicious-looking, almost medieval. It caught him in the top rim of his right eye socket, and his weight did the rest. He fell forward, the point gouged into the bone of his skull, his legs left the tailgate, and then he was lodged there, hooked like a great flailing fish. The plastic pot he was carrying hit the lawn without breaking, although potting soil sprayed everywhere, and the colorless bloom was crushed. His body went out of control then, legs kicking and spasming as if he were trying to pedal up Mt. Everest, hands and fingers slapping and clawing at the smooth vinyl siding of the eave in a vain attempt to lift himself up. While all this went on, his throat opened up and spouted a veritably Pentecostal string of gibberish that seemed to have something to do with screaming for help.

Then Susan was grabbing his legs. She was grunting and lifting him up, heaving, thrusting, while her impossibly loud and long scream still hung in the air. At last she succeeded. The hook ripped free, taking a few bone splinters with it, and he dropped to the truck, slammed into the open tailgate with the small of his back, and hit the lawn still writhing.

That was when the blood began to spurt from his eye in red gouts like finger-paint. The pain was a white-hot ball searing its way inward from his eye to his brain. Susan was pawing at him in panic, weeping, asking him what to do. And in the midst of it all, rather absurdly, he vomited.

༄༅

"He puked? So what happened then? Tell me everything!" Cornelia's eyes shone with eager interest. Lafcadio drew in a sharp, tobacco-laden breath and let it out slowly, trying to buy time to fathom the reason for her eagerness. This time they were at their favorite bar, the Twilight Lounge. The decor was an edgy mix of Goth and camp imagery: ABBA posters and black candles arranged into arcane geometric patterns, G.I. Joe dolls tangled in faux spider webs. Cornelia was dressed for the occasion in a black velvet catsuit with a denim jacket.

"No, he didn't die." Lafcadio floated the words out on the tail-end of a smoky exhalation. Cornelia interrupted him before he could say more.

"What?" She blinked and leaned closer, bringing with her a mingled scent of sweet perfume and sour gin. "Did you say 'he sits and cries?' Lafcadio, my darling, you're incomprehensible when you mumble, especially amidst all the lovely musical accompaniment." A bassy club beat was throbbing in the atmosphere around them, overlaid with a glassy texture of synthesized strings.

"I said he *didn't die.*" He repeated the words with a hint of annoyance in his voice. "People usually don't die in their own dreams, right? And after all, he is me." He held up his cigarette before him in an attitude of detachment and regarded the cherry-red ember glowing on the tip. "Things seemed like they were getting better before I woke up. Susan took care of him. She dialed 911, and an ambulance came and rushed him off to the hospital. I opened my eyes just as they started to wheel him into the ER."

"Interesting..." Cornelia took a sip from her gin and tonic. "So, Susan saved his life. But then, she's the one who installed the hook in the first place. And you say it hurt his *eye?*" She mused for a moment while the smoky air continued to throb around them like the interior of an artery, and while Lafcadio remained deliberately absorbed in his cigarette meditation. In his mind, a fiery orange sinkhole had opened up in the abdominal arctic waste. Volcanic flames were beginning to lick out from the edges and melt the snow to slush. The water first dripped, then drizzled into the hole, and its touch only seemed to fuel the flames.

"Hey." Cornelia's ruminations seemed to reach a point of sudden synthesis. "Do you think that's symbolic—'eye' equals capital 'I'? Maybe the hook in your eye represents a buried feeling of hostility toward your deathly-dull dream life." She smiled with an almost childish glee, and he thought she seemed just a little too pleased with herself.

"It's a fundamental tenet of my belief system," he said in a far frostier voice than he had intended, "that there is ultimately no such thing as a fixed center of identity." He saw her eyes roll in a familiar expression of boredom, but he went on. "These chairs underneath our asses right now are just as much a part of who we are as anything rattling around inside these juicy little heads." He raised his right hand, the one holding the cigarette, and tapped his index finger against a veiny temple. A tendril of smoke found its way from the tip of the cigarette to the corner of his eye, where it brushed a stinging tail against the tender pink tissues. He waved it away and tried to ignore Cornelia's look of amusement.

"The injured eye once again," she said. "Do you think someone is trying to tell you something?"

He refused to acknowledge her comment. "I have no reason to be hostile toward Brian or his life," he continued, "because he may as well be me, and his life mine. My life may as well be his. Just as yours may as well be mine, and mine yours. Our souls are both located in this cigarette I'm smoking here. They're also in that gin and tonic you're sucking down." She was in the midst of downing the rest of her drink, and she made a face at him, holding the liquid in her cheeks for a moment before swallowing it.

"Really, darling," she said with a sigh, "sometimes your attempts at Zen-like wisdom are too much. What the hell are you talking about?"

"I'm saying there's no boundary between identities, so what's to be afraid of?"

She shrugged. "Who said anything about being afraid?"

"It's the same thing with my art," he went on, ignoring her question. "I deliberately make the perspective unknowable. The viewer might be looking at any one point from any other. Have you heard of Indra's net?"

NIGHTMARES, IMPORTED AND DOMESTIC

She shook her head, clearly having lost interest in his monologue. But that did not prevent him from continuing.

"It's a metaphor in Hinduism for the infinity of perspectives in the universe," he said. "Indra's net is an endless web that has a jewel located at the intersection of every strand. Each jewel reflects all the others, so you have infinity contained in every finite point on the net. A long time ago I decided to use this idea as the philosophical basis for my paintings. When you view any one of my pieces, you don't know where you're supposed to be seeing it from. What's more, this means the frame itself isn't the boundary of the scene. My landscapes fold in on themselves and create a self-contained infinity. In this way, my work mirrors the reality of subjective personal existence, just like the metaphor of Indra's net. Because ultimately, there's nothing outside the frame for any of us. There's just an endless hall of mirrors with no boundary." He started to say more, but then he abruptly shut his mouth and sucked on his cigarette as he realized that the words he had never spoken, and never wanted to speak, were rising to his lips. These words expressed a fear that had dawned on him one day in a quiet moment when he was reiterating his credo to himself for the thousandth time: *No boundary means no escape.*

"Is there anything else?" Cornelia asked. She was watching him with her ruby red lips screwed up into a wry grin.

"Just the fact that your eye/I theory doesn't hold water," he said. "The injury wasn't a threat at all. In fact, it might turn out to have been a liberation. Brian and Susan's marital relationship has been at kind of a low ebb lately. Then he ran into trouble and she saved him. Maybe this will revitalize things between them."

"Yes," Cornelia said, "but Susan put up the hook, remember?" She smiled at him with eyes that were as pretty and hard as the rest of her. "If I remember correctly, you also told me that I'm Susan. Is that how you see me—a disturbing mix of destroyer and savior?"

Lafcadio barked out a small, sharp laugh. "Hardly, my sweet. Listen, we could spend all night on this. This autopsy of my dreams. But do you know what? Sometimes a cigar is just a cigar, a rose is a rose is a rose, and diamonds are forever. Let's just say it's all really interesting, and leave it at that. Will you indulge me?"

"Oh, darling!" she cried. "This is too much, coming from the enlightened Zen-master of the avant-garde art world!" She laughed and laughed until he feared she would hurt herself. When she had recovered, she said, "Certainly, my sweet. But one question first: Doesn't it bother you to know that Brian-world is now a painful place to be? You've talked so much about how realistic it is. Well, I'm not so sure the marriage or anything else will be better now. Brian may be disfigured, and he'll definitely be blind in one eye. He'll probably suffer brain damage. I'm surprised you haven't acted more concerned about this. What will your dreams be like now, my wise Lafcadio?" She looked deeply into his eyes, and even in the midst of his consternation, he wondered again whether he loved her.

"Don't know." The artist slumped back in his seat, his meditative mood broken. The arctic landscape remained unaltered in his mind's eye, although the drizzle of water pouring through the hole in the ice had grown to become a steadily flowing waterfall. The flames were hidden now, but they were still there, still burning below the frozen crust, as evidenced by the flickering orange sheen they imparted to the ice around the hole. He had a momentary flash of something new: a human figure curled into a fetal position, located deep within that fiery pit. Its eyes and mouth were open. He couldn't tell whether it was laughing, crying, or screaming. Perhaps it was doing all three.

He frowned at Cornelia as he ground out his cigarette in the glossy black ashtray on the table. "You're just a sweet little ray of sunshine, aren't you?"

◡∴◡

Of course the dream was monochrome. How could it be otherwise? And yet Brian sensed that something was different. Something was missing from the room around him, some indefinable aspect of solidity whose absence made everything seem vaguely flat and unreal, like cardboard stage props and scenery.

(Lafcadio, hovering in extra-dimensional space somewhere near the ceiling, shared his alter ego's confusion.)

Brian was parked in a wheelchair in the center of his black-and-white living room, slumped in front of a black-and-white television set, watching a black-and-white program unfold on the screen. He couldn't budge an inch. The insipid TV world was inescapable, and he was positioned to face it for a full frontal assault. Susan had engaged the wheel locks on the chair to prevent the incessant squeaking of the spokes he had been causing by rocking back and forth, back and forth. She was in the kitchen behind him right now, making his lunch, from the sound of it. She must be chopping celery—*crunch-crunch-crunch, crunch-crunch-crunch.* To his right and left, adorning coffee tables, walls, and windowsills, a tangled profusion of potted flowers bristled with muddy gray blooms that emitted an incongruously sweet perfume. It filled the atmosphere of the room like a syrupy fog. He almost thought he could see it shifting and shimmering in the cold light of the television.

Drool was gathered in a heavy glistening lobe on his lower lip, but he lacked the energy to care about it. He felt nauseous and dizzy, and he had no idea what was happening on the program before him. Something about a perky family stranded on some planet with a prissy bad guy and a robot with floppy arms. A black rotary telephone was perched atop the set with a ridiculously long cord dangling down in front of the screen. It slithered across the convex surface, unevenly dividing the flickering image, and ended up as a bunched pile of gleaming black coils on the gray-carpeted floor.

His injured right eye was smothered in bandages, as were most of his cheek and forehead. His exposed left eye kept blinking, rolling, and refocusing as he tried to fathom what the characters on the television screen were so concerned

280

about. The prissy bad guy was bitching at the robot while the robot waved its accordion-pleated tube-arms.

His poor wounded head was filled with an odd liquid surging sound. In his grogginess and sickness, he imagined that he must be hearing the primal sound of the ocean deeps, where colorless fluorescent fish glided with rippling fan-fins through an eternal night, and where the currents murmured of secrets too ancient to be spoken aloud. Such thoughts were new and strange, and they scared him. He longed for his accounting forms and the familiar taupe walls of his office. But the ocean sound seemed to be a permanent addition, and he feared he would never see the comforting interior of his office again. Now, one week after the accident, he still rocked to the sound of the tidal rhythm, but the wheel locks kept him from creating the soothing back-and-forth motion that had been the only comfort he could find in this new half-conscious existence.

Susan entered the room holding a plate with a sandwich on it. She was smiling and talking to him, but her words sounded like gibberish. When he tried to raise his hands to take the plate, his arms felt as if someone had tied them down with lead weights. Her voice came to him as if through water, all murky and muffled, and the words sounded like *blah, blah, blah,* spoken in relentlessly perky tones, so upbeat they rang utterly false.

She held the sandwich to his mouth, and his nostrils were suddenly filled with the clean yet musty smell of whole-wheat bread. With the cloying perfume of the flowers now mercifully muted, he found that his nausea had concealed a fierce hunger. He was positively ravenous. His lips parted of their own accord, and the bead of spit on his lower lip was sopped up by the spongy bread as Susan fed him the sandwich bite by bite. While he ate, he couldn't help noticing that she was wearing low-riding pants with a high-cut shirt, and that her navel was staring at him from the smooth white expanse of her stomach like an unblinking eye that mirrored and mocked his own newly monocular face. It fascinated him for some reason. He felt he should be reminded of something.

He still had four bites left when the phone rang. Susan set the plate on his lap and took two steps over to the television while he stared down at the unfinished sandwich with a mute cry of frustration sealed off within his throat. His hands clenched and unclenched, but his wrists were pinned to the arms of the wheelchair by invisible straps.

"Blah, blah, blah?" Susan chimed into the black mouthpiece. She listened for a moment, then "Blah, blah, blah!" she replied. A look of pleasure crossed her face as she brushed past him to the coffee table, where she consulted a phone book for the caller. Her smile faded as her finger stopped on the page before a name and number.

"Oh, blah, blah, blah," she continued in a more serious tone, moving behind him toward the kitchen on some errand, dragging the long black cord in her wake so that it pulled up against his arm. He flinched at its stiff spiral touch and continued to look with longing at his sandwich.

After a moment, she returned on some other errand. "Blah, blah, blah!" she enthused, racing in front of him toward the phone book again, still chatting away to that all-important caller, still pulling that super-long springy cord so that it worked its way up and encircled his neck. The coils were as smooth and cool as snakeskin against his throat.

From some point buried deep within his brain, out of some black well of selfhood where the ocean currents murmured in soothing tones, a thought emerged. The whispering voices coalesced into an intelligible sentence, and the sentence began to flow toward his throat. He opened his mouth and grunted, but the cord was slowly strangling him. He coughed as if he were trying to expel some bit of sandwich lodged in his windpipe. The words were almost there, they would almost form. His mouth worked and his lips gathered more spit, but his voice would not come, it could not break free of the constriction around his throat. In desperation he mouthed the words silently with his crumb-covered lips, wondering as he did so what the thought might mean, and where it might have come from: *No boundary means no escape.*

(Lafcadio, who had been watching these events unfold with growing agitation, felt his disembodied heart skip a beat.)

Susan was now out of sight in the dining room, or perhaps even beyond that, and the cord was growing tighter and tighter. The television world continued to blather with incomprehensible characters and concerns while the cold spiral coils dug deeper and deeper into his Adam's apple like a garrote. Straining, trembling, he jerked his arms against the invisible straps, but try as he might, he was immobilized. He may as well have tried to batter down the walls of prison.

As the dull throb of medicated pain in his bandaged eye blossomed into a bright burning agony, and as the robot continued to wave its arms and the prissy bad guy went on with his outrageous accusations, Brian finally realized the nature of what was wrong with the room: *There was no difference between the world around him and the world on the television.* The gibberish spouting from the mouths of the TV characters was no more comprehensible than the gibberish his wife was still spouting in the other room—or, come to think of it, from the gibberish he had spouted himself when he was hanging by his eye socket from the porch ceiling. None of it made sense. All of it was insipid and pointless. There was a tangible lack of *realness* to his surroundings, an absence of something that would have given everything more weight and made it all make sense again. But what exactly was this indefinable quality whose absence made life nothing more than a TV show where people spoke nonsense, and where there could be no escape?

It wasn't until rivulets of red began to seep out from beneath his bandages and spatter onto the colorless sleeves of his pajamas that he found his answer.

No boundary means no escape.

When the change came, it came quickly. The room receded suddenly and sharply, as if he were backing down a tunnel at incredible speed. The pain in his face and the constriction in his throat faded as if someone were turning down the volume on the television. For a time, he knew only an insensate bliss.

When he opened his eyes—his eyes, both of them intact and functional—he found himself lying in a bed that was not his own, located in a room he had never seen, where the walls displayed a dazzling array of surreal painted landscapes, and where he somehow knew that nobody had ever slept beside him more than once, not even Susan.

His throat finally opened and released an impressive array of shrieks when he realized that his name was supposed to be Lafcadio, and that he had awakened into the wrong life.

⁓

"So is he dead?" Cornelia asked. "You haven't talked about him for—what is it, two weeks now? I can only assume that he died from his injuries. What's Susan doing with the life insurance money? Installing a greenhouse?" She smiled and laughed, but he refused to look at her.

This time they were sharing a pizza in their favorite trendy restaurant, Mad For Pie, which served every sort of pizza one could imagine—except the traditional sausage, cheese and tomato sauce sort. The entrée steaming on the table before them now was the specialty of the house, an exotic melange called The Swordfish, Artichoke, and White Sauce (with Just a Touch of Cilantro) Dream Pie. Lafcadio's stomach was out of sorts. He sat back in his tall wicker-backed chair and tried to avoid the overpowering scent of seafood and cilantro that rose toward his nostrils in heady waves.

"To be honest," he said in his best nonchalant voice, "I'm not sure what's going on with Brian right now."

"What do you mean?" She shoveled another lump of swordfish-laden crust into her mouth, and he watched the motion of her jaw with a sickened fascination: its determined scissoring and champing as it ground the fishy flesh to a pulp, then the spasm in her throat as she swallowed the pungent lump and it began to stretch its way downward through her esophagus toward her waiting stomach. His own stomach lurched ominously, and he looked down at his cigarette.

"I, uh—how do I say this?" He picked up a heavy burgundy-colored napkin and mopped his sweating brow. "I haven't dreamed about Brian for sixteen days now."

She stopped her chewing and regarded him from across the pie with an expression of disbelief.

"Yes," he said, "I'm serious."

"Lafcadio," she said. The swordfish suddenly stuck in her throat, and she groped for her glass of water. When she had taken a drink, she licked her lips and continued to look at him. "What's happened? Hasn't Brian been with you for years now?"

"Yes," he said.

"Aren't you concerned about this?"

"Yes."

"So why haven't you said anything?" Her wounded pout dismayed him, and for a moment he considered telling her the tale he had been concealing for over two weeks: of how he had awakened in his silk-sheeted bed thinking that he was Brian; of the profound panic that had gripped him for hours as he struggled to remember how he had awakened into someone else's life; of how the delusion had hung on until mid-morning, when for no apparent reason his own name had seemed to attach to him with a new assertiveness, and the dream-identity had evaporated from his consciousness like a moist fog; of how he had found himself standing in his kitchen, holding a cup of Jamaica Blue Mountain and wondering where somebody had hidden the Folgers.

For the rest of that horrible day he had been unable to stop the trembling in his chest. He had canceled a dinner date with Cornelia (she had gracefully declined to ask the reason) and spent the night in his studio looking at his easel and allowing the arctic vision to gain further clarity and intensity in his mind's eye. He had known the time would soon arrive for him to begin committing the vision to canvas, but on that night some inner impulse had told him to wait, and he had heeded its restraint. Later, when he slept, he had found that his classic TV dreams were gone for the first time in over a decade.

Instead of watching Brian's soothingly banal ramblings, he had found himself floating high over an arctic tundra, watching a volcanic sinkhole widen into a veritable crater amidst the icy furrows, wondering whether the abdominal ripples stretching away toward the horizon might ever meet with the rest of the torso, with breasts and a neck, and with a face. It was the first time he had ever dreamt himself into one of his own artistic visions, and he hadn't known how to feel about it the following morning. The next night the dream had been the same. And the next, and the next.

He considered telling Cornelia this. But how could he, when he knew that it was her face he half-feared to see past the icy horizon?

"I just needed time to adjust," he finally said with a weak smile. "You know you're my most beloved confidante, Cornelia. Please don't be upset with me."

"I'm not upset, dearest. I'm just surprised." She shoved away her plate and began looking around for a server to take away the remains of the pie. Once their table was cleared and wiped down and they were alone again, she leaned forward with her forearms resting on the glossy brown surface and looked into his eyes.

"Do you know I talked to my therapist last week about you and Brian?"

For a moment he thought she was joking. He kept expecting her serious expression to break into a smile, but her mouth was a determined line, and her eyes were as hard as sapphires.

"You told Dr. Breckenridge about this? About my *dreams?*"

Her severity broke easily in the face of his indignation. Immediately she was pouting again, but now in a rather hard way. "I was missing you, Lafcadio. I really wanted to hear about the latest episodes of the Brian and Susan Show.

NIGHTMARES, IMPORTED AND DOMESTIC

I always look forward to our conversations. I just called Dr. Breckenridge to change my appointment, but we ended up talking about you. How could I not mention you, when you were the main thing on my mind?"

Lafcadio could not sit still. He twisted in his seat and tried unsuccessfully to find a comfortable position. He picked up his drink, but his hand shook so badly that he had to set it back down. He looked around at the waiters and waitresses servicing tables, at the upscale couples and college students, all of them wearing trendy clothes and devouring various nonstandard delights. The sight only angered him. As a last resort, he turned to examine his cigarette, but its usual soothing influence was nowhere to be found. Then he gave up and looked at Cornelia's face.

"So what did you tell him?"

"I only told him what you've told me. I described your dream life, all black-and-white and cozy. He found it quite fascinating. I could tell he wanted to ask me to introduce you to him, but he was too afraid of crossing a professional line."

Lafcadio considered this for a moment and then began to nod, slowly at first, then with increasing vigor. "Of course." He recalled the sensation of a curling phone cord pressed cold against Brian's throat, and he snickered a little, then laughed. "Of *course.*" Once again he gazed into Cornelia's eyes, considered her toned and taut physique, now tastefully attired in a green sparkling jacket with black satin shirt and pants. He drank in the sight of her masculine femininity, and found in it an impression of dawning realization. The full knowledge waited just beyond the horizon, like an arctic mountain range chiseled by the elements into the shape of a familiar face.

She was speaking to him. Her words came to him all murky and muffled, as if through water. "After all, Lafcadio, you were the one who said…what was it? Sometimes a dream is just a cigar? Something like that. You were quoting somebody. But the more I think about it, the more I believe you had the right idea. Don't take any of this seriously. Dr. Breckenridge didn't know what he was saying when he told me your dreams are unlike anything in the history of psychology." She shut her mouth when she realized she had said too much, but he found it funny. It was all funny now. She was a million miles away, and her confusion and misery were of no consequence.

It also just so happened that her face and clothing were losing their color. He blinked rapidly as the color drained away from her like dye being leeched from a canvas. Her blue eyes became a stony gray. Her ruddy expression became a murky white. Her sparkling green jacket became a sickly weak shade of gray, like library paste flecked with glitter. In just a few seconds, she was flushed of all color. He was so startled that it was a moment before he realized the same effect had overtaken the restaurant around him. Mad For Pie had taken on the appearance of *Father Knows Best.* The pies and pizzas were gray cardboard, and the patrons and scenery were colorless stage props and cutouts.

(Somewhere close by, in some nonlocalized portion of extra-dimensional space, another center of identity began to make itself known: a buzzing unit of self-consciousness that felt somehow like a vein protruding from the back of his head; an unknown self whose reality ran much deeper and held more solidity than the Magnificent Artist identity he had cultivated for most of his life. This new self was sharing his vision and consciousness, watching his life unfold like a fiction. And it was judging everything about him and his life, considering it all impassively, and finding it all to be quaint and comforting in a banal, white-bread sort of way.)

He felt his hand rise to his mouth to suck in a lungful of nicotine smoke. His lips curled into a smile, and for a moment he almost felt like his old self. "Cornelia, my sweet, don't worry about it." His voice carried through the stale air with a vibrancy that was almost visible, as if its very timbre might bring back a hint of color to the room. He felt a strange power surging in his breast, a kind of exhilaration beyond anything he had ever known. The landscape in his mind's eye pulsed with an intensity that almost obscured the sight of the restaurant. For once, his inner vision was stronger than the world around him, and in this fact he found his release.

If life was unbounded, he thought, just like his landscapes, and if no boundary meant no escape, then the only way out, the only way to achieve the ultimate transcendence, was to turn inward toward the source and center of consciousness itself, and find his longed-for infinity *inside the* world. Just like the self-contained infinity of Indra's net, which he had never truly understood until now.

(The newly-awakened higher self nodded behind him in approval of his insight. He could sense its benevolent attention upon him.)

Cornelia's face loomed in front of him, and also beyond the icy horizon in his mind's eye. In the restaurant she appeared gray and flat. In the arctic waste, her features were chiseled from crackling blue ice, and the light of a slivered moon overhead glinted in silver sparkles on her face like flashes on the facets of a diamond.

"You're not mad?" the Cornelia of the outer world was asking. "Are you sure, Lafcadio? Because I don't think I could bear it."

"No," he heard himself say. "Far from it. In fact, I think you may have liberated me. I'm thinking that maybe Brian is gone now because he woke up. I'm thinking that maybe he and I have finally come together."

She looked at him somewhat suspiciously. "Should I congratulate you?"

"Perhaps. What say we find out for sure?" He rapped on the table with the knuckles of his free hand and sat forward abruptly in his chair. He felt positively giddy with good will. "Will you come over to my place tonight, my dear? I have something prepared to show you. I haven't told you anything about my latest project, you know I always keep them private until they're finished, but it's about time you saw it, even if it is only a work in progress. Because you're directly involved in it."

NIGHTMARES, IMPORTED AND DOMESTIC

Her smile returned then, and he saw that her teeth were still icy white, a flashing beacon in the grayness surrounding her. "Lafcadio! Do you mean that I'm featured in it somehow?"

"Oh, yes!" He laughed and allowed her to grab his hand. "Yes, you are! I think you'll be positively amazed at the role you've played."

After that, he found he could simply allow himself to act the part of Lafcadio for the remainder of their time together at Mad For Pie. He laughed and chatted, and she laughed and chatted back, and they made plans for her to arrive at his flat at eight o'clock, at which time he promised to reveal to her a facet of herself that she had never suspected. He even managed to keep up the old appearance of the Magnificent Artist when her chattering words lost all meaning and began to sound like "Blah, blah, blah."

When they parted, each was riding on a wave of giddiness, although he knew that hers did not match his. She thought she was going to be immortalized in one of his paintings. He, on the other hand, knew they were both going to be immortalized in a scheme much bigger than any she could ever imagine.

✧⁓

He labored all afternoon in his studio. The painting seemed to shape itself.

He had to take extra care to blend the colors for the fiery crater, since his color blindness precluded his assessing it with a simple glance, but he felt his hand being guided by a higher power, and he knew, even without being able to judge the quality of the work with his eyes, that it was the best thing he had ever painted. And after all, he would soon awaken to the actual scene of the vision, and the pathetic oil-based facsimile would no longer have a significance.

As he continued to work toward completion, he began to feel as if a key had been fitted into a lock. The door that opened allowed a flood of insights to spill through his brain. Brian's world had been less real than Lafcadio's, and its unreality had been reflected in its monochromity. That much Lafcadio had always known. But he had never suspected that perhaps his own reality was being viewed from a still wider perspective by another layer of himself, a layer that was even more awake, more vibrant, more *real*. The thought of the sensuous delights, the manifold impressions, that might be available to that wider identity, sent him into paroxysms of aesthetic delight.

Brian had awakened to the insubstantiality of his position. It had seemed impossible—in fact, neither of them had ever so much as considered the possibility—but it had happened nonetheless, through the agency of an unexpected injury, brought about by Susan's unwitting help. Now Brian was gone—or, more accurately, he was more fully *here* with Lafcadio than he had ever been before—and it was Lafcadio's turn to wake up.

Dull-brained Brian would never have thought of the possibility of intentionally inducing an awakening, even if somebody had described it to him. He had even proved incapable of realizing that the half-consciousness of his new mutilated existence was a blessing in disguise, since it limited his external options and forcibly opened him to the enhanced consciousness of the inner world. Lafcadio was not so dull. He knew what had happened, and he was able to recognize its value and purposefully work to take himself to the next level. The only question that remained was how to accomplish it. What means would he use to rouse himself from the relative dream of his life and rise to a greater reality? And again, it was not really a question in need of an answer, for Brian had already provided the solution. His awakening had been accomplished through involuntary suffering. Having reflected on the situation, Lafcadio had come to realize that he could engineer his own circumstances, and awaken himself through a voluntary act.

It had to be the right eye, of course, the one most directly wired to the left side of the brain. Once the channel of vision leading to the logical, rational, intellectual hemisphere was destroyed, all that would remain would be the channel leading to the intuitive, emotional, mystical half. Then all the visual impressions of the sensuous world around him would be funneled exclusively to the wider mystical self that even now was hovering behind him in extra-dimensional space. And he would see himself left behind and transformed.

The gods bless you, Brian, he whispered to himself over and over again during that long afternoon of creation, as he shaped the world on the canvas and contemplated the stainless steel hook he had hidden in his pocket. He would have gone ahead and mounted it on one of the exposed ceiling beams in the studio of his loft apartment, if it were not for the fact that this would have disrupted the correct sequence of events.

There was a protocol to follow.

The mounting of the hook, of course, was Cornelia's job.

⚘

She arrived at eight, right on time. She wore the same satin black shirt and pants, but had exchanged the sparkling green jacket for a sparkling blue one. In her right hand she clutched a bottle of red wine. In her left she carried a rose, which she intended to present to her beloved artist in gratitude for including her in one of his magnificent creations.

She remembered the walk up the narrow dark steps to his loft all too well, even though it was three years since her last visit. The one-time exception to their formerly platonic relationship had been disastrous. They had both known immediately that it wasn't working, even though the physical pleasure had been exquisite. It had seemed too much like incest, and she could tell from his pained expression afterward that he was experiencing his own private regrets. When he had moved down to bring his face level with her stomach, and when he had placed the palm of his hand across her belly in a lovingly gentle way, she had fought back tears that threatened to squeeze from beneath her lids and sear them

288

both. After a moment he had climbed from the bed and thrown on his clothes. She had done the same, and they had never spoken of the incident again.

The staircase had not changed. The off-white walls were still too narrow, and the brown wooden steps still creaked and popped even under the modest weight of her lean, toned body. At the top of the stairs, on the right, stood the brown wooden door to the artist's lair. She smiled and felt a rush of happiness, thinking that this visit would surely turn out better than the last.

She rapped on the door with the hand holding the rose. The delicate bloom, so deeply red that it seemed almost to ache with the saturation of its own hue, bobbed on the end of the thorned stem like a human head. She watched it for a moment and then knocked again.

"Lafcadio?" Her voice rang out with a hollow resonance in the cramped stairway. Tentatively, she reached out with her left hand and tried the brassy knob. It turned smoothly, and the door whispered open to reveal Lafcadio's living room.

She shut the door behind her and took the wine to the kitchen. The rose she laid on the dining room table. Then she went in search of the artist.

His studio was still located in the same room he had used three years ago. The walls and floor were dark and immaculate. The ceiling was high and crossed by wooden beams that gave the room a rustic ambiance. There was a sheet of tarpaulin spread beneath the easel, and upon the easel rested the artist's newest creation. She stopped before it and took in the scene it displayed. After a moment, her heart began to pound.

The icy waste stretched away from her in barren rolls like lumps of fat. She could tell they were meant to mimic the human form by their arrangement into abdominal ripples, and by the snowy hillocks that sprouted like breasts in the upper half of the scene, and by the visage that gazed upward from the diamond-like mountains at the far upper edge. Overhead, a waning crescent moon cast a sickly light onto the surreal landscape.

When she looked back down to the ice itself, she saw that where the navel should have been, there was a gaping hole, like a wound ripped open from the inside. Streaks and splashes of crimson and orange jetted out from the hole like liquid fire, like hot blood and pus, and she thought she could see, buried somewhere deep within the chaos of ripe colors, the shape of a body curled into a fetal position. Its head was bony and bald, with an almost catlike aspect. When she leaned closer, she saw that its mouth was opened in a scream, and that one of its eyes—the right one—had been gouged out.

She knew who it was, of course, just as she recognized the chiseled face at the top of the picture. She almost had time to gasp before Lafcadio pounced on her from behind.

"My sweet!" he cried as he grabbed her shoulders and spun her around. She shrieked, then tried to laugh with relief when she saw his wild-eyed expression.

"Dear God, Lafcadio! You scared the living hell out of me!" Her hands trembled violently, and she rubbed them against her upper arms while still laughing in a shaky voice. "You look like you've seen a ghost. Not Brian's, I hope?"

He stared at her for a moment. Then he laughed with her. "Ah, yes. You always see more than I give you credit for, my dear Cornelia. Let me thank you right now, since it may be the last chance I have, for your many years of friendship."

"Well, of course, darling," she said. Her weak laughter died down to silence. "And why should this be your last chance?"

He laughed again and said, "No, I don't think so." While she puzzled over this non sequitur of an answer, he reached into his pocket and pulled out something silver and shiny. He then took her hand and placed the hook gently on her palm. She saw that it was long and vicious looking, with a sharply curved point. The other end was threaded for screwing into a wall or ceiling.

"Up there," he said, pointing to a ceiling beam high above his painting. "I've already set up a ladder, as you can see. Now, if I know you at all, you've probably brought some wine. Why don't I open the bottle and let it breathe while you mount that hook?"

"Lafcadio, what is this for?"

"No, I don't think so," he said again with a laugh. "Believe me, we understand each other very well. It'll be fun! No matter how unpleasant it might seem for a time, it will be fun, believe you me." He patted her shoulder lovingly and then departed for the kitchen, where she heard him pop the cork on the bottle. The hook was cold against her palm, and she looked at it almost in wonder.

As she climbed the ladder and labored to screw the hook into the tough oaken beam, she felt as if she had stepped into a dream. It was not her own, but somebody else's. Yes, she was a character in somebody else's dream. Below her, the painting was visible on its easel, and she stared down at her own icy face with mixed feelings of dread and awe. From her vantage point near the ceiling, the painting was inverted. Her icy reflection stared back up at her with an expression of almost supernatural peace and wisdom. In the arctic waste of Lafcadio's vision, she had become an avatar of spiritual insight. She could discern this without his giving her a word of explanation.

From the bottom of the painting, the fiery-bloody hole gaped with a fierce determination, its hot and juicy depths standing in stark contrast to the supernal peace above. The counterbalance left her feeling sick for some reason. When she looked up and saw that she had finished screwing the hook into the beam, she descended the ladder quickly and turned her back on the canvas.

Lafcadio returned and saw that she had accomplished her mission. "Excellent!" he said. "Would you please go and pour two glasses for us, darling? I've set them out for you already. Everything is waiting." He stepped closer, and she forced herself not to flinch. "Thank you, too, for the rose. A wonderfully symbolic gesture, and all too appropriate in light of recent developments." He leaned down and kissed her cheek. When he stood back up, his smile was warm and his eyes were calm. She felt herself relax, and allowed herself to hope once more for a pleasant evening.

"Will you explain this to me when I get back?" She gestured toward the canvas. He glanced at it, reflected for a moment, and nodded.

"Whatever you say, Cornelia. It's our night."

She smiled then; it felt good to break through the icy numbness that had overtaken her face without her even noticing it. At some point between her arrival at his flat and his return from the kitchen, her face had grown cold and stiff. Smiling was an effort, but it brought life back to her cheeks and eyes. Still smiling, she went to the kitchen and poured the wine into two stemmed glasses that were waiting on the countertop.

"Lafcadio," she called. "I think you should tell me about Brian again. I've been thinking about it, and I have a theory. Maybe the incident with the hook was a dream of emasculation. Maybe it represents some sort of archetypal male fear of living in a matriarchy. A lot of intelligent people have been saying in recent years that we're turning into a matriarchal society. Or I guess I should say, *back* into one. Do you think maybe you've tapped into a hidden fear in the male subconscious? Maybe you dreamed Brian into a situation where his fear of women had to come out." She set the bottle down and lifted a wine-filled glass in each hand. The bouquet rose to her nostrils with a delicate aroma of vanilla and cloves.

"What do you think?" She turned the corner and stopped inside the doorway to the studio. "Lafcadio?"

The wine spilled, of course, when the glasses hit the floor, but the area of the stain was relatively small. Some droplets hit the cream-colored carpet of the hallway, marking it forever with a permanent speckling of purplish-crimson. The rest of it pooled on the hardwood floor like blood. It was a long time before Cornelia or anybody else thought to wipe it up, and by that time most of it had seeped through the cracks and into the pores, leaving an equally permanent stain on the wood.

Cleaning up spilled wine was the least of Cornelia's concerns at the moment. She was transfixed by the sight of Lafcadio dangling high above her from the rafter, the silver hook buried deep in the socket of his right eye, his legs and arms twitching in spastic birdlike motions, his mouth working silently to shape a whispered stream of veritably Pentecostal gibberish. The gore spattering onto the hardwood floor touched everything around the painting. Some of it splashed onto the canvas itself, adding its own crimson hue to the reds and oranges of the fiery crater. Below the flailing artist, above the deep-gouging sinkhole in the belly of the frozen wasteland, the supernally peaceful face of Cornelia the Ice Goddess brooded silently in eternal bliss.

When the flesh-and-blood Cornelia had recovered from her horrified paralysis, she raced up the ladder and began tugging madly at the legs of the artist, whose spastic motions were growing less vigorous as his strength expired. She grunted and lifted him up, heaving, thrusting. At last she succeeded. The hook ripped free, taking a few bone splinters with it, and he dropped ten feet to the floor and landed with a meaty thud.

Of course the blood began to spurt from his eye then, in red gouts like fingerpaint. It looked red even to him, even with his colorblind field of vision rapidly fading and growing distant, as if he were backing down a tunnel at incredible speed. The pain was even more vicious than he had anticipated: a white-hot ball of electric agony, searing its way inward from his eye to his brain. Cornelia was crouching beside him, pawing at him in a panic, weeping, asking him what to do.

In the midst of it all, rather wonderfully, he found himself floating in an airy sea of transcendent bliss, gazing down from a dizzying height at the outline of an arctic tundra below. The furrows stretched away toward the horizon like lumps of shiny vanilla ice cream, until they met with the mountains of two icy breasts, and even farther north, with the glittering-diamond surface of a gargantuan icon that presented its face eternally to the gaze of vast, moonlit sky.

I am home, he thought, even as the borders of his consciousness began to crumble and allow the pure seed of awareness to expand outward to the next level of selfhood.

The next thought was unexpected. It was different in tenor from any he had ever thought before, and yet it seemed familiar. Coming from his higher self, it was more intense and profound than what he was used to; the sheer truth of it seemed to touch the landscape below, to fill the frigid atmosphere between them, and to saturate the glaze of moonlight cascading down onto the icy hillocks like iridescent milk. The sound of it was the sound of the primal ocean depths, like a million voices whispering into his ear from every direction at once. For a moment, just a final moment of private desire, Lafcadio held onto the perspective of his small self and translated the thought into the language he was accustomed to thinking and speaking in. The million voices coalesced into one, and it was the familiar voice of his own private self. He stared in stark horror at the words that seemed almost to float before him in visible waves upon the snow: *No boundary means no escape.*

For an instant he refused to believe them. He refused to believe that even in this new, blissful existence of ultimate transcendence and freedom, he was still unable to escape the clutches of his deepest-held fear. It simply could not be true, not with the unbounded horizon of a mystical frozen landscape stretching away from him on all sides like the receding outer edge of an ecstatic dream.

Then the grip on his old perspective proved too difficult to maintain. Even as he contemplated these mysteries, he lost his hold on Lafcadio and expanded fully, finally, into the wider perspective of the ancient Self that had always been floating and lurking behind the facade of his consciousness like the ghost of a future incarnation. At last the transition was complete, and he could leave behind all his fears, the old and the new, and glory forever in the exuberance of an unbounded aesthetic delight.

NIGHTMARES, IMPORTED AND DOMESTIC

It wasn't until he fully used his new eyes for the first time that he recognized the flaw in his plans.

Lafcadio was long gone, left far behind in that dull, flat other realm where the senses could never get their fill, because there was simply not enough to fill them up. But the *memory* of Lafcadio was not gone, and in this new existence, where consciousness had no boundaries, he discovered that there could be no distinction between memory and present reality. The incarnate ghost of Lafcadio the Magnificent was still a presence, still a reality, and Lafcadio's subjectivity was still inextricably intertwined with that of the higher Self who was even now dreaming him back into existence.

The dream placed him in the belly of the beast, deep within the womb-like innards of the arctic landscape, where molten fire burned in scalding jets of orange and red, and where self-inflicted wounds assumed all the permanence and significance of religious stigmata. The old Lafcadio screamed in this fiery, freezing hell, and the new-ancient Self screamed with him. They were locked together in twin perspectives of mutual suffering.

There could be no escape, for there was no boundary.

(And somewhere in a black-and-white world of cardboard lives and flimsy stage-prop dreams, Cornelia crouched over the body of her beloved artist and wept as she saw his dying features twist into an expression of horror. He gave one final, mighty convulsion, and then turned onto his side and curled inward upon himself like a slug. She could not force herself to raise her eyes to the painting that presided over them like an icon of everything they had ever hoped to gain from each other. She dared not gaze at the image and see, within the glowing depths of her own icy belly, a transformed image of the bloody artist stretched out before her. As she fell backward onto the rough wooden floor and felt its warm, sticky wetness stain her hands and clothes, a momentary desire flashed through her mind, a habit ingrained from years of brash conversations. Absurdly, she wanted to demand, "Tell me everything." But she knew that even if he could answer, she would not want to hear what he had to say.)

293